The Precious Jules

ALSO BY SHAWN NOCHER

A Hand to Hold in Deep Water

The Precious Jules

SHAWN NOCHER

BLACK STONE
PUBLISHING

Copyright © 2022 by Shawn Nocher
Published in 2022 by Blackstone Publishing
Cover and book design by Alenka Vdovič Linaschke

The characters and events in this book are fictitious.
Any similarity to real persons, living or dead, is coincidental
and not intended by the author.

Printed in the United States of America

First edition: 2022
ISBN 978-1-0940-5831-3
Fiction / Literary

Version 1

CIP data for this book is available
from the Library of Congress

Blackstone Publishing
31 Mistletoe Rd.
Ashland, OR 97520

www.BlackstonePublishing.com

For the muse, for family.

1

The Children

Roland Park, Maryland
Winter 1974

Their mother opens the bank of doors between the mammoth dining room and the sunroom every morning to let the space warm while the children have their breakfast. Afterward, she escorts them in to play. Today a low winter sun streams hard through the long windows.

Her feet are swollen again, as they are with every pregnancy, doughy loaves rising out of her slippers. Little George, kneeling at her feet, pokes a finger at the top of one foot to watch a sphere of white quickly bloom and then fade when he pulls away. He is only three and this is a fascinating thing to him. Jax, having celebrated his sixth birthday the night before, is on his knees with six shiny new Matchbox cars, swishing them across the floor to rev the tiny wheels. Nearly five-year-old Belle watches her mother as well, stares at her feet, and notices the way the sun spatters across her ankles. Belle draws her eyes up over the great mysterious mound of her mother's belly to Ella, Belle's twin sister (who looks just like Belle but is actually nothing like her at all), perched awkwardly on her mother's fullness, tangling her fingers in their mother's hair, pulling strands of it to her mouth, Ella's head tilted to the crook of her mother's neck.

"Be a good girl," their mother says, reaching around to unwrap Ella's arm from her neck like a scarf. "Everyone be good."

The children don't acknowledge this. They know she is talking to Ella.

By comparison, they are always good. Ella is the one who spits out her food at the table, randomly kicks their collective shins, screeches when startled by the banging of pots in the sink or the beeping of the timer on the stove. That morning at breakfast she flipped her bowl of Cheerios to the floor, forcing their mother to ease herself and the mass of her pregnant belly under the table in order to clean the mess. All the while Ella sat banging her spoon overhead, dragging her hands through the slop of milk, and flinging her legs wildly so that the others—Jax, Belle, and George—scooched their chairs farther from her, afraid of being kicked.

"Ma-a-a," Ella says, pulling at her mother's hair as her mother slides her down to the floor. "Ma-a-a." Her voice, like the bleating of a lamb but guttural.

Ella's speech is thick, the few words she knows falling from her mouth in broken chunks. Sometimes a word gets wedged in her throat and replays itself on a loop. "Ma-a-a." She heaves the sound out of herself with what seems like a painful effort and then, without rhyme or reason, the sound stumbles out of her again and again, landing in the midst of the three siblings. "Maaa-aa-aa."

Ella is not fully able to walk, though she can right herself with something to pull up on, maybe manage an unsteady step or two. For this reason, her mother sets her in the center of the sunroom where she is unlikely to move and is usually content to drift off into her own world or watch her siblings play.

Hillary Jules leans over to dig in her children's toybox and pull out toys to set in front of Ella, things that don't have sharp edges and things she can't swallow. Ella tries to swallow everything, and there are rules about what she can have. The children all know a toy has to be bigger than their own hand before they give it to her. Nothing that comes from a Cracker Jack's box, no army men or Silly Putty, rubber balls, marbles, Lincoln Logs. No Matchbox cars or Mr. Potato Head pieces. No pennies that she can swallow in an instant and no one the wiser. No Tinkerbell Toilet Water or Mexican jumping beans or crayons and especially no hair barrettes, which, they all know from experience, can tear a small child's esophagus and temporarily steal what voice she has. Even little

Georgie knows the rules. He anxiously scans the floor around Ella and, spying a Lego within arm's reach of his sister, grabs it quickly and hands it to his mother, proud of himself for having noticed it.

His mother thanks him and tosses the block to the toy bin. George feels a small swell of pride in having been helpful. His mother proceeds to surround Ella with colorful things—fat stacking rings, oversized blocks, a Nerf ball—and leaves the room, her robe flying behind her, to head upstairs and dress for the day. The children know to expect her return shortly. Her blond hair will be pulled back with her favorite black velvet headband that brings out the dark in her lashes, her cheeks and lips blushing with pink, pearl earrings set delicately in the lobes of her ears, though lately she wears them less and less as Ella has taken to pulling on them.

"Maaa-aa-aa."

"Shut up, Ella," Jax says from where he is sprawled on his belly with a Matchbox car. He continues to rev it, dragging it across the floor, making a small ripping sound. When he lets go, it shoots across the floor and smacks into the wall across the room.

Jax is a thinker, and the first thing he said last night after unwrapping the sixth car was that next year he was going to be seven and would get seven cars, and the next year eight, and he continued doing the math aloud until George announced that he, too, would get six cars for his birthday.

"No, George. You get four cars. You are only going to be four, so you get four cars." This had sent George into a fit of tears and had required a great deal of effort on their father's part to explain to George that *some*day he was going to be six and get six cars, but not for his next birthday, at which point he might not even want Matchbox cars. But George was certain that they were exactly what he wanted, and furthermore, he wanted six of them.

George has not forgotten about the cars. On this morning he is now intently watching his big brother, Jax, play with his gifts and is perfectly happy to jump up and fetch each one after its fabulous crash into the wall.

Jax lets another car rip across the floor, but it hits the edge of the braided rug where Ella sits and the car tumbles over, landing inches from her. Ella smacks her hands down to snatch the car but misses it. "Ma," she says. She lifts her eyes to the ceiling. "Ma-a-a."

George knows the rules. Knows that this is something Ella is not allowed to have. He scrambles on his knees from where he sits watching, shoots across the three-foot span of floor, and reaches to grab the car before Ella's spastic slapping hands can land on it. But Ella surprises them all and manages to bring her hand down on the tiny metal car and lift it from the floor in a swift jerk before slamming it down again on the back of George's head.

Belle is on alert now. Ella has surprised them all. It's so confusing. The way her twin sister can be so remote, so unengaged with Belle and her brothers, so placid, and then suddenly transform into something to be reckoned with. And furthermore, Belle cannot understand how it is that Ella hasn't the muscle strength to walk on her own and yet she can lock her fingers around hair and yank it out at the roots, latch onto an arm or a shoulder with her teeth and tear out a chunk of flesh, stab a fork so hard into a plate that it cracks in two, and that she is able to bring that car down so hard that blood is now gushing out of the back of George's head, shooting as if from the lawn sprinkler.

George touches the stinging place on his skull, feels the sloppy wet of it, and brings his fingers—shiny and bright-red—down to his face, stares, reaches again to the back of his head.

Belle feels the fear creeping over her, turning her legs to Jell-O, urging her to move back, turn away. She watches Ella, her eyes glazed over and unfocused, her body rocking, the shiny blue metal of the car protruding from her mouth. And there is Georgie, again touching the back of his head and looking at his fingers, a slow look of horror rising on his face, touching and looking as if he can't believe this flood of blood is his own. And then, long after Belle anticipates it, George lets loose a curdling scream so loud and shrill that it startles Ella and her entire body gives a great shiver. Ella snags George by the hair and yanks him to her, the car tumbling from her mouth, his face smashed to Ella's own.

"Get her off me!" Blood seeps through his blond hair, smearing down the back of his neck. George slaps blindly at her, at the air, unable to pull his head from her grip.

Belle is frozen, terrified that Ella will turn her attention to her. She watches Ella fall backward, taking her little brother down on top of her, his head twisting, Ella's fingers snagged in his hair. His face angled just enough that Belle can see the blood now, so unnaturally crimson, a Christmas red, smeared between the two of them, and Ella, open-mouthed, blood running in tiny rivulets between her teeth.

Belle will forever remember the low *thunk* in her belly, the way she scooted back across the floor, that she couldn't bear to look and yet couldn't turn away and instead clapped her hands over her eyes, staring through her fingers.

It is Jax who flies across the room. He rips Ella's hands from George's hair and pins her flat to the floor so George can escape, shooting like a spider across the rug and back into the corner of the room where he sobs and wails for their mother.

Belle can hear her mother coming from the second floor, her steps thunderous on the stairs overhead.

Jax pins Ella by sitting on her chest and the two of them slap-slap at one another until Jax rolls off and kicks her with the bottom of his foot. Ella moans. The sound, pitiful and vulgar, repulses Belle. But then, seeing her twin flat on the floor, her head weaving side to side, the gush of her breath in and out, Belle has a strange urge to reach for her, quiet her, wants to slip Ella's thumb in her own mouth and disappear into a long-ago warm wet darkness with her.

Their mother must have been in the middle of dressing. She has pulled a huge tent of a dress around herself but only managed the few snaps at the neck so that her belly, rippled in blue veins, protrudes, and the dress flies behind her as she comes through the dining room, her body tilting as she rounds the dining table and streams into the sunroom. She has no panties on and below the mound of her belly is a patch of downy hair that—for a brief second—makes Belle think she is hiding the new baby down there, that it has been under there and between her legs all this time. Much like a kangaroo hides her young in her pouch, their mother has been hiding the new baby from them. It isn't safe to let it out just now.

"Oh, my lord, oh, my babies!" Their mother looks from one to the other and clearly doesn't know which child needs her most. George is crying so hard in the corner that he can't get any breath into himself. But he sees her, sees his mother look from him to Ella and back again, sees the way she hesitates. Ella is on her back, her arms wrapped over and around herself, rocking side to side. George chokes, the blood pouring from a bite over his brow and a rip in his nostril that hangs like a small flap. He wipes at his face, smearing himself crimson. "Georgie, Georgie, don't touch it, honey." Their mother squats to the floor on her knees, scoops him to her.

"Ella was killing me," he manages to say, spitting and choking into her neck.

"No, honey, no. She wasn't killing you. Don't touch, Georgie. Let me look." She cups his face in her hands and tries to lift it. George allows it, his lips trembling, tasting the blood that runs from the rip in his nose. He squints the eye beneath the torn brow, blinking scarlet tears. His mother holds his head firmly at a short distance to look at him, study the wounds, but he can't bear the distance between the two and peels her hands away to dive into her chest again.

Jax knows that head wounds bleed excessively. He has heard his mother say so. He believes her, tells himself that this is not as bad as it looks. Only a few weeks ago he had hit his head on the blade of his sled when it flipped on an icy patch and the bleeding had been hard to stop. But he hadn't even needed stitches, much to his disappointment. Still, things look bad for his little brother.

Jax is still on the floor, keeping Ella at bay with an icy glare. To Belle, he seems terribly brave. Then, his teeth still locked together, Belle hears him say, "I hate you, Ella. I hate your guts."

"Don't say that, Jax. Shame on you!" says their mother.

Belle sees the sudden tears bloom and gush, a brief burst of rain on her big brother's face. Though Jax sits up quickly and wipes them away with his fingers, now tinged with his little brother's blood so that no one but Belle will ever know he has been crying, and it only looks like George's blood has smeared across his face in the struggle.

A bloody wash among all of them, watery pink in the run of Jax's tears, on Ella's mouth—as if she is an animal coming up from its kill— and George's head and face, his hair, their mother's neck and breasts where George buries himself. Red splattered brightly across the paned windows. Only Belle, her back to the wall, her small lips trembling, her arms crossed over her shoulders, is untouched. She will forever think of herself as having been spared.

Will forever wonder why.

George would need stitches, and the scars, both the one on his nose and the one on his brow, would fade to silver by the time he was grown. But still, there would be days when Belle looked at him, especially when his face was still soft and young and he hadn't yet begun to drag a razor across his cheeks, that she would see the scars and think of Ella, her blood-tinged teeth, her groans.

In the weeks that followed, their mother did her best to keep Ella away from the others. It couldn't have been easy. George, with bruises spreading from his wounds, his face too tender to touch, the itching of the stitches a particular discomfort, could only watch and ache for his mother. He wanted to curl in the curve of her waist, bury his bruised face in her neck. But she carried Ella everywhere. Up and down the stairs, into the kitchen, down to the cellar to do laundry, Ella on one hip and a basket of laundry on the other and the mound that would soon be Finney thrust in front of her. Ella, now the monster on his mother's hip, a slick trail of drool running down their mother's neck from where Ella tucked her head, sliding down her breasts beneath the loose maternity dresses she wore. Georgie watched from a distance that pained him, and the wanting of his mother was its own kind of agony. If she tried to pry Ella from herself, even to offer her food, a grumbly noise would rise out of her and she would cling harder to her mother's shoulders, trying at times to latch onto Hillary with her teeth, at which point the children would hear their mother snap at her "No, Ella, bad," as if she were a teething puppy rather than a nearly five-year-old child. But their mother could not hold Ella forever. Sooner or later she would have to let go.

2

Lynetta

Beechwood Institute, Owings Mills, Maryland
Friday, April 17, 2009

That woman wants Ella back and it rankles Lynetta to the bone.

Ella and Lynetta cut across the expanse of lawn, down a weed-patched trail they have worn flat and dusty over the years. The two women pass by the abandoned beehives at the edge of a dead orchard, the knotted apple and peach trees naked and gnarled. Eight hives, formerly five-story cedar contraptions, have weathered and caved in on themselves like small sets of dresser drawers—the kind that might be found in a child's nursery. Rotting in the elements. The bees long gone.

Ella Jules, the younger of the two, lags behind, dragging her tennis shoes through the damp thatches of grass, watching the dew spit from the tips of them. Her body sways side to side as she walks, her shoulders dipping with each stride. Ella enjoys the exaggeration of her own movements, likes the feel of the world around her and the way her body parts the air when she walks. She is lumpy, but not large, her belly rolling pink over the waist of her sweatpants that gather at her ankles but are still too long and fall in a tumble of fabric over her Velcro-fastened shoes. Her upper arms are loose, a soft arc of flesh hanging from them and swaying when she reaches her open hand to touch the forsythia bush that is woven into the gate she is now heading through.

Lynetta, ahead of her, turns on the pathway of cracked concrete, spindly bright-green straggles of chickweed bursting through fissures, and waits patiently—at first.

Just as Ella likes the way her shuffling footsteps send up sprays of mist from the grass, she also likes the way her hips drag along the overgrown shrubbery that roughly frames the walk, flipping the wiry boxwood branches as she moves clumsily along.

"Come on, missy," says Lynetta, tossing her arms over her chest. "Let's get a move on here." Ella trails a leopard-print purse behind her. The strap is too long and Lynetta had meant to shorten it before she gave it to her, but Ella had spotted it on top of Lynetta's mending bag before she'd had a chance to make the adjustment. It bounces at her heels, snagging on the broken concrete walk. "You're dragging your new pockey-book," Lynetta says.

At the rise of Thom Hall, Lynetta stops again, her key chain jingling from her wrist, shifting her weight from hip to hip, trying to get comfortable while standing still, and waits for Ella. "Come on, I say," but she doesn't say it roughly, and she says it more to herself than anyone. It is like this most mornings, even the coldest mornings when Lynetta wants nothing more than to get from point A to point B, when Ella takes her own sweet time, stopping to squint at the sky or rubbing her hands too roughly up and down the trunk of the paperbark maple to watch pieces of bark peel away. Sometimes she even licks the bark, something that drives Lynetta a little crazy, this constant licking of things. Stones and pennies, paper clips, pencils, hair barrettes.

Lynetta looks at Ella now, dragging her purse up the walk and reaching out to run her other hand along the branches.

"We go to work, Nettie," Ella says. She uses the heel of her hand to push her glasses up her nose.

"That's right, missy. And we're gonna be late, too, if you don't get a move on here."

Ella stops at the steps, just as she does every morning.

"Don't be lazy," says Lynetta. "Take those steps and get on up here."

"I not lazy," Ella huffs at her, and she takes the steps with a great deal of concentration, making certain that Lynetta understands just how exhausting an effort it is. "See what I do for you?" Ella says.

"Yeah, I see all right," Lynetta says, and smiles to herself. "Thank you so much for all you do for me."

"You welcome."

Thom Hall is cavernous and smells sour. The smell cannot be gotten rid of, no matter how hard the place is scrubbed and sanitized. Instead, over the years, it seems to have taken on layers: urine and sweat, blood, and—Lynetta knows this smell now—fear. She cannot only smell it, but she would swear to anyone who will listen that she can taste it where her tongue meets the roof of her mouth. A steely and bitter taste that takes the moisture from the back of her throat, and while she smells it less and less often these days, she knows that is only because there are fewer residents in Thom Hall to produce the vile scent.

Ella follows Lynetta into the front office to punch the time clock. Lynetta lets her scan the time cards fanned down the metal slats alphabetically, in search of the one with Lynetta's name on it. Ella knows to point to it first rather than snatch at it, checking with Lynetta to be sure she has selected the proper card. Too many times in the past Ella grabbed the wrong card and punched it before Lynetta had a chance to stop her. Ella slowly draws her fingers down the cards, tapping at *Krietta, Laurence*, and then shaking her own head, no, moving down to *Lehman, Lenore*, no again. Ella squints behind her glasses, and finally taps a finger to *Lezinsky, Lynetta*. She turns to Lynetta, waiting for the nod that allows her to take the card and punch it into the time clock, at which point she always gives a little shiver of her shoulders with the chink of the machine before removing the card and sliding it back in its proper place.

Lynetta pulls her mail from the wooden wall cubbies, slipping her paycheck into a deep uniform pocket. Standing over the trash can, she shuffles through junk mail flyers, saving one from Applebee's that offers a BOGO Sizzlin' Entrée special. One by one, she drops the rest into the trash can but stops at a long thickly packed envelope. The return address reads *Law Offices of Coldwell, Dannzinger, Myers.* This, she knows instinctively, cannot be good.

Hillary and Stone Jules want Ella back. This is the letter Lynetta was told by her attorney to expect. She has an appointment with her next week and she will give it to her, won't even open it. She's paying her to deal with it anyway. Her fees are making a deep dent in her savings, and she knows she can't afford to go at this with the Jules family for very long. They know that. Are likely counting on it.

3

Belle

Belle's cell phone is ringing on the kitchen counter, playing the theme to the movie *Jaws*, which, unbeknownst to the caller on the other end, is the ringtone Belle selected for her younger sister Tess. Tess's calls are almost always an alert to the latest crisis. But at this moment, on this rainy spring morning, Belle is too busy getting her children out the door for school to pick up her sister's call. No matter. Tess is tenacious and will call back every three minutes until Belle finally picks up.

Spring in Massachusetts, to Belle's way of thinking, is nothing more than a series of broken promises. The buds of the oak trees pearl on the branches and birdsong trickles from the tops of the trees in the early morning, but the sky remains thick with a gray mist and the ground is mud-soft, sucking at her kids' feet as they and a myriad of other rain-coated children stream from their homes to converge on the corner and wait for the school bus. A spring snow is still a possibility.

Mothers up and down the street peek from their side doors and from under the eaves of garages. Belle buckles and buttons her children in sync with all the other mothers of Longmeadow. Admonishments are tossed out reminding the children to neither lose nor remove their rain-coats on the way to school. Belle looks up and down the street, straight up into the sky, and wonders if there will really be a spring this year— with the sky so dark and the air so heavy—and here it is, April already.

The phone starts up with its percussive ringtone again. Tess is relentless. She doesn't have children, and so she can't possibly understand what Belle's mornings are like or the fact that every minute is choreographed. Belle's three children, but especially Jack, must be pushed, prodded, and herded through every step of their day.

The street is slate black and shining, last night's rainwater and a small stream of runoff gurgling along the curb. Six-year-old Jack is like a cat, rising on the tips of his toes to sidestep a puddle. Though he'll stop in his tracks to squat down and watch a worm wiggling on the asphalt. But his twin brother, Tobi, will undoubtedly slap his own small rubber-booted foot down—*smack*—into the running water and the only question that remains is will he manage to splatter his big sister, Kitty, with enough rainwater to cause a shriek and the hurling of at least one insult. Belle does not like discord amongst her children, would forbid it altogether if she could.

This time Tobi manages to do the inevitable deed with Kitty already safely clustered among her friends. She hardly notices his foolishness, and Belle is relieved. Watching from under the eaves of her side porch, she is left wondering if the water flowed over his boot and poured down into it so that he will spend the day in a sodden sock. It is likely that Belle will think of this at least two more times today. It's a long drive from her Massachusetts suburb to Baltimore, and she has plenty of time to think of these things. She worries that Kitty will leave her raincoat in the fifth-grade classroom again. She has three raincoats. Every child in Longmeadow has three or more raincoats. Two of Kitty's are MIA and if she leaves this one at school, she will be without a raincoat for tomorrow. The missing raincoat will be at the center of tomorrow morning's chaos—Saturday's donut run, chauffeuring to skating lessons, birthday parties. Belle's husband, Ben, capable as he is, will have no idea that it has been left at school, likely in the company of her other raincoats. He will flip through closets, dig in backpacks, search the car, and continuously instruct Kitty to find the darn thing. She will have no recollection as to where it could possibly be. Eventually, he will force her to put on her winter jacket instead. There will likely be a few tears.

At breakfast this morning, Jack and Tobi wanted to know how long their mother would be gone. Belle told them she wasn't sure, a few days, maybe longer. She knows this is hard on Jack, especially. Kitty, on the other hand, knows it all to be an adventure, this unplanned stretch of days without her mother at the hub of it. She is eleven and looks forward to slipping into her mother's role, so long as she is assured of her return. "I'll take care of the boys, Mom," she said.

"Well, thank you, Kitty. I'm sure your father will be a big help as well."

"That's right." Ben came around the corner with his coffee cup in his hand. "Kitty Kat and I will hold down the fort." He patted the top of his daughter's head with his free hand. "Don't worry about a thing," he said.

It is important to Belle that the children know she understands their concerns about her absence. Also important that they know she is not worried, that she knows they are in good hands with their father. And that she will be back. She will always come back.

Jack stops and turns to where she stands at the door, runs his small hands beneath the wide straps of his backpack, and rocks his body side to side. She urges him on with a blown kiss. The other children have gathered at the bus stop by now and Belle can see the flash of the yellow bus beyond the pine grove across the street, making its slow way to their block. "I'll be okay, Mom. Don't worry," she hears him say. And in this way, he is much like his namesake, Belle's older brother, Jackson—or Jax as they call him—trying to ease whatever misgivings have worried their way into Belle's head.

But unlike Jax, school doesn't come easily to Jack. He's too distractible, according to his teachers, unorganized, constantly forgetting or losing things. Up and wandering the classroom in the middle of a lesson, drawn to the rain dripping down the windows or the way the class guinea pig is chewing up an empty paper towel tube. Sometimes singing bits of songs out loud at his desk. When he's not at school, Belle is good at getting him back on track, steering him with a gentle hand to his shoulder when she needs to hurry him through the grocery store, knowing when to stop and give him her full attention and in that way head off his frustration at not being heard. She's tried to tell this to his teachers, tried to explain that there are ways of handling Jack that are much more productive than calling him out in class in such a way as to embarrass him. Sending him off to school in the morning often feels like she's sending him into enemy territory.

Belle tightens the sash of her robe as she makes her way back to her kitchen. She has three missed calls from Tess. But before Belle can decide whether to call her back now or wait until she's dressed, the house phone rings.

"I was hoping you'd left already," Tess says.

"Nope—it's a little crazy around here in the morning, Tess." Belle feels the resentment blooming, the seed of it unfurling whenever she is pulled from the business of her own young family and back to the complicated one she was born to. She can hear Tess huff on the other end. "What's wrong?" Belle knows the huff is a foreboding thing with Tess.

"Are you kidding? Everything, everything about this is wrong."

"I know. We'll be there soon, Tess. We'll figure this out."

"They're both insane," Tess says. "Mom more than Daddy. I *know* this is her idea, Belle. Daddy can't be on board for this. He always said Ella was better off there, always said that. Always said it was best for all of us—remember?"

Belle can only nod her head, knows Tess is asking a rhetorical question. "Have you talked to the boys?" The boys, Jax, George, and Finney, are now grown men but will always be referred to collectively as *the boys*.

"Oh, yeah. It's a mess, Belle." Tess tells her that George's bitchy wife is insisting he see the girls' ballet recital tonight, so he won't be coming down until tomorrow. Finney—well, who can know with Finney? He will likely find a way to back out at the last minute—patient emergency or some such shit. And Jax, the one they can usually count on, is flying standby out of California so who the hell knows when he'll show?

Belle feels a small flip in her stomach. "Goddammit," is all she can say. Jax has to be there. She doesn't want to do this without him. To her way of thinking, he's the only one who has any chance of convincing their parents that this is a terrible idea, a dangerous and half-baked idea that can only end badly. Still, the possibility of changing their minds is a long shot, at best. It's not like their parents actually consulted them. No—they just made up their minds to do this precarious thing and bring Ella home to live with them. They didn't consult the young Jules children when they sent Ella away thirty-two years ago—didn't even tell them until the night before she was to leave. So it would follow that they would suddenly, on what appears to be a whim, decide to bring her back. Permanently.

By the time Belle hangs up the phone, her husband, Ben, is back in the kitchen, picking up banana peels from the table and stowing the milk in the refrigerator.

"Why does it always look like a troop of monkeys has been through here every morning?" he wants to know.

"Damn it!" she says, suddenly spying Jack's math book on the floor beneath the kitchen table.

"I got this," Ben says. "I'll drop it off on my way to the office."

Between the two of them, she and Ben manage to be a safety net of sorts for Jack. It's a team effort. *Team Jack*, Ben often jokes.

Belle sighs and leans her head into his back where he stands at the sink. He turns and wraps his arms around her.

"Hey," he says. "It's going to be fine." He indulges her with a kiss on the forehead. "You guys can handle this. But be careful driving. It's sloppy out there." He nods out the kitchen window to the street. "And take it easy, lead foot. There's no rush."

No, she thinks, there's no rush, not now that her brothers are straggling in. But there is an urgency to deal with what has been recently revealed. Up until last Saturday when Tess made her first frantic call to all the siblings, the Jules children were blissfully unaware that the family fiat—to always do *what is best for the family*—was about to be violated.

Now the Jules family finds they are in a quandary. It turns out that the Beechwood Institute where Ella lives is closing. Stone and Hillary Jules have known this was on the horizon for two years but neglected to share this information with their children. Apparently, at least according to what Tess reports, their parents failed over the course of the last year to participate in formulating a plan for Ella's care. Instead, Ella's caretaker, a woman the family has spoken of (however rarely) as *Ella's angel*, has petitioned for and been granted guardianship by the state of Maryland. This, Belle now knows, had been the plan all along: Ella would live with Lynetta once Beechwood closed. But something has shifted recently and, for God-knows-what-reason, Hillary and Stone Jules have recently filed an appeal and are looking to bring the estranged Jules sibling home.

The five remaining Jules children—but especially Belle, having spent a lifetime adjusting to the strange jagged hole left by Ella's departure—believing themselves finally settled comfortably around the wound of it, now stand on the edge of a sinkhole. The idea of Ella coming back to the family home changes everything they once understood regarding her banishment to Beechwood.

"You better get dressed and get out of here," Ben says, smoothing his hand up her back and then nudging her toward the stairs.

When she returns, her overnight bag slung from her shoulder and wearing a long-sleeved T-shirt, socks, and no pants, she finds him sitting at the kitchen table, his suit jacket thrown over the back of a chair, the newspaper spread before him.

"Nice outfit," he says, nodding to her naked legs.

Her favorite jeans are still in the dryer. "You're going to be late," she says.

"I wanted to be sure you were okay. Got your cell phone charger?"

"Check." She slides her bag off her shoulder to the kitchen floor. "Look," she says, tapping her finger to the large color-coded schedule on the refrigerator. She starts to remind him that Tobi and Jack have skating lessons tomorrow morning, their activities color-coded green and blue respectively. Kitty is done in red.

Ben leans back in his chair and lifts his feet to the one across from him, puts up a hand to stop her. "Belle, I'm fine. We're fine. I've got this."

Of course he does, or thinks he does. She wants to remind him that her friend Jeannie will meet the kids at the bus stop this afternoon, that she will get Kitty to her riding lesson and keep the boys until he gets home. That he'll have to get Kitty from the barn by five thirty. Sometimes she can stay until six but never any later or the barn manager gets pissed. And she wants to remind him not to let Kitty talk him into stopping for snacks because the boys will be waiting and they get antsy. And Saturday—somebody has a birthday party. The gift is wrapped in her office and the invitation is on top of it. She wants to remind him that Kitty needs a poster board for her science project due on Monday and there may be some behind her desk, but she can't recall and if not, he'll have to pick it up for her. She wants to tell him all these things, but he has interrupted her, dropped his feet to the floor, his hands, palms up, beckoning her to him.

"My Belle of the ball," he says. She moves to him, grateful and perturbed at the same time, lets his hands move to her hips where he holds her solidly, looks up into her eyes. "We will be fine."

She can't help but think of Kitty's inevitable meltdown tomorrow morning when she can't find her raincoat. She loves this man but has always resented the way he can make everything she does look easy, as if it's no big deal to juggle three young children, her freelance gigs writing grants, and their beautiful home in a pricey neighborhood where weeds are not tolerated and potluck suppers with the neighbors are gourmet affairs.

When she first told him about the impending family crisis, when she had stormed into the house and tossed her cell phone to the sofa as if it were the cause of all this trouble, when she had stood before him wide-eyed and incredulous and said, *You're not going to believe this, you're not going to fucking believe this*, he only stared back, blinked, waited patiently for her to explain.

"They want to bring her home."

"Who?"

"Ella." Saying her twin's name felt strange to Belle in the same way she finds it strange, after her fifteen-year marriage, to be called by her maiden name. Something once a part of her and shed over time as she merged into her life with Ben, her children, the family they have built together.

But now, she and her siblings need to meet at the family home back in Baltimore. They will need a few days, maybe more to figure this out, talk some sense into their parents, get to the bottom of this disturbing revelation. The idea of having to leave her children and go back to her family home to confront what strangely feels now like the botched exorcism of Ella rouses a small terror in Belle that had been (she believed) long buried. Like a worm under her skin, she had felt the niggling of it but hoped never to see it in the light of day.

As for Ben, she had expected he would at least have some worries about manning the helm. But no, Ben was completely at ease with the idea—sorry to see her go, of course—but not at all doubting his ability to manage on his own.

She had tried to explain this to her mother once, the way he seemed to think everything she did was simple, but her mother had said it was because Belle was so good at it, such a good mother, a good wife, that she made it look easy, that it was a compliment if she thought about it. But Belle did think about it and she couldn't flip it on its head in a way that made it a compliment, at least not in the same way her mother could.

She reminds Ben now that they have a tour and meeting scheduled at the school they are considering moving Jack to. She has every intention of being there but acknowledges now that there's no way of knowing how things at the Jules home in Baltimore will go. Ben assures her he can handle it, won't make any decisions without her. There has been talk of moving Jack to a private school "more equipped to handle his needs," as it has been put to them. Belle is not inclined to make the move, not inclined to separate Jack from his twin in this way. The idea of doing so pinches at her mind in a way that makes her squint every time the idea is discussed, as if she has been forced to eat something sour. She is doing it now, in fact, and Ben notices, as he always does, and reminds her that no decision has been made. They have plenty of time to think about this.

Twins run in Belle's family, both sides and all over the place. There have been at least one set of twins in every generation of both the McDonally and Jules families as far back as Belle knows. Most are fraternal, some are identical. Belle is always asked if twins are hereditary. Fraternal twins are, but identical twins are not. The McDonally and Jules families are filled with both.

Belle's mother, Hillary, has identical twin sisters who have become, in their later years, Facebook aficionados and have mastered the art of jutting their chins just so and turning three-quarters for the most flattering selfies. Aunts Fiona and Frances have a substantial following for their pics showcasing the many times they arrive *accidentally* wearing similar if not identical outfits, bold primary colors, great swaths of scarves around their necks, matching pumps, and delicate but still formidable jewelry. At eighteen, they both were brought to their knees within minutes of one another in the twilight hours following their debutante ball with synchronized rotting appendixes. They married bankers who are cousins to one another, bore three children apiece, in sets, first each bearing a daughter and two years later each delivering twin boys on the very same day. Strange coincidences befall the McDonally aunts. Both of their husbands won a hefty Maryland Lottery by playing their birthday numbers, both tickets having been purchased by their wives and slipped in a birthday card. Both of their homes have been struck by lightning. Their own daughters married brothers.

When Belle thinks of her aunts, thinks of the way their lives weave around and through one another, colliding in spectacular ways, she cannot help but admit that she herself once spent most of her early life foraging—by way of friendships, the promiscuity of her early twenties, and eventually the bearing of children—for a similar connection.

But now, and in part because of her husband, Ben—because of the way he can finish her sentences, the way he knows she likes a beer poured into a thin glass, the way he asks if she is okay even before she knows she is not—she believes herself reconciled with the longing itself.

The Jules family had fulfilled its twin destiny in 1969 when Ella and Belle were born. Annabelle and Eleanora, *Belle* and *Ella*, the second and third children of Hillary McDonally and Gaston "Stone" Jules.

Belle was born first, the winner by thirty-six minutes. Ella, on the other hand, an afterthought, locked in her mother's womb while the unaware doctor tidied up after Belle's birth. By the time Ella had made herself known she was wedged into the birth canal, a pulsing umbilical cord lassoed around her neck. Finally, Ella was ripped from the wedge of her mother by the tight grip of forceps, and Hillary McDonally Jules had awakened to a blue and lifeless Ella.

Belle's mother didn't talk about Ella much after she was sent away, and so when she did, the Jules children listened and listened carefully, as if something might be revealed to them that would make everything fall into place.

"Honest to God, babies," she once said. She always called them *babies*. "Honest to God, babies," she said. "Your sister Ella was born as blue as that china." And she had waved a finger in the general direction of the china cabinet.

"Is she skin color now?" Finney asked. "I hope she's blue. I want to be blue, too." Finney was only five at the time. Already he wanted to be anything other than what he was.

"That's stupid," George said. "You're so stupid. You're as stupid as she is."

"Darling," said their mother. "You do not want to be blue. You are perfect the way you are."

In nearly every regard, Ella had been perfect, too. Only a few ounces lighter than Belle. Bore the requisite ten fingers and ten toes. But even as the color eventually streamed back into her little body, she never actually *woke up*, as their mother put it.

Five days after Belle and Ella were born, Hillary and Belle came home from the hospital but without Ella. The pictures of them coming up the walk frame Stone Jules cradling his wife's elbow that cradled Belle. A look on Hillary's face that Belle came to understand better as she got older, sad but hopeful, suggesting her mother knew too much and feared the worst. A look she wore when Belle was fifteen and got caught out all night with Duke Larson and swore that nothing happened. It was the face she wore when Finney brought home the love of his life, and Belle remembers the way it pinched at her mother's face and threatened to pull the tears from her eyes. Just a few years ago she had seen that very same look wash over her mother at Belle's youngest sister Tess's wedding. And only last year the same sad smile had graced her face when she announced that her dear friend Bets had taken a turn for the worse.

Ella spent weeks in the hospital before she was finally brought home. And because there had been no preparation for twins (and Belle thinks now that perhaps there was no expectation that Ella would ever be coming home), she was placed in Belle's crib with her and they were reunited. Belle was told that during the first year of their lives, Ella did little more than lie in the crib while Belle blew through the milestones of smiling, rolling over, and crawling. She was often found snuggling against Ella on cold nights and known to suck on Ella's thumb rather than her own.

Ella wasn't completely passive, however, and was often inconsolable, raging and wailing until she sent herself into fits of hiccups. And she was a biter, able to lock down her jaw like a piranha and tear flesh. Eventually, as she learned to scoot around in the crib and could actually seek out Belle, she had to be moved to another crib. Belle still has a small scar on the top of her foot where Ella's two tiny bottom teeth pierced the flesh. They all have scars from Ella, of one kind or another.

Belle likes to think that she and Ella knew each other in a different kind of way when they were in the womb together. She likes to think that the sound of one another's heartbeat purring beneath that of their mother's was a comfort to them both and that they nestled peacefully in a warm dark world, squirming to rearrange their limbs against one another. What she does know, what she can be certain of, is that within her mother's womb were two identical babies, peaceful and dreamy babies, with similar natures and endless potential. But on the other side of that womb, nothing would ever be even slightly similar between the two of them.

It's still gray, dreary, and damp by the time Belle leaves, and the windshield wipers slap away a misty veil that settles on the window every few seconds. The streets in Longmeadow are wide and lined with massive oaks. The homes are large and solid. Many are historical (or hysterical, as Jack says), and so they have settled into the ground and nestled into their lawns in a way that suggests they have always been here and always will.

Belle likes permanence, likes to know that things will stay familiar. When she returns from Baltimore, the golf course at the Longmeadow club will still be unnaturally green for so early in the spring. The Dunkin' Donuts on the corner will still be overflowing with teenagers every morning and she will still have to pull cautiously through the light as they are careless and foolish, bouncing and whirling in their brightly colored jackets like confetti caught in the wind. Her friend Jeannie's house, a slate gray saltbox with red shutters, will still stand guard at the entrance to the neighborhood, and Elmo, her fat and often muddy golden retriever, will still curl by the front door waiting for the kids to get home from school.

Belle's cell phone rings on the seat next to her. She can see that it is Jax, but she is a rule follower and refuses to pick it up while driving. Though she is anxious to know if he will make it. Jax, her beautiful big brother, the one they all need but who needs no one.

Sometimes Belle imagines that he is her twin, rather than Ella. Only fifteen months older than Belle, they shared the same group of friends growing up. Furthermore, he was the one who sent her emails full of postpartum advice after Kitty was born and Belle had spent an entire summer dragging herself around the house with aching soggy breasts and the same pair of too-tight gym shorts that she couldn't muster the energy to toss in the wash. Five years later, when the twins were born, he spent part of his summer break from teaching crashing on her sofa. He was good company and excelled at walking and shushing babies, gathering stray balled-up diapers from the sofa and coffee table, and cooking strange casseroles (that Kitty refused to touch). He once chauffeured Kitty to a birthday party where she balked at being left and so he had spent the next two hours playing freeze-tag and racing around with an egg on the end of a spoon. He even took to adding a silken splash of Baileys Irish Cream to Belle's morning coffee and handing it to her with a wink, Ben at his back and never the wiser. "Relax," he whispered. "You're not driving." Belle worried that it was bad for her milk, and he argued that it was good for her, even went so far as to find an article on the Internet stating that one drink per day was beneficial for milk production. She couldn't imagine how deep into the Internet he had to go to find that article, but she loved him for it just the same. Even now, she is soothed with a kind of nostalgia for the creaminess of a spiked mug of coffee sipped in the company of Jax and the hosts of *Good Morning America.*

It is still mind-boggling to Belle that Jax is single. So many of her friends over the years have had mad crushes on him. But nothing has ever lasted more than a few months. His relationships are short-lived, expiring just around the time Belle starts to wonder if a particular girlfriend is *the one.* He's happy, he tells her. Marriage isn't for him. Belle suspects he's telling the truth. Unlike Belle, Jax doesn't seem to be searching for a connection, likes his own company well enough, and apparently enjoys the freedom being single affords him.

By the time she reaches the Jersey Turnpike, traffic has picked up and she slides into a faster lane, spies a rest stop ahead, and moves over again to exit and calls Jax back.

"Got a flight," he says when he picks up. "I'm boarding in five."

She is relieved, though she never doubted he'd make it. She knew he'd find a way, even if he had to hopscotch across the country.

"Do we have a plan?" she asks.

"Nope. We're winging it."

She tells him that Finney and George won't arrive until Saturday, hopefully before the dinner planned for Saturday night when Ella will be joining them.

There is a long pause and she can hear a mumbled boarding call in the background. "You know, she's actually spending the night," Belle says.

He knows, he tells her.

"She's not so scary anymore, Belle. It's not like when we were kids."

She doesn't know what to say to this. The guilt thumps in her chest. Jax is the only sibling who has seen Ella since she was banished thirty-some years ago. He has nudged Belle over the years to go visit, and she has said she would think about it. But then she only doubled her efforts *not* to think about it.

"Yeah, well," is all she can think to say.

When they hang up, she is uncomfortably snagged on the guilt she has worked so hard to shed over the years. She can't explain it, even to herself, but she knows it is rooted in something deep and primal—love and fear and self-preservation. A strange sense of relief that still nibbles at her core and nips even more ferociously whenever good fortune befalls her. And always, there is the sense that she has escaped something by virtue of a tragically consequential coin toss.

She pulls back out to the freeway, rolls down her window to whip the thoughts out of her head. Tomorrow will be the first time Ella will join the family in thirty-two years. Belle shakes her head, can't imagine what that will look like. What Ella will look like at thirty-nine years old. What their family will look like with Ella back in the center of it. She imagines it as a kind of distortion, her estranged sister pulsing in the center of them all, pushing all of them to the edges of an old familiar space that Belle, for one, does not want to return to.

4

Tess

Tess arrives first. Always the first. Last child born, first to show up when duty calls. The price for having only moved to Silver Spring, an hour's drive (on a good day) from her parents' Baltimore home. When Stone and Hillary had slid off I-83 last fall and ended up in the hospital emergency room with lacerations and minor airbag burns to their faces, Hillary cradling a broken wrist, her father doubled over by two busted ribs, Tess was the one to rush to Mercy Hospital in a torrential downpour. She spent the next four days back in her childhood bedroom caring for both of them, but glad—on some level—to have an excuse to avoid going into the law firm. It wasn't too hard to work remotely, and thankfully she didn't do litigation work and so her actual physical presence wasn't required. In fact, given what was going on with her then-husband, who also happened to be a partner in the firm, it was likely a relief for the entire firm to have Tess out of the office. Now, at thirty-one, childless, and logging the recently failed marriage behind her, she is the available one.

Today, having arrived first, she is hugged heartily by both of her parents, encouraged to have a cup of coffee, and forced to deflect questions about her work. She changes the subject by offering to sweep the kitchen floor. Her father has been doing yardwork and the floor is littered with grass clippings. Her mother rises from the table and grabs the broom and dustpan from the pantry, insisting that Tess stay seated at the table with her father, finish her coffee.

Tess is certain that (though they would never say so) her parents feel abandoned by their other children, flung far and wide. Except for Ella, of course. With Jax on the West Coast, Belle in Massachusetts, George and Finney scattered north and south respectively, Tess considers Hillary and Stone to be her responsibility.

Her father takes a sip of his coffee and settles the mug back on the table, runs a finger over the rim. Tess knows him well enough to know he is gathering a question in his mind, trying to find just the right way to phrase it. "How's the new place?" he finally asks. "Comfortable?"

The question is a loaded one. What he really wants to know is if she's settling comfortably around the loss of her marriage. The short answer is no. She hasn't been at this long enough to get used to it. Tess has never been comfortable with failure, but a failed marriage is particularly complicated. Again, she deflects and tells him she has two tickets to the Annapolis Spring Sailboat Show next Saturday, a day she knows her mother is planning to go to a garden show with her own sisters. Would he like to join her?

"Then it's a date," she says when he agrees to it.

When her father took his annual fly-fishing trip to Montana last fall, Tess was the one to schedule dinner with her mother and a Saturday shopping excursion that had her trekking north to Baltimore twice that week. And when Hillary took off last spring on a five-day cruise through the Bahamas with her sisters, the infamous aunts, Tess once again headed home to join her father for a round of golf and dinner at the club.

Tess was also the one to accompany her mother to the funeral of her good friend Bets back in December. Stone had come down with a wicked cold and couldn't go with her. Tess didn't mind so much. She'd been fond of Bets, had known her all her life, and the loss of Bets had triggered in Tess a surprisingly painful wave of nostalgia, an ache for the childhood she remembered. Her loss dredged up memories of magical tours through Bets's garden, the late-night laughter of adults *cocktailing*, as her mother called it, on the bluestone patio beneath Tess's bedroom window, and the many Thursday mornings Tess had spent at Bets's kitchen table playing checkers while her mother visited Ella (the older children having been shuttled off to school). But she hadn't planned to spend the entire day, from the morning service and into the early evening, beside her mother, who was oddly quiet and not extending herself the way she usually did to a grieving family. It would have been more like her mother to orchestrate the wake and spend the evening wrapping the offerings of food in foil and securing them away in the Garrisons' refrigerator with heating instructions taped to the various dishes.

Thinking back on it, Tess should have known something was on her mother's mind. She'd been different somehow, preoccupied, maybe. A little distant. Not her usual steady self. But at the time Tess attributed it to the death of Bets Garrison and the lingering aftermath of that loss.

This latest emergency, the impending and wholly ludicrous—the downright dangerous—idea of bringing Ella home, only revealed itself on a recent Saturday when Tess had come to Baltimore to attend a national meeting of the regional garden clubs at her mother's request. Hillary was to be a speaker at the event and Tess felt it her duty to support her from the audience.

It was only afterward, on the way back to the family home with Hillary driving, her nose lifted over the steering wheel, her arms sheathed in a dusky pink suit that flattered her coloring but made her seem more matronly than Tess liked to think of her, that her mother had casually mentioned she was thinking of bringing Ella home. Tess had slammed her foot down to the floor of the car as if she herself had been driving, as if she could put the brakes on the whole thing with a fierce stomp of her foot. What Tess would find most infuriating, in the days to come, was the fact that by telling Tess first, her mother had set her up to have to be the one to tell the others. When Tess asked (her foot still slammed flat to the floor of the car), "When did you decide this?" her mother had only squared her eyes to the road and refused to answer.

Tess's father is now back to his morning yardwork. The coffee cups have been washed and put away, and Tess is following her mother around the house, scooping up stacks of newspapers, sliding books back into the shelf. Her mother stops to run her fingers over the edges of a framed photo before setting it back on the sideboard. An old photo of Jax, George, and Finney, *the boys*, lined up by height in front of the massive hedges. Jax is probably thirteen in the photo, George would have been ten, and Finney seven. A first-day-of-school photo.

The children attended Our Lady of Mercy, a prestigious prep school known for its shallow Catholic roots, shortage of actual nuns, and only a small campus chapel, but it was, Tess recalls, gratifying to their father to know that his children attended a school with expectations of morality and decency, where cursing would not be tolerated, and sex education would never be on the docket.

In the photo her brothers are dressed in matching khaki pants, white-collared shirts, and miniature blue blazers, except for Jax, unusually tall for his age and requiring a man's blazer, drastically tailored for his wispy frame. Her mother sighs and tilts the picture just so. Reaches for another—*the girls*—Tess and her big sister Belle. In the photo Butter Bean leans into Belle, his tongue lolling, a paw lifted as if he's begging to be petted. Belle is twelve, her long blond hair hanging to her waist, her blue eyes as clear and bright as her father's, her chin thrust in the air, and a plaid skirt landing way too high on her thighs. Tess remembers the way Belle used to roll the waistbands of her skirts to make them shorter, much to her mother's dismay. Belle is square to the camera, grinning, caught in the act of flipping her hair off her shoulder. It would have been 1981, Tess thinks, which accounts for the fact that Tess herself is not in a school uniform but wearing a bright yellow dress, smocking across the chest. She would have been off to preschool for the first time, only four years old, and this likely accounted for the deer-in-the-headlights look the camera captured and the way she held her big sister's hand, the two of them, just Butter Bean and the two sisters. Ella would have been gone almost four years by then. Tess never knew her, but that didn't mean she didn't feel her absence, rising like the glaring sun between her and her big sister.

There are no pictures of Ella.

Ella was something of a secret that—as a child—Tess had pried out of her mother in tiny jagged pieces—the mysterious missing child, the one whose room Tess now occupied.

What does she look like? Tess wanted to know. What does she sound like? Is she pretty like Belle? Does she go to school at the place where she lives? Who are her friends, is she a Girl Scout, is she mean? Who tucks her in at night? Who fixes her hair in the morning if her mother isn't there? And is she coming back, hmm?

Hillary must have done her best to answer such questions without getting sucked into an abyss. Ella looked like Belle, only different, too. She was not a Girl Scout. She had aides who tucked her in at night. She went to a special school. She was not mean. And no, she wasn't coming back. She was better off in the other place. *For the best*, her mother said. Tess couldn't be sure if this was something her mother said wistfully, as if she wished it weren't so, or if it was meant to be an assurance of some kind. The *why* of it all hovered over Tess's childhood. What were the rules? What transgression merited banishment? Was redemption a possibility? Eventually, Tess stopped asking about her. What clung to her throughout her childhood, however, was the thin awareness that a child could be erased. Tess's mother fluffs the throw pillows and pats them into place along the arms of matching chairs. Stands back and surveys the room. Satisfied, she motions for Tess to follow her upstairs.

Tess thinks of her mother as soft, in all ways. She was soft with her children and soft with her husband. And so, one could find some degree of comfort in such a mother, wrapped in her embrace, tangled in her arms. But, like a warm quilt and a deep bed, there was no real safety in it. The boogeyman could still find Tess, tucked away under the layers.

She needed a fortress to hide behind. That was her father.

Gaston "Stone" Jules grew into his name much as a Dickens character does with the turning of each page. "Stone" was a powerful shortened version of his given name, and surely it made demands of him.

Even as a small child, Tess knew he was a beautiful man. Women stared at him, store clerks and waitresses were both solicitous and coy in his presence. These things did not go unnoticed. At social gatherings—whether it was a church coffee hour or a club formal—she watched the way the men gathered near him, listened attentively, and measured the weight of their own contributions with a quick glance to Stone Jules. When he spoke, people listened. Over six foot, her father is still a tall man, and he seems especially tall now that he is about to crest seventy years old and does not appear to have lost an inch of height. He still has a full head of silver hair, chiseled cheekbones (that Belle and Jax inherited), and piercing blue eyes that glitter when he laughs, as though the sun is passing over his face. Disappointment, on the other hand, brings his brows together like clouds converging. Tess hates to disappoint him, hates the way it makes the muscles in his jaw flex. She reads him easily. Knows that the dragging down of his face is a failure on someone's part to meet what he perceives as reasonable expectations.

He is, as his name suggests, firm and unyielding, often rigid and demanding, but for young Tess, there was some comfort in that. She trusted him and thereby trusted in his expectations of her. All the Jules children were expected to achieve, play sports, excel in all endeavors. Tess did what was expected of her because she loved him but also because there was a certain sense of safety that came with having fallen into his favor.

Perhaps she is most surprised now by the fact that he seems to be on board with her mother's harebrained idea to bring Ella home. It seems so unlike him. Even though Ella was not often mentioned by name when Tess was growing up, there had never been any doubt that sending her away had been the right thing to do. Stone constantly alluded to the fact that sending Ella away had been in everyone's best interest.

If they went as a family to the club for dinner, and assuming the meal had gone well and George hadn't melted down with a fit of tears and Jax hadn't sat like a rock-faced lump of belligerence, but if it had been a pleasant meal with gentle talk and a few laughs, Stone would almost always say, as they were preparing to leave, "Ah, so nice to have such a lovely family that we can do this with, isn't it, Hillary? Such wonderful and well-behaved children." It was no secret that the insinuation was that they certainly couldn't have taken Ella anywhere like this restaurant, this club, this dinner theater. Stone would look around the table and Tess would always feel his gaze on her because she was, she knew, the best behaved of them all, always sitting up straight, putting her napkin in her lap, saying *may I have* rather than *CAN I have* like Finney always did when he gave the waiter his order. She never ordered the most expensive thing on the menu, even if it was her favorite, like steamed shrimp cocktail and Maine lobster, and she always said *please* and *thank you* and *give my compliments to the cook*, which never failed to make her father smile. So, when he happened to mention how wonderful his family was, how well behaved, how stunningly handsome, she had no doubt that he attributed much of that wonderfulness to her. Her mother, on the other hand, would always look ashen and, Tess noticed, never looked him in the eye when he said these things. Her eyes would flit over her children instead, and Tess was certain that she was counting them off one by one and coming up short a child.

Ella will be leaving Beechwood and those gates will close behind her forever in less than a month. Tess's understanding, what little understanding she and her siblings have of the situation, is that the state has been parceling out its residents over the last two years to group homes. A precious few have returned to their families, though it never would have occurred to Tess that Ella would return to her childhood home. In fact, that was quite improbable. But, as Tess learned, her parents have recently petitioned the state for guardianship. This involved filing an appeal against the previously approved guardianship of Ella to Lynetta Lezinsky.

The state approved Lynetta's guardianship over a year ago, and there had been no complaints at the time from Stone and Hillary Jules, at least not that Tess was aware of. Ella has been a ward of the state's Beechwood Institute since she was eight years old, first as a resident of Thom Hall and then having spent the last twenty-seven years living with her aide, Lynetta, in a small cottage on the Beechwood campus. Now her parents and Lynetta are embroiled in a custody battle. Tess, armed with a law degree, has reviewed the paperwork at the request of her mother. Her parents had engaged the family attorney and Tess suspects that her mother's request—that Tess take a look—was merely a courtesy. Tess had agreed to look everything over in the hopes that she might discover a huge flaw in their plan, but sadly, to Tess's way of thinking, her parents stood a good chance of winning their appeal.

Now, Tess's mother is flitting around the house, getting ready for her return as though Ella is coming home from college. She's had a bedroom painted and moved in new twin beds—as if Ella might be having sleepovers with her girlfriends. She put up new drapes, had shelving installed in the closet, and even put a telephone in the room.

"Who is she going to call, Mom?" Tess asks her. She is following her mother around the house because Hillary doesn't give her much choice.

Tess follows her into the bedroom—Tess's old bedroom, soon and according to the ill-conceived plan at hand, to become Ella's bedroom again. Hillary hands her a set of sheets and motions to the other twin bed. Dutifully, Tess begins to make the bed. Hillary holds a pillow tucked under her chin, tugging and jiggling the pillowcase up over the pillow, releasing the pillow from under her chin and shaking the case to urge the pillow down into it. Pulling the spread up over the bed, she motions for Tess to do the same with a wag of her finger and then she stands back and surveys the room. "Looks nice, don't you think?"

Tess has to admit that it does.

"Like the color?"

"I do." The walls have been painted a soft mossy green, and the ceiling is now a buttery yellow. "It's nice, Mom."

"Soothing, don't you think?" She pats the bed. "I think she'll like it."

"Oh, Mom, I don't see how this can possibly work." Tess follows her out into the hall and down the wide stairway, anticipating the creaks in the steps midway down and again on the last step. "I mean, really, have you made any sort of plans, have you even thought about this?" she says to her back.

Hillary stops abruptly on the last step and turns to Tess, her hand coming down firmly on the finial.

"For God's sake, Tess, I have thought about nothing else for more than thirty years."

5

Lynetta

When they first brought her in, Lynetta didn't like her very much. She wasn't easy to like. No matter how much they had tried to dress her up, there was no way they were going to make that child likable. They must have tried to put a bow in her hair because there was a funny little knot of hair pouffing up on her head like she had gone and ripped it out and been none the worse for the pain of taking strands of hair with it. She made nasty little noises that included a gurgling growl that came from the back of her throat, and she kept reaching under her dress and pulling it away from her body. It would have been new. Maybe it itched.

Such a silly waste of money, Lynetta thought, to buy a child like her a pretty new dress like that. Soon they would take it away and use it for dress-up days, visits and such, and maybe it would fit another child as well.

Lynetta knew she had been asked to Dr. Dyson Carter's office to meet a new patient (later to be referred to as *residents*, but this was 1977 and so she was a patient) but she was surprised to find that the child was only eight years old. It was not often that they arrived so young. The little ones were usually abuse cases, or abandonment, horrible neglect. But this child was different. She was clean and she was, as far as Lynetta could tell, cared for. The mother's blinking eyes, swollen and red-rimmed, watched the child on her lap but never looked to her husband or Dr. Carter. There was a strangeness to this, and when at one point she buried her cheek into the child's head of hair, Lynetta considered the deep breath the woman took to be something intimate, something between the two of them that had nothing to do with any of the others in the room, as if she and the girl breathed the same air. When the child leaned forward from her mother's lap and banged her head, once, twice, on the sharp edge of Dr. Carter's desk, the mother wrapped her fingers over the girl's forehead and pulled her to her chest with such maternal ease that it made Lynetta ache. The mother winced when Ella tried to bite her ear, and then scolded her sharply— even hopefully, like the scolding might mean something—*No, Ella, no!*

And while Lynetta couldn't for the life of her understand how a mother could send her child—even this child—away, she also couldn't understand how a mother could be expected to care for a child like this at home. Especially, she thought at the time, a mother with so many more young children at home, so she had been told. She had heard about the Jules family and their children. And this one, Eleanora Jules, would have to be placed if this mother was going to be able to properly raise her other children. *For the good of the family.*

The handsome Mr. Jules kept crossing and uncrossing his legs. Lynetta, even though she was standing quietly in the back of the room, could see the swing of his legs, one over the other. She understood that he would be anxious. But in spite of his discomfort, he stayed focused on his wife, and everything he was saying came out soft and tender, as though each word was meant to wrap around his pretty wife, keep her from feeling too much.

"One of the finest state institutions, we researched that," he said. "We have a lot of faith in this program, and of course, my wife, she's carried most of this burden as I'm sure you can understand," and he nodded at her. "And we think you can help Ella and teach her, and of course, it's best for the others at home, the other children." He smoothed his hand down his wife's arm, the arm wrapped around Ella. Mrs. Jules might have flinched, Lynetta couldn't be sure. There was a small movement in her shoulder that ended with the mother brushing the hair from her daughter's forehead.

"We have a large brood, Dr. Carter." He looked at his wife as he said it. "My wife is a wonderful mother, a wonderful mother."

"No doubt," said Dr. Carter. And even Lynetta had nodded imperceptibly from the back of the room.

It was going to be important to make a good impression on the Jules family. This was a family of some means and that mattered to an institution like Beechwood. Most wealthy families sent their afflicted children to private schools and hospitals, but the Jules family wanted their daughter close by, *for holidays and such, and visits, of course, and we'd like to bring her home sometimes—once in a while.*

Lynetta watched Dr. Carter when Mr. Jules said this. Families said this sort of thing all the time. But the emotions that would be churned up today would not be something they would want to experience again. Bringing a child like this home again, and then bringing her back to Beechwood would be painful. Certainly not something they would want to repeat. Knowing this and knowing the guilt they would feel not living up to their best intentions always led Dr. Carter to offer consolation in the form of a preemptive strike. He would hand them their excuse and they were free to draw upon it as needed.

"Certainly," Dr. Carter had said to Mrs. Jules. "I understand, but often our families find that bringing the children home for holidays and such only makes things more difficult. Eleanora . . ."

"Ella," said the mother, and she brushed her hand down the back of the girl's head to try and still her. Ella reached up into her mother's hair and pulled it to her own mouth. "We call her Ella. She won't know you're talking to her if you call her Eleanora."

"Of course," he said.

"We never call her that."

"Ella," he said carefully, "may find it difficult to make the transition back and forth between two homes. She'll have a very comfortable routine at Beechwood and fine care from our aides like Miss Lynetta here." He nodded to Lynetta, standing in the back of the room, wearing her squeaky white shoes and her white dress. She loved her uniform, was proud to wear it, and always kept it the brightest white with a combination of good soap, bleach, and baking powder. She knew it didn't flatter her pale coloring because Lance had told her so the first time he saw her in it. "Makes you look like a giant marshmallow." She couldn't tell if he was being cruel or truthful.

If the Juleses were happy with Ella's care, there might be some extras. A Christmas tree in the dayroom, perhaps, though it would have to be set up in such a way that the children couldn't reach it, maybe a field trip to the zoo for some of them, or a birthday party with cupcakes, but no gifts. Personal possessions only caused trouble in a place like this.

Ella reached to the top of her own head and pulled at clumps of hair like something was in there that she needed to dig out from under her scalp.

They always do that, thought Lynetta. *Don't like nothing in their hair. Don't like pants too tight or socks with toes turned under or collars that tickle at their necks.*

Lynetta sensed the meeting coming to an end and quietly moved to the side of the room, waiting for the director to nod her over and say it was time for her to help Miss Ella get acquainted with the school. She couldn't help but notice the way the handsome husband was looking at his wife and talking to her like he would drink up all her pain if he could and let it soak and simmer on his insides if only she would stop hurting so.

Dr. Carter always prescribed a little something for parents to give incoming patients on the day they arrived. A little something in the morning. Something to keep the fuss out of them. Ella was trying to keep her eyes open and rubbed at her face, dragging her hand over her lower lip so it pulled down like a flap.

Dr. Carter looked to Lynetta now, tipped his chin to signal it was time. Lynetta came to Mrs. Jules's side and helped take Ella from the woman's lap. Ella shrugged her off and dug more deeply into her mother.

Lynetta was not surprised. *Funny thing about these kind of folks,* she thought, *is they're dumb as cows but they know—just like cows know— they know when something's not right. They know when bad things are coming, like a bath or a thunderstorm, and this one won't be any different.*

In the years to come, Lynetta would come to understand that

comparing her charges to animals often revealed more about the person who said it than the patient. Sometimes the comparisons were crushing to her—*like a wild animal, a rabid dog, crazy as a loon*. And while some comparisons were meant to be endearing, Lynetta would know that beneath the words was a need to see the afflicted as less than human. She would grow to be more thoughtful about her observations. But on this day, still relatively new to her job, she had begun to notice among the patients a kind of instinct, heightened, she thought, by an inability to grasp meaning from words so that they—particularly the children— relied on other senses instead. A change in tone, a disruption in the schedule, a sudden commotion, all served as a warning of things to come, and most of them bad.

Mrs. Jules struggled half-heartedly to untangle Ella's arms and legs as the child's breathing became more rapid and her fingers spun at her mother's blouse and buttons. But Ella was sleepy and her mother was finally able to take the child's wrists in her hands and place them in Lynetta's own. Eventually, Lynetta got Ella standing, though she was unsteady and wobbled on her feet. Mrs. Jules reached out to brace her child's hips, but Ella leaned into Lynetta without hesitation. Hillary put her own hands back in her lap. Her fingers fluttered as if she wasn't used to being empty-handed.

Ella's bags had already been unloaded from the family car and so there wasn't much else for the Juleses to do. Mrs. Jules told Lynetta she had packed some licorice for Ella and that she liked licorice. Mr. Jules agreed with her like it was very important to remember the licorice.

Lynetta couldn't help thinking about who would have unpacked that bag and what were the chances of her licorice still being there. Patients weren't supposed to have much of anything anyway, least of all some- thing everyone would want to have a piece of.

"I'll take good care of her, Mrs. Jules," Lynetta said. "Promise." And she meant it.

Hillary put her arms around Ella's waist and started to pull her back. "Be good, darling. Be very, very good."

All that business gnawed at Lynetta's own womb so that she thought she might bend over double for a second with the sudden pain of it. She knew what it was like to lose a child and all the dreams you attached to her. The whole time she was carrying the baby, she had been wondering if it would have her blue eyes, and then, when the baby girl was born without ever taking a breath, she never knew. Lynetta never saw her eyes. They were closed and when she asked, *What color is her eyes*, no one ever answered her and no one thought to open the lids and look. Then she was gone. Never held her or nothing. Hours later, recovering in her hospital bed, she asked a nurse if there was any way someone could look, tell her what color her baby's eyes were. The nurse said all babies are born with blue eyes, but Lynetta wasn't sure that was true.

Only a few weeks later, her bottom still itching from the stitches and an ache between her legs when she stood too long—which was every day, as she never sat down on her shift—she could only recall the waxiness of the baby's skin and the heart shape of her little lips. When Lance heard about it, he said it was just as good that way anyway. "Probably for the best," he said.

A stupid thing for Lance to say, she knew that. But he never wanted a baby in the first place, never wanted to get married at seventeen and move in with Lynetta and her father, never wanted to try to go to school all day and work all night at Gino's so that he came to bed smelling like greasy fries, his hands all sticky with Coke syrup.

Lynetta knew he would be leaving soon. He'd spent the last two nights back at his mom's house, not even bothering to call. But the good thing about the kind of pain that came from having her baby die was that it left no room for the pain of his leaving her. It was no matter to her.

She named her Becky, though no one cared whether she had a name or not. But in Lynetta's memory, she is Becky and she has blue eyes.

6

Tess

It is George who first conjures Ella for Tess. George who manages to summon the specter of Ella into Tess's life—even though Ella was gone months before Tess was born and she has never seen her in the flesh and blood, knows her only as the missing *something*.

Tess has Ella's former bedroom, and George appears to take perverse pleasure in showing Tess around her own room and recalling Ella's occupation of it. Under the throw rug is a one-foot-square metal grate from which the heat once rose in the circa 1910 home. The grate shaft falls two stories to the basement and with a flashlight, Tess can peer into its depths and vaguely make out the shape of things Ella has fed to it—hairbrushes, possibly a GI Joe doll, a man's belt, a pair of glasses, lipstick tubes, and, most disturbing of all, the small pink arm of a baby doll.

"She used to live down there," George tells Tess. "Because she was very very bad."

Tess flips the corner of the carpet back over the grate and clambers onto her bed where she snuggles into Butter Bean, the huge beast of a yellow Lab spread across her pillows.

Hillary and Stone seldom speak of Ella, though the children know their mother goes to visit her on Thursdays. She always takes a bag of red shoestring licorice, and her pocketbook smells of it for days after.

Georgie is showing Tess his scars—the tiny tear in his nose and another more jagged and angry inch of scar tissue that cuts across his eyebrow and divides it neatly—explaining in great detail that Ella once tried to eat him, face-first, but that Jax had saved him. George flops across Tess's bed, Butter Bean between the two of them now and nuzzling Tess's small hands to solicit an ear scratch. Tess can hear the tapping of her mother's feet coming down the hall and then the slight squeak of her weight shifting as she pauses outside the bedroom door. George's eyes lift over Tess's head to the empty doorframe and he is suddenly quiet.

Their mother shows herself in the doorway and stops, motionless now. She isn't angry, but stands at the threshold, not really looking at the two of them, her eyes moving around the room as if she spies a ghost flitting about. Then she says quite calmly, "She can't hurt you, Tess."

"She tried to eat George," Tess reminds her.

"No, honey, she didn't." But Hillary still will not look at the two of them. "Can we get Butter Bean off the bed?" she says kindly.

George is twelve. Tess almost five. George likes to tease Tess and she doesn't completely trust everything he tells her, but he does have the scars to support his claim.

"It was an accident, Georgie," says his mother.

He looks at his mother and back to Tess, his eyes suggesting that this is best left alone right now.

Hillary bends over and picks up Tess's sneakers from the floor and tosses them into the closet, ignoring, apparently, the fact that neither of them has made a move to encourage the dog off the bed. With her back to them, she says, "I'm sorry, Georgie. I'm sorry she hurt you like that. But she's gone now. You're a very handsome boy, you know that?" And then she does turn and look at him. "Very handsome." She takes a breath, as if she has something else to say, and then releases it, turning and walking out of the room.

"They keep her in a cage," he whispers.

Tess doesn't believe him and tells him so. George looks around the room, shrugs, seeming not to care if she believes him or not. "This room was pink when she had it," he says. "But she wiped all her boogers on the wall, so it got painted yellow."

In that moment, the sound of her mother's steps moving away, and only George's voice, childish and raw, possibly still frightened, but speaking nonetheless, telling tales of the boogeyman that no one else dares speak of, Tess begins to see the shadow of Ella in the corners of her own room.

At night, under her covers, which she insists upon tucking all around her on even the hottest of evenings, and even with Butter Bean (when she can coax him from Belle's room and into her own) on his side next to her, she is certain that Ella is the source of every small sound, from the wail of an alley cat to the small squeaks and creaks of the floorboards and the trill of the old plumbing. They have all become *Ella noises*. Soon she is everywhere. In the windy bang of a door, in the clang of the radiator pipes. If one of her siblings wakes in the night to use the bathroom, the flush of the ancient plumbing can wake Tess with a start, certain that she will find Ella prone on the floor and shoving small objects through the metal grate.

In time, Ella becomes the family gremlin. If you can't find a shoe or a jacket, it is whispered among the children that Ella took it. If a photo falls off the wall, a glass is found broken, a cupboard left open, it is Ella who takes the blame. Missing bookbags—Ella. Coins missing from a dresser drawer—Ella. Stains on clothing, muddy footprints, burned toast, the pop of a light bulb, it all falls to Ella.

7

Lynetta

Beechwood Institute
Friday, April 17, 2009

Lynetta brings Ella to the dayroom and settles her on the sofa next to Maisy. Maisy turns fifty today and Ella had worried herself silly and driven Lynetta completely crazy jabbering on and on about a birthday party. Maisy sits on the sofa gumming the remains of her breakfast. She doesn't exactly smile when she sees Ella, but she sits a little straighter when Ella comes in the room and scooches beside her. Maisy leans into her and rubs her head on Ella's chest like a kitten. Ella puts her arm around her. "My friend Maisy," she says proudly. "Happy birthday, Maisy."

"Happy birthday, Ella," Maisy says.

Ella makes a deep guttural sound that Lynetta knows to be a laugh. The sound tickles Lynetta's funny bone and she will never tire of it, a noise settling halfway between an extended grunt and a true belly laugh. Lynetta knows it takes some kind of smarts to see the joke in what Maisy has said, and for that reason, she is pleased as punch to hear Ella's laugh.

"She's silly, isn't she?" Lynetta says.

Ella nods. "She my silly friend."

Things have changed. Kindness seeps into Thom Hall every once in a while these days, but Lynetta knows it is too little and too late and certainly not enough to erase the insufferable stink of the place. It won't be long, though, when the last 127 residents of the Beechwood "campus" will be gone. The doors locked and the place allowed to continue its rot from the inside out. It is hard to believe that only a few years earlier, the place housed over 2,000 residents. Now, the last residents have been brought together in Thom Hall as they await their reassignments.

Already the kudzu has taken over the entire southern wings of both Thom and King Halls. The wide green leaves have spread across the windows and rambled over the crimping rusted gutters and through the shingles. Lynetta thinks it fitting, and while she is a little wobbly on the whole God thing and the ways in which the heavens are said to reward and punish, she has no trouble imagining the vine is an enchantment of sorts—a way of cloistering off the place as each resident is released to group homes and, in some cases, to homes of their own. It seems to her that as each resident moves on, the kudzu grows stronger, faster, and thicker, smothering entire wings and preventing re-entry. No point in trimming the vines from the south wing windows. Those residents have all moved on. In fact, there isn't much of a grounds crew left to attend to the job, either. The vine now plaits its way across the roof and eagerly laps the crumbling stonework and copper flashing that peels away from where the stone chimney meets the slate shingles.

Lynetta's wish—if she dares to have one—is that all the fear, and the ghosts of dread that swell and shimmy in the corners of the rooms, will be trapped beneath layer upon layer of creeping greens and never again be able to slip beneath the wide double fire doors that separate the medical wing from the dayroom. Or wrap around the cold metal feet of the beds in the dormitory wing or condense like the meanest rain cloud and drip its way down the communal shower walls and slime along the slippery tiles.

Lynetta slides her fingers into her uniform pocket, feels the letter, folded in half within its envelope, deep in her pocket. It seems to her that Ella should have some say in it all, for once in her life. She's had no say in anything that has ever happened to her, not in coming to Beechwood in the first place and certainly not in anything that has happened to her since. Lynetta has tried to make up for it the last twenty-seven years, as best she can, and at the same time, she has kept the secrets that weighed heavy on her, doing her best to walk the line between the Jules family and Beechwood with Ella at her side.

Ella was thirteen when she was sterilized, a full hysterectomy. The policy, an unwritten policy, but a policy nonetheless, was to wait until their first cycle, until the first blood stained the sheets or the dingy panties or even the fingertips that had dipped into a curiously aching place. It was then that the young girl, often sprouting fresh pink pimples and small buds of breasts, would be reported to administration and scheduled for sterilization. The parents or former guardians were always told, but there was no room for discussion. For heaven's sake, no reason to watch her suffer cramping and bleeding every month, no reason to try to explain the purpose of this cycle and the integral discomfort when the womb was to remain a vacuum, an empty vessel, a cruel joke.

Parental permission was not required. The girls, the women, the children were wards of the state, and so the decision was not a decision at all, but a mandate that required all female retardants be sterilized. No exceptions. But it could be made all the more palatable if it was explained to the parents that the young girl found the whole messy experience both painful and confusing.

But for Ella, things had been different.

Lynetta had been putting Ella to bed, tucking the nightgown down around her and pulling the sheets to her chin the way she liked them at night, in spite of the heat. The night was thick, and the crickets chirped in frenzy. Lynetta reached across the bed and squished two mosquitos on the wall. Ella was thirteen at the time. Her hair was oily and slicked to her scalp even though Lynetta had washed it just three days ago—no easy task—and a brackish smell clung to the folds of her skin. She'd begun to fuss at night and didn't like Lynetta to leave her. She had grabbed at Lynetta's hands and pulled them down under the sheets.

"Settle down, now," Lynetta had said. "What's wrong with you, girl?"

"Stay, Nettie, stay."

"Don't be silly. I'll set a bit till you fall asleep."

Lynetta was tired. Her shift was coming to an end and her feet ached. Her patience, too, was worn a bit thin. But Ella was one of her favorites (all the aides had favorites, couldn't be helped) and she was so much easier now than she had been five years ago when she first came in. And Ella, likewise, favored Lynetta, and always asked if Lynetta could put her to bed.

Ella had been fussy all day, clutching at herself, rocking in the dayroom, rolling her head on her shoulders. But she always had good days and bad days, though she weighed in heavier on the bad days of late, not wanting to let Nettie go at night, trying to follow her all around the dayroom and into the nurse's station. And her teacher (Ella was one of the few who followed the rules obediently enough to be allowed to go to day instruction in Wyman Hall) had sent her back to Thom Hall on two occasions recently, claiming she had been acting out and disruptive rather than her usual more cooperative self.

Brody had brought her back early from school that day. Brody drove the small minibus across the campus delivering the more capable residents to school, out to the agriculture building and barns, down to the auto shop, and over to the small canning plant, where patients worked to bottle honey, can peaches, and make applesauce. He had been angry when he brought her back, red-faced and sweating, as was often the case. Brody was an *in-betweener*, a higher-functioning resident sentenced to Beechwood by the courts. And thus, on the one hand, a resident and, on the other, a kind of indentured servant. Not free to leave the grounds, he was, however, given much more leeway within the boundaries of Beechwood, accountable only to a lax supervisor and bound by a curfew that required him back in his dormitory by seven o'clock every evening. Bringing Ella back to Thom Hall had made him late for his pickup at the auto shop. The bus had no air-conditioning, and the heat, as well as his great bulk, aggravated his asthma. He had to drag Ella into the building, his fingerprints still fresh white pressure points on her arm once he deposited her outside the nurse's station with a shove that landed her on a bench. Ella had turned to her side, raised her fingers to her face, and banged her head against the wall until Lynetta came to her. There was a pattern to her headbanging, *rock, rock, bang, rock, rock, bang.* Lynetta had peeled Ella's fingers from her face and cupped her own hands around Ella's head, even letting her fingers be smashed between Ella's head and the wall as the banging continued and finally slowed.

It had been a bad day, but Ella had settled some after dinner and Lynetta hadn't expected the way Ella was fussing over being left for the night. She still clutched at Lynetta's hands and held them against her own heart. "You stay," Ella said again. She rubbed Lynetta's hands up and down her own torso and that was when Lynetta felt it—the wet slick that spread over her soft belly. Lynetta pulled back the sheets and saw the blood that smeared her pelvis and winged over her thighs.

"Oh, sweet girl," she said. "Sweet Jesus, we got to deal with this."

First periods were always last periods for the girls at Beechwood, but they were still a nightmare for the staff to deal with. The girls couldn't be made to understand what was happening, and the cramping struck terror into most of them, often requiring heavy sedation or, worst case, that the girl be restrained.

Lynetta did her best not to frighten Ella, but now she would need to get her to the toilet room, clean her as best she could, and then struggle with a sanitary belt and pad. "We're going to the potty room," she said to Ella, swinging the girl's legs to the floor and urging her to stand. And that was when she saw it, sliding down Ella's thigh like a raw chunk of chicken flesh. This was no regular period. This was a miscarriage.

8

Belle

Belle is nearly back to her childhood home, having pulled off I-83 and now heading through the lights of Cold Spring Lane. She opens her window to a warm Baltimore spring. Closing in on her childhood neighborhood, she is always struck by how little has changed.

Roland Park is an old neighborhood where turn-of-the-century homes are bumpered by old-growth hydrangeas and lilac bushes, and the trees reach over the eaves and twist between one another, scratching at attic windows and dropping wind-snapped branches on rooftops. The homes are large, mostly shingle and wood-sided with stone porches and foundations and interesting architectural details unique to each—stained glass windows, charming porticos, second-story exterior doors that walk out to tiny fairy-tale balconies, deeply carved soffits and corbels, the occasional turret. The streets are wide and lined with mature oaks and most homes boast a charming carriage house that has been turned into a studio or office or a guesthouse but will always be referred to, in a nod to a pretentious past, as *the carriage house*. It is, quite honestly, like coming home to a Norman Rockwell painting.

She turns left into the heart of the neighborhood and the road almost immediately splits in two with Hawthorn veering left and Woodlawn splitting right to frame a long pie-shaped lot where the Morgenfrier family still lives. Clarissa's mother is in the front yard, kneeling along the walk in her gardening Keds, troweling weeds from between the cracks in the walk. Belle can't help hoping the woman doesn't notice her, as she would almost certainly be on the telephone in minutes calling her daughter, Clarissa, and urging her to call or come by. It's awkward for all of them, this friendship with Clarissa.

Clarissa, a former classmate of Jax's, had been an odd child and suffered a rough adolescence. Honestly, as best Belle can recall, she was a mess. Her pens were always leaking in her mouth and leaving blue-black stains on her lips and tongue. Her skirts tended to twist at the waist and, more often than not, were secured with a safety pin. Her notebooks were stuffed until they exploded with only the slightest provocation. She was guilty of making herself an easy victim and the kind of prey that boys especially (though never Jax) liked to toy with before going in for the final kill. Her frustration when under attack, her pitiful attempts to protect herself with a defensive vocabulary that overreached its target audience, amused the most vicious bullies.

Clarissa is married now, to a quiet and apparently brilliant man of Korean descent with whom she works, another researcher at Johns Hopkins. When Belle met him years ago at their small wedding, she was astounded by how tall he was. When she said so to Jax, he had scowled at her. Dae was handsome in a way Belle hadn't expected but she kept that to herself, already embarrassed by Jax's reaction to her assumptions. Clarissa and Dae have two young boys about a year apart who look more like Dae than Clarissa, with their father's straight dark hair and eyes. But they remind Belle of Clarissa back in fifth grade, with gurgling voices and a habit of prefacing their sentences with *quite honestly* and *in retrospect* and even, on one occasion Belle heard the older one say *parenthetically*. It's all too much for Kitty and Jack and Tobi. Even Ben stares at them incredulously at times.

Clarissa, her children, and her husband almost always make at least one awkward visit when one or more of the Jules children happens to be in town. Belle knows their mothers encourage these visits. It's always a stiff occasion, Hillary serving coffee and everyone sitting in the living room trying to balance a cup on their lap while playing the *remember when* game because they have little in common other than their shared memories of this neighborhood.

But their parents have been dear friends as far back as Belle can remember, and the Jules children have always been encouraged to welcome Clarissa as an extension of that friendship. Clarissa's awkwardness, even as an adult, is tiresome, but the Jules children circled the wagons around her many years ago and they tend to stay in formation. Even George, who is most impatient with people who simply don't interest him, is kind. Jax is careful to keep an eye on Tess, however, as she has a habit of toying with Clarissa and it gets under his skin. When Tess tells Clarissa she likes her sandals—and clearly, she has only said so because they are bright orange and heeled with what looks like fat tire treads and, much like the elephant in the room, cannot be ignored—Jax always shoots her a look that says *enough already*.

Belle doesn't know exactly why he's like this, why he always has to feel like he must protect everyone.

The Jules family is a family of some—though certainly not limitless—means, but this wasn't always the case. There's no extensive lineage of wealth trailing Stone and Hillary Jules. College educated, Stone at Colgate, Hillary at Mary Washington, they had a good education and strong upper-middle-class families at their backs when they met through mutual friends forty-five years earlier. But Stone worked hard in mergers and acquisitions, responsible at first for smaller deals—restaurant acquisitions, the sale of a cluster of owner-operated gas stations to a local mogul—and worked his way up to more lucrative deals over the years. The family was certainly more than comfortable and had grown increasingly so through the years, but it was Stone's business success and genuine affability, Hillary's graciousness, that had ingratiated the Jules family to the community. They never pretended to have more than they had and never flouted what they did have.

This is all something Belle knows of her family and appreciates. She appreciates their beautiful home, the opportunities that came her way, and understands that they are a fortunate family and have seamlessly been enveloped by the blue-blooded old money of Baltimore. As a parent now, she can't imagine that her parents didn't stress to some degree over putting five children through prep school (though a Catholic school was slightly less costly than the prestigious Gilman or Bryn Mawr Schools that some of her neighborhood friends attended). She knows that putting her and her siblings through college in overlapping fashion, one year with three kids attending simultaneously, had to have been at least a small strain. But Belle was never made to feel guilty. And her spending money, *pocket money*, as her mother called it, was her own responsibility. Each of the Jules children worked summers to earn their spending money for college. Camp counselor, reading tutor, swim instructor, babysitter, there were always those willing to hire the exceptional Jules children. Belle's husband, Ben, having made his way through Williams on grants and scholarships and backbreaking summer landscape work, once remarked to Belle's good friend Jeannie that Belle came from *a moneyed family*. It was said good-naturedly, but irritated Belle just the same. They were at a neighborhood potluck and the topic of escalating college costs was being bandied about. Jeannie wanted to know how Belle's parents had managed it, with so many children. It was admirable, she said, and Belle had agreed. Until Ben said what he said, deflating her quickly.

"I worked summers," she offered up pathetically.

"Oh, I know, babe, but face it, you were born with a silver spoon in your mouth."

"Silver plate," said Belle.

Once again, she was saddled with the feeling that what the world saw of the Jules family hid something deeper. That with Ella stowed at Beechwood, all that remained was a picture of perfection.

The cherry trees are blooming in excess, the blossoms swirling as Belle opens her car door and steps onto the street. It smells greener here, and less wet, as if spring really has arrived and settled in for the long haul. Her mother swings open the front door and stands, smiling, watching Belle grab her bag from the back seat and heft it over her shoulder before Hillary turns her head to call back into the house—*she's here!* And then makes her way down the steps toward Belle, holding the railing as she walks. Belle notices the way her mother watches her feet as she descends the steps. She can't help but recall how her mother used to bounce down the steps in her tennis whites, shouting to all of them to be good, she'd only be at the courts an hour. *Stay out of trouble,* she would say, *and don't leave the yard!*

"Tess is here already, darling!" Hillary throws her arms around Belle, and Belle's bag swings down from her shoulder and nearly knocks the two over as they embrace. Belle steadies her mother and Hillary lifts the bag back to Belle's shoulder, pats the strap, smooths her collar, touches her face, and says, "How was the drive, Belle." But it isn't really a question. She is too excited to wait for an answer. "It's going to be so nice to have everyone together again!" It is not lost on Belle that she means *everyone,* even the ghosted sister most of her siblings have not seen in decades, and who, in their mind's eye, is pasted over with a slackened version of Belle's face.

Ella. The identical twin who is nothing at all like Belle. Ella, the unknowable sibling at the center of this very bad idea. And just what does Ella think of all this? Belle can't imagine. Does Ella know? Does she understand that the very people who sent her away are waging a small war to get her back? Belle knows nothing of what Ella thinks, if Ella thinks about anything at all. For one thing, she hasn't seen Ella since she was sent away thirty-two years ago.

Unlike most twins, there is no synchronicity between the two of them, no intuitive hunches, strange coincidences, unspoken understanding. Instead, there is a void in Belle—that birthright of which she has been robbed. And what is worse is that she actually fears the possibility of any psychic connection between the two of them.

She is afraid of feeling Ella's feelings. For a time, when she was perhaps thirteen or fourteen and her hormones raged, her emotions so raw that it hurt to be touched by any sort of kindness, Belle had imagined that she and Ella had once been, in their mother's womb, the same person, but once they had been torn from that space, they had landed in two separate worlds. Belle believed that she herself had been gifted all of their feelings so that her feelings were always double the intensity they deserved. It was the only way she could account for the potency of her emotions at that time, the wide swing of them.

Ella, on the other hand, was a void, a shell, without conscience, a doppelgänger of sorts. Belle imagined her as completely reactionary, like the amoebas under the microscope in Belle's biology class, bumping up against the watery limits of their world and setting off in another direction.

It was only Belle, then, who had to bear the burden of thinking and feeling. And it all weighed too heavily. Now, with her mother clucking over her, she feels the pressing down of a responsibility she doesn't want to bear. Her mother has aged. She is still beautiful and has the fine features and gentle demeanor that draws the admiration of friends and family alike. But there is a fragility that has sifted over Belle's mother in recent years (and more rapidly since the loss of her mother's dear friend Bets). The way she so carefully descended the steps, the way her fingers flutter at Belle's face, and the way her eyes dart over her daughter. Her mother is lucky to be a healthy woman. But how long can that kind of luck hold out? And now, to take on Ella, a perpetual child at best, goes against both nature and common sense.

Tess comes to the doorway and stands framed in it, shaking her head back and forth, something resembling a smirk on her face as if to say, *Yep—you're right, this is one hot mess.* She holds open the door as Belle and her mother pass through. Hillary pats Tess's shoulder as she sweeps past.

"Welcome to the loony bin," Tess whispers as she hugs Belle.

"That's not funny, Tess," their mother says. She does not like loony-bin jokes.

"I nabbed the carriage house," says Tess. "First come, first served."

"Yes!" Belle drops her bag and pumps her fist in the air—and then immediately feels guilty, as if she is abandoning her parents after having just arrived.

Hillary only smiles. This is something she is used to—the scramble for the carriage house. "I will never understand it," she says. "Why would you want to sleep in that drafty, dusty old garage when you can have a perfectly nice bed here in the house?" She sighs good-naturedly. "I scrubbed the shower and put fresh sheets on the beds, and your father checked the stove."

Belle loves the old carriage house. When she and Ben visit, they always sleep there. Kitty opts for Belle's old bedroom in the house, and the boys head to Jax's room with its Grateful Dead posters curling on the walls and a dusty lava lamp on the dresser. But two bedrooms are tucked upstairs under the eaves of the carriage house and one room has two twin beds in it and the other room is just large enough for a double bed and a night-stand. She and Ben sleep on a huge king-size bed back in Longmeadow, where Belle is free to toss and turn at night and Ben remains unscathed, but sometimes it's a treat to curl up together in the double bed. They almost always make love because it would seem awkward not to, their bodies so tangled around one another and the way the mattress caves to the middle and piles them both in the center of it. And, quite honestly, she cannot feel that man's shoulder against her cheek or his breath on the hollow of her neck and not want to touch him. Afterward, they sleep so close to one another that she is reminded of heaps of puppies in a basket.

Belle makes her way to the back of the house, through the swinging doors of the original butler's pantry, and into the old kitchen with its wallpaper border of twined ivy and the Corning stove top that has baked itself to muddy gold. Hillary refuses to remodel, claims it is the kitchen she always wanted when she designed it thirty-some years ago and it has served her well. The refrigerator paneling is whitewashed to match the cabinets and the old toaster oven still sits on the counter. No microwave. Hillary fears they will affect a pacemaker—not that anyone in the family has a pacemaker, but there's no need to flirt with danger. Still, it is comforting to Belle that the kitchen is just as she expected, that nothing changes over the years and she can effortlessly find a tea bag, the aluminum foil, the matching lids to the Tupperware bowls. The car keys are in the ceramic bowl on the counter, the to-do list clipped in a massive magnet to the refrigerator, and if she turns on the water, she knows it will take a full minute to run to the perfect chilled temperature.

Belle looks out through the picture window to see her father coming across the lawn dragging a garden hose. She raps on the glass and he breaks into a wide smile, dropping the hose and heading toward the back door as she makes her way to greet him.

Stone Jules hugs his children with his whole body. Even the boys are hugged and patted, squeezed, stepped back from and admired, and then hugged again, as if he can't believe that any of them are comprised of real flesh and blood. He hugs Belle in that familiar way and asks about the grandkids.

"Fine. They're great." She can't help but think about Jack when she says it, wonders if Ben dropped off his math book and if Jack was embarrassed again by his own forgetfulness.

He asks about Ben and then asks about the kids again. She is compelled to elaborate. Kitty is still bossy as hell. Jack and Tobi continue to humor her.

He chuckles. "In charge of the world and everybody in it," he says. "Wish the family could have come with you."

"It's nice that Ben will get some time alone with the kids," says Hillary. She pats Belle's arm. "And so good to have you here all to ourselves!"

Belle has to admit that even though Jack is on her mind, the distance has eased some of her worries over raincoats and riding lessons, pickup times and the struggles with a balanced meal in a home where one child won't eat anything red and another can't bear to have foods touching on his plate.

Just as she is making her way back to the bag she dropped in the foyer, the front door creaks open and Jax steps inside. At the sound of the door swinging on its ancient hinges, Stone follows her to the foyer, Tess and Hillary behind him.

"You took a taxi, son?" Stone asks, peering over Jax's shoulder and through the open door as the taxi pulls from the curb. "I would have picked you up at the airport."

"Hey, Dad." Jax is quick to explain that he flew standby, wasn't sure when he would arrive, and it was just as easy to take a cab. Stone shakes his son's hand, steps back again, and then hugs him deeply with a slap on the shoulder blade.

Belle is always taken aback when she sees the two of them together. Jax has grown into the father of her childhood, tall and lean, graying at the temples but still with a thick head of dirty blond hair. Both of their pants snag on their hips in the same way and their feet turn out when they stand. Belle can detect the beginning of a thickening jowl on Jax that will surely pleat in the same way as his father's in the years to come.

Hugs are relayed all around. Hillary is slower to move toward her son. She waits for him to come to her, her fingers twisting delicately, taking small steps forward, and when he comes to her, Belle watches relief trickle down her mother's face as he leans down to hug her. Theirs is a strained dance and Belle has no idea why. It has always been this way. Nothing that anyone but Belle would notice but it is there, in the air, floating between them, a thin veil that shrouds her mother's delight in seeing him. She is careful with her oldest son.

"Better get your backpack into the carriage house," Tess says. "Belle and I took the twin room. You can grab the other room before George and Finney get here."

"Nice work, roomies." He can't hide his grin as he hefts his pack and heads out the back door. "I'm just gonna go piss on the bed—mark my territory," he whispers in Belle's ear.

He always makes Belle smile.

9

Lynetta

Beechwood Institute
Friday Evening, April 17, 2009

She needs to pack an overnight bag for Ella and she doesn't own one. Lynetta's shift in Thom Hall is nearly over, but she hopes to scavenge an overnight bag from all the cast-off supplies in the basement before she gets off.

Ever since taking Ella on twenty-seven years ago, Lynetta has only worked one or two shifts per week, usually when someone calls out and they are shorthanded. But lately, knowing that Beechwood is closing, staff has been moving on and Lynetta has been forced to cover more shifts in a week than she used to. This is her third shift this week.

Right now they are in the dayroom along with Maisy, Terra, Colin, and John-John, who is strapped securely to a gurney and weaving his hands over his head as if tossing pizza dough. The evening shift is expected on duty any minute and she will snag someone to watch over the small group so that she can go down to the cellar. The others are in the dining hall. The noise is deafening.

Sometimes Lynetta wishes she could just hose them all off after dinner, what with their fingers digging in the bowls and their faces covered in mashed potatoes. Mashed potatoes at every meal. Lunch and dinner. She never eats mashed potatoes herself, having spent three decades watching it spill from the mouths of residents and smeared in their hair, in the whorls of their ears. Maisy, Terra, Colin, and John-John are particularly susceptible to the noise in the dining hall and inevitably the chaos leads to one or the other of them slamming their hands on the table and then covering their own ears, elbows jutted to the sides, and screeching, sometimes headbanging. Often there are fights, chairs thrown, a biting incident. Whenever she is on shift, she takes the most sensitive ones and brings them to the dayroom to eat. They're not supposed to have food in here, but the rules have crumbled in the last years.

No one even bothers to record in the nursing log anymore, so no one knew whether or not Clay had had a bowel movement in the last week, and thus the obstruction was missed. He is in the hospital now—a real one, not the medical wing, which has been essentially closed the last two years. And no one has been keeping tabs on the dental appointments, either, and so the relocated patients have required—so she has heard—extractions and rounds of antibiotics after their moves.

The broken collarbones of late, that's a different thing altogether.

There's been an increase in the use of restraints. Short-staffed, they often have no choice but to restrain a patient. The struggle often leads to injuries, a broken collarbone being the most common. And no one knows how to use the restraints properly anyway. There's no training for this job anymore.

John-John's arms are not restrained. But he has occasional seizures and so he is lashed to the gurney at his waist and chest and it is all he has ever known, but his arms are free to flail about. If forced to sit up for too long in a wheelchair, he passes out, his chin slumping down on his chest and his shirt going damp with drool—a strange condition that no one seems to understand. He is going to be among the more difficult ones to place.

Colin is in his fifties. He has pica, real pica (not like Ella who just happens to like putting things in her mouth as another way to explore objects and so had been misdiagnosed at first). He is forced to wear a football helmet with a screen over his face. Everything goes in his mouth, from the dead flies on the windowsill to the scraps of asbestos tiles crackling up from the floor. Lynetta has had him eat already and if he doesn't try to chew on the plastic plate itself, she will leave the helmet off a while longer. He always sinks to the floor when she goes to put it back on and it makes her stomach thud. Ella will hold his hand while she attaches it and call him her friend. It is no easy task, even with Ella to distract him, as the strap must be threaded rather than snapped so he can't remove it himself. The skin under his chin is calloused and thickly scarred. There is a smell in his hair that can't be gotten rid of—like old cooking grease.

Ella is reading *Hop on Pop* to Maisy and Terra. Actually, she is reciting her favorite parts. She turns the pages randomly and finds herself finished reciting but with many more pages to go. And so she starts over again. *cup, pup. Pup in cup.* When John-John, wide-grinning, his hands flailing, says *up-up-up*, Ella laughs with him. "John-John is down, down, down," she says.

Whenever Lynetta and Ella travel to Ocean City, Lynetta piles everything into laundry baskets. Quick and easy and no fussing with digging in bags. Everything gets folded and flopped in baskets, loaded into the back of her old Camry, and they're off. But this overnight at the Jules home requires a proper bag. While the neighbors in the park may assume she's traveling back and forth with her dirty laundry, and she's never been one to care what anybody else thinks, she can't afford to have Mrs. Jules judge her harshly on this when she delivers Ella tomorrow evening for the overnight visit, her first ever since coming to Beechwood.

Lynetta's trailer in Ocean City is a block off Coastal Highway, down Thirtieth Street, and across from the Jolly Roger Amusement Park, only a three-hour drive, but worlds away from Beechwood. The trailer is neat and tidy. And it's a double-wide, meaning it has three bedrooms and a nice big kitchen. A real laundry room instead of a laundry closet like some of the others in Sunny Days Park. Wally, the manager of the amusement park, power washes it for her in the spring and fall and stops by on weekday mornings to water her petunias that spill from the window boxes and the pot of marigolds at the rise of the trailer steps. First thing she does when they arrive on Friday is roll out the awning and set up the lawn chairs. Ella runs the vacuum and sweeps the small concrete pad. Lynetta scours the toilet and shower. They eat a late dinner on the patio by the light of a citronella candle and the roaring neon of the park. They fall asleep to the tick of the roller coaster climbing and the swooshing descent of screaming patrons.

Wally lets them in for free during the day because they never ride the rides but spend a hefty amount on caramel corn, cotton candy, and sno-cones. Ella likes to call him *Nettie's boyfriend*, which he definitely is not and Lynetta has repeatedly told her so. They never go over at night, even though Ella asks to. The teenagers and drunks come out at night and Lynetta doesn't like the looks Ella gets. The small children who swarm the park in the afternoon are kinder, though they do stare. They know there's something different about Ella, the way she shuffles, the way her words fall in thick clumps, the hard bounce of her consonants. But they can't quite put their finger on what it is, and so they watch, sometimes asking her name, sometimes asking how old she is, maybe sensing that this is a child in a grown-up's body. Ella will talk to anybody and most encounters end with Ella asking the child if they can be friends.

Lynetta won't be making the trip this weekend, as she is dropping Ella off at the Juleses' house on Saturday evening for one night and picking her up the next afternoon. She didn't bother to make this point to Mrs. Jules—that she would be inconvenienced in this way and would miss her weekend trip to the home she had planned to move to permanently with Ella. It seemed best not to remind the woman of the distance she was putting between her and Ella. Lynetta suspects, though she can't be sure, that this is part of what has Mrs. Jules opposed to Ella's living with her once Beechwood closes.

Maybe Lynetta will have Pap over for dinner tomorrow night. Since buying the trailer three years ago, she sees less of her father once the weather warms and she and Ella are spending their weekends in Ocean City.

Up until a few weeks ago, Lynetta had no problem with the Jules family. She especially likes the brother, Jax, though she hasn't seen him in years.

But she liked the way he always sat with Ella, asking her about herself, wanting to know what she was learning in school, her favorite color, who her friends were, and what she liked to do with them. And she likes his friend Clarissa who still visits on occasion. Oddly quiet, awkward even, but kind to Ella. She sits patiently with Ella and encourages her to read to her, even though it's obvious that she's hardly reading but flips the pages and tells the story as she knows it. The woman dresses strangely, even by Lynetta's standards, long skirts and chunky sneakers, often wearing an open man's shirt like a jacket. The first time Clarissa visited with Ella she came with Jax just before he left for California. He explained to Ella that Clarissa was a friend of his and he wanted the two of them to meet. Ella said she already knew Clarissa, but Lynetta doubted her. "I know you," she had said, and Clarissa had only looked from Ella to Jax and back again and said it was nice to see her.

Lynetta hardly knows Mr. Jules. Thought he was nice enough when he made an occasional visit, thanking Lynetta for her care, asking after her father. But he always came alone, never came with the mother on Thursdays. He was more of a holiday visitor, always stopping by on Ella's birthday, the day before Christmas, the Saturday before Easter. And always alone. Sometimes he brought flowers for the two of them. Sometimes chocolates, like an old-fashioned courting.

Lynetta has never mentioned other visitors to Mrs. Jules. She once overheard Ella tell her mother that Jax had brought her a poster for her bedroom, a picture of kittens curled in a basket, and she had seen the startled look on Mrs. Jules's face. Ella urged her to come to her bedroom where she could show it to her. Something about the way Ella said *my brother Jax*, had made Mrs. Jules catch her breath, look curiously to Lynetta and then away. Lynetta expected her to ask about these visits, but she never did, never mentioned them again.

Mrs. Jules. She comes every Thursday. Sometimes she takes Ella out for ice cream, always bringing her back neat as a pin. That was confusing to Lynetta at first because Ella eating ice cream was about the same as any four-year-old eating ice cream. It was bound to drip down her wrists, ring her mouth, and stick in her hair.

Turns out Mrs. Jules carries a wet washcloth in a baggie in her purse and wipes Ella down spotlessly after the ice cream. She even uses one of those little stain sticks on her clothes and always reminds Lynetta—has been reminding her for years now—that the stain stick will keep the stain from setting for at least twenty-four hours but to be sure and get that shirt into the laundry.

At first, Mrs. Jules took Ella off the campus for most visits, just the two of them, but after a few years and when the weather turned cold, she began to visit in the cottage. Lynetta would go to her small bedroom and catch up with her mending while the two of them visited downstairs.

Ella loves her mother, always needs to sit nearly on top of the woman, and the affection is mutual. Mrs. Jules always brings her licorice, new dresses, shoes that she makes Ella model for her before she leans down and presses her thumb to the toes to check the fit. If a dress or pair of pants is too long, Lynetta always offers to hem it.

Mrs. Jules brought them a new television, far too large for the room, and a small stereo system that took CDs. Lynetta and Ella like to dance to Whitney Houston and The Bangles, especially. Lynetta hadn't listened to much music when she'd lived with Pap. Lance had liked rock music, *heavy metal* he called it, and listened to it on a massive stereo system he brought with him when he moved in with her and her father, but she never liked what she heard back then. Iron Maiden and Judas Priest were his favorites, and she was constantly turning it down—or off—if he left the house without doing so himself. The banging and screeching hung in her head afterward.

Seven months. That's how long he stayed. And the weeks following Becky dying probably didn't count anyway as he spent most of that time at his mother's house before he stopped coming back at all.

Pap was just as happy to see Lance and his loud music go. Lynetta simply didn't care one way or the other. Fine if he stayed. Fine if he left. She didn't care much about anything after Becky died. Until Ella. Until Ella had the miscarriage and then Lynetta sure as hell cared about that.

Heading through the medical wing, making her way past the old metal gurney that creaks and slides at the weight of the wide door against it, and around the beds—once lined up perfectly, eight to a side but now haphazardly askew, some teetering on three legs or shoved up against the wall—she weaves through the near dark and wholly abandoned ward. The only light leaks from the clerestory windows high on the walls where the kudzu, she notices, has made its way through a crack in the glass and is now snaking three feet across the ceiling. A stack of bedpans has tumbled, and in the dimness, looks like a pile of mammoth turquoise boulders in the far corner. Plastic sheeting has torn free of a metal rod and falls in a frozen wave to the floor. She steps over a toppled metal pole that once held an IV bag and tubing and around a mammoth old centrifuge machine, spattered in ancient coppery stains and covered in grime, to head toward the doors in the back of the ward that lead to the cellar. They're heavy and make a sucking sound as she pulls on first one, then the other, borrowing the twilight that has found its way to the ward and sheds light on the first steps. She feels along the wall for a light switch, six toggles across, but when she slides her hand up to flip the switches, only one of the overhead fluorescents at the farthest west end of the cellar buzzes and flickers to life. The cellar is endless, stretching beneath the length of the building itself, with the stairs coming down in the center of it and a long angled concrete ramp running beside it and deeper to the middle of the room. The east end remains completely dark, but the end that is now bathed in a cold pool of light is precisely where she needs to get in order to find a suitcase for Ella. She can see them, stacks and stacks, row upon row of various trunks and suitcases, old wooden packing crates. A century and a half's worth of one-way trips to Beechwood.

Lynetta is forced to make her way carefully down the concrete steps, damp and crumbling on the edges. Water puddles at the end of the steps and she has no choice but to step in it. She wishes she had asked someone to come with her, though she would never admit her discomfort. She doesn't like spiders and she's not fond of the camel crickets that hop in every direction and that—she could swear—are hopping right at her so that she jumps back at the last step and nearly sends herself down on her bottom. The walls are heavy rock and there are siftings of stone dust and mortar, like piles of cornmeal, all along the edges. The wooden shelving lining the far wall is dressed in cobwebs as is the raftered ceiling. A row of metal desks lines the wall on her left, an open drawer snagging her shirt so that she gasps aloud and must unhook it from the hem, leaving a small toothlike hole in the fabric.

She passes a stack of metal carts missing wheels, thin mold-covered mattresses tossed in a sliding pile like spreading cards, a metal crib frame—the slats, she notices as she gets closer, gnawed so that the raw metal beneath the painted exterior slashes through—a row of wheelchairs and, lastly, right next to the aisle of shelving where the suitcases are stored, three simple pine caskets set in an undisturbed row, earmarked for indigents, just like the one Brody had been buried in.

Beechwood had picked up the minimal cost of Brody's burial because he had been a court-ordered resident for many years, coming in at fifteen when he was found incompetent to stand trial after having beaten his mother in a rage. He'd been put to work with other capable boys and men in the orchard until it was discovered he had a severe reaction to bee stings. Eventually, he'd been reassigned as a driver and general maintenance man. He, like some of the staff, was housed on the campus in Mason Hall, a small building of sixteen men in a total of six bedrooms that served a mix of higher-functioning residents and—what Lynetta considered to be—lower-functioning staff. Housing a limited maintenance staff—someone who could fix a boiler, turn off a burst pipe, key kitchen staff, and a handful of aides—was important, particularly in inclement weather when other staff couldn't make their way to the campus.

Now Brody is six feet under in the Beechwood cemetery adjacent to the neighboring St. Thomas Episcopal Church. A low stone wall separates the burial sites of the church parishioners from those of Beechwood patients. No headstones for the Beechwood patients, only simple markers in the ground with a last name. Often there are no dates. It once surprised Lynetta that the graveyard wasn't massive, given the thousands of souls who had departed from Beechwood over the years. But she learned that some were buried by family—accounting to guilt, perhaps. Others, it turns out, were donated to medical schools. Brody, she knows, is right where he deserves to be. Not that she doesn't feel some guilt, but she doesn't feel remorse, either. The guilt is its own kind of almost-living thing, lodged in her gut and rising out of her, merging into her nightmares to show itself at various angles. Ugly, jagged-edged, but with a pulse that matches the racing of her heart when she breaks free of these dreams and wakes, breathless and clutching at her chest.

She refuses to look at the coffins and gets to work pulling dank suitcases down from the shelving. The steamer trunks and packing crates are on the lowest shelf and many are tagged in brass with names or initials. Some likely date back to the late 1800s when patients arrived by coach to what was then the *Maryland Asylum and Training School for the Feeble Minded*. A driver would have unloaded their belongings and the trunk would have been stored. But she's looking for something smaller. Maybe even something more modern, and hopefully something that has resisted the damp a bit. She spies a round black patent leather bag, probably from the seventies, with a looped strap and a zipper that runs around the circumference and takes it down from the shelf. It's dust-coated but zipped completely and she sets it on the floor to unzip it, hoping mold hasn't crawled into it. The damn camel crickets are everywhere, and one jumps straight at her. She unzips the bag, and immediately the sting of mustiness hits her nose, but she can't see any actual mold and thinks she can clean the liner with vinegar and baking soda and air it out overnight.

Turning to head back to the steps, she slams her thigh into one of the caskets. She can't get out of the cellar fast enough but refuses to run, refuses to give whatever haunts her that satisfaction.

On her way up the steps, something thuds behind her and she looks back to see a suitcase tumble to the floor. She watches as more topple. One, two, three, they fall, one hitting a casket and bouncing so hard the latch pops and the bag splits open. She takes the last steps two at a time and slams the doors behind her, not bothering to turn off the light.

There's no comfort to be found in the medical wing, even darker now than before she descended the steps. Lynetta was never assigned to the medical wing, but she knows it well from the week she spent here with Ella years ago. She still worked her shift that week, trudged home with an aching heart to shower, and then returned to spend her nights in a hospital bed beside her. There was no way she was leaving that child until she found out what happened to her.

What made her angry, what got under her skin and blistered, was the fact that no one else was asking. When she asked one of the doctors, *Just how do you think this happened?* he had looked at her like she was stupid and like he felt sorry for her.

"These things happen sometimes, Miss Lynetta," he said as if explaining a sad universal truth. He spread his hands and *tsk-tsked* his tongue. "But it won't happen again. We took care of that."

It was clear to Lynetta what he meant. They'd done a full hysterectomy, carved out the evidence as far as Lynetta was concerned, but that didn't have anything at all to do with who had done this to her and making sure it didn't happen again. Not to mention the fact that there were two hundred or more other young girls in her ward that she had to worry about as well.

Ella had spent the week heavily sedated and was as incoherent and confused as she had been when they first brought her in five years earlier. But no seizures. When the sedation began to wear off, she growled low in her throat and asked for her mama until they knocked her out again. They restrained her when Lynetta was on her shift and couldn't be by her side but allowed her to be unrestrained when Lynetta was there, trusting her to handle any disturbances. And, of course, they had the foresight to not restrain her when her mother came to visit. The Jules family was only told that Ella had a hysterectomy. This was something they had been warned to expect at some point, and so Lynetta knew they were not surprised.

Mrs. Jules only came once during Ella's infirmary stay, sticking to her Thursday schedule. Lynetta was taking her shift break and had gone to check on Ella just as Mrs. Jules arrived. The staff had pulled a curtain around her bed to give the impression of some privacy and a chair had been set by her bedside.

Mrs. Jules was still standing, her purse slung on her shoulder, a pink helium balloon floating over her head. Lynetta stood a few feet back from her until Mrs. Jules turned and recognized her. The staff nurse was explaining that Ella was to be sedated throughout her recovery and likely wouldn't wake at all while Mrs. Jules was there. When Mrs. Jules turned to see Lynetta, there was a strange helpless look on the woman's face, a twisting of her mouth and a falling of her brows. Her eyes bleary and damp. Lynetta thought at first that she knew the truth of it. Mrs. Jules settled herself in the chair, looking around anxiously and up at the balloon floating over her head as if she were embarrassed by it, and then said, "I knew this was coming. Her sister started her monthly back in April and I expected the same with Ella." Lynetta knew then that Mrs. Jules didn't have a clue that anything was amiss. She stared at Lynetta over her shoulder. "Identical twins," she explained. "They always start at the same time." She handed the balloon to Lynetta. "Her sister and I celebrated at the tearoom at Hutzler's." She patted Ella's arm, ran her hand up and down the length of it.

Lynetta had been to Hutzler's once. A magical four-story department store, with a top-floor tearoom, an expanse of wall painted with a pastel landscape of what was once the fields and farms surrounding the area and, opposite that, floor-to-ceiling windows that looked out over the town of Towson. Her mother had taken her, only the one time, as a young girl, to have lunch and buy a new dress for her confirmation. The table, Lynetta remembers, held a miniature salt and pepper shaker at each place setting, and in the center of the table sat a porcelain bowl filled with sugar cubes and a small set of tongs. She had been allowed to suck on a sugar cube as they waited for their lunch of tomato aspic and tuna salad on a wide leaf of iceberg lettuce. Only once. But Lynetta imagined that Mrs. Jules frequented such a place with her other daughters, maybe even had a regular shopping day just as she had a regular day to visit Ella. Maybe Lynetta's mother would have taken her again. Another special occasion, graduation or prom dress shopping, but she had died later that summer from cancer in her breast they hadn't even known she had.

Lynetta makes her way back through the wing, stepping around a tipped wheelchair and over a blood pressure cuff, the suitcase at her side. Passing one of the beds, she is reminded of the way she had tied Mrs. Jules's balloon to the foot of it, and the way she had found it sunk to the floor that evening when she returned. Ella never saw it. Lynetta bought her another one for the day she was to be released from the infirmary and tied it to the arm of the wheelchair. She let her keep it there long into the afternoon when another patient, a boy who had delighted in patting it around on the end of the string, had finally pulled it to his mouth and bitten into it, startling himself and Ella, and then he had cried at the sudden pop and disappearance of it. Ella told him her mama would buy him another one.

The day before Ella was to be released back to her dormitory, Lynetta had sat by her bed to feed her Jell-O. At first Ella had batted her hand away and sent Jell-O splattering across the bedsheet.

"I do myself," Ella said.

Lynetta handed her the bowl and the spoon. Ella's hands were shaky, and the Jell-O kept sliding off the spoon and blobbing on her nightgown, but Lynetta let her continue. She had always been capable of feeding herself, but the meds she was on made her clumsy. When she spilled a huge glob down her chest that rolled under the sheet, she looked up at Lynetta. "Mama gave me my quiet medicine," she said.

Lynetta had no idea what she was talking about. "The doctor gave you medicine."

Ella nodded.

"I been wondering some, Ella." Lynetta smoothed a hand down the back of Ella's matted hair. "Anybody around here been hurting you?"

Ella pinched her face. "Penny, she bite me. She bite my arm." She lifted her arm that held the spoon and the Jell-O slid down her wrist. "All the time."

Penny bit everyone. She spent a good part of the day in isolation, a room with only a mattress and thick frosted windows so that she couldn't look outside, the current wisdom being that reducing stimulation would reduce the outbursts.

"Anybody else? Mr. Flay?" Mr. Flay was her teacher, the one who had sent Ella back to the dormitory on more than one occasion lately.

"He nice. He mad at me." She set her mouth in a pout and looked at Lynetta.

"Why's he mad at you?"

Ella shrugged.

Lynetta liked Mr. Flay, what she knew of him. But now she was suspicious of everyone. She moved to the edge of Ella's bed, sitting beside her, raising one arm around her. "Why's he mad at you?" she asked again. But Ella ignored her, holding the Jell-O bowl to her face and licking the inside of it.

Lynetta pulled a comb from her uniform pocket and began to work the tangles out of Ella's hair. Ella tossed her head at first and then settled, allowing Lynetta to work gingerly at the mat on the back of her head. Such pretty hair, Lynetta remembers thinking, thick and straight, blond as sunshine. In that moment—Lynetta's one hand on the top of Ella's head, her other working at the edges of tangles, Ella's breath coming slow and easy, her body tipping toward Lynetta until she was tucked in the curve of Lynetta's waist—it was in that moment that Lynetta felt it, the pull, as she would forever think of it, to this child. As if Ella were her own.

Lynetta heads back to the dayroom to gather Ella and walk back to their cottage. There is a strange emptiness in her chest, as if something has flown out of it. Tomorrow will be the first night she will spend alone in twenty-seven years. Might as well get used to it, if the Jules family has their way.

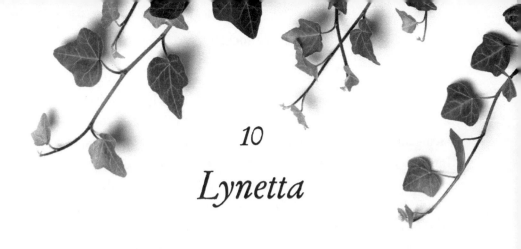

10

Lynetta

Mr. Flay.

  Brody Myers.

  Gill, the new night orderly. But no, he's only been on staff two months now and the timing, to Lynetta's way of thinking, doesn't work out. The assignment sheets are filed in the nurse's station and Lynetta had no trouble getting into them and reviewing Ella's whereabouts the last months.

  Lynetta is bound and determined to find out what happened to Ella and she makes no secret of it. Furthermore, her anger over the stench of it all has ratcheted up over the last week, and she has stopped being coy about what she wants to know—no more *how do you think this happened?* asked sympathetically of the doctors, nurses, custodians, the other aides, and orderlies. She has been in a mood, she has to admit, slapping a male orderly's hands away from Greta when he went to lift her from her wheelchair and his hand had slipped along her breast as he threaded his arms under hers, not even apologizing—just saying *I got this.* Stopping by Mr. Flay's classroom earlier that morning, asking him—demanding to know—who takes Ella to the toilet when the need comes up in his classroom. Cornering other aides and asking, point-blank, *Who done this?* Checking and rechecking the nurse's log to track Ella's whereabouts the past few months.

Brody Myers.

Every Thursday morning for the last six months, he had driven Ella, only Ella, to her classroom in Fryer Hall at eleven in the morning after having already brought the others earlier at nine o'clock. Ella spends Thursday mornings with her mother. It is an accommodation not made for everyone, but the Jules family and their deep pockets make way for allowances. The new medical library room, modest but still impressive to the state inspectors, had been partly funded by their generous donation. Two additional teachers have been added to the staff. The holiday staff party now included a yule log cake and spiked cider. Word has trickled down over the last years. Take care of the Jules family.

Lynetta runs her fingers down the log. Every damn Thursday.

Brody Myers.

"It ain't the first time," Nira is saying. Nira has been at Beechwood as long as Lynetta and they had gone through their orientation together. Sitting in the dayroom with their charges, Nira leans back in her too-tight uniform that bursts into a gap at her breasts, eyes rolling like she is resigned to both the constant pulling of her shirts and also the harboring of ugly secrets. She tilts her head to indicate Rose, who sits quietly—always sits quietly, never any trouble at all—at the game table.

Somehow, over the last five years, Nira has slipped into the role of Lynetta's closest friend. They couldn't be more different, Nira with her ocher coloring, her long, stick-straight, dark hair. She has a mixed heritage that fascinates Lynetta. Born to an Indian mother and a white military father, she was raised by neither. Her mother died when she was an infant and her enlisted father turned her over to his own mother, a woman who never combs the back of her head so that her short gray hair is always smooshed against the back of it. She smokes long skinny cigarettes and drives around in her bedroom slippers so that when she picks Nira up some days, Nira has to hurry out to the car for fear her grandmother will get out while she waits, lean her backside along the door while she smokes in her slippers. Nira jokes that the women could be assumed to be a patient. The loss of their mothers is something they have in common, though not much else. Sometimes Nira's grandmother offers to drive Lynetta home after her shift. She welcomes the ride when it's offered in spite of the fact that her hair and clothes always smell like smoke when she gets home. Nira's grandmother always says "there you go, girlie," when they pull up in front of the house. Sometimes she flicks a cigarette butt out to the street and Lynetta waits until she has pulled off before she grinds her heel to it and then picks it up and drops it in the trash cans set by the side of the house. Nira doesn't smoke, says she's inhaled enough secondhand smoke to consider herself a smoker anyway. But the smell clings to her, rising up over the herbal scent of her shampoo. Lynetta doesn't think Nira realizes it, but sometimes she runs a long swath of her hair under her nose as if she suspects.

Today Lynetta and Ella are sitting with Rose who is putting together a puzzle meant to have six large wooden pieces that fit in a frame, but there are only five pieces and she stares at the indent where the sixth piece should go and jabs her finger at it. She has Down syndrome and like similar patients, her tongue tends to work at her mouth, in and out, when she thinks hard on something. Rose is deaf and likewise mute. Her chart, Lynetta knows, still states she is a *mongoloid female*, but the staff has been encouraged in the last two years to refer to these patients as Down syndrome. Still, original files bear the outdated diagnosis, and no one has bothered to correct them. Her original file also lists her as *Negro*, another outdated term that should have changed by now, but hasn't.

"Her, too." Nira nods to Rose.

"No," says Lynetta. "What?" She instinctively raises her hand and draws it down the back of Rose's head, feels the coarseness of her short hair.

"Same thing."

"Oh, no."

Nira nods sadly, pats Rose's hand, and Rose smiles up to the ceiling.

"When?"

"Maybe seven, eight months ago? Thought you knew."

Lynetta shakes her head; no, she had no idea. "Why didn't you tell me?"

"I just found out. Joeline told me. I figured she told you, too, knowing how upset you've been. We're not supposed to say anything."

Confidential, Lynetta had been told—warned—by her shift supervisor within minutes of getting Ella down to medical that night. Not to be shared with family or—and at this her supervisor had spun in her squeaky white shoes and pointed a finger at Lynetta to drive the point deep into her—staff. If gossip were to start up, Lynetta was told, she could lose her job. It was that simple. Files would reflect a first menstruation and subsequent sterilization, per standard protocol.

In this moment, Lynetta doesn't give a rat's ass about whether or not she could lose her job. She can clean houses, flip burgers, maybe get a union job at the Giant. She watches Rose next to her lift the puzzle in its frame, looking, she suspects, for the missing piece. Lynetta goes to the shelf and pulls down another puzzle, the box edges softened by time, and brings it to her, clearing a space by sliding the unfinishable puzzle away from her. Sweet Rose. Lynetta watches her rub her face with both hands before digging into the puzzle pieces.

"Joeline says it was bad," Nira says. "Five months or more along before anyone noticed."

"Holy Moses," says Lynetta. She is afraid to ask what happened from there. Did they let her birth it, did they take it away, could a baby survive at five months—did they *kill* it? There are more questions banging around in her head than she can set in order, but rising over the top of them all is why the hell hasn't anything been done?

"Who you think it was?" she asks Nira, not letting on as to her own suspicions.

Nira shrugs her shoulders to her ears, huffs. "I got my usual suspects." She leans forward to Lynetta and lowers her voice. "Samson, for one, but then he left last winter so that wouldn't account for Ella. There was that new orderly around a year before Rose—Thomas—but I got my eye on him and it doesn't add up. Least not in Ella's case. He was moved to Manchester Hall for eight weeks in the spring when one of the orderlies there was out with back surgery. Timing doesn't work there, either." She flattens her stare at Lynetta. "Brody," she says. "Bet my life on it."

Lynetta is moving so quickly, such anger buzzing in her chest, that she is forced to stop her forward momentum—feel the near spill of her upper body—to take a step back and reach behind to pull the heavy door closed. She reminds herself not to slam it, does her best, but feels the heavy whoosh, the distinctive click of the latch catching. She stands before Dr. Carter, not at all inclined to take a seat in spite of the way he beckons to the chair in front of his desk. It takes two waves of his hand before she moves to the chair, but sits forward in it, noting the way Dr. Carter leans back at the same time.

She had called his office from the nurse's station only moments earlier. She needed to see him, she said. Now they are squared off over opposite sides of Dr. Carter's mammoth desk, a sea of mahogany between them.

The briefest of pleasantries are exchanged before Dr. Carter expresses his sadness over *the incident*, his gratitude for Lynetta's dedication to Eleanora Jules.

"I know who done it."

Dr. Carter's brows arc and relax. His fingers tented, he tilts farther back in his fancy chair, swivels left and right, swings back to center, and leans forward. "And who would that be?"

"Brody Myers," she blurts on the heels of his question. "He drives the bus. I checked the logs. Every Thursday for months now he's been driving her all by himself. No one else. What are you gonna do about it?"

"Miss Lynetta . . ."

"You gonna call the police?"

"Am I what?"

"Call the police. Have him arrested."

He only stares at her, shocked, she figures, by her abruptness. She makes herself hold his gaze until he is forced to exhale deeply and push back from his desk, dip his chin before looking at her again, raking his bottom teeth across his upper lip and pulling the lip into his mouth, swallowing so thickly that Lynetta can see his Adam's apple rise and fall in his throat. "Miss Lynetta, that's not the way it works."

"Sure it is."

He places both his hands flat on the desk. "I know how upsetting this is to you . . ."

"Damn right it is." She kicks one leg out and crosses it over the other as she says it.

"But there's a lot to consider here. First and foremost, we have no proof of what you're alleging of Brody Myers. Second, he is a resident here, court ordered. And while we may have given him more freedoms and access than is wise in retrospect, we still don't know the nature of his relationship with Eleanora Jules."

Lynetta can feel a bubbling in her chest, something percolating deep under her sternum. She can't believe what she is hearing. Her throat thickens. There is so much she has to say to this, but Dr. Carter smooths a hand down one of his long sideburns, looks up at the ceiling and back at her, holding the hand up to stop her.

"Hear me out," he says.

"His *relationship*? All due respect, Dr. Carter"—she has no idea why she has phrased it this way, has never uttered those words in her life— "but that's horse dung. She's barely thirteen years old. I got no idea what you're thinking could be a relationship, but what you got here is rape and a miscarriage. And it ain't the only one. I know that, Dr. Carter. I know what goes on." The bubbling in her chest is at a full boil and she can feel the tears pressing behind her eyes. "Shame on all of you," she manages to say. "Shame, shame, shame." She will not let herself cry. She will not call back the feeling of that child's hands gripping at hers, shoving them down her belly, the wild animal wail when Lynetta had forced her to stand and watched the blood and clotting slide down her thighs. She sucks air between her teeth, steels herself to be dressed down, a finger waved in her face, threats—maybe a hand slamming to the desk, dismissed from her job at the least. The tears come anyway, and she is surprised that Dr. Carter holds his tongue while she lets them fall.

He reaches into his drawer and sets a box of tissues on the desk, plucks one from it, and hands it gallantly across the desk to her. She takes it, swipes her eyes, pats her now-running nose.

"I can see how much this upsets you."

"You got no idea."

"I'll look into Brody Myers. I will do that. And if it looks like he's the problem, I will have him reassigned so he can't be near patients anymore. But you'll need to do me a favor as well."

"I can bring you the logbooks," she offers. "You can see for yourself."

He swivels left and right in his chair, thinks for a moment as if an idea is coming over him. "You haven't mentioned this to the Jules family. Correct?"

Lynetta nods.

"That would be terribly painful for them, as you can understand, and there's no way to undo what has been done. You live with your father not far from here?"

Lynetta has no idea how he would know this, but yes, she lives close enough to walk to work.

"How would you feel about becoming one of our resident aides?"

Lynetta looks at him, sees the way his shoulders ease, the way he almost smiles, like this is a brilliant idea. She has no intention of becoming a resident aide, living in a dormitory with the other aides, constantly being on call when someone doesn't show up for work, eating in a communal kitchen. No, thank you.

"No, thank you," she says. "I like my job the way it is—most days."

He ignores her. "It's come to my attention that one of our smaller two-bedroom cottages typically assigned to nursing staff has become available. What I'm suggesting here is that you move into campus housing and Eleanora be permitted to reside with you."

Lynetta can only stare at him. It makes no sense to her. She shakes her head, trying to clear the clutter and understand what he is saying. "Why?" is all she can manage.

"You're obviously attached to Eleanora—"

"Ella," she says. "Her name is Ella."

"Ella," he says. "She does well with you, relies on you, or so I'm told. You've seen her through this ordeal."

Lynetta nearly snorts. *Ordeal.* He has no idea.

"And, to be frank, I know you have her best interest at heart and that you clearly understand that discretion—respect for this young woman's privacy—is paramount. It would be difficult for everyone if the family were to get involved. You understand that, right?"

Lynetta nods again, not sure if she agrees or not, but willing to see where this is going.

"Of course, this would be an increase in responsibility for you. You would be Ella's primary caretaker, days and nights. The bulk of your hours would be with Ella. Privately. That means that when she is at school, training classes, or otherwise occupied, you would essentially be off duty."

She knows the little cottage he's talking about, has always thought it cold and lonely, the way it sits at the edge of the cornfield, nearly hidden in the summer by the monstrously high stalks, and then reveals its pitiful self every fall when the field is cut to stubble.

"What would the family say?"

"I think the Jules family would be pleased."

She thinks now of Mrs. Jules, her perfectly coiffed blond hair, her pearl earrings, her neatly trimmed and blush-painted nails. Thinks of the way she had cupped her palm on the child's shoulder and sighed. Trailed the backs of her fingers across Ella's cheek. She had watched Mrs. Jules place a kiss on Ella's forehead when she lay in the hospital bed before pulling the strap of her purse over her shoulder to leave. As she walked away, her patent leather pumps clicking across the floor, Lynetta had felt the gathering of something in her own heart as she herself then reached to put a hand to Ella's breastbone, felt the rise and fall of her breath, and the enormity of what she imagined—wanted to imagine—had been passed to her in that moment. As if Mrs. Jules had relinquished something and it had come now to Lynetta.

"There would be a raise that comes with the increase in responsibility," he is saying. "A stipend for meals and such."

But Lynetta isn't hearing him anymore. This is a bribe, a way to buy her silence, but at the same time, it is a way to keep the promise she hasn't uttered aloud, a way to keep Ella safe. At least until Brody is dealt with.

"What about all the other girls?" she asks. "Who's gonna watch out for them?"

Dr. Carter rests his elbow on his desk, sets his chin in the heel of his hand. "I'll take a look at those logbooks," he says.

"Then what?"

"Then I'll decide how to handle this."

"Well," Lynetta says, standing up from her chair. "Then I'll decide if I'm interested in this career move."

She sees the shock on his face, the way the thoughtfulness of a moment earlier gives way to indignation, feels her own surprise at what she has said. Fully expecting to be sent packing, she considers an apology but just as quickly decides she has nothing to be sorry for.

Lynetta doesn't fancy herself a gutsy woman. In fact, she can't recall ever having really stood up to anyone, not the woman in the checkout line at the KwikSave who huffed at her when she tried to get eleven items through the ten-or-less aisle, not the teenage girl at Kresge's who had literally knocked her hand away when they both reached for the last pair of L'eggs Sheer Energy white pantyhose, not even Lance when he had shoved a plate across the table and demanded to know how stupid was she—feeding him hamburgers for dinner when all he did six nights a week was flip burgers? But this, this is different. This isn't Lynetta taking care of herself. This is Lynetta taking care of someone else. What she has begun to feel for Ella has shifted something in her.

She turns to go, fully expecting to hear that she is fired and wondering what that will mean to Ella. But then in her mind's eye, she sees Rose and so clearly understands what is on the table. All the girls are on the table, the full deck exposed.

"I'll phone down for the logbooks," she hears him say. "If the timeline is as you say it is, I'll have him moved to the machine shop by morning."

"When can me and Ella move in?"

11

George

PHILADELPHIA, PENNSYLVANIA
Friday Night, April 17, 2009

George is urging his young girls into the house, his wife ahead of him and unlocking the side door. The girls, not actually twins, might as well be. They're both nine years old and only ten months apart in age. Irish twins. The fact of it would forever shame him, as if they were some kind of proof that he was a cad, impregnating his wife with Abigail only a few short weeks after the birth of Amanda. They look exactly alike, with the Jules family lineage of blue eyes, but otherwise look like his wife, the slender jawline, broad forehead, the tiny upturned nose, and matching heart-shaped faces. They won't be tall women. More petite, like Tammy. When a store clerk or a stranger in line at the sno-cone booth asks if they are twins, he sometimes nods absently, yes, and never feels guilty about the lie.

The girls are carrying massive bouquets of yellow roses that his wife had reminded him to pick up from the florist before the recital. Amanda drags hers along the brick wall that lines the walk and never notices that she is decimating the bouquet and leaving a trail of petals.

Tammy is swinging her hips into the door to bang it open and there's no heft behind her hips, she is so thin. When she finally gets the door open and turns to enter, her back to him, he thinks her butt looks like that of a scared dog.

He will ask her if she has eaten once they get inside and she will say she has. She will be lying. There may be a fight, maybe, maybe not. He doesn't have the energy to argue with her and so he trudges up the walk, puts a hand to the back of Amanda's head, his other to Abigail's, and urges them on, as if he can put his daughters between him and his wife, the glue that holds them together and keeps them apart.

"You girls were so wonderful tonight!" Tammy says as they stumble over one another in the laundry room, removing their shoes, dropping the pricey bouquets to the floor. The alarm is beeping and Tammy punches in the code. "I was so proud of you. Daddy and I both were." She looks to him, compelling him to carry the balance of this praise.

"My girls were the best," he says. He isn't sure this is true because the entire thing was a mess as far as he could tell, with one of the younger girls in the ensemble running off the stage in tears and another falling steps behind through the entire routine.

"Lucy Govans kept screwing up," says Amanda. "She bumped me."

"It was great," George says. "How about ice cream to celebrate?" He doesn't look at his wife when he says it but goes right to the kitchen and pulls a gallon of mint chocolate chip from the freezer. Peeling back the lid he sees that it is half empty. He only bought it yesterday. He won't look at Tammy. It is better not to make eye contact. He grabs four dishes from the cupboard.

This is some kind of insanity. He imagines she gorged herself in a fit of anxiety before the recital and then purged twenty minutes before they left, accounting for their late arrival and the fact that the girls had to suffer the rebukes from their dance teacher. There was that fine film of sweat on her upper lip when she climbed into the car, last to load in. The forced smile and false enthusiasm when she told the girls it was going to be *such a wonderful night!*

He sets a stack of four bowls on the table and the girls perch in their seats, wiggling their bottoms side to side in anticipation. Tammy keeps her back to him at the sink, wiping down the already spotless counter. He loads three dishes to overflowing and a fourth with only a single scoop, noticing the way the gallon has been spoon-scooped from the outside rim creating an island of ice cream in the middle. She must have sat with the entire gallon, continued to dip her spoon, never bothering to get a dish, until she had likely surprised herself by the little that remained, the cold attacking her teeth, the sugar revving up her anxiety so that she might have even begun to shake.

"What time are you leaving tomorrow?" she asks.

"Where are you going, Daddy?" says Amanda, her spoon clinking against the bowl.

"I have to go to Nanny and Pop's house."

"We want to go!"

"Sorry, kiddos. This is a grown-up trip." He sees the disappointment in their faces. He doesn't take them to Baltimore often. He's not sure why, but his parents seem perfectly happy to make the trip to Philadelphia in order to see the girls, so he never feels he's depriving them in any way. It's a lot to pack up a family of four and even harder to watch his mother cluck and fuss over the food in light of Tammy's inability to gorge herself in true Jules family tradition. His mother is the type who must extend a fork or spoon throughout the food preparations, urging everyone to *taste, try it, what do you think—more balsamic? Too much pepper? Does it need some lemon juice?*

He is conflicted about this trip. He doesn't want to go but he definitely wants to weigh in on this ludicrous idea to bring Ella back. What in God's name are they thinking? He sure as hell won't be bringing the girls to visit with her in the house. Jesus—it's like bringing home a pit bull as far as he's concerned.

He fingers the scar on his brow, feeling with the pad of his finger the dip—a small crevice where the brow hairs have never filled back in—and then with his pinky finger, the scar on his nostril, the one Tammy claims not to notice anymore, though he is certain she is staring at it right now, looking at him over the center island, waiting for him to answer her question. When will he be leaving?

"I'll get on the road around ten o'clock," he says. "How about pancakes for breakfast tomorrow?" George says brightly to the girls, not looking up as Tammy makes her way to the table.

The girls nod enthusiastically. Tammy ignores the dish of melting ice cream that he slides in her direction and takes the empty container from the table to bury in the trash.

It wasn't always like this. He had fallen hard for her years ago at a local dive bar that claimed to be Irish but only carried Guinness and Murphy's stout, though it stocked an excellent selection of whiskeys. They had been so young, Tammy fresh out of Temple's theater arts program and George packing an impressive MBA from Dartmouth. New, also, to their first *real* jobs, Tammy working as an assistant to a small production company and George having landed a promising job in finance with Deutsche Bank. She caught his eye the moment she burst into the pub with a gang of rowdy bridesmaids all wearing tight-fitting T-shirts, glitter-emblazoned with *I Do Crew* across their bouncing chests.

Looking at her now, her thin arms lost in a billow of sweater sleeves, because she is always cold, even in the dead heat of August, he imagines she could topple at any moment. But he has felt this way for years now. When she bends her arm to scrub the spotless counter, he can see the poke of her elbow bone, like a pebble caught in her sleeve. The tendons of her neck are thin and ropey, her breasts flat beneath her sweater, not even the smallest rise to them. He can't reconcile that old memory of the young woman in the bar—throwing back the pricey glass of Blackadder single malt he had bought her (and told her to sip, but she had smiled and tossed it with a glint in her eye, paying dearly for it an hour later when he drove her home and she had hung her head out the window the entire way)—with the woman shoving a carton of ice cream down in the trash so hard that her lips peel back and her teeth grit with the effort of it.

He brought her home to her roommates that night, though in her drunkenness she had asked to go to his place. He was chivalrous, of course, digging in her bag for her keys while she leaned drunkenly into him when no one answered his knock, only to have an equally lit-up brunette with running eye makeup open the door so that Tammy slid from his side and into her arms instead.

"I got this," the brunette said. She had glared at him, doubting his intentions. He worried, as the door slammed to his nose, that her drunkenness wouldn't be monitored, that she would throw up and choke on vomit, stumble down a set of stairs, turn on a stove, drown in a bathtub. At least he'd had the foresight to slip his business card in her purse.

She had rolled into that bar years ago and mesmerized him with her softness, the way her thighs widened into her hips, the curves of her in tight jeans and the rise of her breasts straining under a too-small T-shirt. Her hair had been long but twisted into a thick caramel swirl on her head, the ends flying around her face. Now her hair is so thin and brittle that he is afraid to touch it. Afraid to touch her anywhere and feel the fragility. Winter vines waiting to be snapped.

The madness started right after Abigail was born. Tammy was desperate to lose the weight. For two years she had waddled around the house incubating these two beautiful daughters, both of whom are now looking up at him with garish pink blush on their cheeks and swipes of blue sparkling their eyelids.

And just who thought it was a good idea to put makeup on these girls for a damn nine-year-old's ballet recital—really?

"Be sure to wash your faces," he says to them, maybe too harshly. "You don't want to sleep with that stuff on your face."

"I like it," says Amanda. She puts her cupped hands to her face below her chin and makes an inappropriately sexy pout, reminding him of his aging aunts and their ridiculous Facebook posts. Always voguing for the camera.

Tammy's postpartum crash diet after Abigail's birth had dried up her milk in less than a month's time. He'd been concerned but at the same time anxious to see some of the bulk she had acquired in the previous two years melt away. He never meant to let her go so far. So far away from him.

Finally, after two years of starving herself, her face drawn and aging right before his eyes, as though she were turning to dust, he had forced her to see her doctor. Even made the appointment himself. Left work early in the day to drive her and insisted on coming into the appointment with her. It surprised him now how forceful, what a bully he had been. She argued with him in the parking lot outside the doctor's office—no, he was *not* coming into the appointment with her, she was not a child, it was her life, she knew what she was doing, and for God's sake, what the hell did he want from her?

"Goddammit, Tammy! You aren't leaving me any choice. You are killing yourself."

That was when she said it, the thing that wasn't fair, the thing that cut into him and gashed his heart. "You should have thought about that when you climbed on top of me and got me pregnant again!"

He couldn't believe she would say it. He watched her face fall after she said it, the fight gone out of her and her lips moving as if to take back her words. But it was too late. Her shoulders slumped. Her breath slowed. The tears rained. "I'm sorry," she said. "I'm sorry."

It wasn't true, what she said. He was stunned, his chin falling like a lead weight from the roof of his mouth. She had invited him, begged him, said she felt fine. Said there was no need to wait. She couldn't get pregnant while she was nursing—didn't he know that? She had missed him.

He had been so careful not to hurt her, so relieved to be with her again. Afterward, he had watched the milk spill from her breasts and she had squealed, laughing, dabbing at herself with the hem of the sheets and he had swiped a tongue across her wet breast and grinned at her, loving the way her body had poured itself out to him.

He was angry. Her words stinging him like a spray of sand kicked up from a speeding vehicle. He ignored the tears, took her by the elbow as though she were a recalcitrant child, and turned her to the doors.

The doctor suggested she go into an inpatient program. Well, no way George was going to let that happen. He knew what those places were like. There was no way he was going to lock up his wife in a nuthouse with those kinds of people. That was not happening. He knew that day in the doctor's office, Tammy slumped in defeat beside him, her spine visible like a string of marbles through the fabric of her sweatshirt—he would never allow his wife to be hospitalized anywhere even remotely similar.

They could put her at the Renfrew Center, the doctor was saying. They had a bed. But yes, yes, it was a lockdown ward and she likely wouldn't be allowed visitors at first. It was all a matter of education and changing behaviors, coping skills. Tammy nibbled on her bottom lip, the closest she had come to putting something in her mouth for days. "With a body mass index of only fourteen," the doctor is saying, "I can't force you to accept help. You're still within the parameters for medium risk, but you are treading dangerous waters here. Heart damage, cognitive issues, seizures. A voluntary inpatient program . . ."

"No," George said. "Outpatient. Find us an outpatient option." He had reached across and taken Tammy's hand in his, felt the sharp edges of her diamond engagement ring under the pads of his fingers.

They left with two referrals that she later claimed she was attending but he knew she wasn't—never did.

He needs to pack, make sure his girls wash the gunk from their faces, and make a call to a client who has requested a review of his portfolio. Tomorrow he will see the sister he sent away. He will make clear that he is opposed to her return. So opposed in fact, that he will propose an ultimatum. Either they will abandon this ludicrous, this preposterous, impossible, and dangerous idea, or he will no longer be a part of their lives and furthermore will take no responsibility for this sister. It's time to see where their loyalties lie. She does not belong in their home and he is not afraid to say so.

12

Jax

ROLAND PARK
Friday Night, April 17, 2009

Belle, Tess, and Jax are gathered in the carriage house, a bottle of wine
in the center of the Formica table and a joint making its way around to
each in turn. They have retreated here following one of their mother's
forced feedings and their father's mandatory round of sherry afterward.
Turning in a little early, Jax explained for all of them. Long day traveling. He had clapped his father from behind on the shoulder and looked
over to his sisters, raised his thumb and forefinger to his lips, and mock-
toked. Belle had agreed that it had indeed been a big day, but Tess had
glanced at her father first, noted the disappointment in his face though
he waved them off. "We're all kind of wiped out," she said.

Ella hadn't been mentioned even once during dinner. The three
present Jules children need all hands on deck for that discussion, and
Finney and George wouldn't arrive until the following day. Ella is a
taboo. The very idea of talking about her with their parents, of digging
into the past—so neatly buried—without the collective courage of all
the siblings, is daunting.

Belle squints one eye and takes a hit before passing the joint to Jax
who puts his hand up to say he's had enough. She swings to her other side
and hands it to Tess who sips from her wine before taking another drag
and then offers it back to Belle. She shakes her head, *no, are you kidding?*
Tess snuffs it out carefully in a dish and sets the remains on the side of

it. She gets up from the table, stretching her arms over her head, and goes to the couch, a relic from the days of *This End Up* furniture, notorious for its inherent lack of padding, nubby blue-and-orange-striped cushions set on a packing crate frame.

Tess pulls a pillow from the back of the sofa to put beneath her head, stretches out her hand and wiggles her fingers, signaling Belle to hand her the wineglass she left at the table. The room is small. Belle need only stretch a few extra inches from her seat to reach her.

"I'm just saying," says Jax, "that the place is a pisshole and I'm glad she's getting out of there. But here, with the two of them, with"—and he waves his hand in the general direction of the household—"with *Ron and Nancy* in there," he says, "*that's* insane."

"Nancy was okay. She sure did love that man," Tess says.

"Nobody liked Reagan," Belle says. She thinks about it and scowls. "Either one."

"Daddy did," Tess says. "And Nixon, too. I think he liked Nixon. Did he like Nixon, Jax?"

Jax can only shake his head and laugh. "Jesus," he says at last. "I was only five. I don't know if he liked Nixon!" Jax runs his hand along the back of his neck, thinking on it. "He voted for Obama," he offers. "Hard to imagine he voted for Nixon."

"But Mom loved Nancy Reagan," she says. "Plus the whole pro-life thing. Oh, my God. Remember those T-shirts Mom bought all of us for Christmas?"

"The red *Just Say NO to Drugs* T-shirts—oh yeah," says Belle. Her phone is on the table and she slides it to herself and slides it away again. "Mom used to try to get me to wear it by telling me it was a great color on me." She breaks into a wide grin and dumps her forehead into her open hand.

Jax shakes his head, still laughing. He had forgotten about the shirts. He had been nineteen, home for Christmas after his first semester at Brown. He grew pot in his dorm room under a grow light and worried his plants would die over break, so he'd paid a sympathetic dorm custodian to water them in his absence. His hair at the time hung halfway down his back and his father had instructed him to cut it before coming home, a gesture his mother would appreciate, he had said. Jax didn't cut it, knew it wasn't really expected of him. Though he'd worn the shirt on his drive back to school after break—a stab at irony and a way to avoid a search should he be stopped along the way.

"What's she like, Jax?" Tess rests the wineglass on her chest and then tilts it to her mouth, tries to drink from it by lifting her head. Wine trickles from the corners of her mouth and she sits up quickly. "Whoa—that was stupid."

He doesn't answer her. He can't say Ella looks like Belle only not at all like Belle. How do you explain that?

His sisters look to him expectantly.

"What kind of *pisshole*?" Belle says.

"The worst kind. There've been documented abuses for years." Belle should know this. She should have paid attention. It's been on the national news lately. Calls for closing what was formerly known as the Maryland Asylum and Training School for the Feeble Minded had begun years earlier, and Governor Martin O'Malley finally made the no-brainer call to shut it down and throw away the key. His mother claims the good governor is throwing out the baby with the bathwater—an eerily fitting analogy, Jax knows, in so many ways.

"Closing that place is long overdue," he says. "In the last year, there've been six cases of broken collarbones." His sisters look confused, Belle's brows rising, and Tess flipping her hand palm up in the air to ask what that even means. "From restraints," he says. Still, they don't understand. "They tie them up," he says. "When they can't manage them, they tie them up in restraint coats. Their arms locked across their body." He demonstrates, crossing his arms to make an *X* across his chest. "It's barbaric."

He uncrosses his arm, rubs his fingers across the table, swirling circles in a small spill of wine and gazing at his sisters. Belle shoves back her chair and looks away. Tess leans forward from the sofa, wanting to know more. Belle sips her wine, gets up from the table, and runs water at the sink while she grabs a glass from the single overhead cupboard and holds it up for inspection. With her back to him, he turns his attention to Tess. "She's okay, though, I think," he says. "She's one of the lucky ones. She's got Nettie—Lynetta."

"I am high as a fucking kite," says Belle, her back to them. "Jesus, Jax, my tongue feels like it has a mitten on it." She keeps rinsing the glass, holding it up to the light, dumping it, and refilling. "These glasses are gross."

Jax watches her, the way she still, after all these years, flips her hair off her shoulder in the same way, the way she tends to stand with one bare foot lifted against the opposite knee like a flamingo so that her legs make the shape of a triangle. She looks exactly—and nothing at all—like Ella. Everything about Belle is long and lithe, like a cat. Ella is more like a plump milk-drunk puppy. But still, they are so much alike. Their blond hair, startling blue eyes, and dark lashes, the way they both tend to tilt their heads and thrust out their chins when they are thinking of something, and the way they curl their shoulders to their ears and bring them down again when they don't want to hear what is being said.

He thinks he understands why Belle never wanted to see her. What it would be like to see the other half of yourself and know that it all came down to luck—heads or tails—as to which of the two of them would have landed on the other side of the fun house mirror. Still, he thinks it strange. *Maybe* Belle would tell him. Maybe someday she would go visit. But maybe never came, and he stopped suggesting it years ago.

Jax has been in California now for over a decade, having moved there to take a teaching job at a private high school where he also coaches a lackluster lacrosse team and organizes poetry slams. He's chair of the English department, which sounds like a big deal, but isn't, as he pretty much comprises a third of the department himself. But summers give him time to write and he's had small successes along the way. A story placed in a small journal here and there, an award from an anthology he admires, an invitation to a prestigious writing conference that he plans to attend this summer.

"I think about her," says Tess, a tad defensively. "I asked Daddy once to let me go see her, but he said it wasn't a good idea."

"Well," says Jax. "If Dad didn't think it was a good idea . . ." He knows the sarcasm isn't lost on her. She scowls at him now.

"He was just trying to protect me—all of us," she says.

"Yeah. That's great," he says. "So what's with this crazy idea to bring her back here now? I guess *that's* a good idea?"

"Who the hell knows what they're thinking," Belle says. She sits back down at the table, stretching her legs across the chair Tess vacated. "They feel guilty. That's what I think."

"They have nothing to feel guilty about," Tess says. She is so certain when she says it. Jax shakes his head. He knows Tess doesn't have a clue what she's talking about.

He had hated her—or thought he did. He knows her having left is his fault. As a young boy, he had wished it into fruition. Had prayed for it every Sunday in the open mouth of the cathedral and God had heard his prayers—and likewise his lack of them.

At night, kneeling beside his bed, his own father's hand on his head, waiting to exhale the *Amen*, Jax would ask God to watch over his mother, his father, his sister Belle, his brothers, George and Finney. But he wouldn't ask for a blessing over Ella, never for Ella. Sometimes his father would notice the omission and whisper her name—*Ella*—and Jax would nod his forehead to the tip of his praying hands in acknowledgment, but he knew God knew he didn't mean it.

The guilt is a layered thing, a crashed house of cards with each haphazardly askew amongst the others, his guilt landing over his mother's, over his father's, the tip of one card touching another, or many, falling flat in small piles and burying one another.

"What time does she get here tomorrow?" Belle asks. Jax and Tess both shrug. "I can't believe she's spending the night," she says. "It's way too much for a first visit. She should come for dinner and then go back until this is all sorted out."

"I tried talking to Mom," says Tess. "But you know Mom. Once she gets an idea in her head. I was going to talk to Daddy, too. But I can't seem to get him alone. Mom is doing her hovering thing." She stops for a minute, looks at both of them as if something is dawning. "You know," she says. "I have to wonder if this has something to do with Bets dying?"

Bets and Renwick Garrison, along with the Morgenfriers, have been the elder Juleses' best friends for decades. But Bets died a few days after Christmas, almost four months ago, after a long battle with lung cancer. Their mother had taken it hard. But that was to be expected. Maybe she was—is—depressed. Well, of course she would be. But Jax can't see how that would translate to wanting to bring Ella back.

"This is some bullshit," says Jax. "I don't know what Mom has against Lynetta. I thought they were friends—sort of." His mother had never said a word against Lynetta. Even called her *Ella's angel*. Hell, Ella has been with Lynetta longer than she'd ever been in the Jules home. And who says Ella even wants to come home? Of course she'd want to stay with Lynetta. "You know," he says to his sisters, "George is pretty pissed about this. He's going to be in a ballistic mood when he gets here."

"What's it to him?" says Tess. "He's never around anyway. When was the last time he even came home? Mom and Dad always have to go see him. It's a two-hour drive from Philly and I'll bet he hasn't been home in what, three years?"

Belle nods and leans her elbow on the table, tilts her head into the cup of her hand. "I'm the one it's all going to fall to," says Belle. They look at her, Jax wondering why she would think so. "It's the twin thing," she explains. "You know how the twin thing works."

"No one has more expectations of you than any one of the rest of us. That's ridiculous." But he can see it weighing on her, the way her lids fall as she tilts her head to the ceiling, and he knows that she believes it.

"Nope," Tess says. "It's going to be me. I'm the closest. I'm the one they'll call if something goes wrong." She sits up as she's saying it. "And what if they want to travel, take a vacation, or if one of them gets sick?" She waves her hand in the general direction of the house. "I'll be the one who has to take care of her." She flops back down with a groan. "It's going to be my problem."

"They're too old to do this," Belle says. "It's ridiculous. Mom is going to be sixty-four next month. Maybe they should just get another dog."

"Aw," says Tess, smiling broadly, "good ol' Butter Bean." She flips to her back again. "I loved him."

"Sixty-four. That's not that old," Jax says. He is thinking of what sixty-four means in California. He has friends near his own age, hovering around forty, who have dated women older than that. No one ages in California.

"They're only going to get older," Tess says, her voice a thin whine that makes Jax roll his eyes and then try to catch Belle's. She's texting on her phone and not paying attention—likely missed Tess's brilliant proclamation regarding their parents' aging.

He watches the way Belle nibbles on her bottom lip. "How's the fam?" Jax says. "Everyone okay?"

"Kitty left her raincoat at the neighbor's. Ben wants to know where her other ones are."

"What are you—a tracking device?"

"Sort of." She goes back to texting, a curiously satisfied smile on her face. "Tobi wouldn't eat his dinner because his mac 'n' cheese touched his chicken."

"Tragic," Jax says.

"Jack had a rough day at school again," she says to no one in particular.

"Maybe that other school would be better," Jax says. He looks at her but she doesn't look up from her phone.

"It just got off to a bad start," she says, "with me leaving and he forgot his math book, and you know, things like that are hard for him."

Jax thinks to relight the joint, but the last two matches only spark and fizzle. He goes to the stove and turns it on, the starter fuse clicking endlessly and refusing to light. He finally finds a box of stick matches in the drawer and brings it back to the table, strikes one and moves the match flame back and forth to the tip of the joint, puts it to his lips, and pulls once, not releasing his breath but smoke has gotten in his eyes and he yanks the joint from his lips, squeezes shut his eyes. "Damn." He rubs at his right eye, the more offended one, and it begins to water. "Damn it."

Belle watches him, cracks a smile. "You should have brought edibles instead," she says.

"I prefer a more organic high." He is serious.

Belle slaps her hand to the table. "You're putting smoke in your lungs, asshole! *Organic?*"

"Jeez, Jax," says Tess. "You flew with that stuff?" Tess has a known aversion to risk-taking and the idea of flying with contraband alarms her.

Jax explains once again that he got it from a dispensary—perfectly legal—and that no one is going to arrest him at the airport. Tess responds with a rundown on the finer points of the law regarding jurisdiction, interstate travel, and states' rights. She is a lawyer and she knows what she's talking about, she tells him.

Jax has only seen Ella a handful of times since he was twenty-nine and left for California. He had promised her he would come and see her whenever he was back in town, but then hadn't. In fact, the last time he had seen her was five years ago and he had been home at least once a year since then. He wasn't proud of breaking a promise, but the last visit had been especially grueling. He does his best to avoid going again. Now he is guilty of a badly made promise.

The last time he saw her he'd had to visit with her in Thom Hall. Lynetta was on shift that day and so he had to see her in the building where she had lived as a child. His preference was to visit her at the cottage where she and Lynetta lived. Ella had, for reasons he never understood, been allowed to live with Lynetta around the time she had turned thirteen. She went back and forth with Lynetta on her shift whenever she wasn't in school. This time he had been forced to walk the gauntlet in order to see her.

That's how he had thought of it, climbing the steps to Thom Hall that winter day, passing through the wide double doors and suddenly engulfed in the noise, the echo of two hundred wretched voices, the clanging, the shouting, the groans and gurgles. He had stood on the foyer's chipped black-and-white tile, the far corners discolored and yellowed, the grout gunked with time. The center of the foyer dipped smoothly, worn by a hundred-plus years of passage, the shuffling of thousands. Instinctually, the residents knew he was there even before he rang the bell to the second set of wide metal doors. He could hear them gathering on the other side, shouting amongst themselves, *Somebody here, somebody here.* And another voice, frustrated, *Move on back, Simon. Gretel, I done told you—move back!*

They would want to touch him. They always wanted to touch him. The aides would tell them to move back, get out of the way, give the man some peace, and finally drag away the stragglers, but first they would run their hands over him, ask him questions, the same questions over and over no matter how many times he answered them. *What's your name? Who you want to see? You know me? You got cookies? You like my shoes? What's your name? Do you know me?*

He'd started visiting her, propelled by equal parts guilt and curiosity, when he was sixteen, old enough to take the car and go by himself, never mentioning it to his parents—never told them where he was—but his siblings knew. He never said it was a secret, something to be kept amongst the five of them, like who crept in past curfew, who was failing chemistry, who had detention for using the Lord's name in vain. But no one ever spoke of it to Hillary and Stone. He was certain that Lynetta would mention it to his mother on one of her Thursday visits, but if she did, Hillary never said so. She wouldn't. He knew that, too.

Sometimes he thinks of telling his mother that he has visited Ella over the years. What's more, he wants to tell his mother that Ella is not at all like he remembers her from his childhood and that is odd to him. That was something he hadn't expected when he first started going to see her.

"Do you remember, Belle, when they told us she was leaving?"

Belle's face pinches. "Not really." She picks up her phone again, sets it down, pushes it a few inches farther back on the table, as if it needs to be set just so. "They didn't say much. I remember them saying she wasn't going to *grow up any more.* I didn't know what that meant. I thought it meant she would always be eight." She tilts her head to her shoulder, as if she is hearing something she would rather not. "I didn't get it. And I wondered, with the twin thing, if that meant I wouldn't grow up, either."

"She hardly talked at all when she left," says Jax. "Last time I saw her she talked a blue streak. She's actually kind of funny." He looks to his sister, not sure whether or not to say more. She never liked to talk about Ella. He waits, and when she doesn't say anything, he goes on. "Remember how she was always tripping and falling over, always stumbling around the house?"

Belle thinks about it. "I don't remember much. I remember her sleeping a lot, with the television on."

Jax remembers this, too. She fell asleep on car rides, in front of the television, in a corner of the playroom. She always woke hungry—and angry, or so it seemed.

"Do you think Finney will show?" says Tess. No one answers her. Who can know with Finney?

"Why do you think Ella got to live with Lynetta?" Belle asks Jax.

He shrugs. "Not sure. Something to do with the hysterectomy. Maybe she needed someone with her twenty-four seven while she recovered?" He has to admit, he always found it strange. "Overcrowding, maybe, too," he says. "Could be they needed her bed in Thom Hall and Lynetta had that staff cottage with an extra bedroom. Who knows? Ella's just damn lucky it worked out that way."

Tess turns to her side on the sofa, an arm tucked under her head. "Mom says Lynetta wants to move to Ocean City with her. Maybe that's the problem. Mom doesn't want her so far away."

"Hard to imagine Mom driving to Ocean City every Thursday," Belle says. "No way."

Tess flops back down to her back with a huff. "Nope—more like I'll have to take her. God, this sucks."

"Don't be dramatic," Jax says. "They don't expect you to take off work to drive them around."

"I quit my job," she says.

"You what?"

Tess rolls to her side, looks from Jax to Belle, clearly surprised Belle hasn't told him.

"What?" says Belle. "You told me not to tell anyone yet."

Tess shakes her head. "You tell Jax everything."

"Jesus, Tess. Not if you tell me not to!"

"Back up," says Jax. "You quit your job?" It is so unlike her.

"Sort of," says Tess. "They were going to fire me anyway. Apparently, it's a bad idea to divorce your husband when he's a partner in the firm." She looks away. "When he's your boss."

"Yeah, well I think it's a worse idea to sleep with your wife's friend. He's the one who should go." Jax never liked him anyway, but saying it aloud was never an option. The Jules siblings are careful with each other in this way, never openly questioning one another's big life decisions. Marriage, a move across the country, lifestyles that butt up against their Catholic upraising. The way they see it, the expectations for how they would live their lives had been firmly put in place by their parents, and likewise, only their parents reserved the right to raise any doubts. Tess had plowed into the marriage too quickly, as far as he was concerned. But then, Jax was more careful with his heart, never handing it over easily. So here he was, just past forty, having never taken a deep dive into romance, having tested the waters but never having found his footing. He doesn't seem to have the same need his siblings have to pair up in their lives.

"I'm sorry, Tess," he says.

She waves him off. "I'm over it."

He doesn't believe her. "Okay," he says.

"I'm curious," she says. She lifts one leg straight in the air, pointing her toe to the ceiling, and then pulls the leg to her chest by the back of her knee. Then the other. "Do you think she'll remember you, Jax?"

"Sure," he says. "But I've always wondered if she ever told Mom I came to visit."

"Mom would have said something if she knew," says Tess.

He doesn't think so.

"She could just come for visits, you know," Belle says, turning to Jax to see if he'll agree with her. "Mom may not see her every week, but she could have longer visits with her once in a while."

Jax shakes his head. He knows that while the impending three-hour driving distance between here and Ocean City may have something to do with his mother's efforts to get Ella back, there's more to it than the obvious. "So, what if this whole thing isn't worked out before Beechwood closes?"

Tess turns to her brother and props herself up on her elbow. "The state can't officially close the doors until everyone is placed. There are only a handful of patients without pending arrangements. I reviewed the paperwork for Ella last week after Mom had already filed her appeal. Which, by the way, was a shock given that Mom told me she was *just thinking about it*, and then I find out she had already filed. Lynetta's guardianship was approved over a year ago. But the courts do tend to side with the biological family. Truthfully, it could take months to work this out. If there's no decision on the appeal in the next few weeks—which is likely, given how the courts move—Ella will stay with Lynetta for now and she can take Ella with her but can't leave the state." Tess rubs her hand over her brow to brush her hair away, rolls to her back again, and looks at the ceiling. "Did you know Lynetta has been there since 1976? She's been there as long as Ella has."

Jax looks beyond Tess, out the window behind her to the darkened lawn and the expanse of warmly lit stone patio with its wrought iron furniture, white and lacy. Pots of pansies sit on the low bluestone wall that surrounds it. Their mother always has to be the first to get her flowers out in pots around the yard and at the front door. A point of pride once, that she could manage so many children and still have her pansies potted, the grill cleaned, and the patio furniture arranged by the first weekend in April. Jax would get the pots from the garden shed and rinse them with the hose, menacing the spiderwebs and egg sacs pearled in the crevices, and then fill them with fresh potting soil. His mother never had to ask him to do these things. It was always his father who would remind him. His mother asked so little of him—only that he forgive her.

They are silent for many minutes and he thinks Tess may have fallen asleep. She never could handle her pot. Belle is yawning, stretching in her seat. She pats his hand. "It's always weird to come home, isn't it?"

"Yeah, somebody ought to warn Ella," he says.

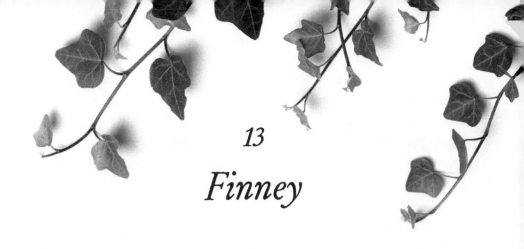

13

Finney

Finney is watching Brad sleep and while he tries not to wake him, he can't help but be grateful when he begins to stir, his legs sliding down under the sheet. Finney has a long drive from Key West to Fort Lauderdale where he will catch a flight he'd rather miss.

"Morning, partner," says Brad, reaching his arms up over his head. They seldom call each other by name. *Partner* is a kind of joke between the two of them, and also an endearment. It serves its dual purpose as they are partners in both their practice and in life.

"I didn't mean to wake you," says Finney.

"Oh, so that's why you've been slamming around the room all morning." But he says it teasingly, opens his mouth to yawn, and lifts his thick brown arms to Finney who goes to him and leans over him to hug him, even considers crawling back into the bed, but can't, won't. He needs to go. He knows this.

Finney and Brad have been together since they met during their grueling residencies at Boston Medical Center Pediatrics. They now share a pediatric practice of their own. Surprising to them still. A ridiculous idea when they first conceived of it—to start a practice, two gay men administering to children. But they dreamed it through the thirty-six-hour shifts back in Boston, in one another's beds, in the hospital cafeteria—sleep deprived and too tired to make their way home—and finally began sharing the notion with their few friends who cheered them on, thinking the times were ripe for the idea.

They'd considered San Francisco, of course, and Philly, and Portland, but Finney had finally suggested Key West when they traveled there for an all-too-brief vacation together. There was something bohemian about it that called to both of them and the need was there. Tess had warned them against it, saying it was too risky, too ripe for a lawsuit—they would be putting their hands on naked children, for God's sake. The suspicions and mistrust were front-loaded in such an idea.

That had been two years ago, around the time that Tess's marriage was going sour, but he hadn't known that then. Now, when he thinks back on it, he can recall the way she kept insisting that it was never a good idea to go into business with a spousal equivalent anyway. But it was different for Brad and Finney. They would be equals. Tess's husband was fifteen years her senior, a partner in the firm when she met him, the balance of power tipped precariously from the beginning. He came prepackaged with an angry ex-wife and, in Finney's opinion, a bloated ego that would be her undoing. Brad and Finney had nothing but medical school debt and a short history of kindness toward one another.

Finney's aunts (the F Troop, as Brad liked to call the three of them when they got together—Finney, Frances, and Fiona, citing an old sitcom he favored) had funded their practice with a modest loan that would be paid off in three more years, right on schedule.

It hadn't been hard to ask them for the money. Brad had flown into Baltimore with him and gone to Aunt Fiona's house to meet with her and Aunt Frances. Finney was their favorite. No question about it. They had taken both him and his mother under their protective wings after Finney was born.

Hillary had been deep in a kind of postpartum depression after Finney's birth, maybe having more to do with Ella than any kind of hormonal imbalance. Of course, Finney never knew this at the time.

Instead, it is something that dawned on him slowly over the years, something that fits like a glove over the breadth of his childhood.

The aunts, he understood, had rotated their days with the Jules family, helping with the other children as well, but mostly caring for Finney. He used to wonder if he had known one from the other of them as a baby. Perhaps he thought it was the same wonderful person coming every day to care for him. But now he knows that he could have likely smelled the difference between the two of them, as newborns do.

The only stipulation the aunts had was that Finney and Brad not mention the loan to Hillary and Stone. Their sister and brother-in-law would surely be offended that Finney hadn't come to his own family.

Brad had set his iced tea on the marble coffee table amongst the four of them, slid his hand over to Finney's, and said that as for telling Finney's parents, that would have to be Finney's call. He would defer to him.

Finney couldn't be sure his father would have given him the loan, and it wasn't pride that kept him from asking. But it felt complicated all the same. His family had paid most of his medical school bills, even though Finney had offered to secure student loans on his own. "You don't want to be saddled with those loans, son." Finney had graciously accepted his father's generosity back then, but now, with Brad by his side, a second ask felt as though it might strain something between the two of them. He would be asking on behalf of both of them and he suspected that his father's generosity did not flex far enough to embrace Finney's relationship with Brad. He might or might not have agreed to fund them both, but either way, he feared the ask itself would put Finney and Brad's relationship under the glare of his family's Catholic scrutiny. The fact that Finney loved a man (a Black man, though no mention was ever made of that, either, making Finney wonder if his mother was trying to live up to her ridiculous proclamation some years earlier that she *didn't see color*) was seemingly ignored by his family. On the single occasion when the two men had made a trip to Baltimore, having recently finished their residencies, the Juleses had hosted a small cocktail party. Mrs. Jules introduced Brad to the guests as *Finney's good friend, also a doctor.* Brad claimed to find this hilarious. But later that evening, after the guests had departed, after his parents had retired to their bedroom (and Finney would swear they did so early so that they wouldn't have to be made explicitly aware of Finney and Brad's sleeping arrangements), Brad had wandered through the den where the family photos sat on a shelf.

"You were adorable," he said, picking up a photo of young Finney and his brothers. Then another, the entire family together on a vacation in Bethany Beach, clustered on the beach, all in breezy white shirts, the boys in madras shorts, the sisters and their mother in brightly colored skirts. And Butter Bean, looking regal in a turquoise collar, his nose lifted in the air. "Jesus," he said. "You're like a little Aryan Nation. Even the dog is blond."

Finney was stung by the comment. It hurt to be seen in such a way. Brad later apologized, said he was only kidding and admitted the comment went too far. There was no truth in Brad's off-the-cuff remark, but it stuck with Finney, the idea that his family could be perceived as someone's warped idea of perfection.

This time, Brad and Finney had flown into Baltimore with no intention of seeing Hillary and Stone. Finney didn't tell them he was coming into town. He and Brad had reservations at a small bed-and-breakfast downtown and a flight back to Florida scheduled for the very next day. This was a business trip, as he saw it.

Of course, Finney agreed to the terms. It would be private, between the four of them. There had been hugs all around, and both Finney and Brad had said how much they appreciated it, how the aunts wouldn't be sorry, how fortunate Brad and Finney were to have them. The aunts had cooed over the two young men, said there was no reason to gush, they were happy to do it—privileged to be a part of it all in some way.

They insisted on taking photos with their new iPhones, and the four of them clustered awkwardly while the aunts held their phones at arm's length and took pictures. (On their birthday a few weeks later, Finney would send them each an extendable selfie stick.)

"We are so proud of you," Aunt Fiona said.

"Of *both* of you," Aunt Frances said.

Finney had beamed, put his arm around Brad, and felt a surge of something deeper than love between the two of them, as if this idea of theirs, now bearing his aunts' blessing, was a kind of benediction over their future together.

Brad rises from the bed and makes his way to the bathroom, not bothering to close the door behind himself so that Finney can hear all the running and flushing of water. Finney waits, sitting on the edge of the bed and glaring at his carry-on bag. He can't remember if he packed a sweater. It can be cool in Baltimore in April, nothing like the weather here, salty-damp and hot, wonderfully hot, so that the weather fits like a second layer of clothing. Finney hates the cold, thinks maybe he always has but just didn't know it until he left it behind. There are so many things he didn't know about himself until he left. That he likes Cuban food, that he has a drive to succeed, that he doesn't have to be lonely, that shame is a dirty word. That he is entitled to a great love.

It's Saturday, a day they typically see last-minute appointments from eight to noon. Afterward, they almost always grab a cold beer at La Te Da and then spend the rest of the day at the beach or on a friend's boat. Brad probably won't be able to close the office until well after two o'clock, having to take Finney's calls as well.

"I am ruining your Saturday," Finney says to him as he comes naked from the bathroom. They are both beautiful men, or so they have been told, Finney the taller of the two and lean. Brad, slightly shorter and thicker, muscular across his chest with the leg muscles of a linebacker, which he once was, back in high school. Finney was a swimmer and a tennis player, not the kind of team player Brad was. That didn't come naturally to him, but he is learning, learning to think as a team. It's easier than he had imagined after being alone for so long in his own head. They complement each other. Finney thinks of Brad as something solid like an oak and imagines himself the pale vines that climb and splay through his limbs.

"No big deal, partner. Family stuff is the big stuff." Brad grabs his robe from the back of the door, an exorbitantly pricey Turkish cotton blend that Finney had given him for his birthday, and wraps himself in it, ties the sash, and rubs his hand up and down the lapel, just as he always does, which pleases Finney because he knows the robe pleases Brad.

"I don't know how I feel about all this," says Finney. "I never got used to the idea that they sent her away in the first place. And now"—he lifts both of his hands, open palmed—"and now, to bring her back . . ." He slaps his hands to his thighs, rubs them the length of them.

"I wish I could go with you."

"None of the spouses will be there," says Finney, feeling a tad defensive but hoping he doesn't sound that way. "Not by design," he adds. "It's just that she's been a kind of secret for so long that George's wife and Belle's husband hardly know anything about her, I'm sure."

Bringing Brad home with him is an awkward endeavor. Twice now they have been expected at the Jules family home and failed to show, Finney panicking at the last minute and cooking up elaborate emergencies that have him missing a flight. His parents claim to be *fond of Brad*, but still, there is always the cloying stink of Catholicism in the air, the crucifixes mounted on the inside door of each of their childhood bedrooms, the rosaries tucked in the drawers of sideboards and nightstands, the prayer cards for lost friends and family that his mother keeps in a file box on the kitchen counter—as if there is a recipe for grief. His mother's relationship to her faith feels unhealthy to Finney, a kind of codependence, whereas his aunts have staked their claim to what they jokingly refer to as *Catholic Lite*. Finney thinks maybe his aunts don't need their religion in the same way his mother does.

"It feels so *private*," Finney says. "Like we're getting together to discuss how to manage our dirty laundry. I don't know how we're going to talk about her. We've *never* talked about her."

"Oh, come on—never? *You* talk about her."

Finney doesn't answer. It can't be explained. Sometimes, and usually only if she'd had a drink or two, his mother would mention her, telling them Ella had been born blue, damaged, and she was in a better place now. That had led Finney to believe she had died until George told him otherwise. She was crazy, George had said. And they kept her in a cage so she couldn't hurt anybody. Finney must have been four or five at the time. He had cried, curled himself on the floor next to the family dog, sniffled into Butter Bean's neck, but whether the tears were for himself or Ella, he couldn't be sure. That dog had sopped up more tears over the years, like a sponge, especially as Finney got older, the horrific dawning of who he was and all the ways he didn't fit into the world creeping over him.

Brad stands in front of him now, reaches to touch him where he sits. Finney doesn't remember Ella, or thinks he doesn't, but there are wisps of memory that come to him now and again, especially if Brad's hand should touch his face, as it does now, if Brad should lean in to kiss him just as he is doing, and if his breath should fall a certain way on Finney's cheek, when Finney hears a small voice, soft but thick, enveloping him.

Be nice to baby, nice baby.

14

George

George never meant to set foot on the Beechwood campus, let alone see Ella. He is only eighteen, about to head off to Penn. His mother has sent him over to their tailor on Reisterstown Road to have clothing altered for his freshman year, mostly khaki pants and blazers that he will never wear but which she insisted he pack. All the Jules men require tailoring of their clothes given their heights and slender builds. George, like Jax and Finney, is tall and thin but with even narrower shoulders and arms that he knows are too long for his body. The Jules men are handsome, Jax more so than the others with a kind of androgynous beauty that appeals to girls, especially. But George knows himself to be the least handsome of all, owing primarily, he tends to think, to the scars on his face. He was twelve when the remake of *Scarface* came out and the nickname had stuck for a few insufferable years. While his mother constantly reminds him that he is *a handsome boy*, it isn't lost on him that she means in spite of the scars. His chin, he knows, is thicker than his brothers' and his eyes are deeper set, not quite the bright-blue that the others have inherited, but more the dusky gray of his mother. Lovely on her, but nothing special on him.

He stands in the tailor's three-way mirror, his hands falling at his sides and fingering the sleeves of the blazer as the tailor pinches the back of it, chalks it, and threads pins down the spine. He is thinking maybe he should start lifting weights once he gets to college. He has failed to fill out in the same way Jax had by this age and is reconciling with the possibility that it will never happen of its own accord.

The door at his back chimes and two women enter the shop, the younger one more girlish, soft and doughy, her feet sliding as she walks, and a woman at least a decade older behind her. He isn't looking in the mirror, but down at his flip-flopped feet. His mother had reminded him to bring his dress shoes, but he had ignored her. When he hears the door chime he looks up to the mirror and thinks for a split second that it is Belle. They look that much alike. But Belle's hair is long and halfway down her back and this girl's hair is cut short at her shoulders. She is thicker, too. Her arms flaccid and her thighs snug in long denim shorts. She is slightly shorter than Belle, too, but there is no mistaking the blue eyes behind thick glasses, incongruously dark lashes, the set of her cheekbones high on her face, and the narrow nose with its deeply set bridge.

"Be with you in just a second, Lynetta," the tailor mumbles through a mouthful of pins.

"Hi, Mr. Goldman."

"Hello there, Miss Ella. I'll be right with you."

"We come get the work," says Ella.

"Bin six, Lynetta, if you don't mind getting it yourself?"

"Sure." She lifts a finger to Ella. "Ella, don't touch a thing. I'll be right back."

"I not touch nothing."

George's stomach is suddenly hollow as if everything has thudded to his bowels. He tucks his chin, glares at his own toes, not wanting to look at her but unable to keep from finally flashing his narrowed eyes to the mirror and watching her. The looseness of her, the disjointed way she walks, as if her joints are gummy. She moves to a row of dress forms, runs her hand over the jersey-covered breasts and down to the waist. "Girl," she says. Then turning to the male form beside it. "Boy," she says, not touching it.

She never looks to him, though he senses she is watching herself in the mirror. George tells himself she won't recognize him, couldn't possibly know who he is. He feels himself tightly curling—like the gift bows his mother used to whip the blade of her scissors up in order to produce a tight curlicue of ribbon—his shoulders rolling over his chest so that the tailor has to nudge him to stand straighter, pull his shoulders back, pick up his chin so he can check the collar. George keeps watch, though, careful to avert his eyes if she should look up. With her back to him, she bends over, using the flat of her hand to hold her glasses in place, her shirt sliding up her backside to reveal inches of skin that pudges slightly over the edge of the denim waistband.

"Pin," she says, as she picks the pin from the carpet. "Uh-oh, pin on the floor." She holds it pinched in her fingers.

"Can you set that on the counter for me, Ella?"

"You welcome," she says, carefully walking to the counter and setting it precisely in the center with a touch of flourish, smacking her lips together and sighing.

"Thank you, Ella." Mr. Goldman shakes his head as if Ella amuses him. George feels himself begin to sweat under the weight of the jacket. He shakes out his arms, tosses his head as if freeing it from a vise.

Lynetta comes from the back room, a pile of skirts and blouses slung over her arm with brightly colored tags dangling and small envelopes likely filled with buttons.

"I not touch nothing, Nettie," Ella assures her, "'cept a pin. I touched a pin."

"She's fine," says Mr. Goldman, looking up to Lynetta. He nods to the pile in her arms. "Mostly repairs," he says.

George feels his chest tighten. He curls his fingers into fists and then splays them out again. Once, twice, tucking his head deep to his chest.

"Almost finished," Mr. Goldman assures him.

George doesn't dare say a word, tries to even out his breath, his teeth gritting in his face so that he can feel the muscles in his jaw bloom and deflate and bloom again.

"I'll have these back by Tuesday next week," Lynetta says.

"We see you Tuesday," Ella says, waving her arm over her head as if it is a huge goodbye.

George holds his breath as the bells tinkle behind him. He can't escape fast enough, shrugging off the jacket and then shifting his weight side to side as he waits for Mr. Goldman to fill out a claim ticket.

Back in his car, he slaps his hands onto the steering wheel before backing out too quickly, almost sideswiping the Mercedes parked next to him. He slams his foot to the brake and thunks the gears into park, adjusts his rearview mirror, and looks at himself, his face flushed, sweat rising on his forehead. The rear end of the family Volvo half in and half out of the parking space. He pulls back in, gathers his wits about him, and eases back out of the parking space to the exit. He should turn right on Reisterstown Road, head to the Beltway, which will take him home, but he finds himself turning left, toward Beechwood.

She had grown up. He had never imagined her as anything more than the little girl he had watched walk out the door, clueless, no idea where she was going or, more important, that she was never coming back.

The aunts had been at the house and he had watched them plant their hands in turn to her head and place a kiss on her forehead, though he can't recall that they said anything at all. There were whispers. Then they had hugged his mother who had stood stock-still beneath their arms, her one hand holding a small purse by the handle, the other holding Ella's. His father had already loaded bags in the car and stood on the street with the doors open as if he were chauffeuring them on a great adventure.

Belle was crying. He remembers that. Aunt Fiona came to her, told her everything was fine, just fine, and let her bury her head against her waist. George would have only been six at the time. When Belle lifted her head from her aunt's waist, he could have sworn she glared at him, slashed the tears from her face, and leveled a hard stare at him. It wasn't his fault. Wasn't his fault that Ella was vicious, dangerous. He wanted to tell her he was sorry but fingered the then three-year-old scars on his face as if they were still new and raw, as if they still stung. His left nostril would always be angled oddly, stitched back together and the tissue hardening as his nose itself continued to grow around it so that the nostril had an odd lift to it. He hated her, but he had never asked that she be banished—only wished it. Wishes, he knew in that moment, were a powerful thing. The realization of such a thing struck terror into him so suddenly that he had felt his chest crack and he burst into sobs. Aunt Fiona reached an arm from Belle and pulled him to her, to the two of them. He pushed her away, squirmed from her embrace, and ran from the foyer to the butler's pantry, where he collapsed in a basket filled with soured kitchen towels, dropped his head to his arms, and sobbed till he choked on tears and snot and rage.

He drives to Beechwood, only a half mile down the road, and stops at the open entrance gate, expecting someone to poke their head from the stone guardhouse, ask after his intentions, but it is empty. He drives on, rounding the curves, eyeing the crumbling buildings, the lack of landscaping so that the buildings rise as if they have broken out of the ground, thrown up by a dark underworld.

It is the tail end of August, the heat visibly rising out of the fields in a way that makes the far-off bodies of men, or boys perhaps, waver as they stoop over their work so that they could be a mirage or a fading memory. He passes a gnarled orchard, the leaves of the peach trees golding on the edges. Between the trees he can make out stacked beehives woven over in clouds of autumn clematis. His mother is forever cutting back the invasive vine from their shrubbery at home, but refuses to cull it altogether, for the sake of its pillowy blooms. He slows behind a short gray bus that swings toward one of the largest buildings and follows it at a distance until it stops at a building that seems to go on forever, rising large in the center and telescoping on its ends. He can barely make out the sign over the door. Pembroke Hall.

The bus heaves a blast of black smoke from its tail end and, as it clears, George watches two women pushing empty wheelchairs come from the building, down a wooden ramp that parallels the steps. A tangled cluster of eight or more bodies disembarks and then unweaves from itself, some wandering toward the building, dragging, scuffing, and others heading in the opposite direction, passing behind the bus, or farther ahead. One of the wheelchair-bearing women, aides or nurses to judge by their white dresses and shoes, settles a spastically weaving and waving girl into a chair and sets off after another wayward patient. Another girl walks, wide-gaited with her hands out in front of her, like a child playing blind man's bluff, and the remaining aide takes her by the arm and swings her toward another chair, forces her to sit in a way that makes her jut her chin to the sky as if she is being pushed underwater. He watches the aides gather their charges and can only think of his father's saying when they were small and he would try to gather them for an outing—*like herding cats.*

A mild nausea is surfacing, and he turns up the air-conditioning, angling the vents to blast at his face. A girl squats on the walk, rocks her body back and forth like the wide-bottomed Weebles he had played with as a child, tipping too far back and forth but never tumbling over.

He needs to go. Can't believe he has come here. He slips his car into gear again and edges forward to move around the bus, resisting the urge to press hard on the gas. Just as his nose edges beyond that of the bus, a woman stumbles seemingly out of nowhere and slaps her hands to the hood of his car. He hits the brakes so hard that even at a mere crawl, he can feel the back end of the car rise up and come down again and he can hear the scuff of his tires. Though he knows she has come from in front of the bus, he never saw her, never knew she was there until she slammed her hands down on his passenger side hood, leaned the whole of her thin frame across it, and spit on his windshield. At a dead stop now, he looks up in horror to watch her clamber onto his hood her face only inches from his windshield. His spine stiffens as her dirty palms *slap-slap* on the glass. He can see clear down her dress, can see the urine-colored stain at the collar and the way the dress hangs from her thin frame and drags across his hood. *Fucker!* she screams. *Fucker, fucker . . .*

Every time she says it, he flattens his head harder to the headrest and watches her too-tiny teeth hook over her bottom lip. She locks eyes with him. He wants, *needs* to turn away, but can't, can't break what transpires between them, can't stop looking at the dried crust around her nose, the angry welts on her arms, the grime on her long thin neck. Just as she unrolls her tongue from her mouth and leans closer, aiming he thinks, to lick his windshield, a burly arm hooks her around the waist and the bus driver drags her flailing from the hood of his car. She kicks and claws as he spins her around and carries her away, never looking back. Never apologizing, never asking if he is okay, just ambling away with the woman twisting in his arms.

George shakes in ripples through his body, his hands gripped to the wheel and his legs trembling as he eases inch by painful inch past the bus before hitting the gas and tearing off through the campus. He can't find his way back to where he came in and keeps following the main drive so that he leaves the campus through a back entrance flanked by a weedy graveyard and a mammoth silo missing jagged patches of terracotta tile so that he imagines a puzzle missing pieces. He lands at the entrance to a country road that unfurls with such grace he isn't sure it is real, that such a thing can exist after what he has just seen. He feels his breath steady as he passes Sagamore Farm, rolling hills and miles of white fences, horses and sheep, rippleless ponds reflecting boughs of weeping willow, tiger lilies bursting orange against the roadside.

He will never reconcile the world he has grown up in against the world of Beechwood. Never reconcile that a Jules sibling lives there. Never ever.

15

Clarissa

BALTIMORE, MARYLAND
Saturday Morning, April 18, 2009

When Mrs. Morgenfrier phones Clarissa to say the Jules children are all in town, Clarissa already knows. In fact, she's on her way to meet Jax now.

It is Saturday, and she is just now making her way from her Fells Point home downtown to the outskirts of the city. It is only eight in the morning, but she is stuck in a schedule of rising at six thirty a.m. Monday through Friday. She shares coffee with her husband, packs her boys' lunches, and sees them off to school. Her husband is out the door at seven thirty, but Clarissa spends the next hour on her computer working from home before heading into her lab. That precious hour without interruption allows her to tend to emails and then jump into the clinical work as soon as she arrives at the lab. Weekends, with their open expanse of unscheduled time, are always disorienting to her. Her husband and boys have no trouble sleeping late and were just rising when she turned breakfast over to them and headed out the door, planning to stall at a Starbucks until at least nine thirty at which point she would text Jax and tell him she was around the corner.

She reminds herself now as she drives down a bumpy cobblestoned street that she must tell Jax how much she liked his last published piece—a strange love story written almost like a fable about a man with a hideous scar, a ropey slash mark across his chest, and he has no idea what its origin is. Whenever a lover asks about the scar, he makes up an elaborate story to account for it, but with each embellishment, the scar grows longer and deeper so that many years later, it encircles the circumference of his chest.

When her mother calls her cell just as Clarissa is coming through the harbor, she has to take a moment before answering to decide whether or not she will tell her where she is headed. Her mother never asks. Instead, she goes on and on about the wonderful news that Ella is coming home, is *ready to come home*, as she puts it, as if this has always been part of the plan.

"We're all invited to come over for dessert this evening to meet her."

"I've met her already, Mom. So have you. That makes no sense."

"You know what I mean."

"Listen to yourself, Mom. You're saying she's *ready* to come home, as if she's been cured. It's not like she's been at some training camp for thirty-two years. She's a person, not a dog!"

"I know that, of course. You're being ridiculous, Clarissa. You're putting words in my mouth. I'm just saying I think we should be supportive of the family. It's really very good news, Clarissa. You have no idea how hard this has been for Hillary, for all of them, for years, and now there is an opportunity to get to know their sister again."

Clarissa can picture her mother with her hand over her heart in the way she tends to do when she feels heaven has answered her prayers and everything is working out, a happy ending on the horizon. "I've prayed for this, you know, for this family to put itself back together. God answers our prayers. It's a miracle, really."

Clarissa doesn't believe in such nonsense. She believes in something altogether bigger. She believes in cause and effect, the science behind patterns, the minuscule changes that alter outcomes, the physics of chaos. "That's ludicrous," she says.

Her mother is silent. Though Clarissa can hear the deep and frustrated sigh she is releasing.

They had agreed to disagree on the subject of God many years ago. Or she thought they had, but her mother can't refrain from pointing out divine intervention wherever she claims to see it. And even when

God doesn't answer her mother's prayers, the woman chalks it up to *God's will*. It is a win-win theological argument for her mother as far as Clarissa is concerned.

The miracle, as Clarissa sees it, is that she and Jax had been in the Jules house in the first place on that day many years ago. That, she thinks now, was some kind of divine intervention.

Jax had texted her earlier in the week.

> Shit show going down at the Jules abode. All hands on deck.

Later that same day, taking a break from the lab, she phoned him. She had waited until precisely 2:10 in the afternoon, knowing it would be 11:10 in California and Jax would be between classes and able to answer his phone. Sitting outside the lab, six flights down on a low stone wall with the fountain making its white noise behind her and where she always took her lunch alone, weather permitting (though usually at noon so the slightly different slant of the sun in the sky spreading across her lap disoriented her to some degree), she waited for him to pick up.

"You are not going to believe this one," he said when he answered, dispensing with the formalities she worked so hard to perfect.

"Hello, Jax."

"Hey."

"How are you?"

"You're really not going to believe this."

"I'm fine, thanks." He had thrown her off script, and there was a moment of empty silence.

"Are you sitting down?"

"I'm eating lunch," she said.

That's when he had told her the unbelievable news, that his parents were trying to move Ella back home.

"Well, that doesn't seem like a good idea."

"You think?"

"No, I don't think it's a good idea at all." She turned to look back at the fountain over her shoulder, the parabolic trajectory of the water stream that allowed for a precise calculation as to where the stream would land and simultaneously mitigating the sounds of traffic, the soothing concentric ripples of surface water spreading from the point of contact. She didn't know what to say now, as was often the case, but something was expected of her.

"What are you going to do?" she said.

Silence.

"Jax?"

"Have you ever told anyone, Clarissa? Does anyone know?"

"No one," she said. She never told a soul.

"Not even your mom, right?"

She never told her mother. "You asked me not to," she said, stating the obvious.

They hung that way on the phone, a great quiet between them, only the heave of his breath coming through the phone.

"I'm coming home this weekend," he finally said. "We all are."

"Can I help?"

"I think," he said, and here he paused again. "I think I need to get a read on this when I get back."

"Yes?" She wasn't sure what he was asking of her.

"This *is* a bad idea, Clarissa, right?"

"Definitely a bad idea."

"The worst."

"Among the worst, yes. I'll come over if you want. Will she be there already?"

"No, but she's coming Saturday night for one night. Then she goes back with Nettie until this is straightened out."

"It's a terrible place, Jax. She has to go somewhere." She could hear behind her the way the fountain failed to do its job of overriding the sounds of cars screeching and thunking through the stacked layers of the parking garage. "I never imagined she'd come home."

"Agreed," he said. "But it's complicated. Nettie wants to take her."

"That's perfect." She felt immediate relief. Clarissa knew Nettie, had met her when she first began visiting Ella years ago. Clarissa had promised Jax she would visit Ella when he left for California and she had kept her promise, visiting every few months and reporting back to Jax afterward. Lynetta, in her opinion, was terrific, like a mother to Ella, only more. What could be better?

"I think so, too, but Mom filed an appeal and claims to want her back. What a fucking mess." Clarissa could imagine him wiping the back of his hand across his brow as he said it, shaking his head side to side in that way he did, even as a child. Maybe even slumping against a wall, the way he had thirty-two years ago, exhausted, frightened, but doing exactly what she told him to do, trusting her.

Clarissa loves Jax, has loved him since that day, but in a way wholly different from the way she loves her husband. She loves Jax the way two children with a secret that could crack the sky wide open love each other.

16

Lynetta

Lynetta had scrubbed the overnight bag and set it open on the kitchen table overnight to air out. She dips her face into it now and takes a whiff. She can still detect a faint hint of something unpleasant and decides she will set it outside in the sun, waiting to pack until a little later in the afternoon.

It is morning, not quite nine o'clock, and she and Ella have already had their breakfast and made the beds. The breakfast dishes are washed and drying next to the sink, though Ella is still in her ridiculous silky pink Victoria's Secret pajamas that she had nearly swooned over on a recent trip to the mall and insisted on having. Getting dressed is always an ordeal. Ella is picky about what she will wear—preferring pink or sparkles to anything else in her closet—and Lynetta had suggested a pair of lavender leggings and a bold purple T-shirt that didn't comply with what Ella had in mind for the day.

"Put on what you want, but tonight you got to wear that dress I laid out," she says to her now.

"I not wear the dress, Nettie."

"Ain't nothing wrong with that dress. Your mama gave it to you and it's a nice dress." She stares at Ella who ignores her, watches her pick at a dried piece of cereal on her lap. "It looks nice on you," she says. "Real pretty."

"Don't like it."

"Why not?"

"Itches."

The door to the cottage is open from when Lynetta set the bag on the steps to air, and a stinkbug has made its clumsy way into the cottage, thumping against the window and dropping to the sofa next to Ella. She screams and throws her hands up to cover her face, hooting and scooting to the far side of the sofa. It is like this with flying insects, especially bees, which terrify her. She has never been stung, not even once, but the fear is real.

"He's not gonna hurt you," Lynetta tells her. She goes to the counter and takes a juice glass from beside the sink. Placing it over the bug on the sofa, she slides a magazine underneath it and walks it to the door where she sets the glass right side up on a low ledge and watches the cumbersome block of a bug climb to the lip before shooting up into the beams of the small portico. "All gone."

"Shut the door, Nettie."

The cottage has only two windows on the first floor and a small back door with a trio of panes. Lynetta hates to shut the door and cut down on the sunshine streaming in, but she does as Ella asks, knowing how afraid she is. The room falls into shadow with only a small rectangle of light stretching across the floor.

Lynetta likes the cottage well enough, knows she is lucky to have had it these many years, and luckier still to have been able to move into it with Ella. There are only a very few small cottages on the campus and one larger one that once housed a series of directors. Now it, too, is empty and tumbling like everything else. *The inmates are running the prison*, she says to herself. There is no oversight anymore, other than the state and Governor O'Malley with his herculean efforts to close the place down. Lynetta, of course, has never met the governor, but she knows she likes him. Is counting on him, in fact, to do exactly what should have been done years ago.

She wonders lately if she will miss the cottage. There are some happy memories. Dancing to Whitney Houston, baking cupcakes with Ella and trying to keep her fingers out of the batter, the time a toad got in the house and Ella insisted Lynetta kiss him to see if he was a prince before she would let him go. Funnier still was Ella's disappointment that he was *just regular.* Nope, she had said, just regular, and later that day, touching Lynetta's shoulder and saying she was sorry. Maybe the next one.

Her favorite memories have to do with the Christmas dinners she has prepared over the years for both Ella and her own father, usually just a large roaster chicken, baked potatoes (never mashed), a green bean casserole that Ella picks the onion rings off of, and a sparkling cider that makes Ella sneeze and sets Pap to laughing.

"Not funny, Pap," Ella always says, but she giggles in that throaty way of hers when she says it because she knows it is, in fact, funny—the way the cider tingles her nose every time without fail.

"Ella-Bella," he always says. "You tickle my funny bone."

"I not Belle," she says. "I not tickle you."

"Well, you'll always be my belle of the ball."

There are memories in this cottage, most of them good ones. But what lies beyond the safety of their little cottage and within the grounds of Beechwood, Lynetta is just as happy to wash her hands of.

Lynetta fills the teakettle with water and places it on the front burner, reaches into the upper cabinet where she keeps a tin filled with the four stove knobs. She pulls one from the tin, slides it into place on one of the small rods that protrudes from the panel along the front of the stove, and turns on the smallest burner. Ella knows where she keeps the knobs, has kept them for years, but the cabinets all have child-protective locks. Lynetta thinks Ella could probably figure it out if she took the time, but she has, over the years, lost interest in them, resigning herself to having to ask Lynetta for anything that lies within the cupboards.

On their first night together in the cottage, Lynetta had watched Ella make her way around the first floor, pulling the dusty blinds up and down and finally leaving them oddly angled when she moved to the cupboards.

Opening and closing them, pulling out pots and pans and baking sheets. Wandering to the bathroom and repeatedly lifting the layers of the toilet lid and seat. Finally coming back to the kitchen where she puttered at the sink and squeezed the dish soap to watch tiny bubbles rise from the tip of it.

Lynetta had no problem with letting her explore. Figured it had been five years since she'd actually been in a home of any kind and that much of this was new to her. The banging of pots and pans, however, got on Lynetta's last nerve. She assumed, and was only partly right, that the novelty of it all would wear off in time.

The next morning Lynetta had come into the dim kitchen to see the four coils of the stove glowing like alien landing pads. She would soon learn that Ella fiddled with everything, doorknobs and window latches, the flushing handle on the toilet, the houseplants on the windowsill. Smaller items sometimes went in her mouth—Lynetta's keys, crayons, coins, the fat fallen leaf of a jade plant—but that behavior, too, had ebbed a bit in the last years. Not that Lynetta didn't keep an eye on it. She'd catch Ella licking a candlestick, the television remote, see her snatch at the cap to a soda bottle, a hair barrette left on a bedside table, and pop it in her mouth without thinking about it. Lynetta had learned to simply put her cupped hand to Ella's chin and receive the sloppy item.

The stove was another beast altogether. Lynetta couldn't risk a fire in the cottage and so she had removed the knobs and stored them in the tin behind a child-proofed cabinet for years now. The trailer was Ella-proofed in the same way. Still, Ella would stand at the stove and pretend to cook, futilely twisting at the metal dowels that protruded where the knobs should have been, sliding the teapot from burner to burner, dinging the stove timer over and over again.

Eventually, Lynetta's father had surprised Ella with a large-scale playhouse complete with its own kitchen. He had built it himself because the children's playhouses were all designed for much smaller children. Ella's "house" was outfitted with a plywood refrigerator, painted avocado green, and a door that snapped shut by way of a magnetic latch. The stove had real knobs on it that spun and clicked. The burners were red spirals painted on the surface. Lynetta stocked Ella's kitchen with plastic plates and cups, cast-off pots and pans, empty Frosted Flakes and Bisquick boxes for the cabinets. Ella could spend entire afternoons in her playhouse cooking elaborate imaginary meals and then inviting Lynetta in to join her. Sometimes they took their lunch in there, their knees touching under the tiny café table.

Lynetta fixes her tea and comes to the sofa beside Ella.

"What's the first thing you gonna do when you sit at the table?" Lynetta asks her.

"What table?"

"At your mama's house."

"I gonna put my napkin in my lap." She pats her lap as if there is a napkin settled over her thighs.

"That's right. Then what?"

Ella shrugs. "Then what?"

"That's what I'm asking you," Lynetta says. And then, seeing as Ella has no answer for her, she drops a hint. "They might say grace," Lynetta suggests.

Ella claps her hands together and holds them in prayer fashion, smiles.

Lynetta can't be sure but figures it is something Catholic families do. She had taught Ella how to fold her hands just in case. She didn't want Mrs. Jules to think she had raised Ella to be a heathen.

"I come home after dinner, right?"

Lynetta explains again that Ella will be spending the night and watches her eyes go wide.

"No," Ella says.

"We talked about this. It's one night. It'll be fun."

"You come, Nettie."

Lynetta shakes her head. "No, doll. I can't come." She puts an arm over Ella's shoulder. "But I'll pick you up the next day after lunch, remember?"

"I just come home, Nettie." She leans her head into Lynetta's shoulder. She isn't defiant in the way she says it, simply stating matter-of-factly. Lynetta is used to these pronouncements, knows it is best to ignore it. "I not gotta take a bath at Mama's house," she says. "Will Belle be there? And Jax?"

Ella hasn't seen Belle in thirty-two years, and so it always surprises Lynetta when she mentions her twin. Lynetta doesn't know who will be there and tells her so. "But your mama will be there, and you love your mama, right?"

Ella nods. Sits back. "I not wanna live with Mama," she says, shaking her head so hard her hair whips.

"Who says you're living with your mama? We talked about this, remember? You're living with me like you always done."

"Down the ocean!" She is suddenly happy again. It amazes Lynetta how she can go from the brink of sad to utterly happy in the blink of an eye.

"That's right." She sips her tea, wraps her hands around the mug, feeling the warmth of it through the ceramic. But it does nothing to settle her insides, churning now at the idea of Ella going back to the Jules family. It makes no sense to Lynetta, this possibility of Ella moving back to her family home. She hasn't even been back for a single visit since the day she arrived at Beechwood.

Eighteen months earlier on a brilliant October afternoon, a meeting had been convened to decide Ella's future. Mr. and Mrs. Jules were, of course, encouraged to attend, and Lynetta had been surprised when they failed to show. It was a known fact all along that Lynetta would offer to take guardianship of Ella. The meeting had been brief, with the powers that be all too happy to have Lynetta take on the continued care of Ella. After all, she had shown remarkable dedication to Ella the last twenty-seven years and even in the years preceding when Ella had lived in Thom Hall. She had long ago been certified by the state for just this kind of thing. There was no question that she would be the best guardian for Ella. What they didn't say aloud was that she had proven herself capable of discretion. The placement plan had been finalized, and Lynetta's guardianship was approved a mere three days later. The news, though it didn't surprise Lynetta, had a strange effect on her. It made her feel as if her life—their lives—was just now starting. The air around her nearly bursting with possibilities. She and Ella were walking home from Lynetta's shift. An autumn breeze in their faces, the official approval letter clutched in her grip. The trees were dropping bright orange and burgundy leaves along the path. They swirled in circles at her ankles, lifted, and dropped with a kind of grace she had never noticed before.

For twenty-seven years she had been careful to cross her *t*'s and dot her *i*'s. She had flown under the radar, always afraid that she was pushing the limits, especially when she started taking Ella to the ocean for weekends. Always careful to fill out the paperwork properly, to keep a detailed calendar that read more like a diary so that if she was ever questioned about anything, she would have records to fall back on. And never, ever, did she ask for a raise, file a complaint, question authority. Most of all, what she had done over the years, the thing that had worn her down and thinned her mind, was that she had refused think about the future. Chained, as it was, to Ella. How could she imagine the days ahead if the possibility of leaving Ella behind was a part of those imaginings? If Lynetta ever left Beechwood she knew without a doubt that she would be sending Ella right back to Thom Hall and the madness that lay within those walls.

It was in that moment, with the wind in their faces, the letter flapping like a bird in her hand, that she decided she and Ella would move permanently to the trailer.

That had been a year and a half ago, and Lynetta never anticipated any blowback from the Jules family, figuring instead that they were pleased, grateful even for the way Lynetta had stepped up to take on what they likely saw as the burden of Ella.

But then there was the strange phone call from Mrs. Jules a few weeks back. She had called to say she wanted to arrange for Ella to visit, a family dinner and an overnight stay. She understood that Lynetta and Ella headed down to *the trailer* (and it wasn't lost on Lynetta the way she said it, like it tasted bad in her mouth) on weekends, but she'd like to arrange the visit for a Saturday. She hoped that wouldn't be an inconvenience, though she didn't say it like she gave a hoot one way or the other if it was.

She then went on to ask Lynetta about her trailer, how close was it to the beach, did Ella like the ocean? (And no, she didn't, but Lynetta only said she wasn't keen on sand between her toes but otherwise she liked it fine.) The string of questions bothered Lynetta. It felt like she was fishing for something. Did Lynetta have friends down there?

"My friend Nira has a place in the park, too," she found herself saying. "That's how me and Ella heard about it." She could feel the conversation starting to take a turn down a road she didn't want to go down.

"Is there a special someone down there, Lynetta?" Mrs. Jules asked, as if she were a kindly grandmother inquiring about a potential beau.

Lynetta nearly snorted in the phone. "No, ma'am," she said. The idea was ludicrous. "No."

A fidgety silence followed during which Lynetta found herself trying to figure if she was expected to say more. "No one on my radar, Mrs. Jules," and she immediately regretted saying it, as if she ever had radar for that kind of thing. No, Lynetta had no interest in bringing a man into her life ever again, and no one she could remember ever offering to step in, if you didn't count Lance's halfhearted efforts.

"Oh," said Mrs. Jules. "Ella mentioned someone named Wally."

At this, Lynetta did laugh. "Just a friend," she said. She was going to have to talk to Ella about this again. She knew Ella liked to conjure up boyfriends for Lynetta. For years she had insisted the tailor, Mr. Goldman, a happily married man with a wife and three grown boys of his own, was Lynetta's boyfriend. But that had finally worn itself out when she bought the trailer and Wally had started stopping by. He never stayed longer than it took to repair a window screen or change the filter on the air conditioner, but that didn't stop Ella from imagining a torrid romance between the two.

The phone call had nagged at Lynetta afterward. Now, given the fact that she'd had to hire an attorney and she knew exactly what the Jules family was up to, well, now it just made her angry.

"Jax is a nice brother," Ella says.

Lynetta agrees with her.

"You come, too, Nettie." She starts to rock her upper body just enough that Lynetta knows she is nervous thinking of tonight. "I be nice to the baby."

"The baby is all grown up now," Lynetta reminds her.

"Baby Finney."

"That's right. All grown up." Lynetta knows it is hard for Ella to understand that her brothers and sisters are not the same children she left behind thirty-two years ago. She understands this about Jax because of his visits, though they slowed down when he moved to California and then stopped altogether. But Ella still thinks of Finney as the baby.

She wonders now if Mrs. Jules understands how Ella sees the world. She wonders, in fact, if the Jules family knows anything at all about Ella. Do they know that she is terrified of bees—of most flying insects, actually—and that she doesn't like raisins or nuts, that apples give her a bellyache, that she has to be reminded to flush the toilet and then she has to be told to stop? Do they know that she saves pictures of cats from magazines, that she has learned to sew on a button but sometimes sticks the needle in her mouth? That she never shuts a door behind herself, struggles over which shoe goes on which foot, likes ketchup on her eggs, mixes her orange juice with milk (which Lynetta finds disgusting but is willing to overlook), and that she gets carsick if she sits in the back seat?

Lynetta looks at her now, wondering what Mrs. Jules sees when she looks at her daughter. She uses the curl of her finger to tenderly loop a lock of Ella's hair behind her ear. One thing is certain. They don't see what Lynetta sees. They see disappointment and tragedy, heartache. They see imperfection, something lost. Lynetta, on the other hand, sees a jewel of nature, a precious jewel.

17

Hillary

Roland Park
Spring 1975

The best way to bury the tiny half a Valium is in a spoonful of sugar. Hillary hums the tune, not daring to sing the words aloud. *Just a spoonful of sugar helps the medicine go down . . .* She keeps the vial out in the open, right on top of the windowsill over the sink, next to the Bayer, the Pepto-Bismol, ChapStick, and a jar of Oil of Olay. The other children are in the backyard and Stone is pulling gardening tools from the shed. The hose is snaking across the lawn, and he is instructing Jax to rinse the pots she plans to fill with early spring pansies. Six-year-old Belle is on her knees along the patio edge, grudgingly pulling the early spring weeds. She's terrible at it. Hillary can see the scowl on her face and the way she refuses to wrap her small hand securely at the base of the weed where it meets the brick pavers and instead pulls from the top so the tender weeds are being removed inch by inch rather than at the root, certain to burst through again after the next rain. She would rather be out there doing it herself, but there is Ella . . . Always, there is Ella.

Hillary snaps the Valium in half, forced to estimate the dosage. Ella is at the post-breakfast table, dragging her hand across syruped plates and then licking it off, heel to fingertip, and the syrup shines her nose and chin. She is not so bad today. Some kicking when Hillary tried to thread her icy feet into socks, but other than that, not so bad. Hillary snaps the half pill in half again, places it in the heaping spoon of sugar, pushing it down into the crystals with her pointer finger, and then balances the loaded spoon on the counter. She runs a fresh rag under water.

Ella reaches to her with sticky hands and Hillary catches them, wraps one hand around both of Ella's small wrists so that Ella is forced to hold her hands together prayerfully while Hillary wipes them down, working the rag between her fingers. Ella is being patient. *Good girl*, says Hillary. As if she is talking to a puppy. Ella looks to her mother, a smile spreading lazily across her face, and it changes everything about her, makes Hillary imagine they are capable of pleasing one another. Reminds her, painfully, that there is love buried between the two of them.

Hillary never wanted the prescription in the first place. Stone had insisted, claimed her sisters were in agreement as well. She needed a little something to take the edge off. It had angered her at the time. He had no idea what was required of her to manage this family. Even with her sisters' help since Finney was born, there was still too much to do.

Stone was up and out the door by five thirty every morning, a long commute ahead of him, but he never neglected to leave the little yellow pill next to a glass of orange juice on the counter. She had taken them, but they made her feel like she was traveling underwater. By the time one or the other of her sisters had arrived every morning, she would find herself oddly at ease with the chaos around her. Half-dressed children, a wailing infant, and Ella, more often than not, still trapped in her crib but shaking it so violently that the floor overhead thumped. And then, once Fiona or Franny or whichever of the two had drawn the short straw (as Hillary saw it), had swept into the house and begun to restore order—clearing breakfast dishes, soothing a damp and neglected Finney, dressing children, sorting through piles of laundry—Hillary would find herself in Ella's room, struggling to raise her thoughts up into a clear space where she could make a call as to whether or not Ella would wear a diaper or they would continue with the futile task of potty training.

No. She could not afford to let her mind slink off with the Valium every day. Not with Ella's temper tantrums, her biting, the need to peel her clothes off on the coldest days, her refusal to sit still on a toilet and thus requiring a thorough scouring of the seat after every bowel movement. Hillary needed her wits about her or—What? What would happen if she regularly let her mind wander into a soft space? Would the dental appointments get made, Finney's bottles sanitized, the Christmas decorations set up or put away, the front door swept, and the pansies potted before spring was long gone? She had imagined back then, nearly a year ago, limp on the floor of Ella's bedroom, the way in which the Valium coursed through her circuitry, taking the turns too wide and softening the corners of her mind. She had watched Ella dump the hamper filled with dirty diapers, the stink of it thick enough to stick in the back of her throat. When Hillary, if only out of habit, had raised her head to the crucifix that hung on the back of Ella's door (exactly like the one on the back of each of her children's bedroom doors), and pleaded for the patience, the strength, *the time*, to make it through another day, she was certain that He had nodded His head in agreement, though it might have only been the swimming of tears in her eyes.

Stone insists that everyone participate in family chores, a mandate. Even four-year-old George has a job and is walking in circles around the yard picking up sticks, bits of trash that have blown into the hedges, lacrosse balls that froze into the ground over the winter. The baby, Finney, is down for his morning nap. She should be able to get at least an hour in her garden before he wakes. She will need to get a trowel between those pavers.

She is always careful about the dosing. Careful, most times, to remember to toss out the broken halves and quarters. Last week Ella had a small seizure, nothing terrible (at least, she thinks it was a seizure). Her eyes rolled up in her head and her limbs trembled in waves. It was over quickly, and Hillary doesn't think it had anything to do with the *quiet medicine*, as she calls it. Still, she hasn't mentioned it to the pediatrician. Wait and watch.

She picks up the spoon carefully from the counter, glances out the window to her family before turning to her daughter, humming as she does so. Ella simultaneously opens her mouth and lunges her face to the spoon, snapping. Her teeth lock and unlock quickly on the neck of the spoon and she pulls back, taking the sugar and scrap of a pill with it.

Swallows.

18

Lynetta

BEECHWOOD INSTITUTE
Labor Day 1982

Pap is manning the Weber, flipping burgers and rolling hotdogs across the grill to make for perfect spirals of char marks. A platter of buns is set on an old weatherworn picnic table that today is covered in a red paper cloth, so no one is the wiser. Lynetta is just a bit worried that she didn't buy enough food. She hadn't expected so many people to take her up on her invitation to come by the cottage after their shift for a Labor Day get-together. More than a dozen people are milling about behind the cottage, dipping into the cooler for sodas and help-ing themselves to a pitcher of spiked lemonade that, after downing two cold glasses on this warm day, has her feeling a touch light in the head. A moment earlier she had snatched a cup from Ella's hands and warned everyone to keep her away from the spiked version while she went inside to make up a second batch for Ella and any guests who preferred a virgin recipe. She had grabbed a chilled Coke from the cooler for herself before heading in, thinking it best she take a break from the alcohol.

The bees are a nuisance, one having trailed her into the kitchen, but it is slow and clumsy, and she shoos it out the open back door with a broom. She pulls a pitcher from the cabinet, thinking she will never adjust to the damn child-protective locks, and sets it on the counter, pulls a can of icy lemonade concentrate from the freezer.

She hears Pap call out for slices of cheese and Nira comes in the back door to ask where the cheese might be. Lynetta hands her a hefty package of Kraft Singles and reminds her to take the plastic wrap off each one. Her father, she tells Nira, has been known to put them right on the burger with the plastic wrap still on them. Nira laughs, calls her father *a sweetie*, and heads out the back door again, shutting it behind her so that Lynetta can no longer hear the chatter in the backyard.

Ella is happier than Lynetta has ever seen her, delighted to show the guests around and point out the two sets of towels in the bathroom, the two bathrobes hanging on hooks, the new curtains Lynetta has sewn for all the windows, and the pretty pink floral slipcover *Nettie made all by herself* now dressing the old ratty sofa. Nira, in true Nira fashion, had said *it looks like Laura Ashley threw up in here* and Ella had said, *Nope. Nobody got sick. It's just new and pretty.*

Lynetta wasn't offended. She knows how Nira feels about anything fussy. It is their differences, she thinks now, that make for the balance in their friendship. Nira likes motorcycles and Miller Lite and men—in no particular order. Lynetta has no use for any of it but somehow, listening to Nira talk about her trips to Ocean City on the back of one bike or another every weekend intrigues her. They don't do the things together that Lynetta imagines girlfriends do. No shopping trips to the mall, no runs to the drugstore for new eye makeup, no fixing each other's hair. But Nira likes to talk and Lynetta likes to listen and out of this a friendship has bloomed.

Lynetta looks up to the front window and sees Carl, the new bus driver, and a skinny young girl who she recalls was her shift replacement but can't remember if her name is Tia or Thea walking down the service road toward the cottage. She hadn't invited the girl specifically, but assuming the food holds out, she's just as happy to have everyone here. Carl has a six-pack of beer snug under his arm. She is a little nervous now, wondering if there are any rules she should be mindful of concerning alcohol on the grounds. A pitcher of spiked lemonade shouldn't be any problem, but she didn't plan on having a six-pack paraded down the road, either. She opens the front door and directs the two of them to the backyard and then, as an afterthought, tells Carl he can stash his beer in the cooler and would he mind drinking his beer from a cup being as she is unclear as to the rules and all. No need to have bottles in plain view if the director was to drive by, right? Carl looks over his shoulder, up the long service road, shrugs his shoulders, and says sure, no problem. She's afraid now that he doesn't feel welcome and so she tells them both how glad she is that they could make it and sends them around to the back of the house.

Back to the lemonade. Another bee has made its way in the front door, and she waves at it with a large spoon. It is more persistent than the last, but finally swoops away and out to the portico. She is unzipping the plastic tab that runs around the can when she looks up at the doorway and sees another figure coming down the service road to the cottage. She can't quite make out who this is, only that he's large and wearing overalls. She pops the tab to her Coke on the counter, takes a sip, and carries it to the doorway. She sets the soda on the low stone wall of the portico and steps down, lifts one hand to shield the sun that glares at her and puts the other to her hip, looking to see who it is.

"For the love of God," she says aloud. It is Brody Myers making his way to her house. Instinctively, she steps back into her doorway. He can't possibly think that he is welcome here. She watches him get closer, can make out the sour look on his face when he is twenty feet from her, can almost hear a growl rise out of him as he nears.

"You and me," he says, pointing a fat finger at her, "got a bone to pick."

"I got nothing to say to you, Brody." Lynetta locks her knees and steels herself. "You turn around now and move on." She shoos him like a fly. He keeps walking toward her until he is at the edge of her step, leans himself against the pillar like he has all the time in the world.

They both can hear the voices in the backyard, and Brody cocks his head. "Heard you was having a party."

"You're not invited," she says.

He is wheezing and sweaty from his walk. His chest pumping at the bib of his overalls. "Free country," he says. He wipes his hand across his mouth, sucks in a rattly breath. "Ain't your house anyway."

Lynetta's throat is dry, and she swallows the gummy lemon taste in her mouth, sees the cold soda set on the ledge but doesn't dare to step forward and retrieve it just beyond the bulk of this man at her door. She watches a bee light on the edge of the aluminum, settle its wings, and walk delicately around the edge. Another hovers, dips to the open spout of the can, and disappears under the rim.

Brody waits, his eyes tracking up and down, looking over her shoulder into the little cottage with its new curtains and a trio of plants at the windowsill, a picture Ella drew taped to the refrigerator. His eyes come back to Lynetta and she makes herself look him in the eyes, tries to ignore the strange bulk in his front left pocket that she thinks for just a brief second could be a gun, but then thinks, no, that just couldn't be.

"Nice place," he says. "Bet you're real proud of what you done to me."

"I didn't do nothing," she says. "But what I should of done is made sure you went to jail."

He laughs and it comes out like he is choking on a joke. He gathers himself, stands a little straighter, leans into her, and says, "You're talking out your ass, Lynetta."

"I know what you done, Brody Myers. And I won't forget it." And damn it, she feels the tears coming and she will not cry in front of this bastard. Will not give him the satisfaction. She grits her teeth together. "Get on out of here. Go on. Get!"

"Beer for the road?" he says, swiping a hand across his forehead to push the damp hair back. Pulls at the collar of his T-shirt and Lynetta can hear the threads pop.

Lynetta shakes her head. "I got nothing for you."

"Well, I got some news for you, Lynetta." He folds his arms across his chest, splays his legs, leans back, and settles squarely into his own hips. "I got a feeling the little retard liked it." He waits. Spits at his feet, raises his hand to his chin. "Yeah, that's what I think."

Lynetta can think of nothing to say to this. Her heart has inched to her throat.

He spits again and it lands inches from her feet. Looks straight at her. "Didn't think of that, did you?" And with that he spins his wide girth around, swipes out with his left hand as if to knock her soda can off the stone ledge where it sits, but instead catches it in his hand, tilts it to his open mouth, and drinks in great gulps.

At that very same moment Lynetta hears the back door open and Ella is asking for her lemonade. Can she have her lemonade, please? No one will let her have any of the grown-up kind.

Suddenly the can clatters to the steps and Brody Myers is spinning in circles like a rabid dog, clawing at his throat, pulling at his tongue, his back slamming against a pillar. The can rolls off the step, soda trickling from it and Lynetta sees two bees flow to the stonework, rise up out of the sticky puddle and into the air. Brody is slapping at his pocket with one hand, dragging his other hand down his face. His tongue is swelling out of his mouth like a strange growth, stretching fat and pale past his ballooning lips and Lynetta can see the bee smashed to his top lip and another still wiggling on his grotesque tongue. His terrified eyes bulge in the crevice of his brow. He stares at Lynetta as his tongue and lips continue to swell and then his eyes recede behind the ghastly transformation. Oddly, Lynetta thinks of a story she read in high school about a man who woke up to find himself changed into an insect. The story made no sense to her at the time, but in this moment she is thinking she understands it now. He slaps once more at his groin, slumps to the ground.

Ella is at her back, her face buried in Lynetta's shirt, her hands grabbing at the fabric. Lynetta turns and takes her by the shoulders. "It's okay, Ella. Listen to me. Go out back and get help."

"What's wrong, Nettie? What happen?"

"He got a bee sting. That's all. Go get Pap."

By the time the others have swarmed in through the back door and out again through the front, Brody Myers is on his side, motionless, his face blue and misshapen like lumpy dough. He is unrecognizable and when they ask, Lynetta tells them it's Brody.

Lenny Greene, an orderly who is studying to be an EMT, gets to him first. Brody carries a bee sting kit, Lenny explains. Always has it on him, and he feels in Brody's pockets, first one and then the other, and comes up empty-handed. "Jesus Christ," he says. He unsnaps Brody's overalls, rips his T-shirt at the neck, and begins chest compressions, tilts his head back but can find no way around the massive swollen tongue. "Fuck," he snaps. "Fuck. Somebody call the medical wing. Tell them to bring a syringe of epinephrine and a trach kit fast!"

But everyone knows it is too late, too late for Brody Myers.

Lynetta makes the call, keeps her voice calm and even on the phone. Then goes to Ella who is curled on the sofa, her knees to her chin, rocking back and forth.

"The bees kill him, Nettie?"

"Yes," Lynetta says.

"Why the bees killed him?"

Lynetta leans close to Ella's ear and whispers, "Because he was a bad man."

19

Clarissa

Jax and Clarissa are sitting outside Starbucks. Jax has quickly downed an Americano and is tapping the bottom of his empty cup on the table.

"Did you remember to bring me a hard copy of the journal your story was published in?" she asks him.

He forgot to bring it with him, he tells her, but he has a copy back at the carriage house in his bag, promises to give it to her this evening. Clarissa thanks him. She saves all of his stories, sometimes reads them aloud to her husband. They both agree that Jax's work is getting better, more complex, and the journals more prestigious. Not that they fancy themselves literary critics, but they both are drawn to Jax's work and always happy for him when another piece is picked up. But Jax doesn't want to talk about his writing now, and Clarissa circles back to the crisis at hand.

"It seems to me," she says, still sipping her own bitter coffee, "that this really has nothing to do with what your parents want. It should be Ella's decision."

"That's like asking a child who she wants to live with in the heat of a contentious divorce," says Jax.

Clarissa nods. Agrees. Still, she thinks Ella should have some say in it all. She watches Jax draw his hand down his stubbled cheeks. It always surprises her when men fail to shave on the weekends. Her husband is the same way, a five-morning-per-week routine that includes a ritual of shaving and the application of a stiff hair gel only to abandon his main-tenance routine on the weekends. By Sunday evening she often thinks she doesn't recognize him at all in his sweatpants and T-shirts, his flop-ping hair, and his chin looking like Velcro.

"See, here's the thing," Jax says, leaning forward across the table and settling his cup firmly in front of him. "I'm not saying that what happened before . . ." And he lowers his voice. "Not saying it will happen again. I'm just saying that *if* something like it happens again, if she loses it, you know—if it all becomes too much—there won't be any backup this time."

"Backup in that they can't send her back? Or you mean . . ." and here she stops, extends her hand, palm up, not sure how to frame this.

He knows what she's trying to say, nods.

Clarissa thinks of Ella as two people. The child she once knew and the adult she was reintroduced to a dozen years ago. It's hard to recon-cile the two.

She remembers young Ella as someone, some*thing*, to steer clear of. The way Ella growled, groggy and cranky if she woke from a nap on the sofa. And she spent a lot of time napping, from what Clarissa can recall. She remembers the way the others stayed clear of her (except for Finney, the two of them sharing an obvious affinity for one another), not even settling on the other end of the sofa if Ella was curled to the corner of it, and she remembers the way Ella clung to Mrs. Jules when she was awake, wrapping around her thighs, lifting her arms and pulling at her mother's shirts to be lifted to her mother's hip. And she remem-bers now, as if it was yesterday, the way Mrs. Jules would sigh and heft her up to her side, her mouth grimacing with the effort of it, resigned. Clarissa remembers the children complaining that Ella had messed the bathroom again, and Mrs. Jules would tell them to use her bathroom instead, that she would get to it as soon as she finished the laundry or washing the dishes or clearing the table or feeding Finney.

"Have you ever talked to them, Jax, to either one of them—you know—about what happened?" She already knows the answer.

He shakes his head side to side and looks around. Roland Park is waking up and the two of them are watching the pedestrians moving along the walk, an elderly man with a walker, his back hunched over the whole of the contraption, a trio of young girls in yoga pants, and a harried woman dragging a small wire-coated dog at the end of his leash so that it has nearly slipped over his ears. Clarissa's boys have been asking for a dog. She has agreed reluctantly to something small and with a calm demeanor. Her research has revealed that her best choice may be a King Charles spaniel, known to be lapdogs, though she's not sure that's exactly what she wants, either.

"Just the one time, when I told my father," he is saying. And she is shaken from her thoughts of dogs. "A week later she was gone." He stares at her, all the meaning implied. "So that's how that went."

They sit in silence for a moment, and it is not lost on Clarissa that this is exactly what she likes about Jax, that he doesn't feel compelled to fill in the quiet between them. An only child, she often wonders if what she feels for Jax is what siblings feel. A knowing that while one is essentially alone, they are also inextricably tangled in the life of another. Jax and Clarissa have been threaded to one another as far back as she can remember.

But the cinching of that tangle, the thing that knotted them to each other, was what had happened.

They seldom spoke of it, even when she made her occasional trips to California for a conference and they made a point to catch up over dinner or drinks. Their conversations, full of comfortable silences that she appreciated, seldom landed on Ella's past, though they talked of the adult Ella—her funny laugh, her fascination with cats, the lunch Clarissa had been forced to share within the confines of Ella's playhouse.

"All of you are so good at dancing around the elephant in the room," she says. "Has anyone told them that this is simply a bad idea? Maybe address the issues—they're getting older, Ella will severely limit their freedom, she can't be left alone, she likely wants to be with Lynetta."

He wears a blank expression, reminding her that the idea of the Jules children talking to their parents about Ella is foreign to him. "That's what we're trying to figure out," he says. "How to go about this."

Again, they are silent, both watching a flutter of little beige wrens at their feet. Jax leans forward to rest his arms on the table, drawing his legs beneath his chair, and they scatter, but don't take flight. "Hopefully, Finney and George will get here before Ella does and we get a chance to talk this through."

"Will your aunts be there tonight? I haven't seen them in years."

Jax tells her they will, but that he thinks it's not fair to Ella, to subject her to everyone at once like it's some kind of homecoming.

"I don't have to be there," she offers, not sure if there is some implication in what he has said. "Though I doubt I'll be able to keep my mother away. She thinks she's witness to a miracle of some kind."

"Truth is, she's not at all like everyone remembers her. I'd be hard-pressed to admit that Beechwood was a good idea, fucking nightmare of a place, but it is something, the way she is now. I credit Lynetta."

"You think this is all rooted in some kind of guilt, like your mom can get a do-over and set everything right?"

"I do." He looks up at Clarissa and quickly away. "If we hadn't been there that day. Jesus. If you hadn't been there . . ." He shakes his head, drops his forehead to the palm of his hand. "I can't even think about it."

But Clarissa does. She thinks of it as one of the times when she did what had to be done, when something hung in the balance and she had what it took to tip the scales. She has that feeling in the lab nearly every day, the way one result naturally leads to a series of next steps until that thing she is looking for is centered. But in life—with her mother, sometimes with her boys, with women in the checkout line at the grocery store, with her son's teachers, even with the Jules sisters—she is confounded by the options, the myriad ways to answer a simple question like *how are you* or respond to a compliment (like when Tess says she likes Clarissa's shoes or the way she wears her hair lately). There are so many options, and she can't get herself ahead of the question or statement to figure out exactly what is expected of her and where this conversation is expected to go. Inevitably, she goes in the wrong direction, admitting she's not so good today, has a headache, or her period started and her back is killing her. And then there is that blank look, that pause that she has come to recognize as the clue that she has answered incorrectly, that no one really wants to know how she is—that the question was simply a warm-up to the matter at hand, a way of greeting, a prelude to *nice to see you again*, before passing one another in the grocery store.

But that day, that day she knew exactly what to do and sometimes when she thinks back on it there is a swell of pride in having done what she did, even if she could never tell a soul.

A shadow falls over their table and they both look up, startled to see Belle standing over them. She wears running shorts and a bright-blue tank top. Sweat shimmering on her collarbones. A sweatshirt is knotted around her waist.

"Hey, guys! I'd hug you, Clarissa, but I'm sweaty."

"Okay."

Belle looks from Clarissa to Jax and back again. She is likely surprised to see them together on this sunny morning in the old neighborhood. Clarissa knows her friendship with Jax surprises his sisters. While she had once longed for a connection to Belle, an actual girlfriend, she let that ship sail long ago. Clarissa always feels like a familiar piece of inconveniently placed furniture when she is around the sisters, like she's the sofa everyone knows how to step around, even in the dark.

Jax pulls out a chair and invites Belle to join them. She says she wants to grab a coffee and asks Jax if he has any cash. He leans to his side and pulls out his wallet, hands her a ten-dollar bill. "I'll hit you back," she says, spinning on her toes to head into Starbucks.

Clarissa watches her walk away, bouncing on her feet as if she might break into a sprint. Belle is beautiful, always has been—in that way most white women tend to measure conventional beauty. But Clarissa's world is bigger than that now. Having married into Dae's family, working in her lab with a virtual smorgasbord of races and accents, she's no longer entrenched in the concepts of beauty that had once made her feel lacking. Besides, Clarissa thinks Belle couldn't care less, doesn't even notice the table of adolescent boys that gawk as she walks by them, her long thighs level with their trailing eyes.

"I think you should tell them," Clarissa says, nodding in the direction of Belle's back as she heads to the doors.

"What?" He looks after Belle, but she is inside now. "Oh, no, no." He trails his hand down his cheek, lifts his eyes to the sky, and inhales deeply before dropping his head. Shakes it slowly side to side with his hands placed firmly and flat on the table. "Bad idea. They don't need to know about this."

"You look like your father right now." It's neither a good or bad thing, just an observation. He has always looked like his father, but in this moment, it is as if she is sitting with Stone Jules and one of his pronouncements. *All the boys are getting a haircut tomorrow*, he would say while watching his young teenagers at a family barbecue. The idea having come from seemingly nowhere as Mr. Jules sat with Clarissa's father on their back patio and watched the kids in the pool.

Mrs. Jules would look to the boys, their hair dripping down their backs, and while she didn't say anything, it was noted. Two days later the boys would come to school with their blond locks shorn and a pale band of untanned skin along their hairlines. Belle needs to see a dermatologist, she once heard Mr. Jules say to Mrs. Jules. A patch of blemishes smattered across Belle's forehead. Clarissa watched Belle, lost in a television show but aware enough to run her fingertips across her forehead as if she was reading braille. Moments later Clarissa wandered into the Jules kitchen to find Mrs. Jules on the phone making an appointment. These things were not said unkindly. *Good day to clean out the potting shed, the kids should see an opera, Christmas Eve at the club would be a nice change. Butter Bean is getting fat, itching at his paws, digging under the rosebushes. We haven't had pot roast in a long time. Belle's skirts are too short. Tess is still chewing her nails. Finney tracked mud through the house again.* Simple calls to action that Mrs. Jules responded to by grabbing a broom and dustpan, making a reservation or an appointment.

Jax looks at Clarissa now, brows raised, asking her to elaborate.

"Just saying." She wants to explain that maybe he isn't in charge in the way he thinks he is. Maybe this isn't his decision to make—regarding the concealment of what had happened or the job of convincing his parents one way or another—and furthermore the past belonged to all of them, the entire history of Ella belonged to all of them. They were going about this in the wrong way, looking at the wrong problem. The problem, as Clarissa saw it, was everything that had not been said, all the pain that had been privately hoarded by each one of them rather than weighed and divided equally. This family, in her opinion, carried seven times, eight times the pain that should have been divided and allotted each one of them. They could, she was certain, take all they know, all they carry, and unload it amongst one another, sort through it carefully, dispose of that which held no real meaning or truth or consequence. She could see it all: the burden of useless guilts sliding off their backs and picked through, examined, held to the bright light to see what is genuine and what is only a cheap imitation of itself. Oh, it would be messy, and there would surely be struggles as to who owns what and who is allowed to carry their own pain and who must swap theirs for another's. But this madness, this cloistering off with the whole of the burden on each individual backside, wasn't helping anyone, least of all Ella. That's what she wanted to say, but sometimes the right stringing of words eludes her. She loves words, the precision of them. But sometimes, like now with Jax looking at her from under the shade of his brow, the exact way to put those words together is beyond her.

"I don't think any of you can do anything if you're not willing to be honest with each other about what you're dealing with," is all she can say. When he says nothing, just shakes his head, no, she says, "Maybe you can't tell them what to do. Maybe you have to approach this differently. It's a hell of a thing," she says, "to carry this around by yourself."

She, too, has carried the secret, but she knows it hasn't weighed on her in the same way it has on Jax. She had gone home that day, run home, actually, to resume her role as the heartbeat of her small family. Jax stayed. Was maybe still there now, in some time-traveling way.

Jax can only shrug. Belle is making her way to their table again. Jax pulls a chair out for her and she sets her coffee on the table, punches her arms and head through her sweatshirt before seating herself between the two of them. He looks at Belle, as if he is appraising her and she raises her brows. "What? Am I interrupting something?"

Typically, Clarissa would feel the division between herself and Jax, with Belle sliding between the two of them, slicing them apart from one another. But instead she sees Jax look to Belle, a strange resignation in his face, and back to Clarissa, and feels a kind of communion, as if Belle is about to come into the fold they have created.

"Belle," he says. "There's something we need to tell you about."

20

Finney

Finney doesn't eat meat. He is certain he has mentioned this to his mother on more than one occasion, so he's not exactly sure how to interpret the fact that she has presented him with a ham sandwich. He and George and Tess are seated at the kitchen table, per her instructions, and she has set a plate in front of each of them. Rye bread with thick cuts of ham, slices of swiss cheese, slathered with honey mustard, which he also dislikes, and a side of her macaroni salad. He picks up his fork and begins to eat the salad. He has to admit that he misses some of her cooking but is disturbed, all the same, by her negligence regarding the sandwich.

It is late in the afternoon, and he has just arrived on the heels of George, hasn't even had a chance to get his bag up to his old room. His mother had hugged him and touched his face in that way she has a habit of doing, smoothing his cheek and looking for a moment as if she is lost in time, before announcing that she was about to serve lunch. She ushered him to the table. George rose eagerly to shake his hand, clap him along the arm. Tess had jumped up from her seat and thrown her arms around him.

"In the flesh," she said. "I wasn't sure you'd actually post."

He had ignored the slight, remembering the way he had earlier dug in the scullery of his mind for an excuse to not be here, even as he had packed his bags this morning.

Belle and Jax, he was told, were out running errands. Their mother needed ice cream to serve alongside the pies she had planned for dessert tonight and she had instructed them to pick up a few bottles of a good red wine. Their father was at Home Depot in search of weed killer. The last bothers Finney. Not only does he not approve from an ecological standpoint, but he doesn't like to think about the many springs his father has spent mixing the toxic substance, spraying it from a gallon mister, the chemical carcinogens dripping down his wrists. Finney had warned him years earlier, but the man considers himself invincible. "I've been using it for years," he had said.

"That's my point," said Finney. But it fell on deaf ears.

Finney finishes off his macaroni salad and helps himself to more from a bowl set in the middle of the table. His mother eyes the untouched sandwich on his plate, a realization drawing down over her and her mouth dropping to a pout. "Oh, Finney, I'm sorry. You're still not eating meat?" It is asked earnestly, as if she assumed it was only a phase. "Let me fix you something else." She reaches for his plate, but he stops her with his hand on hers, can't help but notice the papery smallness of it, the way her diamond engagement ring turns, clunks to her pinky finger.

"I have tuna. You eat tuna, right?"

"I'm fine, Mom."

"Well," she says, drawing back her hand. "I commend you for your commitment to this vegetarian thing. I can fix you a cheese sandwich."

"No," he says. "I'm good." And then he adds, "Brad packed me a lunch for the flight." It's not true. He has no idea why he says it. Brad had handed him a power bar and an orange as he headed out the door, but the insinuation that Brad had actually packed him a lunch in the same way their mother used to labor over an assembly line of lunchboxes every morning is a gross misrepresentation of the truth.

His mother looks at him and blinks. "That's nice," she says. "Very thoughtful."

Finney is embarrassed now and peppers George with questions about Tammy and the girls. Tess joins in and asks about the girls' ballet recital.

George mimics young Amanda, tosses his head side to side, twisting his lips, and whines, *Lucy Govans bumped me!* He tells them about the ridiculous bouquets of roses, the overzealous parents who cheered and hooted when their children took the stage, the fact that Abigail was still onstage contorted in a prolonged curtsy, even as the other girls were led away, and he had to catch her eye and swish her offstage with a wave of his hand at which point she stood tall, put her small hand over her eyes to block the glare of lights, and proceeded to give him a *bon voyage* kind of wave.

Everyone laughs appreciatively, especially their mother. "Oh, I wish I could have seen it," she says wistfully.

"Well," says George, so quickly on the heels of her sigh, "I don't see how you're going to be able to visit once—" But then he stops, as if he cannot say her name.

Finney catches the way George's eyes have narrowed, hears the very slight tremor in his voice, like something beginning to bubble.

They are all quiet, eyes dropped to their laps. Eventually they watch his mother rise from the table, stacking plates as she stands. Finney catches Tess's eyes just before she rolls them to the ceiling. When Hillary moves to the sink, George glares at his mother's back and then shakes his head, looks to his siblings and grimaces, his lips thinning.

With her back to them, their mother apologizes again for the ham sandwich.

"It's okay, Mom, really," Finney says as tenderly as he can. "The macaroni salad was great, more than enough." It is a small lie. "Thanks, though. Thanks for making lunch."

George and Tess nod, yes, thank you. But she still has her back to them, has no idea that they are watching her, that they have been watching her for years.

She makes a small sound, like a hiccup swallowed. "I try," she says softly. "I do," said so softly that Finney is not sure if he hears her right.

"What's that, Mom?" he says.

She doesn't answer, but he sees the straightening of her back, the realigning of her head on her shoulders. "Mom?"

"Let's just try to have a nice evening," she says. "Let's make this nice."

Tess wanders into his room as he is opening his small carry-on bag, digging around for his iPod and headphones. He wants to flop on his childhood bed, stare at the ancient poster of Andre Agassi he had pinned on the far wall a million years ago, and lose himself in the music of Tom Petty. Tess doesn't knock, just stands at his doorway and says, "George is right, you know." She rolls her eyes dramatically, uses a puff of breath to blow her bangs into a flutter on her forehead.

"I guess."

"This is some shit, right?" She plops on his bed, pulls one leg up under her, and looks around the room. Nodding to the curling Agassi poster, she asks him, "You heard about his hair? The wig? Crazy, huh?"

Finney agrees. "I can't look at that mullet without thinking about it," he says. "That wig cost him the French Open. Turns out that keeping secrets has a price."

They both stare at the poster. Agassi's long locks are backlit, his androgynous face turned three-quarters. "He was hot," Tess says, and Finney agrees. Tess looks away from the poster to Finney. "Do you remember her?" she asks.

"I'm not sure," he says. "But, no, I don't think I do. I couldn't. I was just two when she left. I don't think I even remembered her name for a long time." He laughs lightly to himself. "I remember her as blue."

Tess screws up her face. "Blue?"

"Mom once said she was born blue and I guess that was how I always thought of her. Brad and I saw the Blue Man Group in Miami and it had me sort of disoriented for a while."

They are silent for a moment, until Tess suddenly slaps her open hands to her thighs. "What are we going to do?"

Finney doesn't know. He hears George on the other side of the wall and bangs twice with the ball of his fist. George thuds the wall back. A moment later he is in the room, closing the door behind himself. The crucifix, identical to the ones on the back of each of their bedroom doors, looms over his shoulder. He nods to the poster. "You hear about the wig?"

"Old news," says Finney.

"I can't respect that," says George.

"I'll let him know," says Finney. "He'll be crushed." He watches Tess fight the beginning of a smile. But then she juts her chin in the air. Looks to George.

"You really hurt Mom's feelings," she says. "I mean, I get it, George, but why do you always have to charge in the back door?"

Finney watches the muscles of George's cheeks pump and deflate.

"Somebody's got to say it. This is dangerous. And I'll tell you another thing. My kids are never coming here with her in the house. That's for damn sure." He leans back against the door and crosses his arms over his chest, as if he is daring them to try and change his mind. "You watch. Tonight's going to be a cluster-fuck."

"We can get through one night," says Tess. "It's the rest of their lives I'm worried about." Finney watches her shoulders fall. "I'm worried about Mom, too. Ever since Bets died, she's been a little . . . *off.*"

"How?" says Finney. "You mean depressed?"

"Well, of course she's down," says George. "But that doesn't have anything to do with this."

"Maybe it does," says Tess. "Maybe bringing Ella back makes her feel like she's needed, you know—like a chance to mother someone again. She's had this loss with Bets, and all of us gone, and now she wants to be needed."

"You don't get it, Tess. She's a fucking monster."

"I'm not saying it's a good idea, George. I'm just saying maybe that's what's behind this."

Finney, though he doesn't know Ella, instinctively wants to defend her. Something deep inside of him doesn't believe in monsters. He's treated hundreds of children in his practice, some with terrible challenges both mentally and physically, and always he is struck first by their humanity. Never has he seen a monster. But he stays silent, knows it is useless to reason with George when he's like this, even if he does have something to contribute.

George is grinding his teeth, sucking air through the grid of them. He points to his own face and Finney could swear his hand is trembling when he does it. "Jesus, if she could do this when she was only five, what the hell do you think she's capable of now? Huh?" He glares at Finney and starts to say something, changes his mind, and then starts again. "You have no idea. You don't remember this, Finn, but when you were little—I mean really little, a baby, you were sleeping on the sofa in that little baby bouncer thing, propped up in it on the corner of the couch. And the next thing you know, you're upside down on the floor, still strapped in the damn thing. Your head slammed to the floor. She had whipped you off the sofa"—he swipes his hand through the air violently—"and *bang*! You were on the floor, screaming your damn head off." George stares hard at him, daring him to challenge the memory of it. "She almost killed you," he says. "But you don't remember that, do you?"

"Of course not," says Finney.

"You're lucky," he says. "Because I remember *this*." Again, he points to his own face, jabbing at the soft flesh beside his nose, pointing to where the skin is harder. Jabs again at his brow. "And this."

"George," Tess says kindly, though there is a hint of exasperation. "It's not that bad. You hardly notice it."

His eyes narrow. "Fuck you, Tess. It's not your face."

Finney fully expects Tess to react, but her face goes blank instead. She is used to George's outbursts. They all are. She stares at George as if she is waiting for him to continue. When he leans back against the door, drops his shoulders as if a weight has slid off them, she only says, "Feel better?"

"Why are they doing this?" Finney asks them both. He's deflecting, but also curious. There are options—a group home, Lynetta.

"Mom is giving her my room," Tess says. "I know it was her room first, but still—feels weird."

"I'm over it," George says. Finney knows this means he's not. George is never over anything, carries each perceived slight in his back pocket as if he's stowing the evidence, whips it back out, unfolds the creases of another's transgressions, and recites them back. Finney knows that when George says he's over it, he means it's been noted. It means his mind won't be changed.

Finney isn't sure how he feels. He doesn't think of Ella as the horror that his siblings imagine—or remember—if that's what is going on. But he knows, in spite of what George says of her, that something in him, something he can't quite access, something on the tip of his subconscious, misses her. And just how is that possible? He only knows that when he thinks of her, he is not frightened and in fact feels a tiny comfort start to unfurl, never quite blooming, but there are tendrils fingering his heart. And with it comes a sense of harmonic motion, a gentle wave that laps and retreats.

Finney is not afraid. He is not afraid.

21
Hillary

ROLAND PARK
December 2008

Baltimore hardly ever gets a December snow and this one is most incon-
venient. It is deep and icy, crusted over with the afternoon's sleet. Hillary
would rather not go out in it, but her dear friend Bets is ill, dying. She
has been released from the hospital because there is nothing more to be
done. And besides, it's the holidays. Her husband, Renwick, wants her
home for the holidays and Renwick deserves what he wants right now.
Only he wants Bets not to be dying, and that isn't working out at all.

Hillary slips on her winter boots. They're stylish and lovely with a
low heel and a trio of shiny gold buttons on the side, more a fashion
statement than a practical winter boot. The hem of her woolen pants
falls and breaks at the rise of her booted foot when she stands. Hillary
is picky about the length of her pants and the hems of her dresses and
skirts. There is a precise length that looks best on her, and all of her
clothes are tailored to perfection. She wraps her neck in dove-gray cash-
mere and puts on her coat and driving gloves. Stone calls to her from the
den. Be careful, go easy. Park on the street if the driveway isn't plowed,
and please, give Bets a hug from me. She's irritated that he's not coming
with her, but willing to give him a grudging pass given his long commute
home in the horrible weather.

"I'll tell them you'll come by this weekend?"

"Of course," he says. "And I'll see them in church on Sunday."

Hillary sets down her purse on the hall table and walks into the den. The light from the evening news program flickers over his face. "You won't see them in church, Stone."

He looks up at her, drops his gaze, waits.

"She's dying, Stone. You understand that, right?" She doesn't tend to talk to him in this way, but she's hard-pressed to understand why he appears of late to be avoiding their good friends at a time when they need him most. Perhaps, she thinks now, he is not so much avoiding them as choosing not to invest in their tragedy. And he has always been so fond of Bets. But since she has taken a turn for the worse, it is as though he has backed away from the friendship, not even accompanying Hillary to the hospital to visit her, not checking in with Bets's husband, Renwick, in the same way he did when all of this started a year ago.

He looks at her for the longest time, his chin quivering, or maybe it's just the wavering lights from the television. She can't be sure. "Stone?"

He has nothing to say, drops his gaze. Something washes down over him and Hillary has no name for it, has so seldom seen this look on him. It makes him knit his brows and draw his hand down his chin, pulling at his jowls. His eyelids lifting enough that she can see his eyes flit to the corners and back, but still not looking at her. Part of her wants to go to him. Part of her thinks she is being sent away. She turns and leaves the room, grabbing her purse from the foyer, and heads out the door and into an icy evening.

The six of them, Bets, Renwick, Hillary, and Stone, along with the Morgenfriers, have been friends almost as far back as Hillary can remember. Bets and Renwick were once next door neighbors until they decided twenty-five years ago to move to Homeland, a neighborhood less than a mile from Roland Park. By the time they had moved, Ella had been gone nearly five years and Bets's daughter was a toddler. Bets had claimed that the huge Roland Park home had begun to weigh on her in its emptiness with just the one child and little likelihood of another. Homeland was a lovely neighborhood with a similar aesthetic to Roland Park but the homes were not quite as grand in scale. A four-bedroom home, as Bets had explained, made more sense than the current three-story, six-bedroom home next door to the Jules family. Hillary was saddened by their move. Bets had felt like her only friend in the world back when Ella was small. She and Stone so seldom got an evening out, with Hillary tied to the house by way of Ella, and so she and Bets had become back-door friends and shared coffee over the fence that divided their yards. Summer evenings were often spent with the four of them in the Juleses' backyard once the kids were down for the evening. Bets usually made a cheese-and-cracker platter. Stone mixed the martinis, poured the wine. The Morgenfriers from down the block sometimes joined them if they could get a sitter for Clarissa. But having a fence-line friend was a gift Hillary had cherished. Things had shifted temporarily between them however, just after Ella was sent away. A bit of uncomfortable distance between the two friends, and for some time Hillary wondered if she was being judged for sending Ella away or if she herself had created the distance out of her own guilt. They seldom spoke of Ella's leaving, and with time their friendship found its niche again and they slipped back into it as if nothing had ever happened.

Hillary relished those long-ago evenings. Her patio parties, as she came to think of them, were her refuge from long days spent caring for her children and struggling with Ella. Sometimes she drank too much, and who could blame her? She never ate enough during the day and so the first martini or the first glass of wine tended to hit her hard, sweeping the ground out from under her in a way she looked forward to. Those days are long behind her. She is careful with her drinks these days and not fond of the way alcohol used to carry her outside herself.

After they moved, Hillary missed their shared breaks over the fence. But they belong to the same church, the same country club, the same garden club, and they have remained fixtures in one another's lives. Bets is the glue. Bets is the one Hillary and Stone are drawn to if only because the three of them are aligned in their assessment of Renwick. Easily over-looked amongst the four of them, content, in a fragile way, to hang in the background while the others laugh and cavort. Bets deftly tends to that fragility, knowing just when to turn their collective attention to Renwick. When Hillary and Stone tell her that her camellia bush is exquisite, she accepts the compliment graciously and then points out that Renwick had insisted that he could get the plant to thrive in their fickle zone seven and she had planted it grudgingly—but he was right! No winter sun, protected from the wind. And just look at it now, throwing up a bounty of blooms.

When Hillary arrives, she finds Bets on a hospital bed in the living room beside a massive tree that twinkles under the twelve-foot ceilings of their old home. "This is where she wanted to be," Renwick explains apologetically, aware that no one expects to find a dying woman under the Christmas tree. Normally, Renwick would offer to take her coat, maybe a drink or cup of tea? But he does neither, stands with his hands at his sides, awkwardly turns to look at his wife and back again to Hillary. She notices the drip of stains down his shirt and a dried white film of spittle at the corner of his mouth. She turns away, embarrassed for him, and looks to Bets.

"She's in and out," he says. "The meds make her loopy."

"I won't stay long," Hillary says.

"No, no. Stay. I just sent off the nurse. Night nurse doesn't arrive until nine. I could use a few minutes in the kitchen if you'll stay with her?"

"Of course." Hillary realizes that he doesn't want her left alone. She has a job to do now. She will stay with her friend until he is ready to return. "Have some supper. I have no place I need to be. I'm happy to stay with her."

Bets is waving a weak hand from across the room, up and back down to the covers, up again. Hillary goes to her, removes her gloves, and pats the hand, squeezes it, presses it down to the covers with the weight of her own. "Oh, Bets," is all she can think of to say.

Bets's dark hair is short and curly now. Since she insisted on ending the chemo two months ago, it has begun to grow back. She had no intention of dying bald, she said.

A plastic tube runs to her nose and Hillary can hear a whispered whoosh of air. The house is too quiet, save for the low pump of oxygen and the clink of radiator pipes. Hillary wonders if the room is warm enough for her friend. These damn old houses and their too-tall ceilings are always drafty. There is no fire in the fireplace and while Hillary thinks it would be nice for her friend to have one roaring, she knows that a fire will only suck the drafty air through the house and up the chimney.

Hillary does most of the talking, lowering her voice in time with the falling of her friend's eyelids. Bets and Renwick's daughter lives with them but is not at home. Bets has always joked that she is a classic case of failure to launch. Twenty-seven and still home. But the lung cancer had been diagnosed just as Theresa was finishing up her master's at the University of Maryland and so she had moved back home, taken a teaching job at one of the local prep schools, and never moved out. It saddens Hillary that this young woman she is most fond of has tethered her early adulthood to her parents in this way. It is, she assumes, the burden of being an only child.

Hillary asks after her and Bets looks around the room as if she is surprised to not find her daughter seated nearby. A flash of alarm passes over Bets's face and then she quickly settles again.

"Basketball practice," Bets says softly, relieved.

Hillary knows this isn't the case. Theresa played basketball in high school. Bets is confused, but Hillary says nothing.

Bets tries to say something more, but a futile cough starts up, unproductive. It lasts a long time and Hillary looks away, as if she is witnessing something private. Finally, Bets calms again. Her eyes have watered and leak at the outer corners, running in shiny tracks down her temples and dampening her hair.

"Stone?" Bets asks.

"He couldn't come tonight, but he'll stop by this weekend."

Bets nods, eyelids falling as she does so.

Hillary wonders if she should say more, make an excuse for his absence. "He wanted to come," she says.

"Probably not a good idea," Bets says. Shrugs her frail shoulders.

The comment confuses Hillary, though she again says nothing, watches Bets turn her head away. They sit in silence for a moment, Bets blinking, a weak smile on her face. "Let's talk about you," she finally says. "Jax?"

"He's good. Flying in next week for Christmas. Still loves teaching, and he placed another story that comes out in February." She doesn't really understand Jax's stories, but she won't say so. They're complicated and abstruse, in her opinion. But still, it is easy to talk about her kids, to simply relay what they have chosen to share with her. "I'll let you know when it's published."

Bets smiles and rolls her eyes. They both know she won't be here. Hillary soldiers on.

"Belle is doing well, kids are happy. We'll see them over the New Year. She's such a good mother, Bets. Kitty's been begging for a horse, of all things, so they're giving her riding lessons for Christmas." Hillary jabbers on and on about her grown children, happy to have something to talk about. George is fine. His wife is still too skinny and Hillary suspects there's more there than he's telling them. Sometimes she wonders if she should intervene, but she won't. Finney's practice is thriving. She doesn't mention Brad, isn't sure how to do so. She is confused by it all, and truly, she likes Brad, but he isn't really family in a way that she can settle comfortably around. Bets asks about him anyway, having met Brad years ago at the Jules home at a cocktail party.

"Such a nice man," Bets says, and Hillary agrees.

Tess has moved out of her home in Silver Spring, Hillary tells her, and is separating from her husband. It's confirmed. Hillary had hoped they could work things out, but it's messy. She can't remember how much she has told Bets about Tess's situation, her husband's transgression.

"It was only . . ." Bets says. "It wasn't anything." Hillary can't remember if that's what she told Bets or not, isn't certain she gave her any details at all, in fact. She watches her friend, sees her squint, her mouth drawn in a thin line, sees tears leaking. Her friend is confused. Hillary doesn't know how to move her away from the moment she is locked into. "And Ella . . ." Bets drifts away. "All of that," she says softly. "Such a long time ago." Her lashes are damp and starlike around her eyes. She twists her head on her neck, left to right, up and back to Hillary. "Oh, Hillary . . ." Her voice now a thin whine, her brows raised hopelessly so that her forehead pleats.

Hillary doesn't know how to soothe her friend. Doesn't know what to say or do, doesn't understand where Bets is residing in her own mind. And what does all of this have to do with Ella? The coughing starts again, like something percolating.

"Easy, Bets. It's okay." She lifts a glass of water with a bent straw in it from the side table, offers it to her lips, but Bets shakes it off, continues to cough.

"What can I do?" Hillary asks, wondering if she needs to call Renwick from the kitchen. "Do you want me to get Ren?"

Bets shakes her head severely, bouncing with the coughing. "No, no, please," she manages. "He doesn't need to know."

Something begins to pinch at Hillary's mind. She can't name it, but it is something sharp and small, gnawing. Her friend is confused, but there is something more. Something Hillary is compelled to back away from. Bets begins to calm, nods at the glass of water and Hillary lifts it to her, tilts the straw to her mouth and watches her drink, drop her head back to the pillow. "Tell me more about the kids," she says.

Hillary gratefully moves on to her grandchildren. George's girls are delightful, almost like twins. They never squabble. Belle's twins, on the other hand, are so different from one another. Tobi is the tougher of the two, very bold, but Jack is the sensitive one. She starts to tell a story about the cat they adopted from the shelter and the way it made Jack cry for days for all the cats they left behind, but she is interrupted by Bets.

"Ella," she says. It is not a question. It is an utterance, a conjuring. Hillary stops in the midst of her story, looks to her friend.

"She's fine," she says. "Ella is fine." She is taken aback. Ella is so seldom mentioned and yet twice now Bets has circled back to her. Bets knows Hillary visits Ella every Thursday, but no one ever asks about her. Bets stares back at her, waiting—for what? "She's going to live with Lynetta, her caretaker, when they close. Lynetta is an angel, so kind." Still, Bets watches her and Hillary thinks she is being encouraged to go on. "It's a good situation," she assures her friend. "She's like another mother to her," and at this her chest clenches. She knows she has been replaced and it is her own doing. There is no going back, no room for regrets, though they are there, piled like a wall of rocks in her chest. "It's for the best."

"Of course," says Bets. "Of course it is." They stare at one another, sad hopeful smiles playing at the corners of their mouths. "Stone never blamed you," Bets says. And at this Hillary draws back sharply, her head flinging back on her neck.

"I should hope not," is all she can say. He can't blame her, not completely. He was the one who insisted. He was the one who found Beechwood, made the calls, met with the doctors before they brought her in. He was the one who always said it was for the *good of the family*. But even as she thinks these things, she knows it is her own fault and that Stone does, in fact, blame her. She has always known, though he has never said it aloud.

"You had so much on your shoulders," Bets is saying. "You didn't mean it."

This last sends Hillary reeling, pulled as if at the end of a line and drowning in the depths of memory. She is a good mother, she tells herself. It is the mantra she taught herself. *I am a good mother.* She wants to believe that Bets does not know what she's saying—*couldn't* know what she's saying. He wouldn't, he couldn't, her husband would never tell. But even as she thinks these things, she knows that Bets is lucid now. Bets *knows*.

"He was so sad," Bets says. "Stone loves you. I love Renwick, always have."

Hillary is confused again.

"It was over before it started."

The pinching in Hillary's mind returns, descends to her chest so ferociously she is forced to place a hand to her own heart. Just what is being said, she can't be sure, only knows she doesn't want to hear it. This is a treacherous moment. There will be no undoing the dawning of it.

"Nothing ever happened, Hillary." Bets licks her lips, draws her teeth across her bottom lip. "He was so sad. Scared."

"Bets, what are you talking about?" She asks this carefully, afraid the answer will sting. But Bets doesn't answer her. The coughing starts up again, this time lasting long enough to draw Renwick from the other room. He looks to Hillary and assures her this will pass.

"Easy," he says. "Easy, Bets."

Hillary watches him lean down, smooth his hand across her brow, and use his other hand between her shoulder blades to lift her gently. She continues to cough but there is no force behind it, as if she is resigned to drowning. When she eventually calms, he lays her back again, wipes a tissue across her mouth, the gesture so tender and his face so close to Bets's that Hillary feels like a voyeur. Bets's eyes close.

Renwick straightens up from her side. To Hillary he seems small, diminished. "It happens when she talks too much," he offers with a weary smile. "She's okay now." He pats her hand that rests on her chest.

"I should go, let her rest." The room is suddenly stifling hot, the radiator pipes banging and pinging all around her.

A moment later she finds herself on the unshoveled front walk, her coat unbuttoned and flapping, her scarf trailing from one hand, her gloves clutched in the other. She fumbles for her keys in her purse and the purse drops, spills to the icy sidewalk. There is a buzzing in her chest and her eyes swim in the hazy porchlight. She feels around in the crusty snow like a blind woman, gathering her hairbrush, her wallet, her lipstick tube, and shoving them all back into the depths of her purse before clutching it to her chest and making her way to her car.

Hillary can't go home, not yet. There is a sorting in her mind that needs to take place. She pulls over at the Starbucks on Roland Avenue, thinking she will get a fancy hot drink, but she finds the ordering so cumbersome—venti, grande, whole or skim, no whip, two pumps, three—and she hasn't the energy for it.

She thinks back to the many cups of coffee shared over the fence with Bets years ago. Sometimes Bets would come into the yard and they would take a few minutes together on the patio, but those moments were always too short with the kids calling for her attention in a way that made Hillary feel less than hospitable toward her guest. At the fence line, it was easier to gather for only a minute or two and the pulling away by one of her children didn't feel so rude. Though she constantly had to say, "Do you see me talking to my friend?" whenever a child pulled at the hem of her shorts or pat-patted her side to draw her attention.

Ella was often on her hip or collapsed to the ground beside her. Hillary had become adept at balancing both a toddler latched on her side and a coffee cup in the other hand. Though as Ella grew older and missed the milestones of walking, potty training, and first words, as her tantrums increased and the slapping and screaming became her only means of communication, it became harder and harder to settle her in any way. Bets, however, still childless at the time, was always sweet to her, saying, *good morning, Ella*, and stooping to look her in the eyes as she did so.

Hillary sits now on Roland Avenue in front of the Starbucks, the car's vents aimed at her face and blasting a dry heat. She closes her eyes. Tilts her head to the headrest. Yes, there is some sorting to be done.

Over before it started.

In the back of her head something is unreeling. An evening, only a week after Ella had been sent away. The footage is grainy, muddled in a dusky light. Stone and Bets on the Jules patio. Hillary is looking down on them from Ella's bedroom. The evening's wine hadn't sat well with her and she had excused herself. Told the others to carry on. She needed to turn in.

Upstairs, she splashed her face with cool water and felt no better. The wine, perhaps, but also the unannounced pregnancy she had not yet faced with certainty had left her feeling unsteady. She hadn't been eating much lately, between the nausea and sending Ella away, she could barely choke down tea and toast in the morning. The children had been oddly quiet the last week. Not even playing with one another, not squabbling over skateboards and bikes and basketballs, but each one retreating into their own quiet world, lingering in their bedrooms or wandering the neighborhood, but never together. If she asked them what they wanted for lunch, they only shrugged. When she told them at night that it was time for bed there were no protests. Only Finney remained unchanged. Two-year-old Finney, just starting to attach names to his siblings, had asked about her. Putting his tiny hands palm up in the air. *Ella?* Only he said it "E-wha." And Hillary could only shake her head. *All gone*, she had said that same night, tucking him in his crib. The pain of it, of the words themselves, had torn through her throat and ripped it raw. *All gone.*

Even now, thinking back to that evening, she can feel the clawing of those words, the tearing of her heart.

She could hear the others outside and there were the sounds of departure, of Renwick bidding good night and Bets calling out that she would be home soon, was just going to finish her drink. Hillary had toweled off her face and walked into Ella's room with its pink walls and the rails on the bed that kept her from tumbling over the edge at night. The bed was stripped, the plastic protective sheeting rolled to the end of the bare mattress.

When she thinks back to it now from the seat of her overheated car, she sees it as if through a screen. She can't quite reconcile the woman standing in the dark of her banished daughter's bedroom with the woman seated now, thirty-two years later, in a running car on an icy evening three short blocks from home but feeling as if she has nowhere to go.

She had gone to Ella's window and looked down to the patio. She can remember now, the way she had looked on the scene as if she herself were not a living breathing being. She was a ghost, not attached to this world, hovering in a flimsy netherworld, neither here nor there and no place of belonging. She had looked down to Stone and Bets as if they were strangers. And perhaps that accounted for the way she felt—or failed to feel (as she thought of it now in the moment) anything at all— when she saw Stone dip his heavy head to her chest, as if he had fallen in a faint, and she had watched Bets's arms reach around him and his back heave with what could only have been sobs. She had watched the way Bets had run her arms up his back, patted him solidly, and allowed this man to crumble and quake upon her. And still, Hillary felt nothing, but perhaps a tinge of sadness for the fact that those emotions were beyond her. She had looked at the both of them and thought, *Oh, there is a man who is sad.*

Did it occur to her at the time, in that moment decades ago, that he had told Bets the why of it all—exactly what had happened that had precipitated the decision to send Ella away? No, it never did.

She leaves her car running with her keys in it, parked on the street as it is, and heads into Starbucks to order a coffee, a plain old regular coffee. A man exiting nods to her car and tells her that her lights are on. "It's running," she says, and steps to the side to let him pass. The barista wants to know what size and she says *petite*, and immediately feels foolish, has no idea why she has answered him in this way. "Your smallest," she says. When did ordering a cup of coffee become so complicated? She sits at a counter along the window and watches her car, the cloud of exhaust that billows at the tailpipe, the way the snow has begun to fall again, the flakes snapping into focus as they drift through the brightness of her headlights. Her thoughts, too, are sifting through her mind, suddenly clear. There all along, but unseen until they fall into the light.

Her husband had betrayed her, had shared their pain with another woman.

Her secret had never been a secret.

She had done a terrible thing and disguised it in her mind as a mercy.

Resentments are rooting inside of her in this moment, spindly and raw but burrowing, tangling in the past that she once saw one way and thought she could settle around, but she now finds instead that the earth is shifting. She doesn't know what will come of it all, but she is certain that something is changing.

22
Hillary

Hillary chops the rosemary and the woody scent fills the kitchen. She uses the heel of her hand to scoop it to the side of the cutting board and begins on the thyme. These things grow in her garden, and though it is early in the season, the rosemary wintered well, suffering only the one deep December snow, and the thyme is starting to creep back, newly green and fragrant. She moves on to smash and dice the garlic. The lamb is marinating in the refrigerator, but the peas will still have to be shelled and the new potatoes need to be scrubbed and oiled.

Lunch was unsettling, what with George lashing out (though he stopped himself and she prefers to see that as a good omen) and Finney's vegetarian *thing*, as she thinks of it. She realizes, in this moment, that Finney will not partake of the lamb this evening and she scours her mind for an additional side she might prepare. Maybe glazed carrots and a salad with feta, pecans, and cranberries. The dinner itself is intended for only the immediate family and as this thought skirts through her mind, she is suddenly aware that she has never prepared dinner for the eight of them. This is the first time that Ella will meet Tess. Silly, she knows, because it isn't likely that Ella will remember Finney, either. She hopes Ella will recognize the others but isn't sure. She isn't sure of anything, in fact, other than that she wants Ella back, in spite of what Stone thinks. She knows she can do this. It's not like years ago when she had so many young children around, a husband who punched out directives and left her to implement them. Not at all like the day she found herself swaying over a toilet, Ella on the floor behind her, swatting at Hillary's hair as she vomited into the bowl. Suddenly letting it dawn that she was certainly pregnant, again, and Finney barely two years old.

She won't think about it, won't think of those last days before Ella disappeared from their family. She was a good mother, all things considered. And there have always been Thursdays. Some harder than others, but she has never missed a Thursday, always adjusting her calendar to be with Ella, even rearranging trips with her sisters or visits to see her children in order to make her Thursday visit.

Really, she likes Lynetta. But Hillary was never keen on Ella living in Ocean City in a trailer, and she suspects there is a boyfriend that Lynetta keeps under wraps and she finds that troublesome. Even so, she feels a bit sorry for Lynetta, knowing all too well the pain she herself felt in having to let Ella go, and she assumes Lynetta is feeling some of that now. But the circumstances are hardly the same. Can't be compared.

Hillary is at odds with everyone and it is exhausting. Finney has low expectations of her, often seems surprised when she remembers his birthday (always, she would never forget a birthday) or calls just to see how things are going. It would have been easy to fix him something else for lunch, but it is just like Finney to refuse allowing her to right a small oversight. It wouldn't have been any trouble at all. Instead he had forced her to sit with her mistake while he ate three helpings of macaroni salad. George is angry, but always has been. There's a raw place in him that Hillary is constantly rubbing up against but doesn't know how to avoid. Tess is being a pain in the ass, following her around and trying to talk about the impracticality of it all. Tess thinks she has the answers to everything, but really, as far as Hillary is concerned, she is parroting her father. Hillary is convinced that if you ask Tess her opinion about anything, she is only capable of trying to figure out what her father's opinion is and then presenting it as her own. She isn't sure how that happened. She thinks maybe Tess picked up early on that Stone's side was the winning side and firmly established herself on Team Dad.

As for Belle and Jax, she can read it in their faces. They are wary and it is tiresome. They think she doesn't see the looks tossed between the two of them, the subtle eye rolls.

She and Stone have been careful with one another since she told him of her intentions. Not because he's angry with her, but because he owes her, and it is guilt that's making him tuck his tail between his legs and defer to her (for the first time ever that she can recall).

When Hillary returned home the evening of her last visit with Bets, Stone had already gone to bed. Hillary wandered the dark bedroom, not turning on the light as she undressed, gently laying her pants, blouse, and bra over the back of a chair (so unlike her, a woman who took great pains with the care of her wardrobe). She took her nightgown from the hook on the back of the door and slipped it over her head, afraid the creak of the door swinging could be enough to wake him. Climbing into bed gingerly, she hoped he wouldn't sense her next to him, wouldn't feel the dip of the mattress as she lay back. She couldn't face him, though she knew she'd have to, eventually.

Sometime in the early dawn, she dreamed she was sitting in the pew of her cathedral. The parishioners were being called to communion, but she couldn't move her feet, couldn't rise up. She was weighted to her place, and though she struggled to twist free, she couldn't release herself. Those in her pew were forced to step over and around her. As she struggled, twisting her shoulders left and right, craning her head on her neck, she felt a sharp jab in her chest. When she looked down she saw, between her breasts, the slow seep of blood, a heart-shaped bloom of it soaking through her silk blouse. Suddenly, her chest split open and hundreds of black birds, beak-first and screeching, were clambering from her chest as if she had birthed them. Tumbling over one another, wings unfolding as they emerged, they swooped to the rafters where they perched, preened their feathers before folding them, and cocked their heads to stare down at her with beady, glittering eyes. She looked to the priest making his way along the row of communicants. Strangely, rather than his traditional vestments—the alb and chasuble—he is dressed in a single flowing robe, hooded, and she watches him turn to her, pull the hood up and over his head and down his face so that he is looking at her through two holes cut in the fabric. She woke, breathless, her heart pounding in her chest, with Stone on his side turned to her. His hand went to her chest, just below her clavicle.

"Hey, hey, shhhhh, it's okay, you're okay," he crooned softly.

She clutched at his hand on her chest with both of her own. Felt the thickness of his fingers. Waited for her heart to slow its pounding as her tears ran from the corners of her eyes to her ears. Without turning her head to him, but her fingers wrapped well around his, squeezing, she said, "You told her. I can't believe you told her."

Stone is oddly solicitous of late and she finds it disconcerting. She knows he's hoping that having Ella back will make things right between them again, but she knows that's unlikely. Some things shift the equilibrium between two people and can't be fixed. Hillary is not bringing Ella back in an attempt to strike that balance again. She's bringing Ella back because she never should have let Stone send her away. In Hillary's mind there had been an agreement of sorts between her and her husband.

She hadn't argued with him thirty-two years ago when he made it clear that it was time to send Ella away. Hillary knew she had done something terrible and that he was proposing a solution of sorts. But they never talked about what she had done. What's more, she had allowed herself to believe that Stone understood. Oh, she knows that was a lie she shrouded herself under. Knows that now. But believing it was what she had held on to the last thirty-two years—that he forgave her, that he knew that what she had done (however wrong it might have been) was not a weakness in her so much as a mercy steeped in love.

The lamb is in the oven and the aromas are thick and savory. Jax and Belle have brought home their provisions, set the wine on the sideboard, and escaped to confer with their siblings. They're all gathering in the carriage house, which she refers to privately as the opium den. They think she's clueless, but she's always known what they do in there. A mother just knows.

Stone, having finished spraying weed killer in the backyard, is coming in the back door. He removes his shoes, tells her everything smells wonderful, what's cooking? She recites the full menu, though she has already told him what she is serving. He places a hand at the small of her back, leans over her shoulder to peer in the pot, turns to watch her tear the bib lettuce leaves, and suggests an addition to the salad. How about some of those slivered almonds? When he goes upstairs to wash, she stows away the pecans and takes a bag of slivered almonds from the pantry. She is not conscious of this small change of plans. It is a kind of muscle memory at work, the suggestions that she instinctively acts upon.

The thing with Bets had thrown her, but she shouldn't have been surprised. She believes Stone, that nothing happened. But that's not the point.

She is in her walk-in closet, standing before her large dressing mirror and threading pearl earrings into the lobes of her ears, spritzing Chanel between her breasts, but not too much. Hillary believes you should not *smell* a woman when she walks in the door. You should, instead, detect something lovely when you lean into her, something that makes one want to linger longer. Her girls used to douse themselves in cheap perfume, something ghastly called Charlie and another lemony one she can't recall. She finally took Belle to Hutzler's and had her select a signature scent. To this day she gives Belle a small bottle of the classic Joy for her birthday every year. She did the same for Tess when she turned sixteen and now gifts her a bottle of L'air Du Temps once a year. She's not really sure if Tess still wears the scent, but Belle, on the other hand, definitely does and it warms Hillary's heart every time she welcomes her daughter, as if she has just emerged from a meadow.

Hillary goes to her bedroom window, the one that looks out on the wide street. The day had started bright and promising, warmed through the afternoon and was now cooling at an alarming rate. The sky is ashen and a gentle wind is picking up. The daffodils are bowing. She had hoped to serve dessert on the patio, but it's only April, the weather so unpredictable.

She turns to see Stone standing in the bedroom doorway. "How are you?" he asks, as if they are acquaintances meeting on the street.

"Fine," she says, too quickly. She is fine, feeling purposeful and determined.

"It should be a nice evening," he says. "A nice visit with her for everyone."

She nods, but deep down inside she knows it's not likely. It will be tense, filled with innuendo, her children side-eyeing one another. Stone will work especially hard to act as if nothing is out of the ordinary, as if this is something he agrees with, has put much thought into and planned carefully. It's hard to look him in the eyes and be forced to see what she had failed to recognize over the years. He is to her, in recent months, like a knight fallen. Where she had once basked in the certainty of his wise counsel, she now sees it as a charlatan's trick, a sleight of hand he practiced on her.

Perhaps she is being too harsh. She ventures a glance at his face and sees, for the first time in months, the remnants of the same look he wore when he told her, gently but certainly, that it was time to send Ella away. It is shocking to see, to recall, and now, in this moment, to see it for what it was. His eyes unfocused, his lips twisting as if to find words that don't exist. On the surface there is resignation. She can see it in the gentle lift of his brow, the expectation that she will follow his lead, but deeper behind that facade, she detects now a kind of hopelessness, an admission, perhaps, that he is only doing the best he can.

"Hillary," he says. He lifts a hand and drops it to his side.

"It's okay," she says.

"I needed someone to talk to," he says.

Hillary had needed someone to talk to, too. And the longing of it is lodged in her throat. She has always needed someone to talk to about Ella. Instead, the words have become stuck in her throat until they scabbed over, never healing completely. "She was my friend," she says. "I can't believe she knew all these years. And I can't believe that whatever happened between the two of you—whatever *that* was . . ." And here she throws her hands in the air, unable to define just what was between the two of them.

"Nothing," he says firmly, transforming before her eyes back into the man she has relied upon for forty years. His back straighter, his jaw firm, his feet solidly planted.

"It was a kiss," he says. "That's all it was, one kiss." But there is a small sting in the word *kiss*, like a rubber band smacked on the most tender part of her neck. There are so many ways to imagine a kiss. "Nothing more."

"I don't know what has me more troubled," she says. At the same time, she allows him to step forward and lift her hand from her side. "That you kissed my friend thirty-two years ago, or that you told her something so private, so easily misunderstood, so . . . so *complicated* . . ." She can't go on, dips her head to his chest. "My God," she sobs. "What did she think of me all these years?"

He presses her to himself, rubs his hand up her back, holds the back of her head to his chest. "Hillary, she thought the same thing I thought, the same thing I've always known. You were in a terrible place and I didn't do enough to help. In that moment back then, you did the only thing you thought you could to save everyone, even Ella."

"I can't explain it," she admits. "I can't explain what happened that day."

"You don't owe me an explanation," he says. "Not me or anyone else."

She's not sure this is true. But it is an olive branch she is willing to tuck away.

23

Lynetta

"You come, too, Nettie."

"I'll walk you to the door, but I can't stay, Ella."

"You stay."

They are parked on the street in front of the Juleses' massive home. Ella is fiddling with her glasses, taking them off and twisting them in her hands. Lynetta takes them from her, wipes the lenses with the hem of her shirt, and hands them back. "Put those back on, doll. You want to be able to see everyone?"

Ella has had glasses since she was thirteen. Too late, honestly, but it apparently never occurred to anyone that she had such poor vision until Lynetta noticed that Ella could recognize large letters on signs—the *K* in Kmart, the *S* in Sizzler steak house—but couldn't recognize the same letters in the books Lynetta read to her. When she had mentioned this to Mr. Flay, he had agreed that she was able to recognize some of the larger flash-card letters he used in class, but had never gotten the hang of stringing the letters together for actual reading. He would put in a request for a vision test. She's good about wearing her glasses, but Lynetta knows that when she takes them off and twists them in her hands it is because she is nervous.

"Do you remember this pretty house?"

Ella shakes her head, no, slides the glasses back up to her face and looks again. "Mama and Dadda's house? I not live here."

"You did, a long time ago."

Ella shakes her head again, no.

"It's very nice," Lynetta says. She says it sadly, though she hopes Ella doesn't notice. It is so much more than their little cottage, so much more than the trailer she is moving to. She sees, suddenly, just why Mrs. Jules said it the way she had, *trailer*, as if the word itself was small. She thinks of hurricanes and storms and tsunamis and the way her little trailer could be carried off in any number of disasters whereas this home has weathered the ages. The huge front porch wrapped in boughs of dripping wisteria, the massive front door with its gleaming brass doorknocker centered in a wreath of dried lavender, and the meandering stone walk framed in bowing cherry blossoms are all beckoning Ella from the car, welcoming her home.

"Let's go, doll," she says in the most cheerful voice she can muster. Her heart is sinking fast as she gets out of the car and retrieves Ella's bag from the back seat. At the last minute, Lynetta had added a small potpourri sachet in the hopes of masking the faint scent of mildew she couldn't scrub away. Ella had then taken it upon herself to add a time-worn copy of *Cattery* magazine, a Tupperware container of crayons and markers, and the jar of seashells she kept next to her bed and carried back and forth to the trailer. Lynetta hears the *thunk* of them in the bag as she swings it from the car. She goes to Ella's door and opens it. Ella doesn't move, just stares at the house over Lynetta's shoulders. She squints and adjusts her glasses as if she is noticing something in the distance. Lynetta looks behind herself and sees Mr. Jules standing in a second-floor window and gazing down at them. He raises his hand in a wave and turns from the window.

"Dadda," Ella says matter-of-factly. She hasn't seen him since the day before Christmas.

"Come on," says Lynetta. "Everybody's waiting for you. You're the guest of honor."

"Nope," Ella says. "They don't know me." She brushes her hands down the fabric of her dress, picks at the parade of buttons down the front of it.

"You look nice," Lynetta offers. "Real pretty. Come on now. Your family is excited to see you."

Ella rises half-heartedly up out of the car, looks to the window again. Sighs. "They don't know me, Nettie." They step up to the curb. Ella feels for Lynetta's hand. "They don't know us."

24

Hillary

August in Baltimore is hot, always hot. The temperature reaches into the nineties, sometimes tickling one hundred degrees, and everyone remarks, year after year, as if they are surprised by it and have no memory of the previous summer, that they never imagined it could get so hot. No one sleeps at night, not even the children. Fans are whirring and streams of warm air rush throughout the house, swirling down the hall and swooping down the wide stairway, but nothing cools. It's only eight thirty in the morning and already flies are pinging into the screens. By late afternoon the children will surely be cranky and melted over the patio furniture or the shady spots in the lawn.

Hillary has a doctor's appointment for Ella. She's sending the children to the Morgenfriers for the morning where there happens to be a swimming pool, and while she knows that the children are indifferent to her friend Mary Morgenfrier's daughter, Clarissa, they will suffer her willingly for a chance to spend the better part of the morning submerged in the pool. Jax may struggle to engage Clarissa. It's just his nature, but the others will ignore her. Mary will pull young Finney around on a raft and never leave him unattended. She is lucky to have two such good friends, Bets and Mary, both willing to spread themselves thin over the Jules children.

Hillary also knows the morning chaos will overwhelm young

Clarissa. She isn't one to join in the shenanigans of the Jules children. Clarissa, according to her mother, goes into the pool twice a day to swim uniform laps and otherwise makes use of the pool only when it's unbearably hot and the shade has spread over the steps that lead into the shallow end where she can sit on the pool steps with a book and read.

On Sunday afternoon, two days earlier, Ella had had another seizure. One of the worst Hillary had seen, and in this case even more disturbing in that Stone had witnessed it as well—the first time he had seen such a thing. Up until Sunday, the seizures, off and on over the last two years, had been small, barely perceptible to the children who accepted peculiar movements and tics from Ella as perfectly normal for their strange sibling. Only Belle was ever concerned, sometimes asking Ella what was wrong, holding her hand afterward and asking her what happened. But they were short—a mere ten, fifteen seconds long, her body going oddly rigid—sometimes trembling—and the snapping or jerking of her jaw, the rolling of her eyes in her head. If she was standing when they came over her, she would fall to the ground, which frightened the children, but they were over quickly, leaving Ella glassy-eyed and sleepy. George called them *Ella's weird thing*. "She did it again," he would say. "Ella did that weird thing," at which point Hillary would go to Ella and sit with her, wipe her mouth and brow, offer her some juice, all the while assuring herself that these incidents were a part of Ella's *condition*, as she thought of it, but never mentioning them to Stone and only telling the children that their sister would be fine, just fine.

But late Sunday afternoon had been different. Hillary was headed to the cellar with a load of laundry. Stone was in the backyard setting up a badminton net for the children. When she passed by the kitchen's open back door, the laundry basket on her hip, she spied the children outside, Ella and Belle lying side by side on their backs in the grass, gazing up through the branches of the ancient magnolia tree that littered the lawn year round with its thick fat leaves. The boys, Jax, George, and two-year-old Finney, tangled in the badminton netting, watching their father hammer the poles into the hardened lawn. Hillary set the basket on the kitchen table to watch. At first, from a distance, she couldn't tell Belle from Ella and found herself puzzling out one from the other. Both of them with their hair spread, a golden halo around their heads, the sun dappling their nearly identical bodies beneath the shade of the tree, legs stretched long and wide. But when Belle sat up suddenly and leaned over Ella, the movement so quick and fluid, she knew it to be Belle sitting up and Ella still flat on her back. Belle leaned in closer to Ella's face and for a moment Hillary thought—in spite of the fact that she had never seen such a gesture on Belle's part—that she meant to plant a kiss on Ella's forehead. Until Ella's feet turned out, the bare toes curling, the legs stiffening. Belle pulled back, hesitated, and reached out again to push her hand down on her sister's chest that rose and fell, as if she could hold her sister's body to the ground. Ella arched and fell, twisted her torso. Hillary saw the way Ella's arms pulled to her chest, twitched like the wings of a damaged bird, her head thrashing, her chin jutting in the air.

Belle was screaming for her father even before Hillary's feet hit the patio stones. George, gawking beneath yards of badminton netting, stood frozen, watching. But Jax was right behind Stone, rushing to Ella's side. Finney rose from where he sat, fat diapered bottom rising first and then pushing up from his hands and toddling to the cluster of them as Hillary made her way across the lawn.

"Hold her, just hold her," she heard herself saying, believing that the tremors and thrashing could be contained in their arms.

Stone waved Belle back and she scrambled to her feet and moved away from the swing of his arm.

"What happened?" asked Jax of Belle, but she could only shake her head. "What happened?" he asked again.

"She did that thing," Hillary heard Belle say. "She did that thing again."

Hillary went down on her knees beside Belle, watched the straining of tendons under Ella's skin—her neck, her fingers—as if they were being pulled from her body. Stone picked her up and Hillary could smell her, the urine soaked through her shorts, and the stink of her bowels released, saw the smear of it along her backside as Stone carried her into the house, the children trailing behind, and laid her on top of Finney's napping blanket on the sofa. The children fanned out, silent, like an audience. Hillary kneeling at Ella's side, pressing her hands to Ella's face, Stone wrapping Ella's wrists with his large hands, her fingers curled like claws. *Shhhh, shhhh, it's okay, Ella. It's okay.*

When it was over, when her body relaxed, she melted like gelatin into the sofa, sweat-soaked and stinking in the heat. Hillary smoothed the hair that stuck to her face and neck.

Stone pronounced it a seizure—the first time the word had been said aloud. Hillary rose and went to the kitchen where she retrieved a towel from the laundry basket, ran cool water over it, and brought it back to the room, wiping Ella's face and neck first and then doing her best to clean her thighs, turning her on her side to wipe her backside. Stone sent the children out of the room and they backed away, Belle taking Finney by hefting him to her hip.

"She'll need a bath," said Stone, stating the obvious.

Hillary bit her tongue and only said, *Of course.* But there was so much more she wanted to say. She wanted to say that she was afraid. She wanted to say that she was trying, trying, every day, she was trying, but that it was only getting harder. She wanted to say that no child, especially a perpetual one, should have to bear such a thing as this. She wanted to say, *For the love of God, what is going to happen to her?*

Stone lifted Ella and the blanket beneath her and carried her upstairs where the two of them bathed her together. She was weak and drowsy, and Stone cradled her head while Hillary soaped and gently scrubbed. When Ella stepped out of the tub, Stone with an arm around her, Hillary waiting with a bath towel, Hillary was struck by how perfect her young body was, how pink and lovely, struck by the dreamy smile on her face, the way she looked from one parent to the other, tipped her damp head to her father's waist and stepped into her mother's waiting arms to be wrapped and patted dry.

"She'll have to see the pediatrician," he said. "Better call him tomorrow."

"Of course," said Hillary. But she knew it was an exercise in futility.

The children are all in the kitchen in their bathing suits, beach towels curled under their arms and Hillary has packed a bag filled with snacks and juice for Finney, extra diapers, a pacifier for naptime that she has yet to wean him from.

Jax suddenly breaks away from the group to search the den for a particular *National Geographic* magazine he wants to bring Clarissa. Something about King Tut's tomb and Egypt. "Clarissa likes things like that," he says. Ever since the Morgenfriers had ventured to Washington, DC, and the National Gallery of Art back in March, Clarissa has been obsessed with the King Tut exhibit—the mummifying of human remains, the labyrinth of the burial chamber, and the ridiculous curse said to fall upon the archaeologists who first broached the chamber. Jax comes back into the kitchen, empty-handed and disappointed. He will find it later, he tells his mother. He will ask his dad where it is when he gets home tonight.

She sends them off to walk the block to the Morgenfrier home, admonishing them to stay together, Belle to hold Finney's hand, and to be good, be very good for her friend, and she will see them this afternoon.

The trickle of morning nausea that she has been doing her best to ignore the last few days is abating. She can't stomach any breakfast and has had only weak tea and a glass of water for breakfast. She drops some saltines into a baggie and stuffs them down in her purse to fight off the wooziness that she anticipates will return. She is expecting a call from her own doctor today but already knows what the results will be. She has been through this enough times to recognize the barrage of symptoms—the bloating, the tenderness of her breasts, the waves of nausea made only worse in the cloying heat.

Hillary places the seatbelt around Ella's waist and Ella bats her hands away. Hillary knows it is pointless, that Ella will take it off at some point before they arrive at the pediatrician's office. But she tends to stay still in her seat—a good thing, given the circumstances—and Hillary tells herself she is only doing the best she can as she has yet to devise a way to keep Ella from unsnapping herself. Immediately Ella begins to fiddle with the belt, looking for the buckle's lever that will release her.

Dr. Aengus Warfield wears a mournful expression whenever he sees Ella. He's kind enough, but there's something patronizing about the way his brows lift in the center when he asks Hillary what's been going on. It's getting on her last nerve. She explains the seizure to him and asks him if there is a test for epilepsy.

Hillary and Stone know Aengus socially, though not well. Their social circles intersect like a Venn diagram, with a number of mutual friends. They belong to different clubs, hers predominantly Catholic and his predominantly not, though no one would ever say so aloud, but his wife is in a neighboring garden club and they once lunched together with friends. Hillary likes her well enough.

Aengus tells her that there is a test, but it can't be done in his office and Ella would need to be sedated and checked into the hospital. Basically, he explains, this is a kind of misfiring in the brain. We may never find the cause, he goes on to say, and the seizures may or may not stop on their own. He tells her she must record the incidences as they occur, write them down and note the duration as well.

Hillary knew this was a pointless trip. When it comes to Ella, there is nothing the medical profession has to offer. He does the obligatory: listens to her heart, watches her pupils dilate and recede from the light of his tiny flashlight, taps her knees, gently pinches the skin on the back of her hand and then again at the collarbone and pronounces her slightly dehydrated, even goes so far as to offer her a paper cup full of water from the small hand-sink behind him. Before handing it to her he lifts one of her hands. "Little bit of a tremor here," he says, matter-of-factly. "Blood pressure just a tiny bit high but still in the normal range and heartbeat is a little quick—nothing I'm concerned about," he assures Hillary. He hands Ella the cup of water and she drinks it down eagerly with both hands and begins to chew on the edges. "I imagine this visit is a little stress provoking for her."

He asks Hillary how things are going at home with Ella's care. Is she sleeping at night, getting fresh air, eating regularly?

Hillary answers yes to everything. Everything is fine. He asks her if she has help at home, with so many children and Ella's needs as well.

When she doesn't answer him, averts her eyes because they are filling with unexpected tears, he takes the mangled paper cup from Ella and holds her hands for a moment before handing her a Rubik's Cube that she tries to pull apart and then puts to her mouth, tasting, biting, dragging the edge of her teeth across the ridges of it, and he turns back to Hillary.

"My sisters help some days," says Hillary. Though the truth is that she asks less and less of them of late. The small doses of Valium that she gives Ella have helped, kept Ella calm, less excitable, helped to lull her through the long days, though she hasn't given her a dose in four days, so certainly the seizures have nothing to do with the *quiet medicine*. Of course, she doesn't tell him this, never mentions the dosing. She had thought of hiring help, had even placed an ad in the paper, but the first woman who had answered the advertisement had looked so pitifully at Ella who sat on the floor beside Hillary, picking at her nose, pulling at the bow Hillary had put in her hair. The woman said she was fond of *the mental children*, especially *the mongoloid ones*, had a brother who was *simple, but not mental, not as bad as Ella, here.* "God's little lambs," she said, and Hillary knew she couldn't bear to have the woman in her house, have her hovering, trying to turn Ella into a blessing of some kind.

There are special schools, Aengus reminds her. Not all mentally retarded children will qualify. But has she checked into any of them? Ella is old enough now, at eight, assuming she's potty trained and there are no medical issues that would exclude her. The seizures, should they continue, might be a problem, but there is the recently opened Claremont School and the Arc of Baltimore, both of which might be an option, provide Hillary with a respite from Ella's care and Ella could benefit from training.

"Training for what?" asks Hillary.

"Basic skills—life skills—personal hygiene, home economics."

Hillary just nods, but inside she feels a stab of anger. *Personal hygiene.* Hillary keeps Ella clean, struggles with the toothbrushing, hand washing, bathing, but the child is clean. If the well-meaning doctor were to lean into Ella and breathe deeply, he would find she smells of soap and the baby powder Hillary dusts her with after every bath. Her nails are clean and trimmed—no small feat, given Ella's penchant for digging in her flower boxes—and her hair is combed and pulled back away from her face so that she can't suck on the ends of it, though she has worked furiously at the elastic so that the ponytail is askew and the hair poufs in places.

"A residential program is always an option," he says. "A program like Beechwood, or a private facility."

Hillary shakes her head, no. She would never think of sending Ella away. "I'm not interested in sending her away," she says, but her voice quivers and the doctor leans back against the cabinet, crosses his arms over his chest, and places his feet wide.

"Hillary, things are not going to get easier with Ella." He waits but she says nothing. "How does Stone feel about this?"

The question infuriates her, but she holds her tongue. He feels the same way she does about it, that Ella is a tragedy of nature and their cross to bear, for whatever reason.

She won't look at Aengus, runs her hand down the back of Ella's head where she still sits on the examining table, grunting at the Rubik's Cube that she cannot take apart.

He goes on to tell her of all the progress being made these days when it comes to caring for *retardants*. "They are often much more capable than we once thought," he says.

"Potty," says Ella. But she says it softly so that only Hillary hears her.

"You have to go potty?" says Hillary in her ear.

"Sometimes, you need to make the tough choices, do what is best for the family as a whole," he is saying. "I would strongly urge you to consider the needs of your large family in light of the burden of Ella."

Hillary is scooting Ella off the table. She needs to get her to the bathroom.

"Research has demonstrated that the institutionalization of children like Ella can be beneficial for the entire family," he says. "It may be a loving option."

"*Dr.* Aengus," she says, because she wants to be respectful to some degree. "My daughter is not going to a place like that."

"Potty," says Ella.

"No one knows what is best for her better than I do," Hillary says, more to herself than to the doctor, and with that, she slides Ella to the floor where she promptly releases her bladder and splatters the floor with urine.

Back home in the bathroom, Hillary is wrangling the wet panties down Ella's legs. The smell of her from the drive in the too-warm car was nauseating and at one point Hillary had to pull over and open the window, stick her head out into the saturated air to calm the spasms in her stomach, thought for sure she was going to heave on the side of the road. The moment passed and she nibbled at the saltines in her purse the rest of the ride home, willing them to stay down and absorb the acids in her stomach.

Ella was agitated by the time they got home. Hillary blamed it on the heat, the urine-soaked clothing she endured the length of the ride, the likelihood that she was hungry. She had handed her a graham cracker as soon as they got in the door, hoping to bathe her before feeding her lunch, but Ella had kicked the cabinet and rummaged through the refrigerator grunting to be fed even as she stood stinking and wet at the open refrigerator, her hands grabbing at condiment jars, knocking over the bowl of marinating chicken breasts and slopping the shelves. She pulled out a block of Velveeta cheese and shoved it at Hillary, demanding it be unwrapped. Hillary cut her a thick slice and lured her to the bathroom with it.

In the bathroom now, peeling Ella's panties down her legs and struggling to get her out of her saturated sundress, Hillary's stomach gives
up the fight and she throws herself over the toilet and wretches up the
crackers she has eaten, hangs over the bowl and gags. Her head sways
and the smell of the bowl sends her into dry heaves. Ella, one ankle still
tangled in the wet twist of her panties and her sundress hanging from
her neck and one shoulder, wraps her arms around Hillary from behind,
pulls at Hillary's hair so that it falls from its sleek knot and sticks along
her neck. With Ella nearly clambering up her back, Hillary gags over
the toilet bowl again. Lifts her head and howls pathetically in a way
she has never allowed herself to do before. A wail that has been locked
in her gut for years. So thick and dark and jagged-edged that she can
feel it tear at her throat, tastes the charred bitter blackness of it on her
tongue, hears it echo off the surrounding tile walls, feels the weight of
it raining back down on her.

Ella, perhaps frightened, slides from her mother's back, crumples to
the floor behind her. Hillary takes in slow shallow breaths to steady herself
before turning around, settling in a limp and defeated squat, letting the
sobs spill as she pulls Ella to her. Ella curls to her mother and Hillary
rocks the damp wiggling bundle of her, feels the sweaty slide of Ella
against herself, smells the salty stink of sweat and urine, the ammonia-
sting of it.

With her arms wrapped around Ella, Hillary tremble-sways on the
bathroom floor, her body splintering with the gush of all the agony she
has carried for both herself and her daughter, as if chunks of rock are
coursing through her, shattering on the shelves of her ribs, ripping at
the twists and turns of her veins and capillaries, surging through her,
seeking pores and orifices by which they might meet the light of day.
She has held these churning rocks deep in her dark gut for years, tried
to still them with the slippery platitudes of her faith, but she is certain
in this moment that her body is breaking down, disintegrating at its
damp edges like the paper cup Ella had gnawed on in the doctor's office.
Everything tearing to the surface, shredding her very soul.

She doesn't try to stop the crying—to *pull herself together*, as she has come to think of it—and instead decides it is a kind of purging that is long overdue. In this mix of tears is the requisite pity for her own self, for the constraints of her life as it is tethered to Ella. But what is back-filling behind her own self-pity is the knowing that Ella's life is a misery that Hillary cannot change the course of. There is nothing for Ella to look forward to, no future to step into eagerly. Instead, there is the like-lihood of more seizures and God-knows-what other complications, the possibility of institutionalization. And just what would happen to this child if Hillary were to perish—hit by a bus, stricken with cancer, inca-pacitated in any way?

Over her own sobs she can hear the frenetic buzz of a fly, ricochet-ing off the ceramic wall tiles, landing in the tub, flipping to its back, and spinning madly. The fly's agony serves as a distraction against her own and eventually she chokes out the last sobs, drapes herself, drained and empty, over her daughter.

Ella pat-pats at her mother's hand that is pressed to her bare chest, jiggles the rings on her mother's finger, tries to slide them off. Frustrated at the way they refuse to glide off her mother's finger, she tugs harder.

The crying has left Hillary empty, but what is taking its place is a rising fear over Ella. Hillary can no longer see around the corners. Always in raising Ella there has been a sense of putting one foot in front of the other and trudging through the overdue milestones that would indi-cate progress of some kind; she never doubted Ella would eventually learn to walk, language is stunted but growing daily and she now has a vocabulary of perhaps twenty or more words, potty training has been progressing and they are through the worst of it (if you didn't take into account that an accident with an eight-year-old child outweighs that of a three-year-old).

But suddenly now there is no way for Hillary to imagine Ella's future around the corners of her own mind. A dark labyrinth she has felt her way through like a blind woman, turning corners by the raw tips of her fingers, the walls only narrowing along the way so that she has begun to feel her own breath bounce back.

She leans away from Ella to reach the works of the tub, adjusting the water temperature from where she stretches. Then remembers the fly and slides Ella off of her lap to rise and grab a tissue, pinching the carcass out of the far end of the tub before the water has a chance to lap at it.

As the tub fills, Hillary encourages Ella to stand so that she can take off the sundress hanging from her shoulder, stoops and lifts her foot to pull off the panties while Ella rests a small hand on her shoulder to steady herself. Hillary puts an arm around her and takes her to the edge of the tub, now a mere two inches deep with swirling water.

With one foot in the tub, and the other lifting over the rim of it, Ella suddenly lolls her head on her neck, tips it up and back down so that Hillary can see her eyes roll up in her head, and pitches forward, her slick arm sliding from Hillary's grip, her head banging into the far edge and crashing facedown with a frightful clunk and splash into the tub.

Hillary falls to her knees, tries to pull her from the tub but only manages at first to flip her to her back where she flails and trembles so that the water sloshes up the sides of the tub, her arms bent and jerking, her feet slap-paddling at the water, her mouth open and gasping, the water rising to her ears.

Hillary leans deeper into the tub, puts her arms beneath Ella's small shoulders and lifts, but Ella slides, a slippery fish through her arms, away, her head slamming again to the bottom of the porcelain tub.

It is—and Hillary is certain of this—a moment of grace offered up. *Shhhh, shhhhh, it's okay, Ella.* She presses the palms of her mothering hands over her child's heart. Watches the water rise over her thrashing daughter. Presses harder.

25

Belle

The Jules siblings are tossed around the carriage house like discarded socks, Jax draped the length of the sofa, George seated but with his upper body slung across the small table, his head tipped to his hands like he's cradling a headache, Finney with his backside against the countertop, and Tess, sprawled across the floor on her belly but with her elbows propped so that her upper body rises elegantly as she instructs them all in the broader points of custody law. It's not her specialty, she tells them, but she does know the basics tenets of it and there's no reason *not* to return Ella to the family. *That's* the problem.

Belle is in the tiny bedroom she and Tess are sharing. The pitched ceiling means she can't stand to her full height beside her bed—even sitting on it has her head grazing the ceiling—and so she stands in the doorway. She can hear every word they're saying below her. Tess is wrong. There is a very good reason not to return Ella to her parents. She is still reconciling the morning's revelation from Clarissa and Jax. There had been no discussion about telling the others. It would have only inflamed George. Quick to burn, as Belle thinks of him. It would be fuel for his constant fire.

And as for Finney and Tess, Belle and Jax agreed that there was nothing to be gained by telling them. Finney having been so young, only two years old when Ella was sent away, and Tess having been born seven months after the banishment. Somehow it doesn't feel like it had anything to do with them. This is something she can't explain, either. As if she and Jax are somehow responsible and should bear whatever guilt has snaked its way to them.

Knowing what she learned from Jax and Clarissa earlier today has shaken up everything about the past in Belle's mind, and none of it has settled into a permanent place yet. She cannot reconcile what Clarissa and Jax had told her over coffee about that day long ago—a day she barely remembers because there was nothing significant about it to notch out a memory—with what she recalls. She has struggled through the afternoon to find a space for it, twist history around in her mind to find a place to insert it. With some nudging, she was able to remember that her father had picked them up from the Morgenfriers' that afternoon—much later than she had expected so that she was hungry and cranky when she had walked in the door, waterlogged, her toes wrinkled and raw, her eyes puffed and stinging from a day submerged in chlorine, her shoulders burned hot and tender. An open block of Velveeta was on the counter, the edges darkened and hard, and she used a crusted knife on the counter to cut herself gooey slices. She remembered this because her mother kept a neat kitchen and it wasn't customary to find food left out or silverware lying about. That was the best she could dredge up, and the rest of what Jax and Clarissa had told her still doesn't fit around the edges of that single memory.

She is dressing for the evening in anticipation of Ella's arrival and it has suddenly occurred to her that it would be incredibly disturbing if she should find herself wearing something even remotely similar to what her estranged sister might be wearing tonight. It is the oddest of thoughts and she knows—or hopes—it is unlikely, but Belle has been raised in an extended family of twins and so if such an unthinkable coincidence should occur, no one would be the least bit surprised. She tries to imagine, among the few items of clothing she packed, which pants or tops are least likely to show up on her twin. Immediately she rejects one of her favorite blouses, seafoam green with a scalloped hem that is perfect with jeans or black pants. It had been a gift from her mother, one of her *saw it and thought of you* gifts that she now fears may have been duplicated on Ella. She steps into jeans—not her most comfortable ones—and a peasant-style top covered in mirrored spangles. Other than the small, blemished medicine cabinet mirror in the bath between the two rooms there's no mirror in the carriage house, but she's worn the top and pants enough times to know what she looks like.

U2 is playing downstairs, and Belle is thinking how fuzzy it sounds on the ancient stereo system that dates all the way back to high school. Jax still can't help fiddling with the bass settings even after all these years. As if he can make an adjustment that will fix it.

"I say we get through the night and talk to them tomorrow after she leaves," says Jax, just as Belle is coming down the steps in search of her shoes. "We'll have a better handle on it by then."

"What about church tomorrow?" says Tess.

"Oh, no way," says Finney. "No way. Not going."

"I didn't even think about that," says Belle. She kicks a pillow on the floor to reveal a pair of black flats and slides into them. "You don't think she'll drag Ella to church?" she asks Finney.

He shrugs and checks his watch. When he doesn't answer her, she announces that she is not going to church, either. She may be the compliant one but on this, she is not budging.

Finney says they should get up to the house. She'll be here any minute. But Belle is headed back up the stairs saying she needs to have her phone in case Ben calls. The church thing is bothering her if only because she knows it hurts her mother that she refuses to go. What's worse is that Belle refuses to explain herself, has always said it is between her and God. "That makes no sense," her mother always says. "If you're mad at God, you should go to church and talk to Father Dougherty about it."

But Belle had talked to God instead, and she figured she and God had come to an understanding and agreed to disagree. Bottom line is, she had fucked up, and, what's worse, she blamed Him for that.

At twenty-three, she had been old enough to make her own decisions but also old enough to know better. That was where the blame fell to her. She should have been on birth control, but it was the height of the AIDS epidemic and condoms were a required accessory among her male peers. She hadn't felt the need to double up on protection. Besides, by abdicating responsibility she was, in some twisted way, adhering to the church's prohibition against birth control. She wasn't using birth control, but the man-boys she slept with were. Not her call, but theirs, was the way she saw it.

She'd been working as an underpaid grant writer for the Bread Box, an organization that brought nutrition education to Baltimore City schoolchildren, sponsored field trips to farms where children learned that chocolate milk didn't come from brown cows and that ketchup wasn't a vegetable. She loved her job, the structure of it, the easy hunt for language that supported a program she believed in, the camaraderie amongst her coworkers. But outside of work, she felt unmoored. She lived in a three-bedroom, eight-foot-wide row home with two roommates and a lethargic iguana in the Federal Hill district of downtown Baltimore where a hookup was steps from her door in any direction and the bar patrons always spilled into the streets.

Within days of missing her period, she found herself peeing on a stick and simultaneously doing the math that would reveal three possible suspects, only one of whom she could attach to a last name because she had gone to high school with him. Even so, she wasn't sure she could spell it—*McCorkle* or *McCorkell*.

From the moment she had peed on the stick, her mind had run on two tracks: the one straight and narrow and leading directly to the Planned Parenthood center on North Howard Street and the other a meandering path that traipsed her imagination. For less than two hundred dollars, she could step back into her life exactly where she had left off. No one the wiser—her sin disappeared. But if she was brave, if she had been a different kind of young woman, if she had been the kind of woman who could operate, boldly, in the face of her religious upbringing, she just might (*maybe*—because she couldn't be sure, couldn't clear her mind in the days leading up to the procedure to see the world outside the walls of religious fiat) she just might become a mother at twenty-three.

She spent the next few days weighing one sin against the other, knowing that what she was about to do was the greater of the two. But knowing also that she was not brave enough, did not *believe* enough to bear the fruit of her sin for a lifetime. That was when it dawned on her that she had been backed into a choice predicated on her understanding of just what constitutes a sin and how far one is subsequently willing to go to hide the tracks of the original.

She finds her phone on the edge of the sink in the bathroom and thinks to check in on Ben and the kids, but the others are calling for her from downstairs and Tess is coming up the steps behind her. Does she regret the choice she made back then? Not necessarily. What she regrets is that she couldn't unpack the decision to do so from the trail of sins that precipitated it. She regrets also the way the decision had amputated her from the church of her childhood. There was no chance, given the string of choices she had made to cover her tracks, that confession felt like an option. No way she could enter a church and not feel like she was squaring off against God Himself.

"You okay?" Tess asks.

"Sure."

"I keep forgetting she's your twin." Tess leans back against the railing at the top of the steps, crosses her arms. "This is going to be weird for you, isn't it?"

"For all of us," says Belle. "You, too. You've never even met her."

"Think she still looks like you?"

"She did when we were little," Belle says.

"I never think of you as a twin."

Belle doesn't know what to say to this. Ella was nothing at all like Belle, and yet, a long time ago, long before Ella was sent away, there had been moments when Belle couldn't be sure where she herself stopped and Ella began. Does she feel like a twin? All she knows is that there has always been a sort of phantom pain associated with Ella's disappearance. She should have gone to see her over the last years. But oddly, her resolve not to visit Ella had become even stronger after the abortion. Somehow the two things had tangled themselves up in her mind's eye.

Suddenly she feels tears welling.

"Belle?" Tess's hand goes to Belle's shoulder. "What is it? What's wrong?"

"I'm afraid she'll hate me," Belle says. She collapses to her sister's shoulder.

"Oh, no, no," Tess says, holding her sister against her, rubbing her hands over her shoulders. "She won't. I know she won't. Why on earth would you think that?"

"I should have gone to see her. I should have visited her over the years."

Belle steps back and wipes the tears from her face. She can't explain it to Tess, can't explain that there had been some relief in Ella's disappearance, in being left behind where she could breathe only her own breath. But now, with Ella about to walk back into the family home, Belle finds herself wondering if the frayed edge of whatever once connected her to Ella is still there and how it will weave around the two of them.

26

George

ROLAND PARK
Saturday Evening, April 18, 2009

Hugging appears to be one of Ella's favorite things. Hillary introduces each one of them in turn, but before she can finish, Ella is hugging Jax, and George watches him relax into it, hears him say, "How've you been, Ella? I've missed you."

"You not come see me no more," she says.

"I'm sorry about that—" but she stops him. "I miss you all the time," she says. George chances to look over at Belle as Ella says this and sees her face softening, her head tilting, hears the catch of her breath. Ella goes into Finney's arms and calls him *the baby*. "You the baby," she says. "All growed up. The baby's growed up now."

"All grown now," says Finney, a ridiculous smile spread across his face. "And you, too," he says. "Just look at you."

After she has hugged her parents, brothers, and sisters, including Tess who she has never met before, she starts back through the lineup of family and hugs them again. George was stiff and held his breath for the first hug, the second he allows as well but steps out of quickly, never lifting his arms to her in the easy way that Jax did or laughing nervously as does Belle.

George cannot understand the tenderness on display all around him. He, for one, is not fooled. He knows she is a monster creeping back into their fold. He steps back from the gathering and watches his mother smooth her hand over Ella's back and the way Ella tips her head to her mother's shoulder. He can't explain the feeling it draws up in him, as though there is a betrayal taking place, as though his mother has left him alone with a confounding ache and chosen instead to give aid and comfort to the enemy.

They are standing in the large foyer and Stone disappears into the dining room, calling back over his shoulder, "What can I get you to drink, Ella?" and George nearly busts out with a laugh, as if she might request a dry martini with a twist, but he catches himself and waits for her response.

"I like Coke," she says. She moves toward the sound of her father's voice and they all herd into the dining room. Hillary catches everyone's eyes in turn as they pass by, a wry smile on her face, and explains that they don't happen to have any sodas but perhaps she would like an iced tea?

"Does Lynetta give you sodas with dinner?" asks Hillary, coming into the dining room, now set magnificently with all the family's best china and silver, crystal sparkling, tulips draped in a low silver bowl.

"No," Ella says. "I drink Coke. Where Nettie go?"

No one answers her. George sees his mother catch his father's eyes and look away. It is Jax who finally tells her Nettie will be back tomorrow. It is the same question she will ask multiple times throughout the evening.

"Let's take your bag upstairs, Ella. We'll get you settled, and then I'll get you that iced tea."

"She's pretty," Tess pronounces to no one in particular.

George isn't sure this is true. Belle, on the other hand, is beautiful. He has always known this, and Ella looks like Belle, but like all things beautiful (at least in George's opinion) the smallest asymmetry changes everything. Ella squints when she talks so that her left eye is not as wide as her right, and her face is looser than Belle's, the cheeks fleshier and her jaw slack. There's a nasal quality to her voice and a bouncing to her consonants that has grated on him.

George goes to the sideboard and pours himself a hefty four fingers of scotch, adds a splash of water, turns to his father, and says, "You can't be on board for this, Dad."

They can all hear footsteps overhead. George nods to the ceiling. "You know this makes no sense." He looks at Tess, thinking surely she will say something, but she turns to Belle instead. Mouths, *You okay?* Belle nods and lifts a wineglass from the table, makes her way to where the wines are displayed, and pours from an open bottle of red.

No one is going to say a thing, not even his father. Everyone is going to play nice and act like this is perfectly reasonable, which it is not, and George, for one, is not playing along. "Tell him, Jax—Tess? Jesus," he says, taking a sip from his drink and then looking around the room. "I'm not the only one who knows this is crazy."

"We'll talk later, son," Stone says, tipping his head to the sounds of footsteps coming down the stairs. "For now, we will have a nice evening."

His mother rounds the corner into the room, announces that dinner will be ready in twenty and why not take their drinks on the patio. George pulls his phone from his pocket and brushes past Belle and Tess, steps pointedly wide around Ella, heading to the den where he will make a call.

There is a missed call from his house phone. But no message. It was likely to have been Abigail or Amanda. He won't give them a cell phone and they're both unhappy about it. He has told them they can each have one for their twelfth birthday and not a day sooner, but Tammy says that is ridiculous and they will need one before then. It's a matter of safety, she tells him. What if they need to reach their parents, if they're at a slumber party or dance practice and something goes wrong? Their tenth birthday is more reasonable, she tells him. In any case, someone has called from the house phone and it obviously isn't important as they didn't leave a message. And there's another message as well from a number he doesn't recognize. Likely a client whose contact information he has not yet put in his phone and it can wait. It's the weekend and he's entitled to his time, even if he is spending it here, in his family home, watching a catastrophe gather some weight before exploding.

He calls Tammy's cell and there is no answer. It rings for a very long time and doesn't go to voice mail which he thinks means that she is on the phone with someone else. Her mother perhaps, or her old roommate. Tammy has friends, but not many. She's still friends with the roommate whose arms he had dumped her in more than a decade ago at her doorstep. George is certain the friend blames him for how skinny Tammy is. Even pulled him aside at a parent coffee once to express her concern. George had told her he was handling it. Watched her mouth edge into a grimace and her brows knit across her forehead as if she was thinking hard on just what might resolve this thing. Her name was Carmen and she was not fat—but layered in small folds he could see along her middle, sheaved in a knit dress that clung to her wider hips. He had wanted to get away from her, but she had a look of urgency on her face, and he feared she would follow him into the crowd and continue to talk about this very private thing. The more she talked, the more he wanted to escape, if only because he found himself also wanting to touch her, touch the place on her back where her flesh lumped slightly at the constraint of her bra, smooth his hand down her side where it lapped just a bit at the cinch of her waist. He wanted to bury his face in a soft neck, put his lips to a blushing cheek. He couldn't remember the last time he had felt the softness of flesh beneath his hands rather than the chink of bone.

"It's very complicated, George. We see this sort of illness all the time, and it can get dangerous."

He recalled then that she was a nurse, a psych nurse, if he was remembering correctly. "We've seen a doctor," he said. "Things are in the works."

"I'm glad to hear that," she said. "That's a relief. Let me know if you need anything, will you?" And she had placed her hand lightly on his sleeve.

He almost shook it off, but caught himself, placed his other hand over hers, and said, "thank you," as earnestly as he could because the truth was—the truth remains—that he can't do it by himself. He cannot convince his stranger of a wife that she needs help without losing his temper, and in losing his temper he only pushes her away and he does not want to imagine what his life will look like without her, without the constant irritation of Tammy's *illness*, as Carmen calls it, as a receptacle for all of his frustration. It is the thorn in his side and the scratching of it—the irritation that builds when he watches her scoot her food around on her plate but never lift it to her mouth, when she claims to have eaten without him, when she emerges dripping from her tread-mill—the picking of that thorn in his mind's eye is what supports his righteousness, his essentialness.

When he heads out to the patio, Ella and his mother are nowhere to be seen and Jax points to the kitchen window where he can see Ella, perched at the kitchen table and his mother just beyond her at the stove.

"I didn't realize you'd been visiting her," his father is saying to Jax. George detects an odd placidness in his father's voice, as if he is resigned to something.

"Yeah, well, not so much lately."

"I guess I just didn't realize." Stone sips from his drink, swallows, and lifts his head to the breezy sky. "That's a nice thing, that you've been to see her."

"It wasn't a secret," Jax says. "Just something I did. Once in a while."

"That's nice," he says.

Tess says she didn't know they were allowed to visit because maybe she would have gone, too. But she didn't know.

"Oh, my goodness," Stone says. "You could have gone anytime you wanted."

"Well, I mean, when she was younger, when *I* was younger, you know. I asked. I asked you if I could meet her."

Stone only nods. He knows what she means.

"What about you, Belle?" George asks and she shakes her head, no. "Finney?"

"No," he says. "I'm sorry to say it never even occurred to me."

The others are seated but George continues to stand. "She wouldn't have known who you were anyway," George says. "So what's the point?"

"The point is," Belle says carefully, "she's our sister, and we should have gone to see her."

"That might have made the adjustment much harder for her," their father says.

George watches his father now, watches the way he looks deep into his scotch before taking a sip, lifts his gaze over the top of the sugar maple, just starting to unfurl its lime-green leaves, and comments as to how much the tree has grown over the years. It was hardly more than a sapling when they had planted it forty-three years ago.

Has there ever been such a perfectly beautiful family? This is what George thinks when he watches his brothers and sisters turn their collective heads to follow their father's gaze into the boughs of the tree. His wise and handsome father, a *well-respected* man. That is how George has always thought of him. His long career in mergers and acquisitions may have been what propelled George into an MBA in finance. He couldn't be sure, only knows that he wanted some of what Stone Jules had, the admiration, the way other men (and in recent years, women) sought him out after church to pick his brain on industry trends, mid-market acquisitions, policy changes that might affect their business's valuation. His clients became his friends with just the slightest imbalance of power, Stone holding their future in his hands. A successful sale or acquisition always brought new friends to a Jules cocktail or dinner party, an invitation for the Jules family to join clients in Nantucket, Rehoboth, or Telluride where they were welcomed as if they had always been part of one another's lives. His father would retire soon, had already begun to cut his hours, the long commute having worn tiresome over the years.

They all have, with the exception of George, their father's startling blue eyes and both their parents' blond hair, though Jax's has darkened in recent years. George assumed Belle and Tess got some of theirs from a bottle these days. Highlights, Tammy had explained once. There's no way they're both still so blond at their ages. But Ella had surprised him upon her arrival by her own still-blond hair and so he will have to tell Tammy that, no, he thinks they're both natural blonds as well. His mother's, however, has turned in recent years and he had noticed a mere quarter-inch of gray tracing her part line when he arrived earlier. But it's more than the collective narrow noses and high cheekbones that makes it impossible not to notice his family's good looks. It's something in the way they carry themselves, the way they all fail to notice their own good fortune, the way they refuse to be accountable to it. Tess, wrangling her hair back in a sudden breeze and securing it thoughtlessly off-center with an elastic from her wrist. Belle slouching down in a patio chair with her legs long in front of her, Finney, up now and pacing, slightly duck-footed when he stops to set his drink on the patio table and quickly adjust the crotch of his pants. There is no self-consciousness among them, and this is something George envies, their carelessness with their own bodies. George, on the other hand, has a practiced way of walking, seating himself, rising. Finds himself adjusting his shoulders when he speaks, never relaxes his breath enough to feel his waist expand over his belt the way Jax's does now. George used to gnaw on his bottom lip the way his father does, but it was a habit he broke years ago. And he used to drum his own fingers on his thighs when forced to sit and wait too long but has squelched that habit as well. There is still his teeth clenching that makes the muscles of his jaw bloom and recede, and his daughters have begun to notice it. "You're doing that thing again," Abigail had said just last night, "that thing with your face." He was staring at Tammy where she stood at the sink and he quickly looked away. He had been noticing the blotchiness around her mouth, the way the redness spackled her face.

George doesn't think about whether or not he loves this family. He thinks instead about how he fits into it—or doesn't. The lot of them, they hang together so easily, but he has always felt like the puzzle piece that got lost under the sofa. No one noticing its absence until everything else has been snapped into place.

Through the kitchen window, he watches his mother refill Ella's iced tea glass and settle at the table across from her. He can see them both in profile and through the old wavy window glass, he could be looking at a slightly plumper version of Belle. He can't imagine what they find to talk about. But Ella is clearly talking, wiggling back and forth in her seat and waving her hands around much like his own daughters do when they are telling one of their ridiculous and convoluted stories about something funny that happened at school—*Johnny Korman farted during the math test, Jennifer Langdon threw her retainer in the trash can by accident and we had to dig it out of the pencil shavings, the class gerbil got loose and Mrs. Pfeiffer jumped up on her chair when it ran past her!* He watches his mother lean into Ella and then startle with a laugh, reach out, and pat Ella's hand that she has captured out of the air. George does not understand love, has always struggled with the pieces of it and how they make a whole, how they assemble themselves into a thing that tethers him to his own beautiful girls. No, he does not understand it, but he knows it when he sees it.

27

Jax

ROLAND PARK
August 1977

Mrs. Morgenfrier calls them into her kitchen for lunch and they all clamber around the kitchen table with their towels under them while she serves them sliced apples and peanut butter and jelly sandwiches, sets a handful of curly Fritos on each plate in turn. She has cut their sandwiches in quarters. Jax's mother only does that with Finney's sandwich, and sometimes George, if he asks specifically. But it feels babyish to Jax to be eating little triangles of sandwich. Still, he is careful to thank Mrs. Morgenfrier when she sets the plate down in front of him, and again when she goes around the table and doles out additional apple slices.

Clarissa doesn't even look at her food as she eats, so engrossed she is in her book. "What's so good about that book?" he asks. She doesn't answer him, and Jax asks again. He doesn't feel ignored. He knows Clarissa often slips off into her own little world when she reads. She's been called out on more than one occasion in school, and it always makes Jax cringe when she is caught reading under her desk, pulled from her own world into a room of giggling classmates. Sister Theodora swishes the book from her lap and Clarissa startles, sometimes even looking a little afraid, like she's just crash-landed in enemy territory. It isn't her fault that she is smarter than everyone else, can do long division in her head, has already memorized the periodic table, even pointing out that there is a pattern embedded in it, all long before Jax understood just what an element was.

"It's about ancient burial practices," she says.

"Mummies," Jax says, nodding.

Clarissa blinks. "Not until 3600 BC, if it's the Egyptians you're referring to."

"Sometimes they buried alive people with the dead people," says Jax, eager to let her know he knows something as well.

"Only the wealthy," Clarissa says, "to serve them in the afterlife."

"No way," says Belle. "That's gross."

"I read about it in *National Geographic*. It's true," says Jax.

Clarissa has been eager to get a copy of that, she tells him. They don't subscribe. And Jax promises to find it for her. Tells her he looked for it earlier and will look again.

"How old are you?" says George.

"Nine and three months," says Clarissa.

"You sure know a lot of stuff," says George. "More than Jax."

"I know stuff," says Jax.

So it is that they find themselves standing in the kitchen of the Jules home in their damp swimsuits. Back at Clarissa's house, Mrs. Morgenfrier had taken Finney upstairs to struggle over a nap that Jax was fairly certain he would not take to, and Jax told the others he and Clarissa were just going to run back to the house and find that magazine he had been looking for. They would be right back.

Jax is surprised to find his mother's car in the drive and wonders why she has not called down to Mrs. Morgenfrier and asked her to send her children home. The front door is kept locked, and so he and Clarissa go around through the yard. They are barefoot and the grass feels good on their feet after walking the hot sidewalks. He finds the back door open, just as he knew it would be. The counter is strangely cluttered with a baggie of saltine crackers, an open box of graham crackers, and a slab of the soft orange cheese his mother melts into macaroni. A sharp knife rests on a damp sloppy rag. He calls out to his mother, waits, but there is no answer and he hears the bathwater running above them. He will find the magazine for Clarissa and then he will go upstairs and tell his mother he is home. He hopes she won't mind if he goes back to the Morgenfriers' with Clarissa. It's such a hot, hot day and the pool has been such fun.

Overhead Jax hears what he assumes at first to be the knocking of pipes and the water choking through the tub's spigot. The banging continues as he makes his way toward the den, calling up to his mother, "It's me, Mom!" He doesn't expect her to answer, assumes she cannot hear him above the sound of the running water, but directly over his head now he hears the stranger sounds of water slapping, thumps, and knocks he has never heard before. He is not worried, just finds it strange, strange that she would leave a knife on the counter, food unwrapped, when she is always so careful to keep these things out of Ella's reach. Odd, perhaps, that bathwater is running in the middle of the day. A loud *thunk* makes Clarissa look up to the ceiling.

"Mom?"

Another. He turns, goes to the bottom of the wide stairway, calls again, and begins to climb the stairs. The splashing now is louder. He can hear it sloshing over the sides of the tub, can hear a wild wet thrashing. Just as his vision crests the top step, he sees through the open bathroom door, his mother leaning deep into the tub, her skirt, water-sloshed and clinging to her thighs, sees Ella's hand clawing at his mother's face, her hair, the collar of her shirt. He hears Clarissa behind him, hears the way her steps quicken so that she has run up against his back, sees what he sees, Clarissa's breath now spilling on his neck, her hands taking hold of his shoulders.

"Mom!"

She leans deeper into the tub and her voice is pitched in a desperate octave he has never heard before. *It's okay, Ella, it's okay, dear God . . .*

It cannot be that he is watching his mother drown his sister. But there is no mistaking what he is seeing when his mother whips her head up and away from Ella, uses her left hand to clinch Ella's that is clawing at her neck, shoves it back to the tub, and then heaves her own upper body over the rim, bearing down on the swinging and flailing of limbs.

Jax cannot move, cannot put one foot in front of the other. His breath is caught in his throat and there is a great pressure in his chest that is spreading and sinking to his bowels. He can't turn around, can't unsee what he is seeing, can't make sense of it. Can't know if it is real because surely, surely, he has misunderstood. He is witnessing one of those things that seems one way and is really another and he thinks in that moment of the time only last summer when he had crept to his parents' bedroom, drawn by muffled cries and a rhythmic thumping. Inching into their room, closer to the odd sounds he was hearing, and he could see his father on top of his mother, heaving his weight over her, could hear the breath coming from the both of them. He had wanted to tear at him, pull him off of her, put his small body and all its might between theirs and swear an allegiance to his mother. But then, he had watched his father's body still, the silhouette of his father's face tipping to his mother's, had heard tender whispers, though not the words them-selves, had watched his mother's hands trail and tap over his father's bare backside.

This, this was surely something like that, something confusing that looked like one thing and was another altogether.

Clarissa's breath trickles down his neck. "What's happening?" she whispers. The splashing has slowed, stops. The water continues to run. His mother is frozen over the edge of the porcelain, her head dropping to her chest and a long cry, like the whistle of a train in the distance that will soon be bearing down on them, *Oh, dear God, dear God, Ella, Ella, Ella . . .* He watches her lift her head to the ceiling, before crumpling back to her heels.

Clarissa shoves at his back.

"Mom?" She doesn't answer him, doesn't see him, she is wiping her wet hair from her face, stares into the tub, and begins to sob. He means to go gently to her, place his hand on her back, but when he gets to the tub's edge, he sees what she has done. Ella is on her back, beneath the water, her eyes open, the blue of them cooling beneath the water. She is perfectly still, like a mermaid with her hair swirling around her.

Jax stands over the tub and sways, his thighs wobbling, and it is only his knees pressed against his mother's back that keeps him from sinking to the floor. His mother doesn't see him, doesn't feel him at her back, doesn't seem to understand that she is not alone. Clarissa nearly sends him toppling as she shoves in front of him and around his mother, lifts Ella's head from beneath the water, and yells to Jax to turn the water off. He reaches in and turns the knobs, first the hot and then the cold, the way he has been taught, and the clarity of the silence is a wind through his head. Suddenly, he is splashing into the tub, lifting the slippery Ella at her waist then sliding an arm under her dripping legs, Clarissa with her arms under Ella's shoulders, dragging Ella up and over the edge of the tub, over his mother's shoulder. They carry her out of the small bathroom to the hall and nearly drop her, hear the thunk and splat of her on the wooden floor. He has never seen his sister naked, has never seen her lips so blue, her eyes so smogged.

Clarissa puts her ear to Ella's lips, shouts at Jax to call 911. "Tell them your address, her age, and that we have a drowning."

Jax doesn't want to leave his sister's side but something about Clarissa's calm, the way she is feeling at Ella's neck for a pulse, the way she has tipped back Ella's head, pinched her nose with her fingers, sucked in a huge breath and placed her mouth over Ella's own, tells him that she knows what to do and he—he has no idea—must do whatever she tells him to. He steps away, watching Clarissa's lips around Ella's, *blow, blow*. She crosses her hands, one over the other over Ella's naked chest, and uses all of her upper body to push down on the bony plate of it, counting between gritted teeth as she does so, *one, two, three* . . .

From his parents' bedside, he makes the call, surprised he can find his voice, surprised how calm he sounds even though he feels the bounce of his voice in his chest. *Yes, she's out of the water. No, she's not breathing.*

"I'm only nine," he says, though the question is never asked. But he is nine years old and he doesn't know what to do, thinks that this shouldn't be happening because he's *only nine*. The man asks if he is alone with her and he wants to say yes, yes because that is how he feels. He is very alone, but when he looks to the hallway and watches Clarissa, *blow, blow*, he is so grateful for her, so relieved to have her here, that he begins to cry. The tears are splashing down his face and he can only say that no, he is not alone, please hurry, and he hangs up the phone, thinking somehow that the same man who answered his call is the same man that must hang up now, must stop talking so that he can come to the house and save his sister.

Jax goes back to the hall, watches Ella's chest rise with each borrowed breath from Clarissa, sees through the bathroom door the slump of his mother over the tub, hears her sobs and they are animal noises to him. He steps around Ella, around the puddle from her hair, and goes into the bathroom where he pulls a towel from the rack to cover her. Clarissa is diving into Ella's chest again and counting, *sixteen, seventeen, eighteen . . .*

His mother isn't moving and her sobbing has stopped. She has turned her back to the tub, collapsed, draping the back of her head over the rim and gazing at the ceiling, unfocused, as if she is looking right through it. Her face is chalky and dark black smudges run down her cheeks. Her hair is stuck in the crease of her neck and her blouse is ripped so that he can see the white lace of her bra and angry claw marks rising on her chest and the tops of her breast.

Ella has begun to choke and Clarissa drops to her bottom beside her. "It worked," she says. "It really worked." She keeps her small hand to Ella's chest and Jax watches the rise and fall of it beneath her hand.

He shuts the bathroom door as he comes back to the hallway, leaving his mother behind, keeping her from Ella. Away from her.

Ella is choking and her breath rattles, but she doesn't sit up. Her eyes are still unfocused, her limbs still limp. Jax drapes the towel over her, stoops down to her side.

"I think my mom was trying to help her," he says.

"I think your mom was trying to kill her."

They can hear the sirens in the distance. "You can't tell anyone, Clarissa. You have to swear you won't tell." He wipes the snot and tears from his face with the edge of the towel he has draped on Ella. "Swear it!"

"I'll go," says Clarissa. "I won't tell anyone."

He believes her. He believes *in* her. "Is she going to live?" he asks her.

"She's breathing."

He doesn't want her to leave. He is afraid of his mother behind the door, the whimpering he hears at his back, the sirens that are screaming down his block.

"How did you know what to do?" he whispers. Clarissa is getting to her feet. She stops and looks at him, the first time she has taken her eyes from Ella's body.

"Tell them you read it in a book. Pinch the nose, blow, blow, and thirty chest compressions, repeat."

There is a fierce banging at the door. Jax jumps up and the two of them run down the steps, Clarissa veering off toward the den and Jax headed for the door. A small army of men flies up the stairs with Jax at their back where they find his mother in the hall, Ella's head in her lap, her hands tucking the towel around the edges of her small body.

His mother lifts her head to look at the men, confused, black streaks running down her face, her jaw hanging limp. Jax can't look at her, doesn't want her to see him looking at her, doesn't want her to know he knows.

He backs to his own bedroom and looks out the window to see Clarissa running down the sidewalk. Hard and fast, can even hear her feet slapping at the sidewalk. He imagines himself beside her, bound for anywhere but here.

Ella is in the hospital where she will stay at least one night. His mother is *resting*, his father tells the children. Don't disturb her. There was another seizure, he explains to all of them. But everything is fine now, just fine.

An hour earlier, he had taken Jax aside, congratulated him on his bravery, on knowing just what to do. The doctors, his father tells him, were quite impressed with Jax's quick thinking. Jax saved her life and he is a fine young man, very bright, to have administered CPR. Ella has a broken rib, but that is to be expected—not Jax's fault at all. He has done a remarkable thing. And just how did he know what to do?

Jax cannot look his father in the eye. "I read it somewhere," Jax says.

"Well, son, I'm very proud of you."

Jax knows he must tell his father what he saw, what he knows, but he can't dredge up the words. He twists on the sofa, cannot find a good place for his hands, and so he sits on them. But then he sees Clarissa in his mind's eye, sees the way she had known exactly what to do, had fearlessly done what she had never done before and never stopped to doubt herself. Focused, intent, calm. And so Jax sucks in a breath and lets it whistle out between his lips, takes another, and launches into what he saw, leaving out the fact that Clarissa was with him, not willing to implicate her.

His father tells Jax he is confused, misread the situation, surely he can't think this of his mother? She would never. She's devoted to Ella, as she is to each and every one of them. She is a fine mother, a good Christian woman, and Jax is lucky to count her as his own. And these seizures, they can be so difficult, so disturbing, so violent.

The strange catch in his father's voice draws Jax's eyes to him. Jax has nothing more to say. Is praying, in fact, that his father is right, but when he looks at his father's face, he sees the man's damp and glassy eyes and knows that what his father says and what his father now knows are at odds with one another.

Jax agrees. He is surely mistaken. He is the squirming witness—the only witness—and he must make his father believe that he will keep this secret, would never betray the family. "I was confused," Jax says. "Let's not tell them," he says, meaning his younger siblings. "Let's not tell them what I did, about the CPR and all." He blinks but keeps his eyes on his father now. "I was scared, Dad," and admitting this one truth is a relief to him. "I don't want to talk about it with them."

His father, too, looks relieved. "We won't speak of it," he says kindly. "It's between us, a private matter. We don't have to speak of it to anyone."

28

Lynetta

After dropping off Ella, Lynetta is headed home. But just as she is prepared to turn into the long weed-scraggled drive through the Beechwood campus, she imagines coming into the cottage alone, an entire evening ahead of her without Ella, without her chatter over dinner preparation, her insistence that ketchup goes with everything. No Ella digging in the silverware drawer to find the fork with the broken tine that she insists on using at every meal, no Ella bumping up against her in the bathroom, the two of them in their matching bathrobes, Ella pulling back her lips to ask Lynetta if her teeth are brushed enough.

Instead, she turns off her blinker and heads farther north on Reisterstown Road, turns left on Franklin to the tiny clapboard square of a house where her father lives. It is modest by any standards, but immaculate, the hedges shorn level within an inch of the two front window ledges, the concrete walk swept clean and lined with perfectly spaced daffodils, the tiny lawn so green that it all looks like a child's drawing.

Pap is at the door before she can even get out of the car, and even though he knew that this was the evening she had been dreading, knew that Ella would be away overnight, Lynetta can still see the small wash of disappointment on his face when she comes from the car without Ella.

He doesn't say anything, just pats her shoulder as she walks past him and in through the wide-open door. As neat and clean as the house is, there is a hint of stale grease in the air. Pap fries everything—fish, burgers, chicken—and Lynetta worries about his health and the way his belly rolls over his belt buckle. A frying pan is set on the stove and a package of ground beef and a bag of buns is on the counter.

"You eat yet?"

She shakes her head, no, and he unwraps the burger meat and quickly pats together two patties. She gets the pickle jar from the refrigerator, and he pulls a box of Kraft Macaroni & Cheese from the cupboard.

"Anything green around here to go with this?" She waves her hand over the counter.

"You got your pickles there," he says, pointing to the jar. Lynetta just smiles. "I had a salad for lunch," he says.

Lynetta knows his idea of a salad is iceberg lettuce piled with ham and turkey cubes and a glob of blue cheese dressing.

"Good for you," she says.

By the time they sit down to eat, the streetlights have flicked on and bathed the street in a warm glow. Lynetta can see Mrs. Fancher walking her ancient terrier down the sidewalk and the Foley family is calling in their fat tomcat. Ella always manages to find that cat in the shrubbery in front of Pap's house and spends most of their visit trying to coax it out of hiding. Sometimes Pap gives her a piece of hot dog and that usually does the trick. They are both watching the big gray animal pad down the walk and dart across the street.

"Going to get her that cat she's been begging for when you move?" he says.

"Thinking on it," she says. "Honestly, Pap, I'm not sure I can keep fighting them."

He puts his burger down and leans back in his chair. Waits.

She looks up at him, feels the sludge of feelings she has been trying to keep at bay. Fear, mostly. Fear that they *deserve* Ella, that perhaps it is not so unreasonable of them to want her back. "They're a nice family," she says. "They're not monsters. They're just a nice family."

"You met them?"

She nods.

"And?"

"She went right in hugging them. You know—how she does. And the house, it's something. And they're all so . . . so *pretty*. Even the men." She is thinking of how the family swarmed the foyer when she arrived, how Ella had hugged her mother, her father, and then immediately went to Jax and admonished him for not visiting. Lynetta had stood back at the entrance, Ella's bag in her hand, overwhelmed by the size of the foyer, its deep mahogany-paneled fireplace, the majestic sweep of the wide stairway, the thick oriental carpet, the way the collective voices floated to the high ceiling, and the warm and savory smells that drifted from the kitchen. She couldn't help but feel some resentment building. She wondered if they had worked hard for all they had or if it was the kind of thing that just seemed to accumulate for people like them.

Mrs. Jules had said, "Please come in, Lynetta. Meet our family." And in those words, *our family*, Lynetta had felt the rip of Ella from her, felt the empty space it left in her.

Pap picks up his burger, drags the edge of it against the rim of his plate to catch a blob of ketchup. "Her twin sister there?" he asks. "She look like her?"

"Belle, yes. She looks just like her—taller, thinner, but just like her. They're something, Pap." The Jules family had poured into the foyer and it had nearly taken Lynetta's breath away to see them all together. All that blond hair and blue eyes, their collective athleticism, the way they moved around one another, even the warm welcome they extended to Lynetta—*So nice to meet you, Lynetta*—and she couldn't help but wonder if she had walked into a Ralph Lauren photoshoot.

Many years earlier, Lynetta and Nira had taken Ella with them to see a Monet exhibit at the Baltimore Museum of Art. None of them had ever been to an art museum before, but when Lynetta and Ella had moved into the cottage, Nira had given them a large framed print of Monet's *Water*

Lilies, because, she said, it went with her sofa. Lynetta loved that picture and had since collected two more framed posters in what she understood to be a series and put one in Ella's room and one in her own. When she read in the Sunday edition of *The Sun* that an exhibit was coming to Baltimore, she invited Nira to go with them. They would have lunch in the museum restaurant afterward, and she even thought to make a reservation when she purchased their tickets.

The path to the exhibit required a long trek through the museum, down winding halls decorated with garden trellises and a mounted timeline of the artist's life. Ella trailed her hands down the trellises, and Lynetta found herself reminding her more than once that she would not be allowed to touch the paintings. Nira claimed to be starving, wishing their lunch reservations had been earlier so they could have eaten prior to the exhibit, and she complained of the stifling heat with so many people pressed up against one another, saying it was worse than when she saw Poison play at Hammerjacks nightclub last year. Lynetta had never been to a concert. In fact, she seldom went anywhere without Ella, and so this excursion was something she had been looking forward to. Nira's whining was beginning to grate on her. Nevertheless, Lynetta was glad to have her along. Lynetta was seeing a lot less of her friend in the last year as Nira had enrolled in nursing school at Towson State and only worked an occasional weekend shift, stopping by the cottage afterward to chat, paint Ella's fingers and toes, and regale Lynetta with stories about her classmates. She was just a tiny bit jealous that Nira had an opportunity that would never be afforded Lynetta, given her commitment to Ella, but she was happy for her friend and loved to hear about Nira practicing giving injections on oranges and hot dogs.

"Oh, my goodness," Lynetta said aloud when they finally stepped into the exhibit and fanned out from the crowd, the air suddenly cooling around them. Even Nira took a breath and said, "Wow, these would look great in your house, Lynetta."

Each piece in its ornate frame seemed to be winking at her. Every painting was lovely on its own—the waves of burnished gold fields, the gossamer of white dresses, the sway of green willow, but most startling of all were the blues of sky and water, the clear cool color of it beneath drifting clouds and sun-swept coasts, the light and dark of it beneath stiller waters. Stepping up to each painting, tempted to lean across the velvet ropes, Lynetta felt the movement of each piece, was struck by the contrast of pale and bright. But when she scanned the room, took everything in collectively, the beauty of it all both lifted her heart and made her feel small, even dull, at the same time. And the collision of these two feelings drew up the strange possibility of tears. Square to a painting of a woman with a swath of fabric on her lap, a small child at her feet—the woman looked to be sewing—Lynetta thought fleetingly of her baby, of Becky, back years ago to the child she lost and everything she lost with her.

Lynetta lifted her hand to Ella's shoulder, pulled her back gently from where she pressed against the ropes in a way that tipped the stanchions, threatening to topple everything. "Remember, no touching. We have to stay behind these here ropes."

Ella turned to her then, her blue eyes behind her glasses as bright as Monet's sky. "I like these," she said. "Can we get one, Nettie?"

Ella in her pink sweater with that yellow hair and those sparkly eyes (and perhaps because Lynetta's eyes were swimming with tears) wavered beside her as if Ella had stepped out of the painting itself.

"We can stop in the gift shop later," Lynetta said. She put her arm around Ella and nudged her to the next painting in the exhibit. For the rest of the exhibit, Lynetta did her best to focus on only one painting at a time, stopping in front of each one to admire the tangle of light and color, the abstraction of the subjects that allowed her to bring something of herself to each painting. But she didn't cast her eyes around the room, refused to take in the exhibit as a whole. It was too much, made her too aware of how she fit into it all—or didn't.

It was like that in the foyer of the Jules home, drawing up the same emotions she had felt that day eighteen years ago at the museum, all the pretty paintings, all the pretty people swirling around her, welcoming Ella, and Lynetta had been so struck by the sight of them all that she couldn't help but know her own drabness, her own inability to glow against the backdrop of this family. And what was worse was that they were reclaiming a precious piece of something that Lynetta had thought of as her own.

"What's your lawyer got to say about all this?" says Pap.

Lynetta has lost her appetite and slides her plate away. "It could go to court, and I don't think I can afford that." Already the retainer had eaten into her savings. Lynetta is frugal, has lived rent-free for years and banks the greater portion of her paychecks, living mostly off the pin money she makes doing piecework for Mr. Goldman. Her savings are considerable for a woman approaching fifty with no formal education. She knows she has been lucky. But she paid cash for her double-wide at the beach and she would need a new car in another year. She might be able to pick up a service job at the beach during the season—Wally had hinted at the possibility that he could staff Lynetta and Ella together at one of the booths—but there would be health and homeowner's insurance, the cost of trips home to see Pap, the monthly HOA fees in the park. All of these things she has accounted for. But even with the small disability checks that will help cover some of Ella's ongoing expenses, she can't take on the burden of going to court and the fees associated with it.

Pap stacks her plate on top of his and takes them to the sink, scraping away the remains of Lynetta's burger into the disposal. Overhead, he digs in the cupboard for a package of vanilla wafers and hefts the box to her, asking if she wants one, but she declines. He comes back with the box anyway and sets it on the table between the two of them.

"Did you try talking to them?"

No. Her lawyer told her not to, she tells him. The idea of losing Ella weighs on Pap as well. She can see it in his face. She knows he wants to tell her that everything will be fine, but his own fear is getting in the way. Ella is as close as the man will ever come to having a grandchild. He carries a picture of her in his wallet and there is a framed photo of the three of them over the mantel. Lynetta doesn't know if he shows the wallet picture to anyone or how he explains his relationship to her if he does. She imagines he calls her *my daughter's girl*. She'd overheard that once when she and Ella had picked him up after a routine colonoscopy.

The nurse had wheeled him out to the curb and they were waiting as she and Ella pulled up. Lynetta got out of the car to open the back door. "Well, there she is," she heard him say to the nurse. "There's my daughter and her girl."

"It would be foolish on my part to let this get to a court. It could wipe me out."

"How much we talking here?"

"Thousands, Pap. And I know what you're thinking." She looks him square in the eyes. "No. I'm not letting you go into your savings."

"Now this is where you cut off your nose to spite your face, Lynetta. Don't be that way. That girl means something to me, too. She's family. We're family. And this is what family does."

Lynetta doesn't know what to say.

"How much has this cost you so far?"

"Two thousand to file the paperwork the first time—when I applied for guardianship. But ten thousand for the retainer for the lawyer once they filed against me, and she told me that won't cover court costs if we end up there."

"What do you figure something like that costs?"

Lynetta isn't sure. Her lawyer won't put a price on it. But Lynetta has checked around. Mr. Goldman said it ran his son near fifty thousand dollars to fight his wife over their three kids. And Nira's cousin is sitting on thirty thousand in credit card debt fighting for custody of her young boys—and she lost.

Pap lets loose with a long whistle. "Jeez," he says.

"And sometimes," she says, "there are appeals." She drops her head to her hands. Rubs her fingers over her temples. "This could wipe me out."

Pap had spent his whole life working the line at the Solo Cup factory. The wages were fair and there was a pension that was adequate, but she knew he didn't have deep pockets. He was seventy-two years old and could live another twenty years (if he would stop frying his way through his meals). She would never forgive herself if she wiped out his pension and then lost Ella in the end.

"What are our chances if we go to court?"

Lynetta shrugs. Her attorney wouldn't say. Says it doesn't work that way, and lawyers don't bet on trials. They go in well prepared and playing their A-game. That's how it works.

"Right now," Lynetta says, "I'm just wondering how she's doing, you know? She's never been without me. And they don't know things about her."

"Nobody knows her like you do."

Lynetta gives a small laugh. "They don't know you got to watch her brush her teeth or she'll just wet the toothbrush and say she did it. And they don't know you can't leave medications lying around—not even aspirin—'cause she'll take it, and that's something I should of told them about," she says, suddenly worried and drawing her hand into her lap. "And she's not afraid to cut her own hair, neither." She gives Pap a weak smile. They both can recall the time she got hold of the nail scissors and had a go at it that resulted in a trip to the beauty parlor and new bangs. "She hates baths—has to be a shower, and she likes to sleep with socks on," Lynetta says. "Her feet are always cold."

Lynetta gets up from the table and goes to the sink.

"I can do that, honey," he says.

"No, you sit. I got this." She tosses the macaroni box in the trash, stows the pickles in the refrigerator, and turns back to the sink where she soaps a sponge.

There is quiet between them, just the running of the water, the sounds of cars going down the street, the trail of headlights over the kitchen walls. She flicks on the overhead light and the sink and counter come into stark focus. Next to the sink is a small white dish, shaped like a turtle on its back, the belly scooped to hold rings—her mother's rings. It's been beside the sink as far back as Lynetta can remember. Her mother always dropped her modest rings in the dish before she did the dishes or dug her hands into raw ground beef to make the Sunday meatloaf. It's been empty now for decades. Likewise, the empty cookie jar shaped like a circus tent, and when she pulls out the drawer to stow the flatware, her mother's favorite hair barrette—shaped like a butterfly and sprung open—rests in one of the dividers. Lynetta is certain her father has wiped out this drawer a hundred times, but always he has put that old clip right back in its place. All these pieces of her long-gone mother, everything empty, their only purpose to remind her and Pap of something missing.

She hears the squeak of Pap's chair across the linoleum. He doesn't get up, just turns his chair to where she stands at the sink.

"I shouldn't have to say this, but I'm gonna do it anyways," he says. "If I thought you were doing this because you wanted what was best for you and not what was best for the girl, I wouldn't get behind it. But I know you, Lynetta, and this is about what's best for her. It's fine to sit and stew in our own sorrow—Lord knows I sat in heaps of it when your mother passed, but truth was, I was praying for her to pass in the end."

Lynetta stops what she is doing at the sink and turns completely to him, leans her backside against the sink.

"Because I stopped praying for what was best for me and started praying for what was best for her," he says, as if she may have misunderstood.

She hardly remembers how it was at the end with her mother, only remembers the aloneness of it all. Her father wouldn't let her go to the hospital to see her mother and she spent the days at Mrs. Fancher's across the street so that her father could be at the hospital. He never told her that her mother wasn't coming home, but Mrs. Fancher's long sighs, her habit in the last days of walking past her and cooing *poor child, poor dear child*, told Lynetta everything she didn't want to know. Pap looks down at his hands that are fidgeting in his broad lap, blinks, and looks back to her.

"The pain got so bad for her in the end, Lynetta—" He runs a thick hand over his chest. "I knew we was well past a miracle and I just wanted it to end for her. I wanted what was best for her. And it's like that with Ella. Sure, you'd be lonely without her, but I know you. You want this because you know she'd be better with you than with them."

"Do I?" Sometimes she isn't sure. Sometimes she thinks she is being selfish and maybe Ella really would be happier in her family's beautiful home with her brothers and sisters visiting, big family holidays, fancy dinners.

"Sure you do," he says. "I know you. You'd do anything for that girl."

He has no idea, she is thinking, how far she would go, has gone, how she's capable of the unthinkable when it comes to Ella. And even though she knows now just what she is capable of, even though she tells herself she only did what she did for Ella, she can't help but ask herself if it was to protect Ella or if it was vengeance. "I'm not as good as you think I am," she says. She feels the possibility of a confession rising and seals her lips, swallows, and tries not to choke.

"Look at how that girl was when she first come in—the seizures you told me about, hardly talking, the way she used to hit and claw at everybody, nobody knowing she needed glasses? You got to wonder what made her that way, and you got to wonder just why it is all that changed."

"She still gets angry sometimes." Lynetta is thinking of just last week when Ella had slammed the bathroom door when Lynetta told her that she had to get back in the shower and do a better job rinsing the soap out of her hair.

"Don't we all? But she ain't hitting on anybody. She ain't screaming her lungs out like you say she used to do. That's all to your credit, Lynetta."

Lynetta has to admit that the child who came to Beechwood thirty-two years ago was not the same woman Ella is now. They all came in afraid—no matter their ages—and there was always a period of adjustment before the routine took hold. Some came in acting out and some came in and immediately shut down, pulled into themselves like a slug with salt poured on it. But Ella had come in more like a hibernating bear cub poked with a stick, growling, snapping, and the seizures . . .

It was a long time ago, but Lynetta has never forgotten the seizures that wracked Ella's small body. The letting loose of her bowels or bladder, and what was worse was the attempts to bathe her after the bad ones. It often took two, three aides to wrap her in a short restraining jacket and submerge her in a tub, and the whole time she would be screaming like an animal caught in a trap. Her breathing coming so fast and hard that she risked throwing herself into a second seizure, her feet kicking so fierce she bruised the backs of her heels, once even bursting a vessel in her eye so that the eye was blood-red and angry for days. But eventually, within a matter of two months or less, the seizures mysteriously stopped.

Lynetta thinks back on it now, can't quite reconcile the two versions of Ella. Baths were scheduled weekly, but the fight never went out of Ella when it came to bathing. Eventually, Lynetta started taking her over to the dormitory wing for the older girls and women on bath night and found that a shower was more manageable.

Even now, when Lynetta takes a rare bath of her own, Ella insists she leaves the door open and parks herself on her bottom in the hallway and jabbers at Lynetta the entire time. "You finished? All done?" she asks incessantly until Lynetta finally gives up on the idea of soaking her tired muscles altogether and announces that yes, yes indeed that had been some relaxing bath with Ella hovering at the door. The sarcasm is lost on Ella. Ella will allow Lynetta the time it takes to wrap herself in a towel and drain the water from the tub before popping in through the open door and—more often than not—wrapping her arms around Lynetta and telling her she—meaning Lynetta—is all better now.

Lynetta turns again to the sink. She is thinking back on those early days when Ella came in and Lynetta was new to her job. She'd been so young and naive back then, having dropped out of school when she found herself pregnant and securing her job at Beechwood with a promise to get her GED in the next few months. She hadn't told them she was pregnant, afraid they wouldn't hire her if they knew.

After a couple of months at Beechwood, there had been a shift in Ella. It was small at first. She was still sticking things in her mouth at every opportunity and for a time had been misdiagnosed as having pica, but so long as there was an aide near her, she was not only less agitated but she was also more awake, alert to the things going on around her, watching, quietly most of the time, sliding behind an aide when there was commotion on the floor, following Lynetta—mostly—around the dayroom and sometimes slipping her small hand into Lynetta's. Ella moved awkwardly, stumbling now and then, but overall there was a new fluidity in the way she carried herself. Her face was no longer scrunched in fear and as it relaxed, as the creases eased around her eyes and mouth, it dawned on them all that she was a pretty child. This won her some favor and extra attention from the staff. With so much ugliness, so much disfigurement around them, it was a relief to look at something lovely. Of course, no one would say it aloud, because, with the exception of a few, the staff was as kind as time allowed given the ratio of staff to patients. But there were always those who found it satisfying to be cruel. Peggy, for instance, had a tendency to slap a patient who gave her too much sass, and Lou was far too rough in moving patients from wheelchair to bed, once tossing John-John so hard he rolled across the bed and landed with a *thud* on the floor on the other side. Tyson was always the first to order restraints, and Joeline took perverse pleasure in saying nasty words to Rose all the while smiling at her so that deaf Rose mistook it as kindness when Joeline called her a jungle monkey. But Ella. Ella had slid into their graces, and it made a difference for her.

Lynetta wipes down the once-white Formica counter, scrubbing out of habit at an old scorch mark from the time Pap set a hot frying pan on the counter. In fact, the counter is scarred and yellowed its entire length. A huge purple-blue stain flowers from where she had set a leaking basket of blueberries over forty years ago, and when she lifts the coffeemaker to wipe beneath it, she knows it is futile to try and scrub away the browning stain beneath it.

It is hard to account for the child who came into Beechwood and the young woman Lynetta now considers fairly competent—fidgety, liable to put her hands where they don't belong, deathly afraid of bugs and baths and even some men, though not all (and she knows damn well where that fear came from). There had been a feral quality about Ella when she first arrived and that was all but gone now.

"You know," she says, coming to the table now and settling in again across from her father, "sometimes I do wonder what went on in that house before Ella came to us. She was neat and clean as a pin, and so attached to her mother, so it stands to reason she was well cared for." Lynetta remembers now how she had watched Ella that first day, curling in her mother's lap but reaching out to her father and patting his leg, and he had placed his big hand over her small one. "Doesn't really make sense, does it? Almost like she was drugged up on something."

New patients were always given a little something to calm them before they came in, and maybe that accounted for her grogginess, but it didn't account for the way she stumbled over her words at first—the few she had—and then the huge leap in her vocabulary after only a few months at Beechwood. It didn't account for the first weeks where she was groggy and unsteady, slapping at the aides who fussed with her, and then, over time, growing calmer and more observant, more eager to join in with other children or try to answer the questions asked of her.

Lynetta has access to all of Ella's medical records, though she knows they aren't completely accurate and make no mention of what happened with Brody or the time nine-year-old Ella got hold of medications that had been left carelessly on a nursing tray when a fight broke out and the nurse had abandoned the tray on top of the radiator. The incident had required a heavy dose of syrup of ipecac and resulted in Ella vomiting up torrents of breakfast over a bedpan with Lynetta holding her hair back and wiping her mouth and tearing eyes. *That* had never made it into her medical records. She had read Ella's intake records years ago when she and Ella had first moved into the cottage, and they included a brief history provided by the family and the family pediatrician. She couldn't recall anything alarming, but perhaps it is time to take another look. All the records had been put on microfilm in the last years, but Lynetta had thought to hold on to Ella's paper files and spirited them away to her cottage.

She doesn't expect to learn anything new but only wants to look them over and marvel at how much has changed, remind herself again that she has done right by Ella.

29
Ella

Ella is seated at the table and trying to remember not to kick her legs. She doesn't know why she is inclined to do so, but there is a twitching in her calves that she can't get loose of. She is anxious to show her mother the way she folds her hands in prayer, but when Dadda tells them to bow their heads for the grace—and she claps her hands together eagerly—she is surprised when her mother next to her on her left peels her clasped hands apart, taking one into her own hand, and Finney on her right beside her reaches out for the other.

"Heavenly Father, it is by your grace that we are all gathered here this evening with our dear Ella . . ."

At the mention of her own name, Ella kicks once and connects just slightly with Belle's legs across from her. Belle's eyes fly open and immediately shut again.

"Sorry," says Ella.

"We are no stranger to your many blessings. We humbly ask that as we welcome her to our family table that You, Lord, continue to watch over her. Bless us, O Lord, and these Thy gifts, which we are about to receive from Thy bounty, through Christ our Lord. Amen."

"I said sorry," she says, on the heels of a round of *amen*s.

"For what?" says her mother.

"I kicked Belle, sorry."

"It's fine, Ella—no worries," says Belle.

Ella looks at Belle and sees herself. It's all so confusing. Belle's shirt is spangly and catches the light when she moves or shifts herself at the table. She is the brightest one at the table and Ella cannot stop staring at her. She remembers Belle, remembers the way she smells—like something both sweet and salty. When Ella had hugged Belle earlier in the evening, she had smelled different at first, but then, underneath it all, Ella smelled the Belle she remembered and it made her feel warm in her face and slowed her breath, as if the scent had been waiting for her. She thinks maybe it is Belle she has been talking to all these years, serving her pancakes or brownies in the playhouse, curling up to hallway whispers of *good night, Ella* in the last moments before she drifts off to sleep, lying in the grass with Belle and holding hands under a swimmy sky. Belle has always been with her even though no one would ever know because Belle is the other half of herself. It hurts inside of her somewhere to look at Belle now, as if she has stumbled across something she was missing and it isn't quite how she remembered it. It isn't a disappointment—but no longer fits in the hole its disappearance had left.

The food on her plate is strange to her. There are red raisins in the salad and she does not eat raisins. She doesn't eat nuts, either, and she is pretty sure the pale half-moon slivers she has pushed to the side of her plate are nuts. The potatoes are different, too, small like stones, and Nettie's potatoes are big and fat with loads of butter and sour cream. When she goes to cut one of them in half, it shoots off of her plate and she grabs it with her hand, drops it back to her plate.

Her mother makes a startled sound and her shoulders rise up but then relax again. "How's the lamb?" her mother says to everyone at the table and they all chime in as to how good it is—*wonderful, delicious*—and it occurs to Ella that lamb is the name of this meat on her plate. Just how could that be? A lamb is a baby. Ella knows this for a fact, and no one eats babies. She thinks she might cry but stops herself, covers the meat with her salad greens instead, and tries not to look around the table as everyone forks the meat—*so tender!*—into their mouths. She thinks of bunnies and baby chicks and feels the tears start to build.

"Ella?" It is Finney and he has put his fork down to his plate and is leaning into her ear. The tears are just now starting to run down her face, and she drops her chin to her chest, won't look at any of them.

Finney whispers, "I don't eat meat either, Ella. It's okay."

Her voice bounces in her chest and she asks again, "When is Nettie coming back?"

There is a long quiet and then the voices start up again around the table.

Ella tries to turn them off the same way she does when forced to eat in the dining room at Beechwood. The difference here is that they are not so sharp—no screaming, no random chirping sounds from Paulette who can't say words but squawks and chirps when she's excited, no bang-slapping of hands on the table like TJ does when he waits for his tray. And this place does not echo so that all the sounds linger too long. She doesn't think anyone here will fight and throw food. But she has an eye on George, notices the way he sits closer to his plate than the others, notices the way his fork and knife clink a little harder on his plate. His voice when he talks goes up and down too quickly.

Sometimes the voices are soft. Tess has a giggle that sounds a little like music. Everyone is very proud of Jax because he wrote a story. Ella wonders if he will read it to her.

The baby is a doctor for mostly babies. Ella doesn't like doctors, but she likes Finney. It is funny to her that the baby takes care of babies and she laughs out loud while everyone is talking. This makes George look at her very hard, and she stops herself, goes back to rolling her peas on her plate with the tip of her finger. She doesn't like peas, either. They make her gag. Lynetta says Ella can have only one *gag food*—there is only allowed to be one food that she doesn't have to eat because it makes her gag. Lynetta says she can't keep changing her mind. Peas, green beans, broccoli—pick one and stick to it, Lynetta says. Ella is pretty sure she will stick with peas.

Jax's friend Clarissa is not good at hugging. But Ella already knows this about her. Clarissa has come with her mother, Mrs. Morgenfrier, and when Clarissa says, "This is my mother, Ella, Mary Morgenfrier," Ella hugs her as well. Mrs. Morgenfrier hugs better than Clarissa and says *God bless you, honey* in a whimpery voice in Ella's ear.

"She knew you when you were a little girl and you lived here," says Clarissa. Ella doesn't know what to say about that because she doesn't remember very much—if anything—about living here. She can remember a *feeling* about living here and it confuses her. It is something like when she had the flu last year and she wanted to be out of bed because there was sunshine pouring in her bedroom window and she could smell sweet waffles and bacon frying—maybe her favorite breakfast thing—downstairs, but her muscles ached and her head felt too big on her neck, and she really didn't want anything in her stomach anyway, though she liked the *thought* of it. She wanted to be different and fit into the rising day, but she couldn't. And that is just how being in this house right now makes her feel—like she should fit into it the way her brothers and sisters do, but she can't.

The wind has come up and Mama is sorry that they can't have pie and ice cream on the patio. She is telling this to the aunts. Ella doesn't remember them, either, but she hugs them just the same. They look exactly alike. There is no way to tell them apart, though one wears a long silky scarf that feels like a whisper against Ella's cheek when she hugs her and the other has sparkly earrings that match Belle's shirt. But she can't keep their names straight and remember which one goes to which aunt. They are so happy to see her, and one of them, the one with the sparkly earrings, keeps her arm over Ella's shoulders when she says, "How are you, dear? It's so good to see you," and "Welcome home," which also confuses Ella because this isn't home at all.

The aunts stand beside Ella and hold their phones out in front of them. "Let's get a picture!" they say. They show the pictures to Ella. Lynetta's phone is different and flips open like a little compact, and Lynetta takes pictures with a real camera.

"Do you know where Nettie is?" Ella asks one of the aunts. They are in the kitchen, and Mama is pulling warm pies from the oven.

This aunt looks at her, blinks, pushes her lips together, and looks away, her eyes going around the room, skimming over all the people, Mama, the other aunt, and Belle, Finney sitting at the table, Tess standing against the doorway.

The aunt doesn't answer her. Through the kitchen window, Ella sees George on the patio, walking, walking, back and forth. Beyond him is a little house, bigger than her playhouse back at home that Pap built, but small enough that Ella imagines it is for playing. George is on his phone and he holds it against his ear and uses the heel of his other hand to smack-smack against his forehead. No one else notices when he shoves the phone deep in his pants pocket and comes down so hard in the little chair that it wobbles. Ella watches him lean back and look up to the sky and then, with his elbows planted to his knees, drop his heavy head to his hands. The tips of the branches overhead bow down around him as if they are trying to touch him. As if they have something to tell him.

Ella watches him rise out of his chair as if there is a great weight on his shoulders that he is trying to throw off. When he comes into the kitchen there is a mixed-up look on his face, sad and angry and it is twisting his mouth into a knot.

Mama notices right away. "What's wrong, George?" and when he doesn't answer, just slides his hand across his mouth as if he is working out that knot in it, she asks again. "Georgie?"

Ella doesn't want to know what is wrong with George. She knows that it is bad. It is always bad when everyone stands around gasping and fidgeting with their hands, not knowing what to do. It was like this with Brody and that was very bad. When people say things like *What happened?* and *Oh, my God!* it is never a good thing, and even if they say later *It's going to be okay,* it never is.

Dadda and Jax come to the kitchen, too, and Ella doesn't want to watch. There is something wrong with someone called Tammy and Ella doesn't know who that is. She wishes Nettie was here. She doesn't know who to hide behind because hiding is the safest thing to do when something bad is happening, like when Miss Joeline slapped Rose and Rose threw her tray at her and Nira had to strap Rose down and give her quiet medicine that made her eyes roll in her head and put her in a room by herself for a whole day even though Nira said it was Miss Joeline who should have been tied up instead but that's not the way the world works, *sorry to say.*

There are too many people in this kitchen. Clarissa is holding on to her own mother's arm and pulls her back every time she tries to move toward George. Mama is hugging George and he has his arms tucked under hers and Mama's arms are up over his shoulders.

"Where are the girls?" says Mama, and George tells her they are staying with Carmen but that he needs to get back home. They must be confused, he says. He needs to tell them that their mother will be fine. Ella watches everyone's eyes poke around the room, sees the way Jax and Belle look at each other with sad faces, sees the way Mama looks up to Dadda over George's shoulders and says everything will be fine and the way Dadda nods like this is a true thing.

"Goddammit," George says suddenly, pulling his face up from Mama's shoulder. "Goddammit!" Ella sees Mama flinch, but she holds on to him anyway until he turns away from her and wipes his sleeve across his face. "I told her. I told her she was killing herself."

Finney has been quiet but stands now at the table where he had been sitting.

"George," he says, and everyone hushes, ready to listen to what Finney has to say. He says they need to move the Tammy person some-where and he can help with that, but George is saying no, is shaking his head back and forth. "No, no, no," he says. "I can't put her in a place like that." Ella feels pricked by his eyes when he says this, when he looks at her and then away.

Then everyone is talking at once, everyone trying to tell George things he must not want to hear and things Ella doesn't understand. She can see the big playhouse out back and thinks she would like to be in it, away from all of this, away from whatever is happening that feels bad even though everyone says it will be okay.

No one sees her slip out of the house. She can hear music coming from the playhouse and she likes music. When she goes through the door she cannot believe how *real* it all is. To her right upon entering is a short length of countertop followed by a sink that turns on when Ella swivels the arm of it, a refrigerator that makes just the right sucking sound when she opens it, and a stove with burners that do not light but *click-click-click* better than the one Pap built for her.

She doesn't like the music playing but when she goes to touch the buttons that blink along the front of the CD player, she can't make the little drawer slide open the way it does at home with Nettie. The music stops and there is only a static sound that she cannot turn off.

"Ella!" It is Belle in the doorway. "We've been looking all over for you."

"I right here."

Ella can't tell if Belle is mad at her or not, but she watches her shoulders relax as she stands leaning in the doorway. No, she isn't mad. She is maybe even happy to see her. "You look like me," Ella says. "Do you have a boyfriend?"

"I'm married, Ella." Belle flicks on the light switch on the wall next to the door and it sparks under her fingers. "My husband's name is Ben." There is a soft look in her eyes as she says this and then asks, "Do *you* have a boyfriend, Ella?" Belle notices the water running in the sink and turns off the spigot before turning back to Ella.

The question embarrasses Ella because there is a boy she likes, a man really, but a little bit more like a boy in the same way she herself is a little bit more like a girl. His name is Elmett, and he works at the Dairy Queen in Ocean City. He had asked Ella if she could be his girlfriend, but Nettie said no, said they could be friends instead, just friends. You have to be friends first, Nettie had said. Then, maybe someday he can be your boyfriend. But not yet. "For the love of God," Nettie had said. "I did not bargain for this." But she said it was okay if Elmett came over to watch *Dancing with the Stars*, so long as he promised to stop trying to show off his own dance moves while they are trying to watch the program.

"You do!" Belle says.

Ella is blushing, can feel the heat rise in her neck. "Nettie says we can only be friends but he's my boyfriend anyway."

"Ooohh, a secret boyfriend. Well, Nettie sounds like a smart lady.

She's right, you know. It's always better to be friends first. Is he nice to you?"

Ella nods, and they stare at one another.

"I've missed you, Ella." When she says this Ella can see her eyes get damp and sparkly. Belle puts her hand to her chest, makes a tapping sound with it as if she is tucking something down. "Ella? Do you want to come back and live here?"

Ella shakes her head back and forth. No, she doesn't want to live here where she can't find Nettie and she can't see her friend Elmett and she can't call Maisy on the phone and sing songs to her and make her laugh. No.

Mama's voice is calling. It is being swept up into the breezy damp dusk, drifting past the open door. Belle sticks her head out the door. "I found her," she calls. "We'll be right in." Turning back to Ella, she holds out both of her hands. When Ella doesn't move, she walks toward her, takes her hands and holds them, running her thumbs over the tops of Ella's own. Ella looks down at the tangle of hands and can't tell her own from Belle's. Their nails are short and clean, the nail beds extraordinarily long, the fingers tapering between knuckles in the same identical way. Ella can feel with her thumb the clumps of rings on Belle's fingers, a chunky blue stone on one and a wide gold band and the mound of a diamond on the other.

Ella releases one of Belle's hands to push her glasses up her nose. They are smudged from her fingers, from the buttered peas and the pota- toes and she can't see Belle's face as clearly as she would like. But still, it is like looking in a fogged mirror and she recognizes herself. There are differences, the delicate arch of Belle's brows, the longer drape of her hair on her shoulders. But they are the same person, or two halves of the same person, and holding on to Belle's hand is like holding on to her whole self.

Belle takes the glasses from Ella's hand, holds them up to the light, and squints. She grabs a tea towel from the counter and polishes the glasses, slides them back on Ella's face, and smiles at her. "Better?"

"You don't got glasses and I do."

Belle doesn't answer her, just cocks her head and looks again at Ella, and this time Belle is snapped into focus. "We can share them if you want," says Ella. "They will help you see letters better."

Belle laughs. "I'm fine, Ella, but thank you."

"You welcome."

Belle is making her way to the stereo system to turn down the static when Ella slips past her and out the door. Belle stops in her tracks and turns to follow, flipping off the light switch next to the door and closing it behind her. She catches up with Ella on the walkway along the shrubs that Ella runs her hands along, watches her stop at a spotted laurel shrub and pluck a hard red berry from it and pop it in her mouth.

"Ella—don't eat that!" Ella obediently opens her mouth, the berry resting on her tongue behind her bottom teeth. Ella waits as if she is expecting Belle to reach into her mouth and take it. But when Belle only says again to spit it out, Ella obliges and the berry rolls over her lip and lands on the pavers.

30

George

George is seated at the kitchen table. His mother has made another pot of coffee, this time fully caffeinated, and is insisting George have a cup before he gets on the road. She is packing up leftovers for him to take along, and when she asks if he thinks he will be able to bring anything to Tammy—and then realizes her mistake—George tries not to glare at her and looks instead to Finney who is explaining just what can be expected in the next few days. They'll need to assess the damage to her heart. And if her BMI is below fifteen, and Finney assumes it is, she runs the risk of having developed myocardial atrophy. And there is the mitral valve prolapse that affects the plumbing of the heart. Some parts of the heart can heal, he tells George, and some can be treated with medications. He is explaining to George that it is not a heart attack that the girls witnessed, but that her heart was taxed by her condition. And, it sounds like, her lungs are stressed as well. There's a lot of cellular damage to organs when the body is undernourished. But she is where she needs to be right now and will likely be moved to an inpatient program in a few days. He should insist upon it, in fact.

"I'm worried about the girls, about what they saw," says George.

Jax and Tess have corralled the other guests and brought them to the living room. But Aunt Fiona keeps wandering into the kitchen, asking if she can help with anything, lingering beside his mother at the counter. "Maybe we should go," George hears her say to his mother at the counter. But his mother says *no, no, no, please stay*, and Aunt Fiona asks again if there is anything she can do to help.

Ella had disappeared earlier and sent his mother into a panic, and George wasn't at all surprised by the way everyone had immediately dispersed from the act of comforting him to wander the house and shout down the halls for her. *Ella? Ella? Where are you?* No, he wasn't surprised at all that his own pain was eclipsed by Ella's meandering.

"Carmen, that's her friend, says the girls called her from Tammy's phone when they couldn't reach me. Thank God she called an ambulance right away. The girls found her in the basement, propped up against the bathroom wall, bloody vomit all over the goddamn place."

Finney looks at him and nods and George wonders if this is the way he listens to his patients, chin down, making a low hum in his throat to acknowledge what they say.

"Conscious," Finney confirms. "That's important."

"Carmen says she was confused, but yeah. I think she uses the bathroom in the basement to, you know . . ." He flicks his hands in the air and leans back harder in his chair. "You know, throw up her food."

"How long has this been going on?" his father asks.

"Years, Dad. Years and years."

"Why didn't you say something? We could have helped."

George knows that's not true. No one could have helped.

He can see Ella through the window now, coming into the spill of patio light with Belle. He hasn't thought of them as twins in a long time—if ever, but here they are, identical in the glow of light except for the shorter stature and slighter thickness of Ella, the merest tipping side to side in her walk compared to that of Belle. But both of them walk with their toes slightly turned out, as do all of the Jules children, and both have a way of lassoing their hair off their shoulders when the breeze whips it in their faces and running the length of it through their hands.

"My goodness, Ella, you gave us a scare," says his mother when they come in the back door.

"I not scare nobody," Ella says softly, looking to Belle as she says this.

"We didn't know where you were!"

"I right here," she says. "With Belle." She breaks into a wide smile that Belle mirrors as she puts her arm around Ella's waist. "I like your playhouse," Ella says over her shoulder as Belle leads her away to the living room. "And I spit out the berry."

"Jesus," says George. "You're going to need a tracking device on her." He pushes back in his chair and drops his hands to his lap.

"She seems very sweet," says Aunt Fiona. "It's amazing, really, how different she is from what I recall."

"I'm sure she's on her best behavior," George says. "But don't piss her off."

No one says anything for a long minute. George looks from one to the other of them, waiting for someone to say something, someone to acknowledge what he is sure they know, that she is a time bomb. Instead, he feels the collective pulling away of each of them, even Finney, who looks out the window when George tries to catch his eye and draw him in.

"I can't believe you don't remember what she's like," he says.

"Things were different then," his mother says. She is snapping lids on Tupperware containers.

"Yeah—she was smaller then. You could fight her off. Good luck with that now." He turns to his mother. "For Chrissakes, Mom, you know what she's like. She's a fucking monster!"

"Stop this, George," she snaps. "Stop. I know you're upset but I don't like when you talk this way."

"Son, get ahold of yourself. This is not the time."

"When would be a good time, Dad? When she slams a door on your fingers? When she shoves Mom down the steps? When she bites the mailman like a damn dog?"

"Keep your voice down," says his father. And at the same time, his mother levels a stare at him. "Stop it now," she says through clenched teeth. "For the love of all that's holy, she's not an animal! She's your sister!"

"I mean it, George," says his father. "This stops now."

George knows he has gone too far. He does his best to stuff his anger down his throat, as instructed, and it is bitter. When he swallows he could swear he feels the pressure of it going down and the gaseous heat of it all expanding in his chest. But he can't hold it down. "What about her seizures?" he asks.

"She has a seizure condition?" Finney asks. "Epilepsy?"

"How are you going to deal with that?" says George.

His mother is pulling a small cooler from the butler's pantry and stacking the leftovers in it. She keeps her back to them when she tells them the seizures stopped a long time ago.

"Is she on medication?" Finney wants to know.

Hillary comes to the table, sets the cooler on the table in front of George, and places a hand on his shoulder. "I packed some pie for the girls. I know Amanda loves that cherry pie from the Amish market. And there's extra dressing for the salad. There's an ice pack in there, but be sure to get it all in the refrigerator when you get home. Will you pick up the girls tonight from your friend Carmen's house?"

George pats her hand on his shoulder, holds it there. He is still angry but wants her near him and it is a conundrum to him, how he can be simultaneously irritated with her and want her by his side. He knows she has forgiven him. It's a curious thing to him, that she could have snapped at him moments before and then move on as if nothing has happened.

"Try not to be so angry, Georgie," she says. "It's never done you any good."

He doesn't want her to move, wants the feel of her at his back to linger. Still holding her hand, he turns to her and takes both her hands in his and looks up at her earnestly.

The skin on her neck is looser than he recalls, three distinct creases coiled around it. Her lips, too, are thinner, stretched taut when she looks at him, gathering her thoughts and holding them back at the same time. She is still a woman who turns heads, but George wonders if a stranger, meeting her for the first time, would say so or if their first thought would be that she must have once been beautiful. He wonders if it would require a leap back in time to recognize the loveliness of his mother. Abigail once asked him if Nanny was *hot* back in the olden days. The question had startled him, and he can't recall now what he told her.

"Mom—"

"Think about it, honey. You're always angry with someone or something. It's tiresome, George, and it pushes people away."

He's not sure she is right but he knows that the anger that simmers in his chest is a constant thing. Whether or not it is what propels him, of that he can't be sure. He is surely angry with Tammy. She has flipped his family upside down and he doesn't know how to set it straight, doesn't even know what that would look like. He is afraid of sending Tammy somewhere to heal, afraid of what it will be like for her, terrified that he will have to visit her in a hermetically sealed ward reeking of cafeteria food. But he also knows that his anger over the situation may be the only thing that propels him to action, that will enable him to force her into a place like that. He's been pushed to the edge and he needs to gather his adrenaline-fueled rage in order to find the strength to leap across the abyss to the other side.

"She's not on any medications," his father is saying to Finney. "The seizures stopped shortly after she moved there. Bit of a mystery."

"That's not unusual," Finney is saying. "Were they bad?"

"Just a few bad ones," says Hillary. She pulls away from George and goes back to begin wiping the counter. He watches her lean into a spill where the cherry juice has dribbled over the edges. She bends down on one knee to the floor to scrub at another spot, going down slowly and placing her hand up over her head to the counter to steady herself coming up again.

"I only saw one of them," says Aunt Fiona. "She knocked poor Finney off the sofa."

George looks at his aunt. "When he was a baby. I remember. Threw him off the sofa."

"Not exactly. He was in his little carrier, propped up on the end of the sofa and she was asleep next to him. She loved to cuddle up next to you, Finney." His aunt smiles at Finney, at the thought of it, and then startles at the memory of what ensued. "She was asleep and so were you, Finney, but suddenly she started twitching and next thing I knew her limbs are flying and you're upside down in your carrier on the floor.

Thank goodness you were strapped in. I didn't know which one of you to go to first!"

"I don't remember that," says Hillary firmly, as if she doubts her sister's recollection. She keeps her back to them, releases a heavy sigh before turning from the sink and crossing her arms over the front of herself. "But everything turned out fine."

"It was the only time I ever saw it," Fiona says. "I don't think I knew what I was seeing at the time. I think I thought she was having a nightmare. But her eyes were open and it was the strangest thing."

George can feel Finney's eyes on him. He looks back at Finney, catches the slightest hint on Finney's face of him reorganizing what George had told him earlier, and looks away. It is not how George remembers it, not exactly what he remembers, but when he digs his way back to it, he can imagine Ella thrashing on the sofa, his aunt holding her down, Ella's strange guttural noises. He can picture Finney, flipped right side up by his aunt and screaming his head off.

"Well, things were different then," says Stone. "A lot has changed, all for the better." He looks to George, rises slowly from his seat at the table. "I know you want to get on the road, son."

"We can help, George," says his mother. "Happy to come up and help."

When George stands to hug his mother, he doesn't want to let go. He wants to stay that way, his mother's arms around him, the scent of her perfume drifting from the warmth of her neck, her arms rubbing up and down his back. The little murmuring sound she is making in his ear. *It's okay, honey. Everything is going to be okay.* If he can stand here long enough, if she doesn't let go first, if she keeps holding him like this, stilling all the flailing in his gut, he just might believe her.

And she does stay. She doesn't let go so that when he finally lifts his head from her arms, he is forced to reach around and unwrap her from himself, hold one of her hands in both of his, head bowed, and the tears come. She wipes his cheeks with her free hand—flicks the tears away— just as she has always tried to do.

31

The Family

ROLAND PARK
Saturday Night, April 18, 2009

They are all in the living room after having seen George off. Everyone's thoughts are still with George, but they are careful to refrain from discussing him. It would seem unfair to speak of his situation without him here, if only because it is too easy to be frustrated with George, to wonder how things with Tammy got to this point without any of them being privy. Still, he is the elephant in the room, and they are all combing their minds to find other things to speak of.

"I like your shirt, Clarissa," says Tess. Clarissa is wearing an oversized long-sleeve T-shirt that reads "Wizards for Obama" across the front of it. "Have you read all the Harry Potter books?"

"It was a gift from my boys," Clarissa says, smoothing her hand down the front and inadvertently brushing pie crumbs to the floor.

"Nice," Tess says.

Hillary is watching Ella eat around the pie filling, breaking off pieces of the thick crust and eating it with her fingers. The plate is tipped forward in her lap and it is making Hillary anxious. She gets up and takes her own napkin from her lap, lifts Ella's plate, and settles the napkin across Ella's lap, extending the edges of it to cover some of the chair as well, before setting the plate back on Ella's thighs. This is Ella's third piece of pie, and she has eaten only the crust from all three pieces.

Everyone is silently watching Hillary and she feels their eyes on her as she goes back to her seat on the sofa across from her friend Mary who offers up a weak smile as if to say she completely understands.

"So, Ella," says Mary, "are you looking forward to moving back home here?" This is followed by the distinct clinking of forks dropping on plates and a collective holding of breaths. Belle freezes, her wineglass just tipping to her lips. Jax lets his breath out between his lips with such force that wisps of hair flutter the crown of his head. Hillary thinks that this friend of hers, who she loves and is grateful for, doesn't have the good sense God gave her.

"No," Ella says, without even looking up from her plate. "I gonna live down the ocean with Nettie. Is Nettie coming to get me?" When she asks this, she does look up, first at Belle and then at Jax, and finally at her mother. "Where's Nettie?"

Clarissa is glaring at her foolish mother and doesn't care if anyone notices. Mrs. Morgenfrier stares back at her daughter, mouths *What?* and looks away.

"Nothing has been decided," says Belle.

"Nettie will be here tomorrow," offers Jax, but he wishes he was closer to Ella instead of all the way across the room. Wishes he could catch her eyes and make her believe him that Nettie will be back, because she doesn't look convinced, passing her eyes around them, over each of these strangers. Wishes he could stop the swinging of her head, now going back and forth emphatically. No, she does not want to live here, maybe doesn't want to be here at all.

"Ella doesn't want to live here," says Belle.

Ella is waving her hands in front of her face now, no, no, no. She does not want to live here. "I not live here," she says.

The aunts blink-blink in strange unison. They have always been good at staying out of the Juleses' affairs, pitching in when needed but never offering an opinion on anything more than their baby sister's health, which was, to be honest, taxed to an incredible degree when Finney was born and Hillary was trying to mother a newborn and take care of the handful that was Ella. They were the ones who suggested to Stone that she see a doctor, consider medication for herself. Fiona even took it upon herself to occasionally check the prescription bottle that sat next to the kitchen sink just to be sure Hillary was taking them because, at first, Hillary had been so reluctant, arguing that they made her sleepy and she couldn't afford to sleep—what, with five children and the demands of Finney and Ella. But eventually, she settled into the routine, perhaps, Fiona thinks, taking either too much or too little on occasion because Fiona would sometimes find half and quarter pieces in the vial. She and Frances kept an eye on her and eventually, between the two of them trading off mornings with the Jules family, their sister found her days slightly more manageable, sometimes even lunching with a friend or getting in a game of tennis if one of the sisters or the other could stay into the early afternoon.

It was Frances who first commented that Ella was regressing. Sleeping more, and in some ways more manageable, but when she was awake, she was demanding and groggy, rough with her siblings, with everyone but Finney who she adored. Always wanting to sit beside him and cooing, her face up against his, her small hands patting his belly, *be nice to baby, I be nice to baby.* But taking Finney away from her for feedings or a diaper change always made her angry and she'd kick her legs in the air, once knocking over a floor lamp and scaring Frances out of her wits. The two of them, Frances and Fiona, took to distracting Ella with cookies or marshmallows—or her favorite, licorice—in order to execute a trade-off.

Neither of them thinks this is a good idea, having Ella home again. But right now, at this very moment, with Ella fidgeting in her seat, her plate tilting precariously on her lap, her glasses sliding down her nose, and her hands waving in front of her face as if she is warding off a swarm of flies, is definitely not the time to bring this up.

"Your sister needs time to get to know us again," Stone says calmly. He leans forward in his chair and sets his napkin and then his plate on the footstool in front of him. "We have plenty of time to get to know one another again."

"I NOT gonna live here!" Ella shouts, her hands still waving in front of her face and her feet tapping the floor. The plate slides from her lap and lands on the Persian carpet, the cherry filling and pie crumbs blending in with the bright-red and gold threads.

"Oh, Ella!" says Hillary, quickly sliding down to the floor on her knees with her napkin to try and retrieve the scattered pieces of pie that Ella's tapping feet are grinding into the carpet. "Stop, darling," she says, placing a hand to her daughter's ankle, trying not to raise her voice, trying to stay calm as she watches globs of cherry filling smear beneath Ella's feet.

Ella doesn't mean to kick her mother, is only trying to free her ankle from her grip, only wants them to know that she can't stay here, that she must go home to Nettie, that they are going to the ocean, should be there right now where Ella can feel the pulse of the ocean blocks away, hear the mechanical sounds of the amusement park—the clacking of rides, the electronic bursts of music, the swell of screams from the descending roller coaster. There would be a citronella candle burning on the patio table and Lynetta would have brought her a jacket to throw over her shoulders, and maybe Nira would be at the table with them and she would let Ella play with her stethoscope and listen to her own heartbeat, and they would be waiting for Elmett to wander over after his shift. She does not mean to kick her. She does not mean to kick her in the face and connect with her mother's jaw in the way she does, making her mother yelp and nearly tumble over on her knees, her face now smeared in bright-red cherry glop from the bottoms of Ella's shoes. She wants to say she is sorry, sorry to have kicked her, but her mother is still gripped to her ankle, has tugged at her in the moment of her near fall, and Ella is wrenched from the back of her chair to the edge of it. Her glasses have slid down her nose, set askew on her face, and her eyes are swimming with defiant tears. She thinks maybe it is blood on her mother's face and something is ticking inside of herself, something like the sound of the roller coaster rising, a low murmur rising up, *oh no, here we go, hold on, uh-oh* . . . Stone is rising from his chair. They are all slowly coming to their feet, letting out whooshes of breath, and then there is that one second of blessed quiet as if they can all perch on the top of this moment, as if the descent will not ensue, as if they will remain suspended above it all. Ella kicks again to free herself from her mother's grip, and the hands are coming down around her, a hundred hands, she is certain, but it is only her mother at her ankle, her father gripping her arms from behind, Tess pulling at her leg snagged in her mother's fingers.

"Stop, Ella," Stone is saying. "Stop this now!"

"Mom? Mommy? Are you okay?" Tess uses her other hand to slap Ella's free leg down, twice, before gripping it, holding it away from her mother who is crouched like a cowering animal, cherry juice stamped on her chin and jaw.

Belle feels a strange pressure rising in her chest, as if she is going deep underwater, and she lifts her face to gulp air, tries to lock eyes with Ella but Ella's eyes are squeezed shut. "Leave her alone!" Belle shouts. "You're scaring her."

"This is unacceptable," Stone says.

"She didn't mean it," Belle cries out, because she knows this, knows it as if she herself had swung her own legs in angst and rage. As if it is Belle herself being wedged back into this family, shoved to fit in a space that no longer conforms to her. As if they had been discussing wrenching Belle from her husband, from the life she has been so lovingly embraced within. "Can't you see she's terrified?" It is so clear to Belle what Ella is feeling because she feels the very same terror clamped in her own throat. As if the blade of a guillotine is at this very moment falling, intent on slicing her away from her husband, from Tobi and Jack and Kitty.

Finney is helping his mother to her feet. Ella is twisting her shoulders from her father and cannot break free of him, but when Hillary rises to her feet, Stone loosens his grip, and Ella, suddenly free, pulls her feet up beneath her, dragging her stained shoes across the buttery yellow damask of the chair, wrapping her arms around her knees, dropping her head to her knees and sobbing. Her glasses tumble to the floor.

The aunts are at Hillary's side quickly, wiping her face, blotting at the carpet. Mary Morgenfrier calls out for club soda. She can get that stain out before it sets. She has not yet noticed the smears on the chair.

Stone backs away from his daughter. "Unacceptable," he mutters under his breath. He doesn't know what to do with his hands, rubs one in a widening circle across his chest, offers the other to his wife but she won't look at him, refuses to see him, to take the offered hand. She cannot look him in the eyes and she slowly straightens her back and moves in a quarter turn to see Jax and Clarissa, standing close to one another, motionless, both of them looking back at her, Clarissa's hands on Jax's upper arms, not gripping, not pulling, just touching him there, reminding him that she is by his side. And Jax, unmoving, has a hand placed over one of hers that rests on his arm. They have always been so close, and she can't understand it. She's fond of Clarissa, but she is such an awkward woman, nothing at all like Jax. They stare at her wide-eyed, and she sees it. Sees the way they are thinking the same thoughts. Knows that there is a secret between the two of them. Could it be that Clarissa knows, too? The shame of it all smolders in her chest, is a flame on her face.

"I need to get my mother out of here," Clarissa says under her breath to Jax.

Belle is on her knees beside the egg shape of Ella huddled in the chair. She is whispering to her, running her hand down Ella's head, and Ella tips to her. Belle has Ella's glasses in her hand, smooths the top of Ella's head, and lifts it to slide her glasses to her tear-streaked face.

"I not want to be here," Ella is saying.

"I know, Ella."

"Where's Nettie? I go home now," she says. "I not like it here."

When Ella lifts her head from Belle's shoulder and looks to her mother, Hillary sees the flash of fear on Ella's face as their eyes meet. Brief, quick, a piercing glance that flitters and melts away, replaced by a wash of something tender. "I sorry," says Ella. "I sorry I kick you."

Hillary wants to touch her daughter, lifts her hand to her and sees the barely perceptible shrug and flinch of Ella's shoulders, and draws her hand back.

Frances and Fiona are gathering plates and glasses from side tables and taking them to the kitchen. Hillary lifts a napkin from the floor and wipes at her face, feels the sticky residue come away, feels an ache in her jaw where she presses the cloth. Stone is pacing, stops at the large front window, and turns his back to her to gaze out over the darkened lawn to the street. Mary is on the floor at Hillary's feet, pouring club soda on the carpet and scrubbing, but having to reach out from where she is down on her knees, keeping herself as far away from Ella as she can. Hillary steps back from them and turns to Finney. There is a look on his face that she can't read, as if he is trying to find the meaning in what has happened. "You okay?" he asks.

"Oh, I'm fine, fine." She looks to Ella. "It was an accident," she offers up. "Just an accident."

Tess goes to her father at the window and there is a murmuring between the two of them. While Hillary can't hear the words Tess says to him, she hears the pitch of it, the way her voice suddenly lifts as if it carries a question, and she sees him nod to it.

Clarissa is watching her mother on her knees. "Seriously, I should get her out of here," she says to Jax. "As soon as she cleans up the damn mess she's responsible for, I'm going to get her out of here."

"It's not her fault," Jax says. "It's all just too much," he says.

"Can I get that journal from you?" she asks. "Before I take her home."

Aunt Frances comes back to the living room to gather more stray plates. She runs a hand over Finney's shoulder as she moves past him, and he claps his own over hers, holds it briefly before letting her go.

Hillary looks down the opposite length of the long room, so warmly lit, and out the French doors that lead to the patio, sees Clarissa and Jax making their way to the carriage house. A sudden heavy rain has begun, the patio stones quickly darkening with the drops. Jax looks over his shoulder once, back to the house, stops in his steps for a moment, and Clarissa continues on. Hillary watches him shove his hands in his pockets before turning his back on them and taking two quick steps to catch up with Clarissa before they disappear behind the shrubbed path that leads to the carriage house. The rain suddenly begins to fall in sheets.

She imagines that in the next hour her children will trickle away to gather there. To rehash what they have witnessed, assign blame, confer as to the best way to manage their mother. When did this happen? She wonders. When did she become a problem to solve? She imagines the way they will each offer up their own anecdote of what has become of their mother.

Did you see the way she looked at Daddy? What's with that?

She hasn't been herself since Bets died.

I think she knows this is a terrible idea.

I heard her crying in the pantry.

Yes, her children will gather, and each will offer up their own understanding of just what is going on with their mother. But she doesn't know if any of them will actually step in and try to change the course she is set upon. George, now on his way back to his own family, will continue to hold his anger close and lash out when it boils over. It shouldn't matter to him at all whether or not Ella comes home, but still, he will hold it against her, proof of something, though she isn't sure just what. Tess will pose all the questions meant to illuminate the complications of bringing Ella home, but she will only go so far as Stone allows her to, deferring to him—judge and jury—in the end. Finney will keep to the margins of the family as he always has, happy to offer his trained medical opinion should it be required, but not likely to invest emotionally. Not because he is unemotional, on the contrary, but because he has taken all of his tenderness and invested it outside of this family in a place that fits him perfectly but leaves little room for Hillary and Stone.

Jax. When he looks at her, she can't help but feel that he pities her. She doesn't know for certain what he saw that day years ago, has a difficult time reeling herself back to it. In her memory there is the moment she put her hand on Ella's thin chest and pushed her below the rising water. Then nothing. Until she saw Jax climb the stairs with the EMTs. And how can this be? That she does not recall the stretch of time in between? Over the last thirty-two years, Hillary has looked back to that day, searched for the missing moments, tried to find an entry from every possible angle, and still, it eludes her—the most consequential moments of her lifetime, the pivotal place that reconfigured her family, her life, frayed the once-tidy seams of her heart so that she is forced to wonder what has leaked from it. But there is nothing, nothing in between, nothing to go back to and examine the deeper meaning of. But when Jax looks at her, she knows what he sees—an enigma. As if she is merely a confusing illusion of what she had once been to him—the good mother (*the bestest mom*, he once wrote on a Mother's Day card). All of his faith in her shattering that fateful day. Like the windshield of their car when she and Stone slid off I-83, the windshield smacking a low hanging branch and crackling into a web of fissures. Still there, still mounted in its framework, but useless, threatening to crumble at the slightest touch.

Belle is the one Hillary knows to be most like her. She is, to Hillary's way of thinking, the least complicated of her children. There is an easiness between the two of them, a recognition of the one in the other. But Belle's allegiance, Hillary now realizes, has swung hard to Ella, moments ago ignoring Hillary sprawled on the floor to comfort Ella instead. It shouldn't have surprised Hillary. Belle explaining that Ella didn't want to be here, that Ella was scared. As if Belle knew for certain what Ella was thinking, as if Ella's thoughts and feelings are Belle's own.

Yes, her children will gather and confer. Even now Finney has noticed the absence of Jax and Clarissa, is gazing out the French doors toward the carriage house. Hillary moves to his side, tips her head to his shoulder to watch the rain course down the windows.

Clarissa steps back at the door to the carriage house, allowing Jax to go ahead. They're drenched. She smells the gas the moment Jax opens the door, a stinking smell like rotten eggs. "My God," she says. She grabs the back of Jax's shirt to pull him back, and though he takes a step away from the doorway at the assault of the smell, he still reaches his long arm around the corner and flicks on the light switch just inside the door.

"You okay, Mom?"

She nods into Finney's shoulder and he puts his arm around her, the two of them, their breath coming together slowly, heavily, before they gaze across the lawn to see the side of the carriage house explode, a blue-orange ball of flame roiling through the shrubbery and across the lawn, the flames licking at Jax and Clarissa, blown like two sacks to the edge of the patio.

32

Lynetta

Beechwood Institute
Saturday Night, April 18, 2009

By the time Lynetta gets back to her cottage after dinner with her father, a lonely wind is blowing across the neglected fields. On the short drive from his house to hers, a light rain had begun to fall. Normally she likes a quiet rain, the way it puts a low shine on everything, but tonight it feels heavy, weighs on her like a long stretch of melancholy. The cottage feels as dark and empty inside as it did the first day she had gone to see it. But once she and Ella moved in, put a grapevine wreath on the door, re-covered the old sofa, hung their robes on the bathroom door, once she had thrown down a rectangle of remnant carpet, wiped the grimy windowsills, and nestled a trio of canisters on the counter, she began to warm to it. Tonight, in spite of these things, the place feels damp and shadowy.

She turns on the television for company. *America's Most Wanted* blooms on the huge screen. A man has murdered his wife and children, burned down his house to hide the crime, and disappeared into the Rocky Mountain wilderness. Tips will come in. The bastard will be caught. They always catch them. It's just a matter of putting the pieces together. It is amazing to Lynetta what people think they can get away with, herself included. It always catches up with them.

Lynetta's visit with her father has drawn her back to those first weeks after Ella came to Beechwood. Thirty-two years is a long look back, but she still remembers how Ella had taken ill within a day or so of coming in. On her second, maybe third day—Lynetta can't be sure—they witnessed her first seizure followed by the onset of fever, trembling, and nausea. She was moved to the medical wing and sedated to nurse her through what the doctors assumed was a virus. But then, once the symptoms abated and she was moved back into the general population, the symptoms would begin again. They usually started with trembling hands (so much so that she struggled to feed herself) and led invariably to a grand mal seizure. And once again, the fever, chills, and sometimes nausea and headaches that had Ella rocking her head in her hands.

Lynetta takes off her sloppy tennis shoes at the door, sliding them to a mat next to her hefty mending basket. She wipes her face with a dishtowel and goes to the cupboard over the refrigerator to pull out an old green file folder with metal tips, the file that once hung in a cabinet in the nurse's station. She takes it to the kitchen table and opens it, coming first upon a referral letter to Beechwood from a Dr. Aengus Warfield, and behind that are Ella's pediatric files from his office, noting a twenty-four-hour stay in the hospital for a bathtub seizure and near drowning just a week before she arrived at Beechwood.

Next are copies of the logbook from Ella's first months, detailing her symptoms and moves to and from the medical wing. An incident report cited seven verified seizures, three of which were labeled as *grand mal*. Her vitals, when Lynetta takes a closer look, were all over the pace, Ella's blood pressure rising and dropping without apparent cause.

By the end of her second month, the seizures were milder, over in a matter of moments. By the end of her third month, there is no record of seizures at all. What isn't noted, and what Lynetta remembers clearly, is that the formerly dazed and angry Ella had morphed over a few short months into a sweeter, more engaging child. In some ways it was to be expected. While some residents came in and their behavior worsened progressively—like Penny, who had spent most of her days in isolation—Ella, on the other hand, went from something feral to a compliant child who had only occasional outbursts precipitated by fearful situations—baths, a fight in the dining room, Penny's attacks, and years later the incident with Brody. Ella's lack of coordination smoothed itself out so that she no longer bumped into walls, dropped to the floor and rocked her head in her hands, or trembled so violently that she couldn't feed herself. Her vocabulary grew in leaps and her understanding of the routine made transitions easier. Within six months she was deemed compliant enough to attend school and she waited with the other children on the front steps of Thom Hall for Brody's bus just as eagerly as any other child outside of the walls of Beechwood.

Somewhere along the way, there was a short-lived diagnosis of pica, given the fact that anything smaller than her own hand got shoved in her mouth. The pica diagnosis weighed heavily on Lynetta. She knew that those with pica were often forced to wear a helmet with a face screen to prevent them from their inclinations. But Lynetta was certain that it wasn't pica at all. She argued that those with pica tended to chew and swallow the items that went in their mouths and that most of the time pica patients picked at paint, or crisping bugs, bits of grout come up in the washroom—not watches and pens. But her argument fell on deaf ears at the staff meeting. Lynetta feared a pica helmet was in Ella's future. Believing Ella could be taught not to mouth everything she came across, Lynetta set about making it happen.

"Don't touch nothing," she had said to Ella, though everything was locked up and tucked away and there was nothing to touch but the deep gouges in the table itself. They were in the dayroom and Lynetta's shift hadn't officially started yet. She unlocked the metal cabinet and pulled out the box of blocks. She heard Ella's chair screech across the floor and turned back around to still her. Everything echoed so damn much in the room, especially when it was empty. "Don't go nowhere," she said. Ella rocked her upper body back and forth but settled a bit. Lynetta pulled the small bottle she had bought from Drug Fair the night before from her pocket. It looked like a bottle of nail polish and she used the brush to coat a few of the blocks, blew on them to quicken the drying, and set them in front of Ella.

Immediately, Ella's small fingers clutched at the blocks and shoved them to her mouth. She sucked loudly, making obscene smacking sounds. The block was too big to fit deeply into her mouth and so she used her fingers to shove it into the pockets of her cheeks.

"Nothing, huh?" Lynetta picked up one of the remaining blocks, coated it with the liquid, and for a brief second considered licking it herself, just to see if the bitter taste was there as it should be, but immediately thought better of it, remembering how many children had mouthed the blocks, put them down their pants, and likely shoved them in unnatural places.

She put the block down and reached across the table to brush Ella's hair from her eyes. She couldn't wear hair barrettes because she was always ripping them out—and of course, putting them in her mouth. "Need to get you a haircut, little girl." Little things, haircuts, teeth brushing, even bathing, were so complicated in a place like this. She brushed the hair away from Ella's mouth.

Ella squinted and pulled the block from her mouth, spit awkwardly, and puckered her lips. She put the block back up to her mouth again, seeming to forget what had just happened only to pull it back out again. A small noise escaped her, something like the sound a startled bird might make before it takes flight.

"Well, there now," said Lynetta. "Now you're catching on. Don't taste good, hmm?" She smiled and handed her another block, the red one with the teeth marks in it.

Eagerly, Ella snatched it and put it to her mouth, only to yank it out immediately. Her breathing began to get a bit ragged, a sign, Lynetta knew, that she was frustrated and could easily begin to throw one of her tantrums that could get her locked up for the remainder of the day.

For the rest of her shift, Lynetta kept Ella by her side, coating any small items she came across that might go into her mouth, even small slips of paper and the wide-tooth hair comb Lynetta had worked through her hair and that of two other young girls that morning.

Her efforts were met with just enough success to keep Ella out of the dreaded helmet.

Lynetta flips through more of the file, not sure what she's looking for. There are no incidence reports from once Ella came to live with Lynetta, of course. Lynetta would never have reported things like door slamming, a meltdown over clothing choices, the temper tantrum she worked up to on the last trip to the ocean when Lynetta refused to stop at the McDonald's on Route 50 because Ella had been sassy and rude to her. Lynetta had warned her while they were packing up the car—you keep sassing me about this, Ella, and we're not going to stop at McDonald's. Ella wanted a kitten, three of them, in fact, just like the three in a basket in the poster Jax had given her years earlier. Lynetta had once said *maybe someday*, and that had been her mistake. Now Ella demanded to know when was *someday*.

"You a liar," Ella had said and plopped to the ground. It only went downhill from there, with Ella pouting, refusing to get in the car, kicking at the tires from where she was sprawled, and, in the end, wailing like a banshee when Lynetta drove right past the exit for the McDonald's—just like she said she would.

Within the confines of Thom Hall, this would have merited an incident report and possibly seclusion. The punishments were swift and harsh, but Lynetta knew Ella was no different from any other frustrated child, even at thirty-nine years old.

Lynetta goes to the wall phone and punches in Nira's number. It's late, but Nira is a night owl. Lynetta knows Nira stays up to watch her late-night television programs, having to pump herself with three cups of coffee every morning in order to get out the door for her shift.

"Hey, doll," Nira says when she picks up the phone. Nira is missing the two of them this weekend, she says, but the weather is lousy, rain coming down in buckets and drumming on her trailer so hard that Lynetta can hear the din of it in the background. She tells her the weather is just as bad here.

"How's my girl?" Nira wants to know.

Lynetta says she doesn't know. Ella was nervous when she dropped her off. She explains that she is looking through Ella's old files, that she is curious—does Nira remember what Ella was like when she first came in? Does she recall all the visits back and forth to medical, the seizures, the outbursts, how different Ella was within just a few months?

"Like she just sort of woke up and joined the party," Nira says with a laugh. "I remember a little bit. I remember those damn seizures. They were a bitch to deal with."

"Listen to this," says Lynetta, and she proceeds to read from the files that note Ella's behavior, the flu-like symptoms, the return of those symptoms every time she was released from the medical ward, and the way it went on for weeks.

"Viruses are tricky," Nira says. "There's no cure, only treatment. She may have come in with something especially nasty and relapsed a few times with the stress of leaving her family. What are you getting at?"

Lynetta isn't sure. It all strikes her as strange. "I don't remember a virus going around. You know how it is here—one person gets it and then next thing you know everybody's got it. I don't remember that happening."

Lynetta gets up from the table, the phone cord wrapped around her waist, and goes to the stove to put the kettle on. She's cold now, her shirt damp and clinging to her. "It's weird, Nira." She reaches up over the cupboard to get the stove knobs from the tin and the thought flashes through her head that if Ella goes back to her family, Lynetta will no longer have to stash the stove knobs out of reach, won't have to have child locks on the cabinets, won't have to stick her keys high on a shelf that requires her to stretch on her toes to reach.

"Read it to me again," says Nira. "And what meds was she on?"

"Diazepam. Four times a day while she was in the medical ward. Three or four days later, she'd be seizing again."

"How many milligrams?"

Lynetta skims the reports again. "Ten," she says.

"That's a pretty hefty dose for a child. What was she—eight? That's way too much, but they were probably trying to knock her out."

Lynetta nods on the other side of the phone line. Of course they were. She is looking more closely now. By the fourth day after coming back to the dorms, according to every entry she can find, Ella would seize again, fire up a fever, and end up back in the medical wing.

How high were the fevers, Nira wants to know.

"Only an intake temperature is recorded, 100 degrees, 101. Nothing too high. Confusion is noted, tremors, sometimes nausea and vomiting."

"That's not high enough to cause a seizure," Nira says.

"It's like she was being poisoned," Lynetta says.

Nira seems to be thinking about this, the two of them not saying anything. "Doesn't make sense," Nira finally says.

"I know."

"So what it looks like to me is that she was going through withdrawal every time she was released from the hospital. Diazepam is tricky shit, Lynetta. You can literally die from withdrawal. But she wasn't on it long enough to get addicted. Makes no sense."

"And the seizures started before she came in, according to her pediatrician."

"Well," says Nira. "Unless she was on it before she ever came in."

"Nope," Lynetta says. "There's a list here of everything her pediatrician ever prescribed. Amoxicillin a few times. Cough syrup with codeine a couple of times." She flips through a few more pages. "She had pneumonia once when she was four and was hospitalized, but I don't see any medications."

"I'm telling you, Lynetta. It sounds like she came in addicted to benzos."

"Benzos?"

"The diazepam, benzodiazepine. Probably something like Valium. It was handed out like candy, but not to kids, not long enough to get them addicted. That's it, Nettie," she says, using Ella's name for her. "Somebody was doping that girl on Valium long before she came in. And every time she'd start to go through withdrawal, we were doping her up again just to keep her quiet."

There is a long silence between the two of them. Lynetta can't imagine it, can't imagine who was drugging Ella—and then she can.

"She can't go back there."

"You can't prove it, Lynetta. We're only guessing."

"I'm picking Ella up at noon tomorrow. I have half a mind to tell that woman what I know."

"Slow down, Lynetta. You don't know anything for sure. You can't just go off half-cocked accusing her family of doping her. You can't do that, Lynetta. You have to talk to your lawyer first. When it comes to this custody stuff, you've got to play smart. Hold your cards close and talk with your lawyer."

Lynetta doesn't answer her, pours her tea water into a mug, and slams the teakettle back to the stovetop. She turns to watch the rain batter the windows, the reflection from the television coloring the run of water so that it is a collage of flickering blues and golds washing down the glass.

By the time she and Nira hang up, she is buzzing with anger, convinced Ella is in treacherous hands. The phone rings as soon as it is settled in the cradle, startling her.

"Lynetta—Hillary Jules here . . ."

"Ella?"

"There's been an accident—"

No, no, no, thinks Lynetta. *No.* She is too late. She should have gotten in her car and driven over to their house and demanded Ella come home with her—home, here where she belongs. She never should have agreed to let Ella go there, never should have left her in their negligent hands. All she can say is, "Ella? What happened to Ella?"

"There's been an accident. Ella is fine . . ."

Lynetta can hear her take a deep breath, can hear her clear her throat to smooth out the bumps in her voice.

"Ella is fine, Lynetta, but I have to get her back to you tonight."

"I'm coming right now."

"No, we have to leave right away. My daughters are packing her up now. They're going to bring her back. Ella is fine, she's confused, a little frightened. There was a fire, an explosion—not in the house, nothing happened to Ella, but my son, my Jax . . ."

Lynetta can hear a gulping sound. Can hear the woman's voice but can't understand what she's saying. *That damn old stove . . . explosion . . . Clarissa . . . my Jax . . .* Her voice chugging out words, and, Lynetta is certain, there are tears are streaming down her face. "I have to go now," says Hillary. "I have to go to the hospital. I have to go be with my son."

33

Lynetta

Beechwood Institute
Saturday Night, April 18, 2009

Lynetta watches the car's lights trailing along the service road. She stands at the open doorway, peers through sheets of rain to watch the three sisters rush from the car, one of them taking Ella's hand to urge her along. Lynetta ushers them in and Ella tumbles to her arms, everyone breathless and dripping.

Ella sobs. She is pretty sure Clarissa is dead. Lynetta, startled, looks over Ella's shoulder to the sisters who both shake their heads, no.

Belle flings rainwater from her face, tells her, "No, no, Ella. She's not dead. She's hurt, but she's not dead. Remember how she woke up, Ella? Remember that?" Belle's phone begins to ring in her pocket.

"It's Finney," she says, putting the phone to her ear and turning to Tess.

"The big playhouse is on fire," Ella says.

Lynetta has no idea what she is talking about.

Belle begins reciting what she is hearing from her phone. "Burns were mostly superficial . . . some spotty deeper tissue burns . . . lacerations to his back and head . . ." She breathes deeply and asks about Clarissa. "Concussion . . . severe lacerations to her back, fractured elbow . . . superficial burns to her ankles."

Tess's eyes are wide and blinking. When Belle hangs up the phone, the two of them hug one another.

"He's going to be okay," Belle says. "Finney says he'll be admitted, but he and Clarissa are both going to be fine. They need to keep an eye on Clarissa, too." The two sisters nod and repeat the assessment to one another.

Belle turns back to Ella, lifts her voice an octave. "It's going to be fine, Ella. They're going to be okay."

Ella shakes her head; no, she saw Clarissa being dead.

"You heard your sister, Ella. They're going to be fine, just fine. The doctors will take good care of them," Lynetta says. She tells the sisters the best thing for Ella is to get to bed, but invites them to stay—unless, of course, they need to be at the hospital. Lynetta is anxious to know the details, relieved that they both agree to stay.

"Finney says there's nothing we can do. He promised to call with updates. Our parents are there, too," Belle says.

"Finney is our brother," offers Tess. "He's a doctor."

"Baby Finney," Ella says.

Lynetta comes down the stairs to find the two sisters perched on the edge of her sofa. Their hair hangs in wet strands, and they are drenched, perhaps chilled. She hadn't noticed at first, too consumed with comforting Ella, trying to understand what she had seen, what Ella understood of what had happened.

There is mud on their knees, blades of grass stuck to their shoes. She turns around on the steps and goes back upstairs to grab two towels from a shelf. She hands them to the women and they pat at their faces in identical ways. They look an awful lot alike, both pale and fine-boned, but the difference between the two of them strikes Lynetta as something more innate, something in their natures. There is an obvious nervousness in Tess, an anxious quality in the lift of her brows and the darting of her eyes that makes Lynetta think she is waiting for someone to put the pieces together for her. And Belle, on the other hand, eerily calm, as if she has set a part of herself aside to be in this moment, as if she is waiting for something to reveal itself to her that might explain what she has been through. Belle folds the towel around a length of her hair and rolls it and Tess follows suit, wrapping the towel around her own hair before looking down to her lap and then rubbing awkwardly at her muddy knees, the towel coming away streaked. She starts to rise. "We shouldn't be sitting on your sofa. We're a mess."

Lynetta waves off her concerns. "It's a slipcover. I can throw it in the washer."

"Your place is nice," Tess says.

"How about some tea? Then you can tell me what happened."

She goes to the sink and begins to fill the kettle. Turning off the water, she pauses and turns to the sisters, kettle in hand. "Who was hurt?"

"Jax and his friend Clarissa. There was a gas explosion. At least that's what they think it was." Belle delivers this bit flatly. "The fire department said it was from the old stove."

"My God," Lynetta says. She can't imagine that, has no idea what such a thing would look like.

They go on to explain, between the two of them, that the explosion happened in a carriage house on their property, that there must have been a gas leak from the old stove and something sparked the explosion, sending Jax and Clarissa flying through the shrubs and across the lawn.

"Where was Ella?" Lynetta wants to know.

"With me, with us. In the house," Belle says. "She didn't see it happen, but she heard the explosion, and then we all ran out of the house once we saw what was happening. It was raining pretty hard, and well"—she flips her head to Tess—"maybe that helped? Because it put the fire out, you know, on Jax's pants." Tess agrees that yes, the rain was probably a good thing. "Still, it looked bad. It looked so bad." She stops and looks around the cottage. "It was terrible," Tess whispers, and Belle rubs her hand up Tess's back to comfort her.

"Ella was pretty scared," Belle says. "We all were. I just can't believe this happened."

Lynetta sets the teakettle on the stove and reaches up to the overhead cabinet again to retrieve a knob for the burner. Sensing that she is being watched and realizing, for perhaps the first time, that retrieving the stove knobs from a stashed tin in the cupboard might be a curious thing, she is compelled to explain herself. "I keep these up here because Ella will fiddle with them if I don't. Can't keep her hands off them, or the spigot here," she says, pointing to the sink. "The whole place is child-proofed."

Belle stares at her.

"Well," says Lynetta, "I guess your mother will be doing the same thing—" She stops, sees Belle's jaw dropping, her hands coming up to her face in horror, and regrets for a moment that her sarcasm is too obvious. She has said the wrong thing, has upset her.

"Oh, my God," Belle says.

Tess turns to her. "What . . . Belle?"

"Ella. I found her in the carriage house." She swings to her sister. "Oh, Tess. I think she might have been playing with the stove, that damn old stove that never lights properly." She looks back to Lynetta who thinks her own heart might stop in her chest. Of course Ella was playing with the stove knobs. Of course she was.

34

Hillary

Ella has been gone a full month. Hillary has not been to see her yet. Dr. Carter suggested they wait at least three months before making a visit in order to give Ella a chance to acclimate, as he put it. Hillary is looking out her kitchen window to the sugar maple, just starting to turn, the leaves going gold and pink. She had planted it as a sapling only nine years ago and now look at it, ready to burst into a riot of color.

Spread on the table behind her is a stack of wallpaper sample books and a large plexiglass board covered in squares of paneling. Her sisters had swooped in this morning to gather little Finney and take him for an outing to the zoo. She is alone.

When they had packed him up, folded his stroller in their car, hefted a diaper bag over their shoulders—checking first for extra diapers, a change of clothes, and a hooded jacket in case the weather shifted—and then waved an enthusiastic goodbye at the curb, Hillary had considered the long vacuous day ahead of her. With Finney gone and without Ella underfoot, it took less than an hour to set the house in order.

She watches from a small kitchen window over the sink as her friend Bets walks the narrow path between their two homes with a garden trowel and a sack of spring bulbs. Normally, she would rap on the window and wave to her friend, but instead, she is avoiding her. There is some discomfort between the two of them, perhaps imagined. A few days earlier, she had come around the corner of the house to find Bets and Stone in intimate conversation over the fence, a shared look of concern on their faces, but when she had made herself known, they had both broken into weak smiles and shifted on their feet, their conversation suddenly breezy and meaningless—the fine fall weather rolling in, the bounty of tomatoes in Bets's garden, the new quiet in the neighborhood since all of the children had headed back to school.

It is a perfect day to tidy the garden, but now, without Ella stealing into her time, the urgency to check off her fall chores doesn't seem so pressing.

Stone had suggested she take on a project. Perhaps remodel the kitchen? At first she resisted, thinking she didn't have the energy to take on a large project, but yesterday she had picked up sample books and a pile of home decor magazines.

Last night Stone had flipped through them, explaining that he thought something light—maybe even a white kitchen—would be nice. Modern, maybe one of those stovetops that blends right into the countertops, smooth and shiny, like the one she had admired at her friend Mary's house. And that other gadget—the thing that instantly delivers boiling water, hooked up to the sink. That would certainly be a timesaver. And would she like a double sink? How about a trash compactor?

Her old sink is perfectly fine, she told him. It's an old porcelain piece with a built-in ribbed draining shelf and requires a good scrubbing with Comet at the end of the day to keep it from yellowing. But she finds it to be a satisfying chore every evening. Maybe it didn't have to be such a big project, maybe just wallpaper and new countertops. A new dishwasher, of course. The old one is freestanding and there is a great gap of space between the sink and the other end of the counter where the dishwasher sits. Maybe add an island, she'd always wanted an island with stools in the center of the kitchen, but then, she said aloud, she would have to give up the kitchen table they gathered around. There certainly wouldn't be room for both. She wasn't sure she wanted to gather around an island at every meal.

They could knock out to the tiny covered porch and make a breakfast nook instead, Stone suggested. Maybe put in a big bay window that would look out on their backyard.

"I hate to have all of this hauled to the dump," she said, sweeping her hand around the room. That was when Stone suggested it all be moved to the carriage house. That could be *his* project. He could put up a couple of the old cabinets, re-install the sink and stove, move the refrigerator out there. The lofted area could easily be converted to two small bedrooms. The building was already plumbed for water and gas. Already had electric.

"We don't really need the extra space," Hillary had said, but already most of their neighbors had done the same thing, converting their carriage houses to guesthouses or studios. A project for each of them, is how he explained it. A distraction, she thinks, from what they are both reckoning with. A distraction that will keep them in separate spaces, each one finding their own way to remodel—rebuild—a life that has shattered around them.

She puts her hand to her stomach now, feels the mounding of it. She's only three months along and still hasn't told Stone, but with each pregnancy, her belly gives her away earlier and earlier. As if it has some memory of what to expect and expands in anticipation. She will have to tell him soon—and the children. She's never kept a pregnancy from him this long. But this one is different. It has tangled itself in the banishment of Ella, and she needs a distance between the two things, needs time to love this child that's coming—and ease the pain of loving the one who has been sent away.

She now imagines clearing out the dark cabinetry, peeling up the old floor and laying something bright and colorful. She sees the way the old linoleum has thinned and discolored in a kind of path trailing from the sink to the refrigerator and back again, marking nearly a decade's worth of traveling between the two. She flips through the wallpaper book and finds a bright white and green border of trailing ivy and imagines it running along the high ceiling, maybe some recessed lighting and a long expanse of that Corian countertop that everyone seems to like so much (though Mary tells her it stains easily so be careful with red wine).

A larger refrigerator with a huge freezer section so that she doesn't have to run down to the freezer chest in the basement every morning to pull something to thaw for dinner.

She will make it bright and light and white and chase the dark out of the corners. She will hug her children when they come home from school and she will find a way to tell them that they are getting another brother or sister, and she will hope like hell that they don't for a second think that she is replacing one with another.

When Stone phones at seven, he is alarmingly chipper. He's running late, he says, but he has a surprise. Don't put the kids to bed, he tells her. He wants them up when he gets home, and he's on his way.

"What is it?" she asks. But he only tells her again that he has a surprise.

It's past dusk, and the house has fallen into shadow. She scoops Finney in her arms from the kitchen floor and goes to the den, where the children are curled over their homework, and flicks on a light, startles them. George, easily distracted, is digging in his sister's pencil bag looking for a pencil sharpener. He's anxious to get his homework finished so they can watch *Happy Days* at eight o'clock and he is hoping his mother will let him stay up to watch *Laverne & Shirley*. Fifties shows are popular of late and Belle is always asking if her mother had a poodle skirt, if Dad slicked his hair back. The show comes on at eight thirty—his bedtime.

She tells him yes, they can watch both shows if they get their homework done and in the meantime, she is going to get Finney bathed. She doesn't mention the surprise and once she gets upstairs with Finney, wishes she had. The best part of a surprise, she realizes, is knowing it's coming.

She uses the bathroom off her bedroom. And still, she has to steel herself to bathe him. She allows him only a mere four inches of water and won't take her eyes off of him, terrified by the way the soap makes him slippery, the way the water trickles down his face when she washes his hair, and the way it makes him sputter and squirm away from her. The bath lasts less than five minutes, and he cries when she lifts him from it, reaching back to the tub for his bath toys that now clutter and bob around the drain.

Freshly diapered and wearing his footed pajamas, he pads down the hallway past Ella's room, stops and pokes his head in the door, shrugs his shoulders, and turns back to look at his mother. "All gone," he says, a little sigh escaping as he says it.

She settles on the den sofa with her children as the theme song to *Happy Days* plays. George sits up anxiously, a grin prepping on his face as he waits for the Fonz to make his entrance, at which point Fonzarelli will break into his signature "Hey," arms spread wide, chin turned, and the studio audience applauds. So engrossed are they that they hardly notice when the door creaks open and their father calls out. "Hello!"

They hear him make his way through the kitchen to the den but hardly look up from the television until he stands in the doorway and says, "Surprise!"

In his arms is a golden bundle of fluff, a squirming little Lab puppy that paws at the air and wiggles to be put down. The children squeal and run to him.

They are beside themselves, crowding up against their father and reaching to pet him. *What's his name? Oh my gosh, I love him! Is he mine? Is he ours? Can we keep him? Can I hold him?*

Hillary watches the grin on Stone's face grow wider as his children shove one another aside to reach the pup. "Easy, easy, you'll frighten him," he says as the puppy continues to bob its head and scrabble at the air to be put down. When her husband looks over their heads to her, expectantly, awaiting her response, she tries to arrange her face in a way that won't belie what she is feeling, tries to appreciate the excitement around her.

He sees something there, something she is trying to hide, blinks, freezes for a moment because he can't quite read her face. She tries to bring a smile to it, digs into her arsenal of appropriate responses, but there is something so painful in watching him cradle this gift that she cannot be accountable for the dropping of her jaw. "Surprise," he says again, but not with the same enthusiasm.

The children look back over their shoulders to their mother.

"What have you done?" she says. And then seeing the freeze of their faces, she says it again as if it is a joke, "What crazy thing have you done?" and she feels herself purposefully arrange a stiff smile on her face. Their faces relax and they go back to reaching for the puppy.

"Let me hold him!" says George.

"No, no, we'll let your mother hold him first." And Stone makes his way to Hillary to place the puppy in her lap, the children trailing as he moves.

She can't help but reach for him. She tries not to reach. She instructs her arms to cross over her chest and refuse the puppy altogether. But then they lift spontaneously, and she catches him in her arms. He is so soft in her lap, the fur so silken, the scent of him like a warm pastry, his tongue flicking at her neck. Her eyes fill with tears and she is afraid to blink, afraid to send them coursing down her face. *How could you?* she thinks. *How could you do this?* She runs her hand down his head, pulls his rump deeper into her lap. *How could you replace my daughter with a dog?*

"He's very sweet," she says instead. "A little butter bean." She won't look at them, keeps her chin tucked to the puppy. She must tear herself away from him, can't spare even the most tenuous attachment to him, and so she lifts him to the floor. He stands on his hind legs, his paws to her shins, and then scrambles away toward Belle, who scoops him in her arms, and the boys clamber for a chance to hold him.

Stone goes to her and sits beside her on the sofa. "I thought he might cheer everyone up a little around here." She nods but doesn't look at him. "He's got the best breeding. He'll be a fine dog and a good companion for you during the day." His voice is soft—for her ears only—but deep and certain. She nods again.

The puppy is running between the three boys, his nose to the carpet, stops suddenly, and squats, his pink tongue hanging out, his eyes blinking, and proceeds to pee on the carpet.

Hillary jumps from the sofa, scoops him in her arms, flicks two fingers down his nose. "No! No, puppy, bad!"

Everyone takes a collective breath. It is as if her reprimand has conjured Ella out of thin air. *No, Ella, no.* Everyone waits, wondering how this is to be dealt with.

She looks at her family, all the unblinking eyes.

"We can train him," Jax offers up. "We can paper train him, Mom. He's just a puppy."

She runs her hand down the puppy's head, feels the needling of his teeth on her fingers, the tongue working its way along the heel of her hand. She hands the puppy to Jax's open arms and turns to Stone. "I'm pregnant," she says. "We're going to have another one."

35

Stone

Stone and Finney are moving through the lawn, gathering up the debris and piling it along the fence line against the alley. It is Tuesday morning and Jax is still in the hospital, though he wants to be released, and Finney has stopped his work to take a call from him and explain once again why he needs to stay, needs to trust the team caring for him. The call sounds like the same one Stone had overheard earlier that morning while the two had their coffee standing at the kitchen counter. Jax is on pain meds and they are making him loopy, Finney tells him now, stuffing the phone back in his pocket.

Together they break down an L-shaped piece of the doorframe and toss the pieces to the pile. Inside the carriage house they roll up the singed oval rag rug. The edges of it are melted and crackle as they roll it. The two lift it like a dead body and carry it to the pile.

When Stone rose that morning at the crack of dawn, Hillary was sound asleep beside him. He is used to her trailing down to the kitchen minutes behind him. He makes the coffee and she appears wrapped in her robe, her hair pulled back neatly, her face washed and bright, and joins him at the table for a minute to finish her first cup before offering him breakfast.

Almost always he says he'll just have toast, maybe some fruit if they have anything, and she cuts up cantaloupe or strawberries and settles beside him with a cup of yogurt and they share the paper.

This morning, however, like the last two, she lingered in bed well into the morning, coming down fully dressed closer to nine, having slept later and starting her morning from her bedside where she called George to check on him, called the nurse's station at the hospital to check on Jax, called her friend Mary to see how Clarissa was doing since she was released Sunday afternoon.

She swept in just as Stone and Finney were donning work gloves and heading into the yard. Stone told her the coffee was old and she waved him off and poured a cup anyway, recited everyone's condition, settled herself at the table, and flipped through yesterday's mail, which she and Stone both knew included a letter from the attorney they had engaged to regain custody of Ella. He had ignored the letter, certain that the unfolding of Saturday, and especially the revelation that the explosion was likely the result of Ella playing with the stove, had dissuaded her from bringing Ella back. But this morning she ripped open the letter, scanned the pages, and said it was just a copy of what had been filed and sent to Lynetta. She then set it flat on the table, smoothing out the creases and placing her hand over it like she was about to take an oath on a Bible, and said that everything was in order.

He and Finney had stood dumbfounded in the doorway, unable to look at one another, incredulous. She looked up to him and only said she had a headache, had too much wine last night. It didn't agree with her.

He went to the cabinet and took out two Tylenol and a water glass, filled it at the sink, and handed it to her. Hillary isn't a big drinker and it is true that two or three glasses of wine over the course of a long evening are her limit. She never got sloppy or stumbled around the house, but she has limited herself in recent decades to only a single glass with dinner, and the admission that she had too much reminded him of earlier years and up until Ella left when she was capable of drinking herself numb. One glass made her chatty, two glasses made her silly, and three glasses shifted her into a quiet dreamy place. Last night as all of them cleared the table from a late dinner of Chinese carryout, Hillary remained at the table and sipped at what he was certain had to be her fourth glass. Her eyes, glassy and unfocused, small sighs escaping her that had her daughters turning their heads over their shoulders at the sink to watch her. Eventually, she had picked up her glass and said she was going to go sit on the patio and look at the stars, it was such a nice evening.

She was still there when Stone had gone up to bed, her glass drained, her arms folded around herself. When she slipped into bed, he could feel the cool of the outside on her, but she drew her legs away from his and rolled to her side.

Stone doesn't relish his role, the task ahead of him, that he must be the one to tell her that no, they cannot bring Ella home. In fact, he resents it, has always resented it. Why is it he who always has to be the one to make these decisions? He has worked hard over the years to refrain from issuing directives, never telling her what to do but simply posing questions, summarizing the state of things so that she might be moved on her own to implement. *I wonder if getting a little help around here with Ella might make things easier for you? Butter Bean can't lift his hind end anymore, poor guy, and I wonder if it's time? It's been weeks since Belle has joined us in church. I wish we saw more of Finney and his friend, too, of course.*

All these things were meant to nudge her to action and preserve the notion that she was a part of the decisions. It would have been so much easier to simply tell her to hire help, allow Butter Bean the passage he deserved, talk to Belle and find out what the heck is going on, give Finney their blessing.

Finney has a flight to catch in the afternoon. He has stayed too long and likely put too much of a burden on his partner, on Brad. Stone is clapping together his gloved hands, surveying the pile they have created, the both of them breathing in the charred stench of it all.

The girls, too, need to get home. Tess, Stone learned last night, has quit her job, but he is determined not to make her think that being jobless makes her their designated caretaker by default. She needs to get back to her life and friends, start a job hunt in earnest, settle the mess of her marriage and put it behind her. She had been a bit weepy the night before, perhaps also owing to the wine, and wanted to know what she had done wrong. He could only tell her that she had done nothing *wrong*, there was no such thing in cases like this. Life just unfolds, and it's how we iron out the creases that matters. She's a smart woman, the more nervous of the two girls, always wanting reassurance that she has done the right thing, made the right choices, as if life is a game show and whoever gets the most questions right will win the jackpot. This, he knows, is his fault—the way he encouraged her thinking when it aligned with his. Choosing this class or path of study or internship as opposed to another—all with an end goal of law school, a fine choice for a bright young woman like Tess. Even as a child she had looked at him to gauge his appreciation when she made better food choices—a fruit cup over french fries, frozen yogurt over ice cream—or when she rose early to get a run in because rain was expected in the afternoon, when she chose *War and Peace* for her high school senior thesis, when she bought a Prius instead of the sportier, high-maintenance Ford Mustang she had once set her sights on.

Finney turns to his father. "She can't come back, you know."

"Agreed."

"Are you going to tell Mom?"

"I was hoping she would come to understand it on her own. I thought, after this"—and he waves his hand over the stinking charred debris—"I thought it would be obvious."

"Ella wants to stay with Lynetta," Finney reminds him. "And she's not a child. She's an adult who needs assistance but has the right to make her own choices about what that means."

Finney is right. Stone claps his hand to Finney's shoulder. "I hope you'll come home more, son. You and Brad both."

Stone knows that Finney has made trips back to Baltimore in the past without visiting his parents. He doesn't follow social media, but Belle had called once to ask, was Finney home? She had seen a Facebook post with the aunts, their arms around Finney and Brad. Stone simmered a bit after the call. Angry with Finney at first, but finally coming around to the obvious—that Finney didn't feel welcome. Stone never mentioned the call to Hillary. Though he did suggest Hillary might want to reach out to Brad in the same way she reaches out to her son- and daughter-in-law—send birthday cards, a Christmas gift.

"For goodness sakes," Hillary said. "They're not married!"

"We'd like to see more of the both of you," Stone says now.

"Sure, Dad." Finney reminds him that he will be back for the Fourth of July, a long weekend that the family has always gathered for, but which Finney has shrugged off in years past. They usually get a bushel of steamed crabs and spread the sloppy mess of them down picnic tables covered in newspaper, hammering away, shells popping and flying, smearing their lips with the spices and cooling them with the chilled beers drowning in a tub of ice tucked in the shade. Belle's kids chase after one another with the loose claws and beg their mother to pick the meat for them because she is the best picker of them all.

Brad has never eaten steamed crabs, Finney tells his father, but he is always up for a culinary adventure.

When they come into the kitchen, Belle is on the phone with Ben. Stone knows she is struggling with the decision to send Jack to a private school.

Belle is the thoughtful one, never rash, her decisions are made slowly and deliberately, carefully weighed and measured. She doesn't seek her father's advice or approval, and in this way, she has always been an easy child.

"I know that, Ben, but I think that a lot of damage could be done by separating the boys . . . and he'll be made to feel different, like there's something wrong with him . . ." She glances up to her father and brother and walks out of the room and through the dining room. They can hear her voice but not her words. Stone hears in her voice a sense of agreement and then a counterpoint, possibilities offered up. When she comes back in the kitchen, the phone stowed, and leans her backside against the counter, lifts one leg in that way she does with her foot placed flat and high on her thigh, and brushes the hair from her face, he knows she is uncharacteristically about to ask their opinions.

"Ben wants to pull the trigger on this. They have one slot left for next year because a family changed their mind, but we have to decide by tomorrow morning."

Stone and Finney say nothing, watch her lift her shoulders and drop them. "I haven't even seen the school!" she says. "How can I be expected to make a decision like this?" She goes to the table and drops herself down in a chair. "All I've seen is the damn brochure, *a learning community fostering scholarship and creativity in students with unique learning needs*," she says mockingly. "What the hell does that even mean?"

"Do you want my opinion?" says Finney, and she nods, yes, she does.

"Now I don't know a lot about Jack's learning style. I don't know what you're working with here, but if where he is now is making him unhappy, if he's not thriving in the same way Tobi and Kitty are, and in fact, is possibly having his self-esteem battered on a daily basis, it might be best to put him someplace that knows how to work with kids like him."

"There's nothing wrong with him, Finney. He's smart, maybe smarter than Tobi and Kitty." There are tears threatening to spill.

"Who said anything is wrong with him? He just doesn't learn the same way most kids do. Maybe his way is better, or maybe his way is just different. Trust me, Belle, the world is built for normal. Anything outside of those lines is . . ." he trails off, corrects himself. "Different is just that. Different. That's all—no better, no worse."

"Switching schools and being separated from Tobi is going to be so hard on him," she says.

"Maybe for a time," Stone says. "But if things are as rough as you say they are, it might be a huge relief for him to get some peace from all that." Stone doesn't know if the move is a good idea or not, has no opinion of it, in fact. But he can see the struggle on his daughter's face and knows how frightened she is of doing the wrong thing, making the wrong choice. "Honey," he says, pulling out a chair to sit down across from her. "Sometimes choices aren't so black-and-white—one good and the other bad. Sometimes they're six of one and a half dozen of the other, if you know what I mean."

She looks up at him, blinks her damp eyes, straightens her back, and nods to say she understands.

"You make a choice," he says. "And then you make it right. One way or another, you make it work."

36

Jax

JOHNS HOPKINS HOSPITAL
Thursday Noon, April 23, 2009

The pain is ungodly, a tidal wave that swoops over him, curls around him, and drags him down, especially when he is being worked on. And afterward it lingers for hours, untouched by the higher doses of pain medication. What is confounding to him is the breadth of it when the area itself doesn't seem large enough to produce such torrents of agony.

Aaida, a Jamaican woman with an accent that rolls in the back of her throat and tumbles like river water when she talks to him, has the task of peeling and picking the damaged skin twice a day. The areas she works on are small, three patches on his right shin and each less than three inches square. He's also had two minimal skin grafts and his ass is raw, sore, and stinging where they shaved the skin in layers like pecorino cheese to plug and heal the deeper burns.

Aaida is patient with him, purring, *I know, I know, let's rest a bit,* and then growing impatient with him moments later, *I have babies who don't give me so much trouble.* He hopes she isn't doing this to babies but is afraid to ask. When she packs up her torture kit and leaves him to rest, she pats his hand and tells him his leg *will not be so ugly as you think.* Women will love the scars and he will have a story to tell.

He is able to walk and gets himself to the chair in his room, though he would like to surrender to the drugs and try to sleep. But the pain is there, even in his sleep, running through his strange dreams. He dreams of valleys and hills, storm-drenched skies, and huge expanses of clear star-spangled night. He thinks the dreams are his sleeping response to trying to rise above the pain.

His father once told him, many years ago when he injured his knee in a high school lacrosse game, to try to think of something else. They were on their way to the emergency room, Jax spread across the back seat, humiliating tears streaming down his face, and he was certain he had torn his ACL, had heard the *pop*. He knew it would put him out for the season, and that was its own kind of misery, but at the time the pain had consumed him.

Little trick, his father said, the brain can't think of two things at once—can't focus on the pain when you're thinking of something else. Think of something else.

He tried, tried to focus on the pretty girl from the night before, the warm trail of her hand down his pants, but his father was wrong. The pain stayed and what was worse, it required he check in, even more consciously, with the pain in order to know if it was gone, which it wasn't. It was there, had been there all along, had even managed to get too far ahead of him while he tried futilely to outwit it.

He nearly nods off waiting for George to arrive but snaps awake when his brother comes in the door. How is it that his brother can walk so ramrod straight, so purposefully, and yet Jax always thinks of him as twisted into a knot, his intestines tangled into a throbbing mass. Even when he swallows, Jax imagines a rag going down his throat.

George looks around the room, brushes his hand across the foot of the bed, and settles himself on the edge of it.

The obligatory questions are asked. *How are you? When are you getting out? How's Clarissa doing?*

When he asks how bad the scarring will be, Jax tells him he doesn't think it will be too bad, but he doesn't know if the hair on his leg will ever grow back—a little manscaping by fire.

George looks confused and then tells him that's ridiculous. Only cyclists shave their legs. "At least it's not your face," George says.

"Really, George? Really? Fuck you."

George is surprised, but not put off, because, Jax thinks, it makes perfectly logical sense to George, is just like him to compare wounds and decide who came out better than the other.

"I'll swap you," Jax says.

They sit in silence for a minute, so long that Jax almost forgets he is here until George gets up and begins to pace, passes by the window, and the light shifts in the room. He leans into the window ledge.

"At least now they'll give up this crazy idea to bring her home," he says. "What a mess."

"It was an accident," Jax says, "and Mom was here yesterday. I don't think she's given up on this." He shrugs his shoulders and looks away from George, exhausted already with where he knows this is going.

"You have got to be kidding me," George says, practically spitting.

It's apparent that George knows the whole story, Ella fiddling with the stove knobs, the carriage house beginning to fill with gas, Jax flicking the light switch an hour later, and the old wiring sparking the explosion. He didn't think anyone would tell George about Ella's role in the disaster. He can only assume it was Tess. Belle and Finney know better than to fuel George's anger. His parents, too, would not have wanted to upset George, especially as they are tiptoeing so carefully around George's own problems back home. Jax wants to ask about Tammy but before he can, George starts building to a tirade.

"What the hell is wrong with them? She nearly blew you up. And you, Jax, should be a lot more pissed off. She could have killed you. Am I the only one that sees this? She hasn't been back, has she?"

"It's Thursday," Jax says. They both know what that means. Thursdays start out hopeful, their mother always happy, chattering, packing up gifts for Ella, but when she comes home, she will go to her room and sleep. When they were small, they all knew to be quiet on Thursday afternoon. And dinner would be simple, boiled hot dogs or a frozen casserole set on the counter to defrost, their mother coming quietly into the kitchen at five thirty, distracted but stopping to touch her children at the table, run her hand down their heads one by one as if she is counting them off. She and their father would eat quietly later in the evening while the children gathered around the television, and Stone often was the one who sent them off to bed, rather than their mother who lingered in the kitchen, packing tomorrow's lunches, tidying her already spotless kitchen.

"You staying tonight or are you headed back home?"

"I've got to get back to pick up the girls from Carmen's at six."

"Nice of you to make the drive."

"Yeah, well." He waves him off.

As much as George feels underappreciated, he's not good at accepting an expression of gratitude. Jax asks about Tammy and watches the rag slide down George's throat again.

George tells him that Tammy has been moved to an inpatient program, but when Jax asks how the girls are doing, George tells him that he won't bring them to see Tammy on the ward, won't subject them to seeing their mother in a place like that.

Jax doesn't know what to say to this. George goes on to say he can't believe Tammy has done this to them. Jax has always made a point to tread lightly around George, they all have. But whether it's the drugs knocking out the brakes he once employed with George or the pain that is just now building to a new crescendo, he can't be sure, but either way, he's tired of George's constant state of persecution. "You're a piece of work, George."

George is startled, sucks in a breath between the grates of his teeth and stares back at his brother.

"It's all about you, right?" Jax says. "Yeah, it's all about you and has nothing to do with Tammy. She starved herself nearly to death to get at you." He shakes his head back and forth, presses his hands to his thigh and kneads the top of it in the hopes of blocking the journey of pain signals to his brain.

"That's not what I'm saying."

"Yeah—it is."

"I'm just saying that she . . ." he stumbles over himself. "She's made a mess of everything. You have no idea what this has done to the girls, finding their mother like that."

"So it might be a good idea to let them know their mother's going to be okay, that she's trying, that she is getting help."

"They know that."

All Jax can think as he looks at his brother is that George is so deeply snagged inside of himself that he can't get out of his own way to look at anything from a fresh angle. "They know what you know. They *know*," he says, air quotes around the word itself, "that you're so pissed at her, you can't get out of your own way to help her."

"Wouldn't you be?" George juts his chin in the air as he says it, challenges Jax to answer differently.

Jax wants to be fair, wants to answer honestly, and so he doesn't answer right away, lets the challenge hang in the air. "Nope, George. I don't think I would. I think I'd be worried sick about her and the girls and would try to figure out how to help her without bashing her around my kids."

"Big of you," says George. "Always the magnanimous one. You don't know anything about my life."

Jax has pushed him as far as he is willing to go. The quiet now is disconcerting. He can hear the dining cart rattling down the hall, and when his tray is brought in, he is immediately nauseated by the fishy smell of tuna salad on soggy toast.

"That's disgusting," George says.

On this, they both agree. He starts in on the less offensive fruit cup.

They find a way to talk of other things, both careful to now avoid the subjects at the forefront of their minds—Ella coming home, Tammy. Jax eventually circles around to Tess. George says he never warmed to her husband and Tess is better off without him. Jax, for his part, says he is more worried about the fact that she is unemployed and Tess flounders when she doesn't have a project and a plan.

They both agree to check in with her more often, and it comes to light that Tess has phoned George daily, checking in on him, instead. "She's in your camp," he says. "She thinks I should get the girls in counseling." Jax can see there is more he wants to say and there is something vulnerable on his face as if what he wants to say might reveal more than he wants known.

In an earnest voice, thin and with no weight behind it, he says, "I just don't think this whole thing with Tammy is my fault."

"It's not," Jax says. But what he is thinking is, what the hell makes George think anyone's blaming him? What he wants to say is, who the hell thinks that way? Who *cares* whose fault it is? But there is a fragility washing over George, and Jax is afraid of kicking him into an angry place again. He gives his brother some time, lets his last remark settle.

"Hey, Jax," George says. "Why do you think they sent her away? I've been thinking about that a lot lately."

Jax doesn't intend to answer him, has no intention of saying what he is about to say, cannot believe, in fact, that the words are coming out of his mouth. It is as if they are some sort of spirit ectoplasm he is vomiting. "Mom tried to kill her, and I told Dad. So that, little brother, was my fault."

What Jax doesn't know in that moment, what he fails to see on his brother's face because Jax is drowning in his own shame and can't lift his head from his smelly tuna sandwich, from the length of his bandaged leg, from the deflating of his own chest, is the sudden wash of relief on his brother's face. What Jax doesn't know, is that all along George had been certain it was his own fault.

37

Hillary

It is Thursday, and Hillary is on her way to visit Ella. She's avoiding the shorter route of I-83 and taking the back roads through the Greenspring Valley. Everything is so lush and lovely today, and she has the window cracked so that the fresh air is slipping in around her. Sagamore Farm, a renowned Thoroughbred farm, is ahead on her right. The pasture is dotted with mahogany mares and their foals. She sees a handful of cars pulled to the side and children clambering on the whitewashed fencing to watch the animals.

In the last days since the accident, Hillary has distanced herself from her family—specifically from their assumption that she will change her mind about bringing Ella back. The separation, grounded by her insistence that she be the one to make the decision as to whether or not she will continue to pursue guardianship, has pitched her into a void she has never navigated before.

On the one hand, it isn't lost on her that Ella's visit was disastrous. On the other hand, she can't shake the conviction that bringing Ella home is a way to right a wrong.

Choice. It's something she has given a lot of thought to recently. How is it, she wonders now as she slows the car to watch the foals scamper behind their mothers, that she has made so few choices in her life. The strange void she feels herself floating in is, she realizes, the place where choices are made unanchored to the demands of another person.

She finds herself pulling over to the side of the road. She's going to be late. Hillary has always been precise about her visits, arriving promptly at the appointed hour, but today, given that she's chosen the scenic route and given also that she is drawn to the sylvan scene at the side of the road, she will be at least a quarter hour late.

She comes to a stop and rolls down her passenger side window to gaze out across the field. A foal, splay-legged and curious, wanders from his mother's side toward the spectators, but the mare whinnies and weaves in front of him, turns him effortlessly away. He swishes his small brush of a tail, shakes his head so that his mohawk of mane ripples down his neck, and falls in place beside the mare.

Like the life she has appeared to have lived, it's all so idyllic. But in spite of the advantages she has been afforded, Hillary has also, in recent days, become keenly aware of the fact that her husband, her church, and the needs of her family have dictated the way in which she has moved through her admittedly privileged life.

She can hear the rhythmic sound of grass being torn from the ground as the mares wander, noses lowered, but never losing sight of their charges. Another mare lifts her head from chomping at the earth and allows her filly to suckle, its neck craned beneath her belly. Hillary knows enough of horses to know that the foals will be taken from their mothers in the fall and she is suddenly filled with such overwhelming sorrow that she can no longer watch.

She takes a deep breath, smelling deeply the onion-scented grass, and swallows. Eases back to the road with a small lump wedged in her throat. Recalling now the many times on Saturday evening that Ella asked for Nettie, it isn't lost on Hillary that taking Ella from Lynetta is its own kind of cruelty.

Bless me, Father, for I have sinned.

How many times over the years has Hillary prepared her confession, imagined herself confessing to Father Dougherty the committing of it, telling of the way she watched the surface of the water heal itself over her child's face?

Father Dougherty was kind to her in the months following Ella's placement, offering to meet with her should she be so inclined, at one point taking Stone aside to suggest he encourage Hillary to speak with him.

Hillary watched the two of them together in the vestibule, saw the serious dipping of Stone's head, the falling of his eyelids, saw Father's eyes track to her and back to Stone. When Stone came back to her side on the steps of the cathedral and she asked him what they had spoken of, he only said that Father wanted her to know he was available should she need counsel.

"I'm fine," she said.

"Of course you are."

She ached for absolution, yearned for a penance that would absolve her. But to put words to what she had done and spill those words to another person, no matter how anointed, was beyond her.

She tried confessing directly to her God, but He felt unreachable as if there was a kind of static between the both of them. Over and over again, she considered the confessional, maybe even visiting a different priest, one who didn't know her personally. But as the months stretched to two years, then three, the despair felt like an appendage she couldn't rid herself of. The Thursday ritual of visiting Ella in Thom Hall, particularly taking her leave of her at the end of a visit—the way Ella clung to her, begged her not to go, refused to get off her lap or unwrap her arms from around her neck—was, as she saw it, part of Hillary's penance.

The apostolic nature of her Church was an impregnable fortress between her and her God. Still, she prayed, though the nature of her prayers changed over time. She learned to live with her sin and eventually stopped praying for herself, for forgiveness, and prayed instead that God would protect Ella. And then, after years of shifting her prayers to Ella, they were answered: Ella moved in with Lynetta.

Within weeks of the arrangement, Ella was a different child. Hillary could quite literally see the relaxing in Ella's shoulders—no longer lifted to her ears—the way she sang snippets of song, hugged a book to her chest and proclaimed it *mine.* The eager way she showed off something new in their cottage, a Monet poster on the wall over the sofa, a throw pillow, new towels, a vase, porcelain figurines on a high shelf—*not to touch!* The playhouse out back that Pap built, the bird feeder that hung from a spindly tree and the bag of seed that sat in the entry closet, also *not to touch.* And thankfully, there were no longer the pained goodbyes between the two of them. Though sometimes there was a sting in the easy way that Ella now waved her off at the end of their visits.

The unfurling road ahead of her swoops down deeply and Hillary feels her stomach float and then settle as she ascends the next hill. A farmer's field is being fertilized and there is a rich and noxious scent in the air. She rolls up her window, but the smell still invades. She finds herself willing to suffer the stink for the sake of having the air move around her and cracks the window again. A mile later it no longer bothers her.

Yes, she thinks now, rounding the last bend on the way to Beechwood, God had answered her prayers and in doing so had eased some of the burden Hillary carried. To spurn that prayer, to take Ella from Lynetta, might be its own kind of sin. And she is grateful for Lynetta, truly. Though she admits to a degree of jealousy. Not just because Ella loves Lynetta. There is more to it. Her jealousy is a faceted thing. There is what lies between Lynetta and Ella, and also the way that Lynetta has been able to do for Ella what Hillary had not, but also Hillary envies Lynetta's ability to make her own choices, specifically the choice to take on Ella's guardianship, unencumbered as it is from the influence of family.

It's not that Hillary is oblivious to the fact that bringing Ella home affects the entire family. It's simply that she's spent a lifetime deferring to others, untangling what feels like everyone's best interests and following that thread. She cannot settle around this decision, make a fragile peace with it, unless it is truly her own.

She turns right into the back entrance of Beechwood, through the empty gatehouse and past the abandoned buildings where saplings have sprouted along the neglected foundations. Resigns herself to what lies ahead and the responsibility that comes with making her own decisions.

38

Lynetta

BEECHWOOD INSTITUTE
Thursday Afternoon, April 23, 2009

Mrs. Jules is expected any minute. Maisy is visiting with Ella, and they are both out back in the playhouse. Lynetta keeps the door open so she can keep an eye on the two of them. She fixes them a plate of peanut butter crackers and bananas and calls Ella to the door to hand it to her. Ella takes the plate carefully to the playhouse and divvies the snacks between the two of them.

Normally, she and Ella would have walked Maisy back to Thom Hall by now and be back for Ella's visit with her mother, but today is a special day and Lynetta doesn't have the heart to separate the two. A group home has been found for Maisy and she will be leaving on Saturday. With Ella's future undecided, Lynetta has no idea when the two will see each other again. Lynetta isn't sure how much Maisy understands of what lies ahead, but Ella is already asking Lynetta when they will visit her, assuring Maisy she can come down the ocean with her if she wants. Maisy says, *okay, Ella*, which is what she always says to whatever Ella suggests.

It has been five days since Ella's visit with her family. Since that time it has become clear that Ella was indeed responsible for the explosion in the Jules carriage house. Surprisingly, however, no one seems anxious to assign blame. Finney had called Ella on Tuesday afternoon saying he was hoping to come by and say goodbye but had a flight to catch and wanted to be able to see Jax at the hospital before he left. He will see her again, he assured her, the next time he is in town. Ella said she might be down the ocean and did he know how to get there? Finney asked to speak with Lynetta and Ella said *sure*, and then hung up on him, so he had to call back.

When the phone rang again, Lynetta grabbed it before Ella could get to it.

He wanted to assure Lynetta that no one blamed Ella.

"I haven't explained it to her," Lynetta said quietly, watching Ella flop to the sofa and start turning the pages of a new *Cattery* magazine. "She has no idea this is her fault."

"It's not her fault," said Finney.

"She's real worried about Jax," Lynetta said, "and about Clarissa." At the mention of their names, Ella looked up from her magazine and watched her, took off her glasses and began twisting them in her hands. Lynetta wanted to take them from her before she mangled them but couldn't quite reach her by the length of the phone cord. She motioned to Ella to put them back on her face, and Ella did so with a huff.

Finney carefully explained the extent of Jax's burns, mostly superficial with a couple of places where the burns had gone into deeper tissue and had required two skin grafts to work against possible infection. He would be fine. Clarissa was fine as well, badly scratched, bruised, but out of danger.

"You know," he said, "maybe Ella could visit him in the hospital. Maybe it would be good for her to see that he's okay." He went on to encourage her to call the floor and time her visit well around any treatments Jax might be getting that could wear him out and after which they tended to increase his pain medications.

Lynetta said she'd think about it, but she knew it wasn't likely if only because she wasn't inclined to run into the Jules family on an awkward visit with Jax.

The next day both of the sisters had also come to say goodbye, promising they would see her again soon. And once again, Ella told them she would be down the ocean and asked them if they knew how to get there. They both assured her that they did. Belle told Ella she couldn't wait to meet Elmett and Lynetta had said, "Oh, Lord," which made Belle smile conspiratorially at Ella.

"And Wally, too. He Nettie's boyfriend."

Belle had looked at Lynetta, unable, apparently, to hide her surprise and Lynetta dropped her chin and swung her head side to side. *No, no, no.*

What surprised Lynetta even more was the hug she received from each of the sisters on their way out the door. "She's lucky to have you," Belle whispered in her ear.

Mrs. Jules comes bearing gifts, her usual bag of shoestring licorice and a pair of gold summer sandals that likely cost four times what Lynetta was willing to pay for a pair of shoes, and an overnight bag—one of her own—made of what Lynetta immediately recognizes to be fine, butter-soft leather, but with a tear in the strap that Mrs. Jules hopes it won't be too much trouble for Lynetta to repair. But if it's a problem, she explains, she can take it to the shoe repairman on Cold Spring Lane who has been there forever and has always done a wonderful job refreshing her shoes and bags.

Lynetta is comfortable working with soft leathers—has special needles and tools for doing so in her massive mending basket—and tells her she's happy to repair the bag. It's all so civil, neither one letting on that there is something adversarial in the air.

Lynetta is quick to explain that Maisy is here, and she motions to the playhouse through the door. Hillary walks to the doorway, stands in the spill of sunlight at the threshold, and when she turns back to Lynetta, there are the remnants of a gracious smile on her face. Lynetta tells her she will walk Maisy back while Ella and her mother visit.

"No," she hurries to say. "Let them visit. It's nice to see them together. I guess I didn't realize she . . . she has"—she lifts her hand, searching for the words—"friendships."

"'Course she does." And Lynetta immediately regrets the snap in her voice.

Hillary brings her full attention to Lynetta, straightening her shoulders and then releasing her breath in a way that lets Lynetta know she has come prepared to say something. "I'd like to talk with you, Lynetta."

"Mrs. Jules, if this is about where Ella's going, I think we need to leave that to the lawyers—"

"Please, Lynetta. I know all that. I know what the lawyers say. I just want to talk, woman to woman, two people who only want what's best for her." A hopeful look rises in her brows, and Lynetta warns herself to proceed with caution.

"Mrs. Jules, I'm not withdrawing my petition, if that's—"

"Lynetta, if there's any hope of having an honest discussion, we should start by getting rid of the formalities. I should have said this thirty years ago—please call me Hillary. It's ridiculous that I've not said so sooner."

This last startles Lynetta, but she will not be disarmed. She offers Hillary a Coke, knowing she will say no to it as she always has, maybe request a glass of water instead.

"That would be nice," she says.

Lynetta grabs them both a cold soda, cracks open an ice tray from the freezer and fills two glasses with ice, brings them to the table, and sets a can beside each. She settles herself at the table in such a way that she can keep an eye on *the girls*. They're thirty-nine and fifty years old, but they play like slow-moving children. They will always be girls. Maisy's head pokes from the playhouse window where Ella is watering the plastic plants mounted in a window box. Water is splattering from the box.

Hillary keeps her eyes to the table, doesn't look at Lynetta, gathering her thoughts. When she lifts her head, she looks around the cottage, as if maybe she is pulling some of those thoughts from the far corners. A small sound escapes her, something like a laugh carried on a sigh.

"I've been thinking over exactly what I wanted to say to you and now that I'm here I'm finding it difficult to put my thoughts in any sort of order." Now she does look to Lynetta. "We both love her," she says. "That's the important thing."

Lynetta agrees to this, then reminds herself to be still and just listen. She has no idea where this is going.

"I was prepared to come here with a proposal, a compromise if you will. Obviously, the visit did not go well. And there was another incident. Nothing terrible, but it was disturbing all the same. She kicked me. She got herself worked up about the idea of coming home and accidentally kicked me." Hillary, in saying this, likely sees the sudden look of confusion on Lynetta's face and rushes to tell her it was an accident, really. But it's neither here nor there. She knows Ella didn't mean it, though it was still upsetting—for everyone. "And then, of course, there was the incident with the stove, which again, I bear responsibility for. I don't blame Ella at all, none of us do." And she does set her eyes to Lynetta as she says this, wants her to know it to be true. "I know she tends to play with things, always has—even as a little girl I couldn't keep her away from the other children's things, the silverware drawer, my pots and pans, and I had to keep a bolt on the pantry door."

Lynetta explains that she has child-protective locks on things, keeps nothing on a low shelf that isn't safe to fiddle with. Hillary looks to the cabinets, appears to note the lack of knobs on the stove, which have always been that way but perhaps she never thought it strange.

"I had to get a master lock installed on my car," Lynetta says. "She kept trying to open the door when we were driving, and she was forever playing with the window buttons. I had a vision of her tumbling out of the car and onto the highway."

Hillary tells her about how Ella used to wiggle out of the seat belts. There is a long pause, and Lynetta waits patiently, tells herself not to interrupt, that all this is leading somewhere, and though she might not like where it's going, she best put on a poker face.

Hillary sips from her soda, swirls the glass on the table, and continues. "I never wanted to send her away. It was not my choice, but the truth was, I had no choice."

Lynetta nods. She understands. Doesn't know how that decision was made and doesn't really give a damn. She is trying to be patient with this woman, but she doesn't want to hear her excuses. What she wants is to know what lies ahead for Ella. And she is snagged on the ominous offer of a compromise. All her life has been a compromise.

Hillary is watching the girls through the open door. She waves to Ella, and Lynetta expects her to start heading across the lawn to see her mother, but she doesn't. Ella waves and smiles and ducks back into the playhouse.

"Yesterday I was thinking I might propose a compromise whereby you and Ella could live in the carriage house. And I'd pay you, of course, to continue to be her caretaker."

Lynetta feels her back bristle. She sits up straighter and recalls years earlier in Dr. Carter's office. Oh, she is angry, so angry. The ground swishing out from under her. How dare this woman put her in this position. How dare she prey upon Lynetta's attachment to Ella and threaten to upend both of their lives so selfishly. How dare she even suggest that Lynetta can toss her own life aside, give up her trailer at the beach, the life she had imagined for them both, just to comfort this woman, bring her daughter home to her and strap her own life to a place she has never wanted to be. She is so angry she can't even form the words she needs to bring up. Just who does this woman think she is, sitting at her table, her hair so perfectly swirled into a knot at the base of her neck, her manicured nails tapping at her glass, her back so straight. But then, she watches the woman slump at the table and hold up the palm of her hand to stop Lynetta from saying anything, and her voice is almost a whine when she says, "But I know that was a terrible idea, a bad idea, very selfish of me."

"Damn right," says Lynetta, because she cannot help herself.

"Please don't be offended," Hillary says. "I know it's not something you would be interested in and I know it wouldn't be fair to you, and what's more"—and here she stops, tucks her chin—"what's more, I think you would do it, too. You would probably reluctantly agree to it because you love her and you know she needs you. But I won't ask that of you. Not now, not since I've had some time to think about it."

"I'm not sure I would do it," Lynetta says, calling her bluff, but she isn't so sure of herself when she says it. There's no telling what she would do for Ella, given what she has already gone and done and had to live with.

"My family wants me to drop the petition. Problem is, I've always done just what everyone else thinks is best. And this time . . . this time I wanted to be sure it was my decision, my call, a choice I was making." Her hands go to her lap, her fingers stretching across her thighs, kneading the fabric of her pants.

Lynetta knows something about choice. She knows that making one often requires sacrificing another. But she has no trouble settling around the choices she has made. She isn't one to think the grass is greener on the other side and is instead comfortable with the decisions she has made, especially the one to be with Ella.

Hillary runs her tongue between her pinked lips, draws her teeth over her bottom lip and holds the lip there, pinched, before releasing it. "Over the past few days, I've gone back over this a hundred times, changing my mind. One minute I think I absolutely must bring her home and the next minute I am recognizing it as the worst of ideas. I'm a rule follower, Lynetta. I'm a good soldier, you might say, who willingly takes orders from a higher authority—my husband, my church. In doing so I've abdicated a lot of responsibility in my life. But this, this desire to bring her back home, was a decision I made myself. I certainly didn't have the blessing of my family on this one, that's for sure." She gives a self-deprecating laugh and swipes her fingers across the table as if brushing away imaginary crumbs. "Likewise, I wanted *not* bringing her back to also be my decision. And I've flip-flopped quite a bit over the last days. I never wanted to send her away. I hope you believe that?" At this, she raises her brows, pleads to be taken at her word.

Lynetta believes her. "Nobody *wants* to send a child here."

"It's a terrible place, isn't it? It's a terrible thing to do to your child."

Lynetta won't lie to her. Even though she doesn't want to hurt this woman, make her pay for a choice she claims was made *for* her rather than *by* her. "Yes," Lynetta says. "But what's done is done."

"And she's had you all this time. And that was a blessing for her."

They sit quietly for a moment. "So it was Mr. Jules who sent her here," Lynetta finally says, something she has suspected all along.

"It was his decision, but it was my fault."

They can hear Ella's guttural laugh, and Lynetta looks to see her and Maisy making their way to the back door. But they stop suddenly, turn and wander to the edge of the stubbled fallow cornfield. Lynetta knows Ella won't go any farther into the field, is afraid of the insects, the grasshoppers, and the scrabble of tiny black spiders that disperse under footsteps.

"There was an accident," Hillary says. "Ella . . . was nearly drowned."

Lynetta picks up on the stutter in the way Hillary phrases it, *Ella was nearly drowned*, as if it was something *done* to her rather than something that *happened* to her. She knows now, according to Ella's files, that there was a hospitalization a week before Ella's admission, that there had been a seizure and near drowning in the bathtub. But something in the way Hillary is looking around the room, the way her breath has quickened, keeps Lynetta from saying so.

Hillary makes a series of little clicking sounds with her tongue, as if the details are stuck behind words she can't form. Her eyes are glassy, and she won't look at Lynetta. When she starts to speak again, there is a catch in her voice. "I was getting her in the bath. We'd just come from the doctor. The seizures—they had gotten much worse." She brings her hands to her lap, twists the fingers into a knot. "It was so hot that day. And she had wet herself." She takes a deep breath, bringing her chest up as she does so. Her eyes still flitting about the room. "I was pregnant again," she says flatly. "I always got sick in the early months. I was pregnant with Tess, and between the heat . . . and the smell . . . it made it all worse." She untangles her hands and waves one across the table. "No excuses," she says firmly. "No excuse for what happened."

"What happened?"

Hillary looks at Lynetta as if she is surprised for a moment to see her sitting there. Lynetta watches her face twist as if she is exchanging one persona for another. "Oh, my," she says. "What happened is . . .

what happened is, I was getting her in the bath . . . and she just crumpled that way she does . . . the seizure . . . and she fell." Lynetta sees that Hillary struggles to go on, watches her place a hand to her chest, pressing as she takes a breath. Her voice dropping to a whisper. "And . . . and I . . . Sometimes there are moments . . . Have you ever had a moment, Lynetta . . . where a curtain parts and it feels like an invitation . . . an opportunity opening up . . . that feels like a divine offering, a moment of grace? So easily misunderstood."

"What?" Lynetta asks quietly. She doesn't understand, has no idea what this woman is talking about, who she is asking her question of, because even though she has said Lynetta's name, it feels like she is talking to someone else altogether. But Hillary says nothing more, and the moment passes. Hillary sips at her Coke, sets it back on the table. "The next thing I knew, the paramedics were working on her. A week later we brought her here."

Lynetta notes to herself that there is a huge gap in this story.

"My husband insisted it was for the best. Like I said, it was his decision, but it was my fault."

There is a secret buried in Hillary's telling of what happened. But Lynetta isn't so sure she needs to know the details of it. She knows something of secrets, about the way they snack at a person, eating away at the core of who a person imagines themselves to be until all that's left is a person you don't recognize anymore. She knows secrets are always looking for a way out and that it is tempting to let them fly in the hopes you'll find absolution. But the point of a secret is to keep it that way, and this one, whatever it might be, could put Lynetta in a precarious place with her own. The thing about secrets shared is that they are a bartering tool. They carry a price. The exchange of another secret of equal or greater value. When you hand one over, it is reasonable to expect one in return. A way to seal the deal, each person carrying a piece of the other and a way to ensure that the secret stays where it is newly planted.

Mrs. Jules looks to Lynetta, and Lynetta feels an assumption passed to her as if Lynetta is meant to know what has been implied. And she doesn't, not clearly, but she believes this woman when she says it is her fault, believes that the blame for sending Ella away rests squarely on her shoulders.

"I thought I could go back and right a wrong. But that's just not possible. My kids call that a *do-over*," she says with a small sorry smile. "But I think that's only possible in basketball and board games."

They can both hear the girls now, drawing closer. Hillary sits up straighter, looks to the doorway expectantly.

"My mama here," they hear Ella say.

"Okay, Ella," Maisy says.

The two of them appear at the back door, both of them drenched from the watering of the window box.

"Hello, Ella, darling," says Hillary. "And who is your friend?"

Ella doesn't answer her, dives into her mother's arms, and after pulling herself from the hug, clasps her mother's face between her hands. "You here, Mama."

"I'm right here, darling." Hillary places her own hands over Ella's at her face. "And who is your friend?" she asks again.

Ella takes her hands from beneath her mother's and points. "Her is Maisy," she says. "Her is my friend Maisy."

"*She* is your friend," says Lynetta.

"I said that," Ella says.

"Sort of," says Lynetta, shaking her head slowly. She catches Hillary's eye, and they both share a smile.

"Well, hello, Maisy. It's so nice to meet you." Maisy looks at the floor and runs her palms down her damp shirt.

"She moving to a new house," Ella announces.

"That's wonderful," Hillary says. "And you'll be moving soon, too." Hillary reaches for Ella's hand as she says it.

"Down the ocean!" Ella says.

"That's right," says Hillary. "You'll be moving to the ocean."

39

Hillary

Two long picnic tables covered in sheets of newspaper are run together on the patio. The family is spread down the length of them. The table is littered with sloppy crab carcasses, wooden mallets, ramekins filled with vinegar (for George and Tammy), and congealing butter for a few of the others. Most of the children—with the exception of one of George's girls who will not leave her mother's side, watches anxiously every small scrap of crabmeat that goes in her mother's mouth—have abandoned the table and are chasing each other with errant claws through the yard and garden. Hillary is delivering two pitchers of iced tea to the table for refills—unsweetened for Tammy, and sweetened for the others, though most everyone is drinking cold beer from sweating bottles, which are piling up at the table. Hillary takes the empties from the table and drops them in the plastic-lined trash can that has been set to the corner of the patio.

Something has grown between Hillary and Lynetta, possibly a friend-ship, though not like what Hillary has with Mary, *had* with Bets. But Ella binds them to one another, and this unfurling thing requires compro-mises between the two. Lynetta has agreed to bring Ella by for this visit while all the family is in town for the July Fourth crab feast. She has also reluctantly agreed to cut back on the sodas she allows Ella. And Hillary, for her part, has promised to stop wiping Ella's mouth with a wet napkin after every meal as if she is a toddler and instead handing her a napkin and allowing her to do it for herself. In fact, right now Hillary is fighting the urge to wipe Ella's hands and mouth, covered in the Old Bay crab spice (in spite of the fact that Ella didn't pick any of her own crab but relied on Belle instead, to do it for her). Still, Ella fiddles with the debris at the table, and her fingers are coated with the spices. When she pushes her glasses to her nose, she leaves smeared prints on them.

Jack comes to his grandmother and asks if they might be allowed to go in the carriage house, but Hillary has to tell him no. The carriage house is kept locked when Ella is here, another concession to Lynetta, a precaution, though it no longer has a stove or oven anyway, only a dormitory size refrigerator, a coffee maker, and a microwave. Jack is disappointed, and she distracts him with a promise of watermelon soon and a chance to have a seed-spitting contest with all the other children. He wants to know if Uncle Jax will join them and she assures him, without even having to ask Jax, that it is one of his favorite things and she is certain he will join them. She reminds Jack that Clarissa and her family will be stopping by later and she will be bringing her new puppy. Won't that be fun?

Ella is up now and wandering, looking over the shoulders of those still at the table and pointing out the parts of the crabs she finds most disgusting. *Eww, gross.* She avoids George and Tammy, and likewise, George mostly ignores her, though he did tolerate a hug from her when she first arrived and set about hugging everyone. Lynetta is at the table as well, though Hillary doesn't think she looks completely comfortable. But she and Hillary both know that Ella will not visit without Lynetta. Hillary is hoping that with time Lynetta will feel more comfortable with the family. Lynetta picks at a few crabs but mostly keeps an eye on Ella, watching her lean over everyone's shoulders, tries to keep her from placing her messy hands on her father's shoulders.

"If you're all finished here, Ella, wipe your hands," Lynetta says to her, nodding to one of the two rolls of paper towels on the table. Hillary leans across the table and rips off two lengths of paper towels, goes to Ella with the intention of gathering her hands and wiping them down for her, but catches Lynetta's eye and hands them to Ella instead.

Yes, compromises have been agreed upon between the two women. Hillary has handed the paper towels to Ella and watches her wipe her own hands.

Brad is perhaps the neatest crab picker Hillary has ever seen. Only the very tips of his fingers are mussed, and she can't believe the precision in the way he deconstructs the crab, pulling off the legs one by one in the way Finney instructed him, setting them in a pile, and then neatly removing the top shell and splitting the remains in two. He uses a knife to dip into the cavities and retrieve the meat. She notices now that Finney and Brad have matching tattoos on the insides of their left wrists. A symbol of some sort that she is unfamiliar with, something like an open flower—or a sun—with a six-pointed star inside of it. Hillary doesn't like tattoos, but she no longer thinks of them as some kind of tragic defacement. They're everywhere and she has been desensitized to them, as she thinks of it. Brad sees her staring and tells her it's a chakra symbol, *Anahata*. Hillary has no idea what that means and looks to Stone. He raises his brows to say he has no idea, either.

"Very nice," she says, and the others set to laughing. She can't help smiling, knowing her children know her too well and can't be fooled.

"Mom, you're ridiculous," Belle says finally. "We all know how you feel about tattoos."

"Not really," says Hillary. "Not so much anymore."

"Really?" says Jax. "Then remind me to show you mine later."

"Oh, no, Jax! You didn't."

He wipes his hands on a paper towel and pulls up the fabric of his shorts on his burned leg to reveal, mid-thigh, a tattoo of a triangle with a stylized flame in the center of it. Smiles broadly. "Yup—had to. Just seemed the situation called for it. Clarissa got one, too." Hillary can't imagine what her friend Mary will think of that.

"Oh, I like it, Jax," says Belle.

"Cool," Finney says.

"Oh, for the love of God," says Hillary. "I will never understand any of you." But she is smiling as she says it. She looks to her girls. "Please tell me the two of you haven't done this to yourself."

Belle shakes her head, no, and Ben, beside her, says, "Not that I've noticed anyway."

"I don't, either," Tess says. "But I've been thinking about it. What's the symbol for divorced?"

"A big *X*," says George.

July Fourth and this crab feast may be one of Hillary's favorite things. She prefers crab cakes to crab picking, but it is such a joy to watch her family together. It's been years since Finney has joined them, but she made a special point of calling him and letting him know that she hoped he and Brad would come this year and she was delighted when he promised to make the trip.

Hillary looks around at her beautiful family, the way they have gone forth and multiplied, the people they have brought into their fold. She watches Ella tip her upper body into Belle's back and the way Belle looks over her shoulder and smiles.

Tammy is quiet, perhaps overwhelmed by her illness, juxtaposed against an event where everyone is gorging themselves. But George said earlier that she was doing better. He claims she's gained six pounds but to Hillary, she still seems pitifully thin. Still, Hillary has seen her eat, has watched the small morsels of crabmeat go into her mouth, and earlier she had accepted the plate of salad George offered her. She left a few nuts and a slice of avocado on the plate but had indeed eaten the rest. When Tammy says now that she thinks she's finished and is just going to wash her hands, Amanda beside her insists on going with her.

Everyone looks to George when the two disappear into the house. Though no one says anything. "She's good," he assures them. "It's hard for her, but she's trying." Everyone nods, and the subject changes quickly. Jax heads off to a writing conference in New England tomorrow. Tess is joining a friend in Nantucket next week and then starts a new job when she returns. And yes, her ex is still an ass—cheated on the woman he was cheating on her with—she tells them all. And George says sarcastically that he is shocked.

A yellowjacket wasp zips to a crab carcass and lands, lifts, and moves to the next. Ella backs away from the table, a look of horror on her face, and Jax, seeing her fear, swats it away with his hand. They are a nuisance, the yellowjackets, but they won't sting her, he tells them.

She shakes her head, no, *They will kill you*. Another lands at the table, boldly treks along the rim of an empty inverted crab shell. Ella backs up farther, pushes her glasses up her nose, and then wraps her arms around herself. Lynetta tells her it's okay and calls Ella to herself, but she is frozen in fear.

"It's okay, Ella," says Hillary. She knows Ella doesn't like flying insects of any kind, bees in particular, but the way she is shivering, the way she is starting to cry surprises Hillary. Ella waves her hands in front of her face, *go away*, and they all watch her. Belle suggests they clean up some of the debris, get some of the mess out of the way so the yellowjackets will be less inclined to invade their feast. Lynetta rises from her seat at the table and makes her way around the end of it to the other side where Ella stands.

Hillary suggests she and Lynetta take Ella inside to wash, give everyone a chance to finish up and clear the mess from the table. When Hillary puts her arm around Ella, she feels Ella's body trembling. "My goodness, Ella. It's fine, everything's fine, the bees won't bother you."

Inside the Jules kitchen, Lynetta instructs Ella to put her hands under the running water at the sink and Hillary takes her glasses from her head and cleans them with a dish towel, holds them to the light, and then runs them under the water before wiping them dry.

"I had no idea she was so afraid of bees," Hillary says to Lynetta, just as Amanda and Tammy are coming down the hall from the powder room. Ella is still whimpering, and Amanda asks if she's been stung.

"No, doll. She's just very afraid of bees," Lynetta explains.

"Colin Washington in my class at school is so allergic, he will *die* if he gets stung," she announces.

"I think you're exaggerating," says Tammy, running her hand down her daughter's hair.

"No, really, Mom. He is. He has an EpiPen, and we can't even go outside for recess without it. Mrs. Pfeiffer brings it with her in the first aid kit. Can we have watermelon yet?"

There is a cooler set by the door and Hillary asks Tammy if she thinks she and Amanda can manage to get it outside to the table. Amanda runs to the door and calls for her father. "Come help us, Daddy!" before turning back to Ella. "You come, too, Ella—Aunt Ella," she corrects herself.

Ella is obviously pleased to be invited and smiles broadly. She is strong, she tells them. She can help carry the cooler. George appears at the door and hefts the cooler by himself. Tammy, Amanda, and Ella follow him out the door and Hillary turns to Lynetta.

"This bee thing," she says. "Has she ever been stung?"

Lynetta shakes her head, no, but Hillary can tell there is something more. She watches Lynetta fiddle with the dishtowel, fold it lengthwise, fold it again, and settle it just so on the counter. "No," Lynetta says. "But she had a bad experience." Lynetta won't look at Hillary, keeps her eyes averted, turns her back three-quarters so that Hillary cannot see her face. When Lynetta turns to her again there is a nervousness in the way she runs her tongue at her lips, a small swell of tears forming. "It was a long time ago," Lynetta says.

Hillary waits for her to say more. What kind of *bad experience*?

Lynetta lifts her head and squares herself with Hillary. "A man died. Years ago. Ella was there, at the cottage. Stung by bees."

"Oh, my lord, Lynetta. I'm so sorry, so sorry. Was he a friend of yours? What happened?" Inside she is flipping through the years, trying to remember ever having been told such a thing. But no, she can't recall ever being told that Ella watched someone *die*.

"Brody was no friend of mine," Lynetta says angrily, "no friend of mine—or Ella's."

Hillary doesn't understand. "Who was he?" Hillary asks, though the name sounds familiar, she can't place him. "What happened?" she asks again.

Lynetta wanders to the doorway, looks out over the lawn where Stone is now slicing wedges of watermelon and handing them to anxious, squealing children. Hillary senses she would rather not have this conversation.

"Brody . . ." Hillary says, urging her to go on. Lynetta turns at the doorway to look at her, nods. "I recall the name," Hillary says.

"He drove the bus," Lynetta explains, and Hillary remembers him then. A big man, rough, she remembers. Gruff, when he would come to take Ella from her at the end of their visits. Ella would cling to her, beg her mother not to leave, and she would be forced to painfully unpeel Ella's arms from around her neck while the man huffed and paced in the vestibule. Sometimes Ella would whimper as he led her away, flinching when he took Ella's arm in his hand.

"He was a bastard," Lynetta says, and Hillary feels her heart jump as if she is being thumped in the chest. "After me and Ella moved into the cottage, I had a little party for the staff. He wasn't invited, but he came anyway."

Hillary can picture him now in her mind's eye. Always in overalls, sweating, even in the winter. Stubble on his face, greasy hair hanging over his forehead.

"He was allergic to bees," Lynetta tells her. "And he drank from a soda can with bees in it."

"How horrible! And Ella saw this?" She is recalling now the bald spot on the back of the man's head when she watched him lead Ella to the bus.

"Not everything. She didn't see all of it." She proceeds to tell Hillary about the way he came to her portico, wanted to join her party, and got angry when Lynetta sent him away.

Hillary has always been a gracious hostess and a part of her admires that Lynetta would so easily send an unwelcome guest away. Such a thing is beyond Hillary.

Lynetta tells of Brody drinking from the soda can, the grotesque swelling of his face and tongue, the way he stumbled and clawed at his throat, the way Ella walked in as he fell to the steps, and how Lynetta sent her to get help. How Lynetta called up to the medical wing, someone tried CPR, that nothing could be done for him, that he died on her porch while she held Ella on the sofa.

Hillary sees that the telling of it exhausts Lynetta. Watches her tip her head to the doorframe, slash off the tears, and Hillary reaches for a tissue from the box on the counter, takes it to her.

"You're probably wondering why I never told you."

Yes, Hillary is thinking. Something like that—she should have been told. But she holds her tongue, pats Lynetta's shoulder, and watches her dab at her eyes, take a deep breath, and stiffen her back.

"But Ella never said a word after," Lynetta says. "We didn't talk about it. Never came up again. Just terrified of bees ever since."

"Of course," Hillary says. "Of course she would be."

As the two women head back outdoors, Hillary thinks of what Lynetta has told her, replays what she imagines happened on that day against what she recalls of the man, and tries to find a way to stitch it all together. She can't help but think that things have been left unsaid and that maybe some things are better left that way.

40

Lynetta

BEECHWOOD INSTITUTE
September 2009

It is their last morning in the cottage, a brilliant September morning. The clouds are curdled across the sky and the squirrels have a manic energy that emboldens them to come right up on the portico steps and stare at the two women through the open front door. Soon enough Lynetta will turn it over to them, certain they will find a narrow opening in the soffits and invade the eaves of the cottage.

Every last resident has been placed. Lynetta and Ella are fittingly the very last to leave. The campus is essentially abandoned, an eerie Gothic expanse of crumbling abandoned buildings, overflowing dumpsters stuffed with furnishings and scrap metal. The kudzu has done its job magnificently and lifted the shingles from the roofing of almost every single one of the thirty-five campus buildings, strangling the gutters and bringing them down to the earth. Every night for the last week, Lynetta has had to call the cops on hordes of teenagers cruising the curving cracked drive, slipping into buildings to break glass, scavenge for artifacts, post their Facebook pictures of leather bed straps trailing from old metal bedframes, wheelchairs tipped into corners, dressers upended, files dumped, the pooling of stagnant rainwater in darkened corners. She's kept the lights on in her cottage all through the night, hoping to convey that theirs is a peopled little house, not something to be ransacked for souvenirs. Pap has been sleeping on her sofa the last two nights, just to be sure they are not alone. He wanted her to come to his place, but she was afraid to leave their cottage unattended.

The basic furnishings came with her little cottage decades ago, and so she has moved most of their belongings over the last few months to their new home. There's little left to pack, but Hillary has insisted on coming by today to help her finish up, Ella's winter clothes, pots and pans, a coffee maker, toiletries, towels, and potted plants, her mending basket, a single lamp, and her Monet posters in their brassy frames.

Tonight the town fire department will come and burn down one of the buildings in a training exercise. Lynetta would like to stay and see that, but it can't happen until she vacates the property. She's sorry to miss it, this last fitting tribute to the horror of it all. Ashes to ashes and all that kind of thing.

She is piling pots and pans in a box and has Ella wiping down the inside of the refrigerator as if they are preparing for a new tenant. She just can't bear to walk away and leave the contents to rot. Though she knows her cottage will be vandalized almost immediately. But when she looks around, she feels a tenderness toward her little cottage, feels it has been the buttress it was meant to be, has served her and Ella well. She's sad for it, for the destruction that lies ahead. Pap has moved the playhouse to his own yard. That was a chore. But a friend who runs a flat hauler had helped him with it, and Ella couldn't be more thrilled to know she doesn't have to give up her playhouse and that it will be waiting for her at Pap's when they visit.

Hillary arrives with a potted mum, one more thing Lynetta will have to squeeze in her Camry, but the woman can't come without bearing gifts.

Hillary hugs Ella at the open refrigerator and tells her she's doing a spectacular job. Such a hard worker.

Ella huffs. "You welcome," she says.

Hillary offers to pack the last of Ella's clothes and picks through a stack of boxes in the corner. When she spies the overnight bag she brought Ella back in April, she grabs that as well. "I can use this for her toiletries," she announces, but when she picks it up, she notices the strap has not yet been repaired. Lynetta watches the bag slip from her shoulder and offers to fix it. "Won't take a minute," she says.

She goes to her monstrous mending basket that always sits by the front door and begins to turn the combination lock on it. It bears a hook and bone latch that is further fortified by the tiny lock because she simply can't trust Ella to stay out of it. Ella can manage some basic supervised mending, but she is known to stick needles absentmindedly in her mouth and must be carefully watched.

Ella is getting a bit put out by her task at the refrigerator, and Lynetta tells her take a break, head upstairs, and pull the sheets off her bed. Ella stomps slowly up the stairs, swaying her shoulders side to side as she does so, and it makes both Hillary and Lynetta shake their heads in unison.

"Sorry to put you out," Lynetta says with a laugh.

"Is okay," says Ella.

Lynetta settles on the sofa with the bag on her lap and the mending basket beside her. Hillary sits on the other side of the basket on the sofa.

"What a wonderful, beautiful mending basket," she says.

"It was my mother's," Lynetta tells her. "They don't make them like this anymore." The basket is a marvel, stiff-sided, a beautiful thick grass weave of burgundy and gold, a curved bone handle, and when she opens it, four layers deep in shelving, each one lifting with a folding handle in the center of it.

She takes out two of the layered shelves, sets them on the floor beside her, and flips her fingers through the third in search of her needles capable of going through leather and a small pair of needle-nose pliers meant to help pull the needle through the thicker materials.

Hillary looks in the basket, lifts a clear plastic tub of old buttons, and marvels at the contents.

"So charming," she says. Lynetta is bothered by her interest in the basket, knows what lies at the bottom. She could stop her, could casually move the basket to her other side or to her feet, could simply ask Hillary to be careful with the precious contents, her mother's old buttons, an ancient mahogany-handled seam splitter, old button hooks, an exquisitely sculpted pair of embroidery scissors shaped like a crane, mother-of-pearl collar stiffs, a walnut sock-darning mold. Yes, she could move the basket, remind her again that the contents are precious to her and were once her mother's, handed down, quite likely from her grandmother, in which case Hillary would apologize, settle her hands quietly in her lap.

But she doesn't. There is a sense of possible release in the air, like when one holds the pinched end of a full balloon, anxious to let go and see in just what way it will rise and fall, shoot into corners, and turn randomly in the air. Lynetta has been pinching the balloon for decades.

Lynetta feels the wooden spool dance in the palm of her hand as she pulls the thick waxed thread from it. She threads the needle, concentrating, not looking to Hillary beside her but knowing Hillary is lifting the last tray, settling it in her lap, and peering into the cellar of the basket.

"Oh, my," Hillary says, pulling the red plastic box from its grave, as Lynetta has come to think of it. Hillary lifts the box, turns it in her hand, and when Lynetta looks to her, their eyes meet. The label is yellowed with age, but the lettering is still clear, *Emergency Insect Sting Kit,* and below it, Caution: *Federal Law Prohibits Dispensing Without Prescription, Store in cool dark place.*

"Lynetta . . ." she says quietly, possibly frightened. Lynetta can't be sure. "Is this what I think . . ." Lynetta nods, barely, maybe not even enough for Hillary to notice.

Hillary snaps open the case. Glued to the inside lid and curling at the edges is another label. *Important: Read Instructions Before Emergency Arises.*

"It's that man's," she says in an awed whisper. "It's that man Brody's, isn't it? Oh, Lynetta," and there is such pity in her voice that Lynetta isn't sure she can bear it.

The balloon is zipping through the room, self-propelled, smacking into walls and changing course on its own power. But Lynetta doesn't care, wants to be free of it, can feel the beginning of an empty space where the guilt once resided, once pressed at her ribs and her lungs and heart, all escaping, all spun out, fittingly, in this cottage, in this moment.

Hillary begins to lift, with one cautious finger, the glass syringe filled with a dark liquid, aged over the years from gold to muddy black, a cracked rubber tip capping the needle, drops it back to its cushioned space in the box. Taps her fingers at the cellophane-wrapped antihistamine tablets, and a sterile swab.

"You said . . ."

"I know what I said," says Lynetta. She knows what she said, what she told everyone crowded to her portico, aghast and screaming, someone crying, Brody's face mangled with swelling. She remembers thinking at the time, when she dragged the kit from his pocket, realized that he could be saved, realized that she could not see his eyes for the swelling, would not have to remember a look in his eyes when she stuffed the kit in her mending basket just inside the door only seconds before the others streamed through the cottage and Lenny knelt down beside him, patted his pockets furiously in search of the kit Brody always carried, yelled for Lynetta to call the medical wing. Which she did obediently.

She is thinking now about that moment of grace Hillary talked about, that fine and narrow slip of a moment when a decision is made—or not—because it feels like it is a heavenly offering.

The two women look at each other, each knowing now with certainty that there is a fine line between selfishness and what passes for love.

"We should get rid of this," Hillary says. "Best to be rid of it."

We.

"I don't know why I've held on to it," Lynetta says, surprised now by the lightness in her chest; she puts a hand to her throat.

Hillary goes to the table, pulls a trash bag from the box on the counter, and stuffs and wraps the kit in it. Folds the bag over and over it endlessly. "I can take it with me," she says. "Get it away from here, away from you."

For just a moment Lynetta is afraid she shouldn't let it go, that she deserves to carry it for the rest of her life, but Hillary reads her mind, or so it seems.

"You've carried it long enough," she says. The two women look at one another across the room, hear Ella shout down to them that she almost forgot her cat poster and when is she going to get a real cat, hmmm? *Because you promised, Nettie.*

"Are you going to get her the damn cat?" Hillary asks.

"We've spoiled her rotten," says Lynetta.

"I do so much for you, Nettie," Ella says, huffing her way down the steps trailing her bedsheets behind her.

"Thank you for all you do for me, Ella."

"You welcome," she says, beaming at the two of them. "You both very welcome."

Acknowledgments

My deepest gratitude goes to Johns Hopkins professors and writers Elise Levine and Elly Williams. I am extraordinarily lucky to have had their eyes on these pages as they took shape. Writing a novel is a lot like walking a maze. There are wrong turns, shortcuts that dead end, and long runs that look promising but only have you right back where you started from. I am fortunate to have had the wisdom of these two writer friends to lead me around the corners.

Thank you also to my generous writing group; Lynn Chambers, Pam McFarland, Linda Wastila, and Insha Hamdan. What a gift it has been to be a part of a writing group that inspires authenticity on the page but also knows how to (kindly) call out BS when they read it. It has been my joy to conspire with you as we find our own voices.

Thank you to my friend and agent, Cheryl Pientka, who saw promise in the early pages of this novel and made me believe I had something to say. Madeline Hopkins, here's to you for the developmental edits that made me think—even when I didn't want to. Ciera Cox, thank you for being our tiebreaker. Alenka Linaschke, you turn words into visual art, and I'm thrilled to have been paired with you again for this book jacket.

I write about family, inspired by the exquisitely flawed one I dwell within. I am forever grateful to my husband John, my daughter, Kelly, and my son, Jamie for their willingness to tap the wounds that never fully heal and ask the questions that often can't be answered. You are my muses and my heart.